THE VIEW FROM MY
WINDOW

THE VIEW FROM MY
WINDOW

Patricia J. Gallegos

atmosphere press

To Minerva, who is my guiding-light and True North.

Misfortune

The stream of my life has a way of changing course without much warning, sending me careening, in search of some measure of equilibrium. The summer of my twentieth year was just such a pivotal, tumultuous time.

As a nomad, the view from my window changed daily. My life was governed by my apprenticeship as a shaman. While others in my clan recalled particular villages and hamlets because of the trading they had done and the friends they had made, I remembered the villages for the medicinal plants that grew nearby, the illnesses I had treated and the babies I had helped to deliver.

I enjoyed rising early with my clan and sitting close to my cousin, Galynda, my dearest friend, enjoying a steaming cup of tea as we discussed our aspirations and our dreams.

On such a morning, Galynda told me she that had been awakened in the night by a vision of something terrible that was to happen in the very next hamlet. Although she was clearly shaken by the vision, she became agitated and withdrawn, refusing to tell me the details of what she had seen.

Because her visions are always so clear and accurate, I was nervous and my muscles were tense the entire day. I was on the lookout for bad things to happen around every bend in the road.

Late that afternoon, we rolled into the fringes of the next village. By this time, I had been jostled about all day in the vardo, I was nervous and jumpy, and I had a tremendous headache. I felt a nauseating knot weighing heavily in the pit of my stomach as our caravan rode into the small, isolated settlement of Stravanger.

Tired and dilapidated buildings covered with a patina of grey dust seemed to sag under the palpable oppression of the place. The air was stifling, humid and so thick that the dust seemed suspended by it, making breathing difficult. Although I could see no one, I felt the weight of prying eyes from every decaying dwelling. Anticipation and anxiety clung to me like sweat and dust.

Cicadas buzzed high in the trees. Flies flew in idle geometric patterns, landing occasionally on our sweaty skin just to annoy us. I could feel the perspiration trickling down my back and between my breasts leaving, I was certain, a trail in the dust which coated my sticky skin.

We had planned to camp our caravan just outside the village for the night and do a bit of trading with the local merchants in the marketplace in the morning.

Because of the oppressive humidity, everything we did seemed to require twice the effort. Every movement we made felt painfully slow and sluggish.

I took small comfort in the familiar, leading the horses to the muddy stream that ambled listlessly along in its bed. I watched as the horses sucked in slow draughts of the warm, murky water as if it were as thick as honey. The salty scent of their sweat eased my distress.

As they drank, I looked out over the gently rolling terrain. The grasses were yellowing from the dry summer weather, the soil near the banks of the stream was patterned with geometric cracks, further telling the tale of the midsummer dry spell.

Along the horizon, great billowy thunderheads pressed in all around us, darkening and rumbling softly to one another. The air was cooling off quickly and the winds were beginning to pick up. By early evening, the static in the atmosphere was palpable.

Galynda, who had been struck by lightning as a small child, had tremendous anxiety during thunderstorms. It was my responsibility to seek suitable shelter to shield her from lightning.

When I knocked at the door of her caravan, My Aunt, Ahnja, called for me to enter. Galynda paced blindly, back and forth, like the caged tigers I had seen in a traveling circus.

Ahnja's outstretched hand followed her daughter, offering a soothing cup of tea. She pled "Please, Galynda, please sit down. All this pacing, you are making me feel jumpy too."

"No Mama, I cannot." She said shaking her head. "Can you not feel it?" she asked, rubbing her arms briskly with her hands. The lightning, it dances on my skin! It boils inside me! I must move. I cannot be still!"

I clambered inside the wagon and greeted both women. "Ahmad went to find out if there are any caves nearby." I explained to the frantic mother. I pulled the curtains away from the tiny window. I could see the swelling clouds looming darkly over our camp. Trees were no longer dancing merrily in the breeze but were bending and yielding to the wind. In the distance, I could see the silhouette of Ahmad returning rapidly, with one hand clapped tightly over his hat to keep it from blowing away.

5

"He is returning already. Wait here and I shall see if he has any news for us." I sprang from the wagon and landed firmly at his feet, startling him.

He leaned in and spoke loudly to compete with the wind. "There is a small cave just up this path a bit." He indicated with his free hand. "No more than half a mile." He reassured me with a wink.

My eyes followed his finger and I quickly identified a stand of willow trees, which told me a convenient water source was also nearby.

I poked my head back into the wagon and said, "Aye. There is a little cave about a half mile up the path that runs beside the stream. We shall have to hurry if we are to beat the storm."

"I shall meet you back here in just a few minutes." I called to Galynda as I leapt from her wagon and ran the few paces to my own.

"Magda, Ahmad has found a cave for Lynd. 'Tis only half a mile away and we should just make it before the storm, if we leave now."

"Willow, you must eat. Let me pack you something." Magda replied.

"Very well, as long as it does not take more time to prepare than it takes me to roll my quilt and grab my medicine bag!" I said.

She quickly sliced some of her freshly baked bread, and deftly sliced some of the creamy white goat's cheese our caravan was famous for. She wrapped them together in a kerchief and grabbed two apples from their basket on the wall and added them to the bundle. She had the package in my hand before I could touch the door handle.

"Willow, fill your water skins so that you shall have something to drink." She reminded. Knife still in hand, she brushed an unruly tendril of hair out of her face with the back of her wrist.

"I shall! I shall! Magda. Thank you!" I took two skin bags down from the wall by the door and kissed her on the cheek before I slipped out the door, bedroll under my arm, dinner in its kerchief sack in my hand and two limp skin bags slung over my neck and shoulder along with my otter skin medicine bag.

I ran the few steps to Galynda's wagon and before I could knock, the door swung open. There stood Galynda packed, just as I was, and ready to go.

"The static is becoming stronger. We had better hurry." Galynda warned.

She slipped her left hand into the crook of my right elbow and we set off walking at a brisk pace.

We worked well together. She was accustomed to keeping up with me. I was skilled at avoiding obstacles that she might stumble upon. She had, long ago, learned the unique rhythm of my gait.

"It shall become dark soon, although I can still see fairly well." I explained, keeping a watchful eye in the weather. "We must get you into the cave and then, I shall return to fill our skin bags."

"That sounds... like a good idea," she agreed nodding hesitantly. There was something in that hesitation that made me question the soundness of the idea, but it was an issue I would have to deal with once we had gotten to the cave.

As we approached the water, the verdant, bittersweet scent of willows became stronger. The stream slid noiselessly over its pebbly bed as it lazily carved its small valley into the earth. The stream was flanked on either side by gently sloping hills. Higher up the slope, and further from the water source, the willows gave way to birch trees and then to spicy scented pines.

"I think I have spotted it, Lynd." I announced.

"Is it much of a climb?"

"A bit, there are some roots to watch out for." I guided her carefully around a large root that was protruding above the worn, dusty path.

It began to rain lightly. The rain spattering the ground sent up tiny puffs of grey dust, which looked like puffs of smoke. The heavy scent of dust and rain hung in the humid air and coated the hairs in my nostrils.

Lightening brightened the sky and illuminated our path. In that brief moment, I was able to pick out a clear route to the cave.

No sooner had we entered the safety of the cave, the thunder clapped loudly in our wake, as if a great heavy door was slammed behind us.

I had not thought to bring a lantern and regretted it immediately. It was dark inside the cave and I had no idea how large it was or if it was already occupied by some sort of unfriendly, hungry animal.

"Did you bring a lantern?" Galynda read my mind aloud.

I ducked my head, gritted my teeth and answered weakly, "Nay."

"Oh Willow," she replied, "You are so helpless! What would you do without me?" She pulled from the pocket of her pinafore a bee's wax candle and the tools to light a fire.

"For someone who is blind, you are always prepared to see in the dark!" I said with relief flooding over me.

"It was Mama's idea. She knows that you are often in such a hurry to care for others that you tend to forget your own needs." She said with a smile.

I offered up a small prayer of thanks to Aunt Ahnja and gratefully lit the candle. I was pleased to find the cave unoccupied and large enough for us to rest on the floor side by side. I found a niche in the wall of the cave and placed the candle there, "The candle is here." I said guiding Galynda's hand to it. It should be fine for the short time I'm gone."

"The mouth of the cave is tall enough for you to stand in,

but the ceiling is much lower near the back, which is only about two paces. Fire surround stones are scattered about on the floor just in front of you. There are a few small animal bones and some feathers, fortunately, I do not see any ferocious creatures." I smiled, wiping my sweaty palms on my pinafore.

"Thank you." She said. "I can tell that it 'tis rather small." She nodded, listening to the echoes in the small space. "Large, enclosed places sound hollow because they echo more, and they seem to make a cool wind when you enter them" She continued. I made note of this new observation. I often employed the tools Galynda used in her world to maneuver through obstacles in my own life.

"I had better go and fetch that water if I plan to miss the rain." I said handing her my bedroll and provisions.

"Very well, I shall just wait here." Her voice trailed off, sounding rather hollow.

Leaving the cave, I sensed that she had an uneasy feeling about something. I suspected that it had everything to do with the storm and the vision. Perhaps it had been one of her premonitions.

I decided to stay near the cave and gather branches from the nearby pines to cover the floor of the cave.

My medicine bag is always well-stocked. Everything has its place and my well-trained hands can nimbly find anything I need in it, simply by touch. Another skill I had learned from Galynda. In the semidarkness, I found my knife and cut several nice, broad pine boughs cleanly and returned it deftly to its sheath inside the pouch. I turned and began the short ascent to the mouth of the cave.

I spoke to Galynda as I neared the cave so she would not be frightened or caught unawares. "Lynd, I'm bringing some pine boughs to freshen up the place and to give us something a little cleaner and softer to lie on." I announced.

"Oh... lovely," she replied, sounding as if she had been

holding her breath. "That shall be a...a nice touch." Her back was pressed firmly against the wall of the cave. She stood stock still twisting the corners of her pinafore so tightly that even in the dim light, I could see that her knuckles were white.

I felt a lump building in my throat. "What is it Lynd?" I swallowed. "I have never seen you like this. Is it the storm?"

"Nay, nay," She answered hesitantly, shaking her head. "I am sure 'tis nothing at all to worry about. You go ahead and get the water. I am sure I shall be all right. 'Tis silly of me to behave thusly. The stream is not so very far away and you shall be right back."

I was not certain if her words were meant to reassure me or her.

"I could stay and forget about the water for now." I offered.

"Nay, you must go." She persisted. "I shall scarcely have time to set up housekeeping before you return. Now, get along!" she said smiling weakly, trying to brighten her voice to keep me from worrying.

"But," I began.

"Go. I'm feeling thirsty already!" She said, shooing me with both hands.

"Oh, very well!" I said rolling my eyes and giving up the argument.

"Give me your skins so that I may fill them." I said extending my hand to retrieve them. I slung hers over my shoulder with the two I had brought from home.

"I shall be right back." I reassured her.

"You would get back sooner if you would just take your leave!" she answered with exasperation rising in her voice. Her eyebrows were raised and her nostrils were slightly flared.

"See you soon!" I stepped out into the growing darkness and hurried toward the stream.

I wanted to get to the stream, fetch the water, and return quickly. I tried not to think about Galynda's strange mood, but it always seemed that the very thing I tried not to think about was the very thing that would wedge itself into my head and stay there until I worked it through.

It was sprinkling steadily, but the storm had not really hit in full force yet. The full moon was beginning to rise, and it shone between the thunderheads enough to light the darkening path.

I quickly removed one bag from my shoulder and began to fill it. Replacing its cork, I decided I would only fill one for each of us, and then return to the cave. I uncorked the second skin and dipped it into the water to fill it.

The raindrops were growing in size and number. Lightening slashed through the sky and illuminated my surroundings. Dust was rising up from the powdered soil as the rain began to pound the earth in earnest.

If I did not make haste, I would surely be soaked to the bone before I could reach the shelter of the cave again. Shouldering the filled skins, I set off for the cave at a trot, holding my head down to shield my face from the pelting raindrops.

My mind was, once again, racing about the thing that was making Galynda so nervous. I was thus, in deep in thought, when a lightning strike followed immediately by a clap of thunder caught me unawares. It gave me such a start that my heart leapt into my throat. I lost focus on the path and struck my foot hard upon the very root I had warned Galynda about.

The storm raged all around me. I crashed soundlessly to the ground. The pain in my left foot was sharp and stabbing. The throbbing pain that crept up my leg told me I had probably broken a bone. The stinging sensation I had on the outside edge of my foot told me I had also excoriated the surface of my foot.

I had been frightened, and I was angry with myself for I had allowed the thunder to frighten me. I knew better than to lose my concentration on a darkened path. I knew I should have been focusing on the path that led up to the cave.

I wanted to lie there and cradle my foot, writhing in pain, but Galynda was all alone in the cave, awaiting my return. I pushed myself up onto my hands and knees and tried to put a bit of weight on my foot. The pain reasserted itself. The throbbing in my foot was so pronounced, I could hear it pounding in my ears. I felt dizzy and a wave of nausea overcame me for a moment.

I steadied myself and waited for the nausea to pass. That's when I heard it. It was a muffled noise. It wasn't rain, or thunder. It sounded human! It sounded as if it were coming from the cave! There it was again! This time, it was the unmistakable, sickening sound of a woman's cry for help cut off mid-scream.

My mind was racing again. I had to get back up to the cave. I was nearly there, but it felt as though it was a hundred miles away.

I gingerly hobbled as fast as I could, carefully picking my way around roots and brambles that seemed to be taunting and torturing me along the path to the mouth of the cave.

Once there, I heard the muffled woman's voice again. This time, I recognized it as Galynda's. She sounded desperately frightened. It sounded as though she were struggling. I took a furtive step forward and listened.

"No one would get hurt if you would... stop fighting... little gypsy girl!" The rough, male voice grunted, struggling between words. "Stop it now!" There was a sharp clapping sound. It was the unmistakable sound of a hand solidly slapping a cheek.

"Now whadja go an' do that for? You stupid, blind bitch! You must want me ta hurt ya!"

I had heard enough. I felt the bile rising in my throat and

could taste the bitterness of anger on the back of my tongue. I suddenly forgot all about the pain in my foot. Without any thought for my own safety, I sprang into the cave.

A throaty, animal-like roar emanating from somewhere inside the cave frightened me and caught Galynda and her offender off guard too. When both offender and victim turned to look in my direction, I realized I was the source of that terrifying roar.

With all attention on me, I knew I had to do something, but what?

He was a heavy man. In one of his massive hands, he clutched a large shock of Galynda's hair at the scalp. He stood over her, breathing hard through his mouth. Spittle mingled with his unkempt beard. His greasy hair, darkened by filth, hung limply in his face. His belt was unfastened and his pants were sagging around his ankles. He was, the portrait of pure evil, *Beng* himself.

A sick feeling came over me again. How was it possible to feel such rage toward him and such pain for Lynd at the same time?

Without thinking, I reached into my medicine bag and pulled out my knife. In one swift motion, I was across the cave and plunging the knife deeply into his right shoulder.

He released Galynda's hair and spun to face me. He raised his right fist raised high above my head. I knew it would be coming down hard and heavy. To avoid the blow, I shifted all my weight to my left foot, which failed to support me. I fell to the floor, which was probably my salvation.

His missed swing caused him to lose his balance and brought his head down near me. Acting purely on instinct, I reached for something, anything. My fingers grasped the nearest object, a rock from the scattered fire surround. I swung hard and landed a solid blow to his head.

He crashed to his knees and then fell forward, on top of me. His gurgling snore indicating that he was unconscious.

"Lynd?" It's me. Are you all right? I gasped, unable to breathe under his weight.

"Aye, where is that terrible man?"

"He's right...here...on top of me." I struggled for breath. "I hit him on the head with a rock. We'd better... do something...before he wakes...up." His weight was crushing the air out of my lungs.

Galynda shuffled over to me with her hands outstretched in an uncharacteristically blind manner. For the first time in all my years, I realized that she was so much more vulnerable than I was. My heart ached and I wanted to cry but there wasn't time for such things.

"Down... here Lynd, follow my... voice." I guided her. "Oy!... He's... a heavy bugger!" I grunted.

"Good," I assured her. "You have found me. Now when I count... to three... we'll push him... off of me. Away... from you, to my left. Ready?... One... two... three." With our joint effort, the burley lump of flesh rolled off of me and landed, on his back, on the floor with another cacophonous snore.

"What shall we do with him?" Galynda asked.

"What did he do to you?" I asked.

Now, having adjusted to the candlelight, I could see a large swollen area on her left cheek. Her chest had been abraded at the neckline. Where the bodice of her dress had been fastened, it was untied and nearly half unlaced. The skirt was torn along the waist and the hem. Aside from the scratches, I didn't see any visible blood, which I took to be a good sign.

"Did he force you...did he force himself...did he..." She had been a sister to me all my life. I loved her so much. I couldn't bring myself to name the offense for fear it would be like committing the sin all over again.

"He tried to." She said hollowly. "He came here drunk." She began. "He knew we were here." She had the far-away look that told me she was reviewing the vision she had refused to tell me about. "He was looking for a 'good time' with a couple of 'ripe gypsy bitches.'" She said harshly, mocking him. "He did not get what he came for." she said indignantly.

Relief flooded over me in waves. Suddenly my legs were as limp as bread dough. "Thank the gods for that!" I breathed.

I gathered all the fire stones and restored the fire pit to rights. In short time, I had a small clay pot of water at the ready for a comforting cup of tea and another for healing herbal remedies.

I helped seat Galynda comfortably on the pine bough-covered floor, guiding her to sit upon her folded quilt and rest her back against my bedroll.

As I was working, an idea suddenly came to me. I opened my medicine bag and withdrew the herb pouch and began to rummage through it in search of something.

"I smell your medicine pouch, whatever are you up to?" her Eyebrow arched in suspicion.

"I don't want this man to ever try this again. I want this to be a lesson to him and to everyone he meets."

"Here is my medicine pouch." I offered it to her. "Hold it for me please. I'm going to mix just a little of this powder with some water. I know I saw a feather in here earlier..." My eyes searched the cave until I discovered just the one I needed. Reaching across the man's body, I grabbed the feather and cut the tip off at a very steep angle so that the point was now very sharp. I stabbed the blade of my knife into the soil and then cleaned it on the edge of my skirt and sheathed it.

I had to work quickly before the anesthetic effects of the rock and all the alcohol he had consumed wore off. "How drunk was he?" I asked without looking up from my work.

"He must have been very drunk because his steps were

very clumsy and his words were slurring together. He smelled of alcohol. And he spit when he spoke. 'Tis lucky for me he had so much to drink. He was not very coordinated." Her voice trembled as she spoke.

I opened the kerchief that Magda had packed and set the food aside. I took a small pinch of several medicinal herbs from my pouch and placed them in the kerchief. These would prevent further swelling and would help the bruising heal quickly. I dropped the kerchief and its contents into the pot of boiling water and soaked it. I offered her a soothing cup of herbal tea and returned to my labors over the gargling lump. I was pleased when I had finished. "Now, then. Let us push him out of the cave." I finally announced.

Together, we managed to pull and push and finally roll his overweight body out of the cave. He tumbled out of the cave and down the small hill into some ferns beyond the path. He was sheltered from the pelting rain under the canopy of the pines. His snoring steadfast.

"Tell me why we had to burn his clothes?" Galynda asked, disgusted.

"He shan't be able to follow us without risk of exposing himself. It should slow him down a bit as he attempts to keep himself concealed."

"That is true." She smiled weakly.

"I have treated a great many women and girls who have been victims of this kind of horrible indignity. It leaves damage to their flesh and even makes it so some young women can never become mothers. I have also heard men boasting about what they have done to women and girls. Some have done it more than once to the same woman and some have done it to many."

"The damage to the flesh is nothing when it is measured against the damage to her spirit. I treated a woman once whose spirit smoke was very clouded and small after she had been attacked by her own husband."

"You are sure he wasn't able to get to you?" I asked, looking for assurance that she was still intact.

"Aye." He was unable to fully get to me. He had not gotten here long before you returned.

"I am so sorry this happened to you, Lynd. I love you so much, and the thought of someone hurting you makes me so upset..." The thought of it made me so angry, I wanted to step outside the cave and stab the bastard to death while he slept.

"I am unharmed, honestly. All that man did was give me a horrible fright!" Her voice wavered as she spoke. She took a survey of her body and began to explain her injuries.

"He bruised my cheek when he struck at me, and he hurt my wrists and arms by holding them so roughly. Oh, and he may have bruised a few ribs when he crushed me up against the wall." She recounted.

"You never told me what the water and powdered herbs were for." She changed the subject.

"I mixed the water with a powder you are already very familiar with. It was indigo."

"Indigo? That is a dye for textile! I'm confused." She stammered.

"It can resolve toxicity as well, but when it is mixed with a small amount of water, it can also be used as a makeshift ink for tattoos." I replied.

"But..."

"That..." I had to stop myself from calling him a bastard out loud. "That...*man*... outside has committed a horrible crime."

"Almost, Willow, He did not succeed." She pointed out.

"Well, now his sins are as plain as the nose on his face." I explained.

"What does that mean?" She asked.

"That means that the *man* lying outside has the word 'rapist' tattooed down his big, flat nose. Anyone who sees him will approach with caution. He has brought that *marimé* upon himself. He will have to live with his sin for the rest of his life or risk disfiguring his own face to hide it."

"You never cease to amaze me!" Galynda said and she reached over and gave me a big hug.

"I want others to know what he has done and that he and others like him, shan't get away with it."

"That should do it." She replied nodding her head.

"It's been a long night and both of us need to rest a bit. Let us wash our hands of this man and our faces of the tears and try to eat a little something."

"Here," I said, "let me help you wash your face." I used the herb-soaked kerchief to wash her face and reduce the swelling.

Her face was bruised under her right eye. I could see a distinct outline as if she had been stricken by a hard object. Her beautiful face was smudged with dust and tears and the grime of that retched man's hands.

I fought back my anger and washed her face gently, lovingly. Looking more closely at her, I noticed that her hair was disheveled too.

"After we have had a bit to eat, I can brush your hair if you would like." I offered.

"Aye, please that would be lovely." She smiled.

I dipped the wet kerchief back into the pot, wrung it out, and used one corner of the cloth to clean the dust out of the scrape on the outside edge of my instep. I then tied it securely to my foot. When I had finished with my self-care, I cleaned my knife, thoroughly with the antiseptic tea I had made, rinsed the indigo from the mortar, and washed my hands again.

I opened the kerchief her mother had packed and discovered several thin slices of roast beef. It smelled delicious.

"I love it when Mama roasts it with onions and rosemary

like that. It makes the whole wagon smell heavenly. And then she adds the small round potatoes and the carrots and turnips and cabbage..." Galynda had a smile on her face as she recalled her mother's wonderful cooking. "Just talking about it is making me hungry!"

I took this as a good sign. "Oh, me too, I love to eat your Mama's good cooking." There is sometimes no better medicine than a warm meal and good company.

I made sandwiches with the bread, meat and cheese. I sliced the apples with my knife, so they would be in manageable pieces and offered some to my companion.

We both felt better now that the offensive man was gone, and we had cleaned our wounds and eaten.

I wrapped my quilt about my shoulders and seated myself in the tailor position against the wall of the cave and invited Galynda to sit, cradled in the space made by my legs, facing away from me, so I could brush the tangles out of her hair. Galynda settled in and I pulled her quilt up around her.

"That feels so nice. I love to have my hair brushed. When I was little, I always begged Mama to keep going even after it was already brushed and ready to braid."

Brushing her hair was like smoothing balm on my wounds too. I was giving her comfort and brushing away my anger and fear and negative feelings. With each stroke, I was feeling better. I know she was feeling better too because with each brush stroke, I felt her muscles relax until her full weight was leaning against me. I spoke softer and softer to her until she stopped replying. Her flaccid muscles began to twitch every now and again. I knew she had drifted off to sleep.

I was determined to keep vigil in case her assailant should decide to return to the cave. I sat and brushed her wavy hair and listened to the rain as it pattered gently against the soil, nourishing the earth. I cradled her in my arms and legs and let her sleep. She was secure with me. I wouldn't let anything happen to her.

The candle on the wall shortened with the passage of time, until it flickered, sputtered and then, it went out. I sat and listened to the receding rainstorm, which, like the candle, was sputtering and near its end.

I awoke to the happy sound of birdsong. Sunlight was streaming through the mouth of the cave and landing silently on the floor in brilliant streaks. Tiny bits of dust floated in the sun streams, drifting everywhere and no where.

I took inventory of my surroundings. Galynda, resting heavily against me, was still in a deep sleep. The pine boughs filled the tiny cave with the crisp, clean smell of the forest just outside. The only evidence of our struggle last night were the heel marks made by the drunkard as we dragged his naked body out of the cave.

I realized I was chilled and stiff from sitting up all night. I knew that standing would be a slow process and that putting weight on my foot would be a whole new visit from the pain demon.

I straightened my leg and Galynda stirred in her sleep. She opened her eyes and asked in a sleepy way, "is it my turn to keep watch?"

"'Tis morning already." I answered.

"Why did you not wake me?" She asked.

"I have only, just now, awakened myself. I shall go outside and see how our naked drunk is faring."

"While you do that, I can fold our bedding and we can eat a little something before we return to the wagons." With this, she stretched and leaned even more heavily into me, squashing my full bladder.

"I think I'll water the ferns a bit while I am out there. You fancy a little outing yourself?"

"Yes, but I think I will cower in here while you see what Sir-Drinks-A-Lot is up to." She sat forward and rose to her feet.

I was glad for the moment that she was blind, because I made a fair number of ugly faces trying to straighten up and stand. Worse still, were the frightful faces I must have made when I put weight on my injured foot.

"Are you all right?" Galynda asked.

"Aye, aye, I am just fine." I nodded vigorously. "Why do...why do you ask?" I replied through my teeth, trying to keep pain from creeping into my voice.

"You are making all sorts of little grunting noises in your throat and I can tell something is wrong. Please do not try to hide that fact from me. I know you too well for that."

"It is nothing, really. It was dark on the path last night. I struck my foot on a root that was sticking up. I tended to it last night as best I could. I need to see it in day light to assess how badly I injured it."

"You best be outside looking at it then, because I want a full report." My dear friend stated as she made shooing gestures with her hands.

"Oh, so now I have a second mother." I teased. "I shall never be able to get into any kind of mischief this way!"

She smiled and pointed in the general direction of the exit and said, "Out with you! I'll be needing to water the ferns too you know!"

I made several more horrific faces as I took the first few cautious steps toward the mouth of the cave. I was able to bear some weight on my foot, but I was not looking forward to the walk back to our camp site.

The drunk was still snoring loudly. He appeared to be comfortable and was none the worse for wear. He would have a horrible headache for a few days. His shoulder wound, apparently not as deep as I had imagined, had already sealed itself and had begun to heal.

By the time I had returned to the cave, I was able to hobble without all the comical faces. The stiffness of sleeping sitting upright in a cave was beginning to fade away.

Not wanting to frighten her, I announced my arrival by speaking to Galynda before even entering the cave. "The ogre is still asleep under the tree. You can probably hear him snoring."

Galynda had already folded our bedding and had brushed her hair and put it up in a thick, black braid by the time I returned.

"There you are! I am ready for my turn in that fern patch." She said brightly.

I escorted her out to another patch of ferns. I walked a short distance away to allow her a moment of privacy. When she was done, we walked together to the edge of the stream to wash up.

Her face looked slightly swollen and bruised but it did look better than it had the night before. Thankfully, her assailant had been so drunk he had not been able to strike her with the full force of his strength.

"The water is very clear here; you can see to the bottom. The bed is made of smooth, round river rock. It is slow-moving and is only waist deep at its mid-point, which is about three paces, flanking this boulder." I placed her hand on the boulder to help her become oriented. Little minnows flashed silver as they darted in and out of the shadows cast by the boulder.

She knelt down and began to wash her face. Suddenly, as if changing her mind in mid action, she rose to her feet and began to strip off her clothing, laying them on the boulder. In a small bag that she wore at her waist, she carried the soap I had made for her. It was scented with rosemary and the petals of wild roses.

When I was certain that she could safely maneuver the stream, I engaged myself by removing the herbal wrap so that I could soak my sore foot in the stream. I dipped the kerchief in the water to reactivate the healing herbs in its folds and laid this aside on a rock.

I too, had brought my soap, although mine was scented with the spicy fragrance of sage. I removed my dress, chemise and pantalets, leaving them on the dry rock with my herbal wrap and waded into the stream deep enough to wash my body. I dipped my hands in the water and splashed myself, rubbed the soap vigorously until it made a nice lather, which I rubbed briskly over my sweat-sticky body. Next, I removed my pill box hat, dipped it in the stream, filling it with water. I poured its contents over my torso to rinse away the soap. The water was so cold that it took my breath away. It felt as though I were bathing in icy cold knives. I washed quickly and waded back to shore to dress myself.

The iciness of the water was invigorating and I realized I was getting hungry again. "Are you getting hungry Lynd?" I asked without facing her.

"Aye. I am, a little. I know I will be famished when I get out of this water! It...is... *cold...* in here!" She splashed around for only a few more moments in the water before she too, had finished her bath.

I sat on a large sun-bathed boulder waiting for her to get out of the water onto the safety of the shore. I examined my foot and decided that it was, indeed, broken. Unfortunately, the bones were displaced. I had scraped off a large area of skin on the outer edge and instep of my foot. I reapplied the medicine wrap and secured it with a knot. "I shall be right back; I am going to look for a walking stick. Do you need anything?"

"I shall fare well enough, go ahead." Galynda replied.

I hobbled into the forest in search of a stick stout enough to support my weight. It would serve as a crutch when I walked.

Fortunately, I was able to find a fine, strong stick not far from the cave. I cut away the smaller twigs and peeled the bark off, revealing the clean, smooth wood underneath. I would whittle away the rough edge at the top, where I had broken it off of the felled tree, but this would have to wait until we returned to camp.

I tested it out by climbing up to the cave. I swept the pine boughs out of the cave, away from the entrance, to leave the place as we had found it. I tied the dinner kerchief with the remaining bread, cheese and apples in it to my staff, and slung all four of the water skins over my shoulder. I tucked one quilt tightly under my right arm and then tucked the other beneath that.

I descended the slight grade from the cave and limped the short distance to the water's edge. I met up with Galynda by the stream. She had dressed herself and was seated on a flat rock, warming her body in the sun.

"I brought everything we had in the cave." I said as I walked up to her. I sat beside her on the rock. "What would you say to a little breakfast?"

"That is a lovely idea," She replied with a weak smile.

"Well, your smile seems to be returning a bit this morning." I said untying the cloth holding our food. "That is a good sign. How are you really feeling?"

"Honestly, I am going to be just fine, although I am a bit shaken. I felt very frightened to be left here by myself when you went to find your walking stick." She confessed. "I found myself not breathing, for fear I would hear something, or worse, not hear something! I was so relieved when you returned! I have never felt so helpless in all my life!" she said.

Her brow was furrowed in an expression of utter anxiety. She attempted to recover her poise and finished by saying, "My confidence has been a bit bruised, I would say, but I am sure that with time, I will recover."

I understood what she meant. I had never, before last night, thought of my Galynda as vulnerable or deficient in any way. It had never occurred to me that others might think she was helpless, or worse, an easy target.

It was all coming into focus for me now. I suddenly realized that this was why the women of our clan had not arranged a marriage for her. Perhaps, I reasoned, the Elders in our clan did not deem her to be marriageable! I was appalled.

Galynda had more than proven her great value. People came from miles around and paid many silver pieces to have their fortunes told by her. I was pleased to think that she earned a considerable amount of coinage. I was sickened when I realized she might be perceived as a spectacle by those who sought her council. She might be seen as "the blind seer" like one of the "oddities" I had seen in a traveling circus show. My heart was heavy when I thought about these things.

"You may be the one who can not see, but I am the one who has been blind!" I suddenly announced in the silence.

"What is that supposed to mean?" she asked, puzzled.

"I have never considered what being blind could mean for you. Because you are blind, that man last night saw you as easy prey. Because you are blind, our own tribe has not considered you marriageable, and for that, you shall never get a marriage quilt. You shall not have daughters to share it with." The words streamed out of my mouth as the tears began to flow from my eyes.

"How could I not see it? How could I miss it? I have always seen you as a very capable person. You can do all the things the other women of the camp can do!" I defended.

"Willow," said the gentle voice. "Willow, I know my limitations. I can not go to the rivers and streams to fetch water by myself. I can not go to market alone. I would have great difficulty getting along in camp if it hadn't been for you.

It was you who decided to tie the clothesline from your wagon to mine so that I could always find you. I have always depended on that. It helps me so much when I am trying to orient myself to new surroundings.

It was you, Willow, who taught me so many herbs by touch and smell, and some by flavor. I find that useful in the kitchen and if I ever hurt myself, I may be able to find just the right herb to set myself to healing," she said, trying to make me smile.

"But why are you not angry with being a spectacle. Do you not feel that you are on display? Does that not make you feel misused?" I was incredulous. Tears were streaking down my cheeks and dripping from my chin.

"Willow, I know all these things. I do not see them with my eyes, but I can feel the hush when people see me on the street. I am blind, not deaf. I can hear them whispering behind my back and, worse still, in front of my face.

I am not the one with the infirmity. Their ignorance is a much larger detriment than my blindness will ever be. Can you not see that?" she sagely asked.

I sat on the flat rock, bitter and angry. I did not want others to treat Galynda as though she were broken or had an impediment. She was capable of a great many things. She was my very best friend, my soul sister.

"I shan't marry either." I suddenly said. "We should share a wagon. We would be two old spinster women living alone together. I could do the hunting and gathering, and you could do the cooking and cleaning."

She leaned her body against mine. "That's what I love about you," she said. "You have always made me feel wanted and included and special."

I whipped my head around to face her. "That is because you are wanted and included and special! You are a legend. You are Chosen and that makes you very special. It makes you a treasure. I can not think about my life without you being a part of it every day. I look forward to seeing you when I wake up. I can not wait to see you when I come home from a long day of learning. It does not matter if we are sitting silently or chatting or going for a walk or hunting for herbs, I enjoy being with you. You are the best part of my whole day."

"Willow, I look forward to being with you too. I feel as though I get to see the world through your eyes. You take me places with your stories that I would never have the opportunity to visit on my own.

You have no idea how special you are! Do you not realize that you are Chosen too? You were my very first vision. I was two when you were born. I knew we would be great and close friends and I knew you would be a great medicine woman. I was the seer who confirmed Magda's premonition about you being her Chosen student. Did you not know this?"

"Nay, I did not." I said, thoughtful. "I am curious why no one told me. Were you told not to tell me?"

"Nay." She answered matter-of-factly. "I just thought Magda would have told you about it. No wonder." she said, suddenly thoughtful.

"No wonder, what?" I asked.

"Well, it always seemed that you thought I was a Chosen One because of the famous legend about my conception and birth. But you never really seemed to believe that you were a Chosen One. Your greatness was foreseen by two Chosen visionaries. That is amazing for one little wispy Willow do you not agree?' she said putting her arm around me.

I was flooded with emotion and a tear rolled down my cheek. "Amazing for a weeping willow you mean." I said, smiling through my tears and feeling humiliated for admitting it.

"I was going to pretend I did not notice; I know how you hate to give in to the 'weakness of your emotions' as you would say. Expressing your emotions does not make you weak, Willow. It makes you human. And, it can be very healing, my little healer." she said, lovingly tugging on my braid, from behind, with the hand that had embraced me.

"Why is it that I can start out defending your virtue and I end up being the one who is soothed by you?"

"I have already cried those tears and experienced that anger. Today, it was your turn. I will have my day, and I hope you are there to put balm on my soul wounds."

"I love you, Lynd." I said as I rested my head on her shoulder.

"I love you too Willow." She replied as she rested her cheek upon my hair.

"I do not know another person as deeply as I know you and you always amaze me. It is tragic that all those ignorant people do not know how truly wise and beautiful you are." I defended.

"I am saving all my wisdom and beauty for the few people I deem worthy of knowing me. The others are not worth the effort." Came her calm reply.

"You really do amaze me Lynd. I hope one day my spirit is half as strong as yours." I admired her.

"And you really amaze me too, Willow. You are so wise and compassionate. I know you are smart, you have been in school all your life, but you are wise beyond your years."

"'Tis no wonder we are such good friends. We are so much alike. Imagine how rare it must be to have three Chosen Ones in one caravan at the same time. I am glad we do not have to bear the burden of such great destinies alone." I said.

"I meant it when I said we should get a wagon together. We are both old enough to be on our own. If we had been marriageable, we would have been married off and in wagons of our own." I changed the subject.

"I heard you the first time." Galynda replied. "It sounds very liberating, but what will happen when you need to go to a village to heal the sick and you are away for days at a time? Where shall I go? Shall I wait, alone in the wagon?" She asked reasonably.

"Do you ever think about living in a house? Not moving around so much? I think you would feel more at home in one place. You could familiarize yourself with that place and get around without getting lost." I said, staring into space as I visualized her following a line tethered from her house to the clothesline outside. Everything would have its place.

"Why do I have the feeling you have been thinking about this for a long time?" she asked arching one eyebrow in that accusatory way of hers.

"Because," I replied honestly. "I have been. It just makes sense. If people needed a seer, they could come to you. You could have a small room to do readings in."

"And," she paused for effect. "What about you? How are you going to reach the sick and infirm if you can not go to them?" again the eyebrow arched.

"I think we could get a house with many rooms and I could treat the sick and infirm there. The people could come to me. If they are really ill, they could stay for as many days as they need to recover."

"You truly have thought about this." She said, deep in thought.

"Aye, I have. I want to know what you think about it." I arched my eyebrow at her, even though I knew she could not see me do it.

"I think..." she said, "We should eat our breakfast and get back to camp so that we do not keep the others waiting. I shall answer your questions, Willow, but please allow me a little time to think about everything." She gave me a one-armed hug again to assure me that she would think about her answers and she would let me know what she thought.

"That is a fair request. I shall try to be patient." I said, putting cheese on a slice of bread before offering it to her.

We ate our breakfast in silence as we both mulled over the events of the morning.

Without a thought, I leapt down from my perch atop the

flat rock. I landed, with startling agony, upon my left foot.

Before I could stifle the cry, I made a guttural moan. I regretted it the moment I did it.

"Just how badly did you hurt your foot, Willow?" my elder sister demanded.

I cringed, shoulders hunched, afraid to look her way for fear I would see her arching an accusatory eyebrow in my direction.

"It is nothing to worry about. I just forgot about it for a moment and leapt from the rock. I was just not thinking." I heard myself babbling on and on like a brook.

"If you were thinking, you would have hidden it from me better. Is that not a more precise assessment?" she asked.

I could see the arching eyebrow without looking.

"How do I answer that question? I just...I am fine, Lynd, really. It is bruised. I scraped some skin off the side. It may be broken, but there is not much I can do about that here. I have treated it with herbs to relieve the pain and swelling and to mend any broken bones. When we get back to camp, I shall have Magda look at it."

"May I see it?" she asked, her eyebrow arched in determination.

"Why do I get the feeling that if I tell you it is wrapped in a bandage that will not satisfy you?"

"Because," she said smartly. "You would be correct. We shall not go one more step until I have had the satisfaction of seeing your foot for myself!"

I felt as if I were a two-year-old being scolded by her mother for trying to hide the evidence of some mischief I had committed. There was no way out of this one. I had to let her see my foot. I obediently seated myself on the flat rock again and submitted myself for examination.

I extended my left foot and she caught it in her hands. She untied the knotted kerchief and bent over my foot and inhaled deeply. Then she cupped her hands and carefully placed one under the arch of my foot and one over the instep.

She was looking past the scrapes and bruises. I could she her spirit smoke as it mingled with mine. She was looking deep into the wound. I could feel it in my marrow.

"I do not detect the smell of infection. But you have broken your foot in two places. The innermost break is clean. The outer one will cause you to walk with an uneven gait."

I was dumbfounded. She rarely did readings for me, but each time she did, she was accurate. How was it she would never see my face, but she could see inside my bones?

I did not reply. I felt humble in her presence. She should have been the healer. She could see inside people's bodies.

"Lynd, I just thought of something..." I began.

"What was that?" she asked, securing the wrap to my foot again.

"Do you suppose that we were meant to be together for all of our lives and that was why you were made blind and I was made Medicine Woman, so we would not marry and separate?" I asked all of this in one breath.

"What?" She asked, genuinely puzzled.

"Well, think about this, while you are thinking about your other answers. You are a Chosen seer. I am a Chosen healer. You can see inside people and I can heal them. Could that not be our destiny?" again, I was speaking in a jumbled manner in an effort to keep up with my mind.

She stopped tying my wrap and stood stock-still. Her clear blue eyes searched the space between us for some unseen answer. Her brow was furrowed in deep thought but there was something else there, something that looked like recognition.

"I shall think about that." She said slowly, her focus far away. Her brows still knit together, deep in concentrated thought. "Willow," she began slowly and thoughtfully.

"Aye?" I responded.

"I have shared this information only with Aunt Magda.

Now, it feels as if it is time for you to hear it as well. Everything that is happening now has been foretold." She spoke with an air of solemnity that hooked my attention. I felt the ser-iousness of it grasping at a sinew in my belly below my umbilicus.

"For more than a moon now, I have been dreaming again and again about a wagon wheel or something like a wagon wheel and travel and change." She spoke slowly as she tried to see her way through the misty veil of her vision.

"All will be well, but change shall come abruptly. It shall come more suddenly than having families leaving us one by one in our travels." She continued.

I had many such conversations with Galynda in our lives together. It never ceased to give me goose flesh when her voice slowed and her eyes squinted as she searched the ethers for clarity.

"Not to worry," Galynda reassured me. "We shall all remain together."

"This is happening now." I asked for clarification. "Or happening very soon?"

"Aye." She replied. "All will be well. I just wanted you to be prepared for these changes." She waved her hand as if to dismiss the seriousness of the subject.

I knew my cousin well enough not to press for more information. More would be forthcoming when the timing was right for it.

"So, may I get down now, if I promise not to jump on my sore foot?" I teasingly asked.

"Aye, you may." She answered. "But you have to tell me if you need a rest. That foot really hurts." She said seriously.

I slid carefully down from the rock and took my walking staff in my left hand. I tucked my bedroll under my right arm and Galynda placed her left hand in the crook of my right elbow.

Together, we slowly made our way back to camp.

Our Return to Camp

We were silent as we made the slow and painful journey back to the camp. Each of us deep in thought about all that had happened in the cave and what we had discussed on the banks of the shallow stream.

I could not imagine what the families would say to us about our injuries when we arrived at camp. It was even more difficult for me to imagine what they would say to us about my request to move out of our family wagons and into one of our own. Now that we had seen how vulnerable we really were, I felt certain that they would deny us that liberty.

As we neared the encampment, I slowed my pace. Galynda noticed the change immediately and asked, "Why do you slow your step? Is your foot hurting you terribly?"

"Nay, my foot is not hurting me over much," I began.

"You are concerned about what our families shall say when they see us battered and limping. You have fears that all that we have talked about shall be decided for us."

"Aye." I admitted, astounded at her accuracy. "'Tis

exactly what I was thinking about."

"Willow, you worry over-much." She said giving my arm a gentle squeeze. "It shall work out as 'twas meant to. You shall see. All will be well." She reassured.

"It shall? I wish I had your foresight or faith or whatever 'tis that gives you such a peace in your spirit." I said, furrowing my brow. Oh, how I did wish I did not agonize over every small detail.

Tiny tendrils of smoke rose from the circle of wagons I could see in the distance. Before I could tell Galynda that camp was in sight, she spoke.

"I can smell the wood smoke of Ahmad's carving scraps." She said. "We must be fairly near the camp."

"We are." I replied. "Are you ready?"

"I can not think of any way to prepare myself more for this moment." She replied honestly.

Judging by the careful manner in which she phrased her words, I gathered she had been withholding more about today. I was resolved to trust in her decision to tell me when the time was right.

I could see Ahnja running toward us.

"Your mother approaches." I whispered quietly out of the side of my mouth. "Now, she is running," I breathed to Galynda. Something must be wrong." I held my breath. My heart was flapping about in my chest like a bat. Galynda's grip on my elbow tightened and I could feel perspiration forming between her skin and mine.

"I am glad to see you both." Ahnja said, out of breath. "It has been a long and difficult night. Much has happened here. You, too, have also been influenced by the night's activities. You are both injured!" She surveyed. "Are any of your injuries serious?" She asked these questions as she held us each at arm's length and turned us this way and that, assessing the damage.

Before I could even open my mouth to deny the severity

of my wounds, Galynda unearthed the truth about my foot and was requesting an immediate visit with Magda.

Embarrassed, I conceded that yes, my foot probably did need some attention, but I had tended to it myself by the stream.

"We have already packed up the camp. We must be ready to move on soon." The frantic mother informed. "The people of this village have become unfriendly towards our people. There have been raids upon the markets, horse thefts, violent acts against women and children!

Our allies tell us that much damage has been done by a drunken, mean hulk of a man and his band of thugs. The villagers are fearful and angry and blame the nomads, who are transient and easy to blame for many of their woes. The men of the village are preparing to burn out any migrants they see, for they want no more to do with nomads."

My mind was swimming in all that had happened. The coldness of the people, the mean nature of the crimes in the community, the anger of the man that had wanted to hurt Galynda, it was all swirling together.

"Is everyone in our camp well? Has anyone been hurt? How can I help?" I asked my questions one following another. I was prepared to help in any capacity in which I might be needed. I was compelled to busy my mind and body in an effort to deflect the growing feelings of helplessness and anger and fear and anxiety which were building up pressure in my chest and making breathing all but impossible.

Galynda cut right through my smoke screen. "First, we must have your foot tended to!" she commanded.

I rolled my eyes at my own weaknesses and sighed in resignation. We were in danger and we needed to move on quickly. It was better to allow myself to be treated by my clan family. I was in pain and they could see it. My painful lopsided gait made me cumbersome and awkward, and any obdurate attempts to help my family would only serve to slow them down which would put us all in danger.

Magda opened the door to our wagon as soon as she saw us approach. She too had been nervously awaiting our arrival.

"Come Willow, come in. Let us have a look at that foot." Her usual calm voice was strangled by tension.

She brought me into the comforting, familiar surroundings of our wagon. She seated me on the nearest of our two upholstered chairs in our sitting room just inside the door. Directly in front of me was the kitchen and woodstove. It was comforting to see and smell the herbs which hung from the ceiling to dry. Behind our chairs in the sitting area was our library of materia medica and other fascinating tomes. Our shared bed was at the head of the wagon.

"What have you done to your foot?" She inquired.

"I stumbled over a root in the forest last night, during the storm. Galynda has looked at it and has said it is broken in two places and that there is some displacement" I dutifully reported, hardly daring to meet her eye to eye.

"This clumsiness is not at all like you. You are always aware of your surroundings, Willow. You are at home with Nature." Magda reasoned, her brows knit together in puzzlement.

"I know this, and I am ashamed that I allowed myself to become distracted. I was frightened last night, Magda." There, I had said it. I admitted to being frightened.

"You were frightened. What was it frightened you?" Her expression changed to concern.

"Galynda was feeling very uneasy last night. She had told me she had another vision, but she had not told me what she had seen. She was very nervous and upset. I allowed her anxiety to influence me." I explained.

"I began to feel nervous too." I continued. "I felt as if

someone were going to leap out of the brush and get us both. I had to leave her to fetch the water. It was getting dark. I did not wish for her to feel she was alone."

I recounted the story to my mother, who was making tea and listening intently. "It was a root I had only just warned Lynd about! I knew it was there, but the lightning and thunder and then the scream had me frightened ... and careless." I allowed my words to trail off.

"Do not be so harsh with yourself Willow." Magda scolded. She sat on the bed beside me, stroked a loose tendril of hair behind my ear, and continued. "You allowed Galynda the right to be frightened, did you not? Why would the right to be frightened not also be extended to you? You are not made of stone. You are flesh. You are human and you have a right to every one of your emotions." She patted me on the knee reassuringly.

"So, when you returned to the cave, was everything as you thought it should be?" Magda encouraged me to talk my way through the traumas of the night before.

"Nay, I found a large, surly man there. He had Galynda against the wall." My voice faltered and choked with emotion. I could not continue. A knot had formed in my throat and I could not speak. I could taste salt in my mouth and then, the tears began to flow from my eyes so that I could no longer see.

Magda put both arms around me and gently began to rock me. I felt safe in her arms. Just being near her was both soothing and healing. It was a long while before I was able to speak again. When I did, I told her everything that had happened in the cave.

"Magda, Lynd knew he would be there and yet, she would not tell me he was coming!" I exclaimed.

"Galynda loves you very much. Do you not see that she did not wish for you to be hurt? She was only doing what she could to keep you free from harm."

"Magda," I sniffed. "I realized, for the first time, last night that Lynd is well and truly blind! I clearly understood for the first time that she is really vulnerable, and that vulnerability frightens me! I do not want for anything evil to befall her!" As I spoke, the tears burned hot trails down my cheeks. The honesty of the emotions I was finally allowing myself to feel was overwhelming.

She could easily lean forward in her seat beside me to fetch the cup of tea that she had set aside to cool, for the kitchen counter top and the tiny wood stove beside it were readily within reach in the close quarters of the vardo. Nervous energy compelled her to move. She rose to her feet, thought better of her action, and feigned the need to wipe down her spotless kitchen surfaces before she retrieved the cup.

Magda offered me the cup as my concerned mother rather than my objective medicine woman. I could smell chamomile, catnip and valerian. I accepted it and took a sip.

"Willow, are you sure that the man did not harm Galynda?" There was concern in her face again.

I felt my throat tighten at the thought of what the man had gone to the cave to do. I nodded my head meekly. I took a second sip of my tea in an attempt to free the knot from my throat. It seemed to work and I was able to answer.

"Galynda said he was far too intoxicated to do much of anything that required coordination."

"Thank the gods for that!" She said this with her fingertips over her lips, as though she could restrain an errant comment before she uttered it. Her jaw muscles were taut, and I knew she was worried by the way she stood with the knuckles of her other hand propped on her hip.

"He struck her in the face, but he was not able to land his strike squarely. I have treated the bruise with a compress of arnica and St. John's wort flowers and a bit of witch hazel bark.

Magda encouraged me to finish my tea in one large draft. "How is your spirit now Willow? Are you feeling better?" Magda asked.

"Aye, much better, thank you. I am so glad you were here. You are good medicine for my soul." The care and support had gone far to comfort me and to soothe balm on my frightened soul. I was also feeling the effects of the valerian and there was something else in the tea, I could not recall having tasted before.

"I am glad I could be here with you as well. It is an honor to see you grow and learn. Last night, you grew a great deal. You learned a lot about yourself and Galynda and the way that some people can become when they do not grow in a healthy, loving community." My mother soothed. She gathered a few of her supplies from various cupboards and laid them out on the small kitchen countertop.

I had to agree. Last night had been an eventful night. I had grown a lot from my experiences. Today, I felt differently about a great many things. Inwardly, I resolved that no one would bare Galynda's vulnerabilities again.

"I can see you have your mind working. Your eyebrows are knit together in the center." She came to me, cupped my cheeks in her hands and stroked my furrowed brow with her thumbs.

I smiled. "I get that from you. I am always thinking about something." My mind was growing foggy and focus was becoming hazy.

"Are you ready for me to take a look at that foot?" Without waiting for an answer, Magda was kneeling on the floor before me, unwrapping my foot.

She examined the abrasion, and then closed her eyes, brought my foot up to her face and inhaled, just as I had seen Galynda do. "It does not smell infected."

"Galynda did the same thing. She smelled my wound." I marveled.

"Aye," Magda smiled. "She is a great teacher."

I was confused for a moment. "You mean you learned that from her?"

"Of course, because she is blind, her other senses must make up for her deficiency and so, are much keener." She explained matter-of-factly.

As she knelt before me, she ran her hands gingerly over my foot. I knew she was feeling the internal structures for displacement. As she did this, her eyes went into a far away gaze as though she were remembering something. "I have a story I wish to tell you now."

"I am listening." I said. "I always treasure your stories."

One day, before you were even born, when Galynda was only a small child, I was tending to her and compounding herbs. A man, who had been bitten on the leg by a wild boar, came to me for treatment. I looked at his leg and was preparing to clean the wound and put a poultice on it. Galynda wandered up to the man and placed her tiny hands on his knee and sniffed his wound. She turned to me and announced that an infection was beginning to set in.

"Everyone you encounter in this life is your teacher. If you can accept your lessons and learn from them, you will be truly wise." While she spoke to me, she continued to palpate my foot more deeply. Her expression was neutral, but I knew Magda well enough to see concern where a stranger would not.

It was better to allow myself to be treated than to attempt to deceive anyone in my clan family. I was in pain and they could see it.

"I can feel the displacement." She said nodding with a serious expression on her face. We need to see if we can convince it to fit back in its place."

I had seen her reduce dislocations before. I had learned from her and had assisted her many times. I knew that the process was not a pleasant one for the patient.

"Will you fetch the book of healing fungi from the shelf behind you please?" She asked.

I recognized her attempt to divert my attention away from the task at hand, but I obliged her request and turned away from her to reach for the volume she requested, which was located just out of easy reach, on the shelf behind me. As I stretched for it, Magda grasped my ankle with one hand and my toes with the other. With a deft tug, she brought my bones back into alignment with a sickening, audible pop.

My quest to retrieve her book ended abruptly. Searing hot pain shot through my foot and ran up my leg. The wagon began to spin and I felt as if I was going to vomit. I gritted my teeth and closed my eyes tightly.

When I opened my eyes, I was tucked into the bed. Galynda was seated next to me holding my hand. Her face was pale and filled with concern. The wagon swayed and for a moment, I felt as though I would pass out again. Then, I realized we were in motion.

"Lynd, what is happening? Are we moving?" I attempted to sit up, my head began to swim, and I decided lying back would not be a bad idea.

"You have been asleep for many miles already. How are you feeling? Magda said she tried to put your foot right. Did it hurt much?"

"Tried to put my foot right? What do you mean 'tried'? Did it not go back? I felt it pop and I heard it!" I felt my stomach flip at the memory.

"She said we shall have to wait and see how it mends. If you want it to mend well, you shall have to rest it for two full moons."

I knew the prescription well. I had advised many people to stay off their feet for as long and never realized how devastating the news was to them. I would be helpless for a very long time. I could not afford to sit around while my family did all the work. I had heard all these arguments before too.

Now, 'twas time for me to sit and learn this lesson from the other side of the table. 'Twas not going to be an easy road. I would gain a whole new understanding of patience.

"There is much to talk about tonight. There has been growing unrest in the villages about other bands of nomads. The villagers have become wary of groups of traveling strangers. Many have vowed to chase all nomads away from their villages with threats of violence."

"That is what happened to us last night. There is a great deal of unrest at this time. There is much anger. 'Tis breeding hatred. Much damage has been done at the hands of a few. Soon there shall be few villages we can trade with." Galynda explained.

"Villagers who once traded with us have fear that they shall be targeted by their own neighbors if they are seen trading with us." She continued.

I listened silently. The villagers had so much pain and anger. I could not understand why these rogue groups of bandits and gypsies had chosen to poison the life-giving waters of commerce.

"Our families have been talking about breaking up the caravan. They are discussing finding settlements and becoming shopkeepers as all the others in our clan have done." She cried.

"This is important Willow, are you still with me?" She pleaded. I squeezed her hand to let her know I was listening and to please continue.

"Willow, my mother had a meeting with Magda while they were awaiting our return from the cave." She paused. I pulled her hand closer to my chest.

"They have decided to stay together and find a safe community to settle into. They have also decided that we, you and I, should not be separated. Aunt Magda and Mama shall share Mama's wagon and horses and you and I are to share Magda's medicine wagon. They feel that while we have not married, we should have some degree of independence. Aunt Magda wants for you to continue to gather herbs and thinks that by the time you your bones have knitted; it shall be time for you to assume the mantle of chief Medicine woman." I squeezed her hand again. I had so much to think about.

"You are a sage." Galynda stated.

"I just know which gods to pray to." I whispered with a small sideways smile. "When is all of this moving and settling going to happen?" I asked.

"That depends upon how fast your foot mends. We are traveling to villages we are most familiar with. Some of the families have already decided which villages they wish to settle in. By harvest time, you should be pretty well healed, and we shall be down to our family. Only Magda, Mama, Ahmad, you and me, three wagons shall remain."

Our caravan had always consisted of between eight and eleven wagons. The thought of only three wagons was surprisingly lonely. These people were our family. Through the years, we had seen some families grow weary of traveling and we had sadly watched them settle in villages.

We understood their reasons for settling and accepted their choice to stay in one place and wished them the best. We would miss them, but we would look forward to seeing them on return visits to their communities. There was always much news to catch up on.

"Our families seem to be thinking the same way you do, Willow. What do you think?" Galynda spoke for both of us. "'Tis truly amazing! If I did not know you were in here with Magda, I would have sworn you had spoken with the Elders about your idea." Galynda stated. Her eyebrow was raised in an accusatory arch but her clear blue eyes lovingly sparkled with warmth.

"I know you told me you wanted to think about everything, but now that it is not just my foolish idea, what do you think?" I asked.

"I can see the thought that has gone into everyone's decision. It does make sense, I agree." She nodded. "I am a little scared to think of being away from our families, but that is what the married women do is it not?" she reasoned.

"Aye," I replied. "But no one says we must live away from our parents. We might have a farm where we can all live and work together, as we do in the caravan. Or, we may choose to live in the same community and visit often. We must allow ourselves to be open to the possibilities that await us."

My companion was silent while she processed all her options.

"'Tis as if our lives have changed over night! I have seen many things in our future, even these changes, but I did not understand how it would feel to stand in the midst of it." Galynda marveled.

"Are you all right?" I queried.

"Aye, I believe so. I just have had so very much to think about." She said, already in thought.

"Magda refers to it as 'growing'. I refer to it as 'exhausting'." I said trying to inject a little humor. "'Tis exhausting!" I defended.

She agreed. "Indeed."

"I do believe I am ready to grow up and become more independent. I can not think of a better companion to spend my life with than you, my dearest friend and sister." Saying this, she laid her head on my chest and gave my hand a squeeze.

"I am glad to hear it. I am honored to think you would share your life with me." I said with a sigh.

When I awoke, Galynda lie asleep beside me in the narrow bed. Stars smiled down at us from the heavens, through the tiny window beside the bed. I was filled with a feeling of calm. The heavens seemed to be telling me all would be well.

The next morning, I was not permitted to help break up camp or load the carts and wagons. In short, I was allowed only to watch.

Our families agreed it would be a good idea to move Galynda into Magda's wagon as soon as possible so that we could develop a good routine for packing, unpacking and housekeeping. I already lived in the wagon, so it was Galynda who put upon to move.

As I sat and watched everyone else working, I could feel a growing frustration inside of me. I did not like feeling that I was helpless or in the way. Rather than to sit and allow the frustration to grow into anger or bitterness, I began to devise a way to keep myself useful.

Since I was sighted, it had become my chore to drive. I could at least feel helpful holding the reins. There could be some difficulty with the brakes, but this had been anticipated and our wagon was settled between the others to keep our horses at a respectable pace. In the event of a hill, a driver from one of the other wagons would come and help us maneuver ours safely.

As we traveled along in silence, I had the opportunity to do some plotting. When we stopped for the evening, Ahmad came to lift me off the wagon. "Ahmad, I have an idea that should help me walk and enable me to be useful around here again, but I need your help."

"I shall do what I can to help you. What is it you are thinking?" He asked as he gingerly set me down on a round of firewood that had been set out for me.

"I have been thinking of a brace that shall allow me to walk and yet keep the weight off of my foot." I explained.

"This is an interesting project," he said scratching his bushy mustache, thoughtfully. "I like your idea. Let me help get camp set up and then I shall return here to you." He promised.

Galynda, climbed inside the wagon and was preparing her share of the dinner we would all eat.

I sat on my stump and watched the men as some tended the horses and others set about chopping and stacking the wood the women would need for cooking. Still others gathered buckets of water for cooking and cleaning.

I was impressed at how efficiently our camp worked. Everyone had a job, and everyone did the jobs expected with no fuss or hesitation.

Before long, Ahmad was back with a roll of canvas under his arm. He untied it and unrolled it. There, in neat little rows, he stored his carving tools.

"Have you a design in mind?" He asked as he withdrew a chisel and began to glide it back and forth across his leather strop.

"Well, I hesitated, aye and nay. I believe 'twill have to be above my ankle and 'round both sides of my foot." I began. My brows were furrowed as no clear picture of this brace had actually entered my mind.

Ahmad tested the edge of his newly sharpened chisel with the flat of his thumb and placed it back in its pouch. He withdrew another and began to strop it. "I am thinking too. I think together we shall have some success in making you a beautiful brace." He said with a bright smile on his tan leathery face.

I would miss him when we all separated. A gifted blacksmith by trade, he was also a genius with wood and leather. He had created many wonderful, useful items from ideas he had in his head. I was always interested in the things he would design, and it was always a pleasure to see him create it right before my eyes.

The air was beginning to take on the scents of baking bread and stewing meats and boiling vegetables and tea.

"I have an idea for you." Ahmad said suddenly. "Look

here" he said, picking up a stick and snapping off the tiny twigs. He began to sketch my ankle in the dust.

"Here is your foot" he said, pointing with his stick. Pointing to the outer edge of my bandaged foot he said, "And this is the place on your foot that is broken, yes?"

I nodded, listening for what he would say next.

"We want to avoid pressure there. So, we put all the pressure on the ankle and in back!" He said pointing at my heel. He began drawing in the dust again and said, "Now we need a way to attach it to your leg without causing you more pain." He brushed his mustache with his thumb and index finger and began to hum a tuneless melody while he worked. This was how I knew he was enjoying the challenge of his new project.

It was time to eat then and after the meal, I joined Galynda and the other women as each washed the dishes for her wagon, dried them and put them away.

I was tired from the long day. I decided to stay put inside the wagon and do some mending on the hem of my skirt, which always seemed to be in some form of disarray.

Galynda, not wanting me to feel abandoned, climbed inside the wagon and joined me. "Are you well, Willow?"

"Aye. I am just tired from the long day. 'Tis quite interesting," I observed. "One mere change in my daily activities has been so exhausting for me. I have decided not to bother anyone about coming to get me out and put me back, I believe I shall simply stay in for the night and do a bit of mending. My skirts always seem to require it."

"Would it be agreeable to you if I decided to stay in with you?" Galynda asked.

"Of course," I nodded. "'Tis your home too. You should be able to do in it as you wish!" I stated. "Does that not sound wonderful to you? 'Tis truly *our* home." I spoke almost as though I were in a trance, repeating the fact over and over as if to make it more real.

"Indeed, 'tis truly our home." She said embracing me. "What a lot of changes we have come through these last few days!" She breathed. She had a relaxed smile on her face.

"How is your spirit doing since the man in the cave? Are you still frightened and jumpy inside?" I asked.

"I am." She admitted. "But I can see that I shall be healed very soon. I feel I am less and less frightened about the past and more and more excited about our future." She leaned in toward me and said, "I have discovered that I do look forward to having a home in one place. I imagine living in a place where I do not have to pack and unpack my home every few days. It shall be a place where I know right where everything is. It shall be a home, Willow, a real home." She seemed far away as though she could see the home she desired so much.

In my heart I was thrilled for Galynda. Having to depend on others for only a few hours was too much for me. I could understand her need to have a home where she could put down roots. I wondered if my wild spirit could be as content to live in one place. I reckoned I could be fairly satisfied anywhere, as long as I was surrounded by those who loved me.

We talked for hours, while I stitched the hem of my skirt. As it began to grow dim outside, I realized I would have to stand to light a lantern. It suddenly occurred to me that Galynda would not see that it was growing dark outside. Since she had no need of light, she had no need to light a lantern. Having made this realization, it became pointedly clear that it would be up to me to light my own lanterns. That night, I simply chose to go to bed instead.

Morning came early for me, since I had not gone out to pass my water before going to sleep. I managed to wriggle my way out of the bed and over to the door. Leaving Galynda asleep. I sat on the top step of the wagon and dragged myself down the steps one at a time, careful not to bump my injured foot.

Since the camp was quiet, I clumsily hopped, one-footed to the far side of the wagon. It was quite clear to me that I could not go much further. This was partially because of my injuries, but more so, because of my painfully full bladder.

I struggled to lift my skirts and lean on the wheel of the wagon so I could void. I nearly lost my balance twice and was mortified at the thought of falling into my own urine and having to wait there, with my underthings around my ankles, until someone awakened and came to my rescue.

Fortunately, I managed to stay standing and realized how much easier my life would be if I could urinate standing up as men did. Dogs, I noted, actually lifted a leg to urinate. The thought of having one too many legs to do the job seemed rather comical for some reason. Dogs lifted the one leg to avoid urinating on it. Seeing the slightly damp edge of my nightshirt, I discovered this was a trick I would have to work on.

I hopped back to the camp side of the wagon. It was usually the duty of the first person to rise to start the fire. I decided that, since I was up, I should start a fire.

I hobbled to the fire surround and placed moss and twigs in on top of the embers. I blew the embers into tiny sparks of life. I added sticks and then logs as the fire grew.

I felt as though I had really accomplished a great task when the fire was ablaze to my satisfaction.

The sun was just beginning to wake and stretch his fiery arms up over the horizon. The scattered clouds shone in beautiful hues of pink against the velvety blue-black of the sky. The stars were beginning to twinkle and fade.

The air always seemed to be freshest at this time of day, it was fresh and new and full of promise.

The log on the fire popped and crackled. In the distance, birds were beginning to waken with cheerful dialogue. The horses, tethered to nearby trees or wagons, snorted at the new day.

I was just about to rise and go to my wagon when I heard a voice beside me. "Good morning, Willow." It was Ahmad. He was walking toward me from his wagon. His eyes sparkled and his mustache bristled happily as it curved into a smile. I could see that he was carrying something behind his back.

"I have something here for you to try on. I had it ready for you last night, but you had turned in early. Are you well?" He asked with concern.

"Aye." I replied. "I was tired from hopping around all day, so I decided to turn in early."

The smile in his mustache returned and spread upwards to become a sparkle in his warm eyes. He brought the hidden item into view. He extended his hand and proffered a small parcel wrapped in a bit of cloth.

I accepted his offering with a growing smile and anticipation and unwrapped it with care. He had crafted a fine brace for me out of leather.

"Oh, Ahmad," I breathed. "This is truly remarkable." I said, stroking the ornately tooled leather with my fingers. I lifted it to my nose and breathed in the smoky scent of tanned leather. I am so excited to try it out! I am growing so weary of feeling useless." I explained.

"That is why I worked to finish this brace for you." He said with a proud smile. He thrust out his chest and planted his knuckles upon his hips, the effect of which caused his belly to pooch as well. "Let us try it on, shall we?" With that, he extended his hand to reclaim the brace.

I sat back on the stump and extended my bandaged foot to him. He knelt before me and fastened the brace to my ankle. It fit rather like the supportive shaft of a tall boot. It was laced in the front with thin strips of leather. My foot was suspended above the ground by a thick, wide heel.

I was surprised at how comfortable it was. He had lined

it with lamb's wool and had padded the heel extensively.

"It fits beautifully! I love it, Ahmad!" I stood and embraced him about the neck.

"You must try it out today. This was not as easy as making the special shoes for horses. That, I can do with my eyes half-closed, my little pony." He said stroking my disheveled hair out of my face with his large callused hand. "Let me know if it binds or rubs anywhere and we shall modify it." He said proudly.

"Oh, I shall!" I exclaimed in a whisper. "I shall, indeed!" I could scarcely contain myself.

"Please," Ahmad began. "Walk about for me a bit so that I may see how well it shall serve you." He gestured with an index finger traveling in a meandering fashion.

I wondered if that is how I appeared to him as I went about my day. I cautiously stood and took a few furtive steps. The brace held my injured foot off the ground. My gait was modified so that my weight was on the heel of the brace rather than the injured part of my foot.

"I love it! Thank you, my dear, dear Ahmad!" I embraced him again and kissed him affectionately on the cheek.

Ahmad smiled warmly as he stood and watched me poke about in the dust with my new brace. His left wrist rested on his hip, his right index finger and thumb brushed thoughtfully through his thick bushy moustache.

He stood and observed my movements as I stumped back to my wagon. I knew he was working out some problem because he slid his hat forward with his thumb and index finger, scratched his head at the crown with his middle, ring and pinky fingers and then readjusted the hat on his head.

Doors were creaking open upon their hinges; bedding was put out to freshen in the air. Pans were clattering from their shelves and hooks. These were the restless sounds of camp waking up. A new day had begun, and I knew that it would be a great one.

A New Day

I hobbled to the wagon I shared with Galynda and found the walk was faster and relatively painless. Climbing the steps was also made much easier with the brace.

"Good morning!" I chirped to a still groggy Galynda. "'Tis going to be a lovely day!"

Galynda lay on the bed with her hair mussed and her cheeks still flushed with sleep. "Hmmm?" She asked, "What?"

"Oh, I am sorry to have wakened you! Did you sleep well?" I asked as I stumped along toward Galynda in the unmade bed.

"Aye, I believe so." Galynda replied as she stretched and hung her feet over the edge of the bed. She sat there, rather slumped, thinking.

"Are you not awake yet?" I asked, amused.

"Awake?" she blinked. "Aye. Lovely? We shall see..." She said sounding cryptic. Her eyebrow was arched in a playful manner and we both had to laugh.

"What say we get our unkempt bed made and enjoy a bit of tea to put some spark into your sleepy eyes?" I suggested with enthusiasm.

"You are in a good humor this morning, Willow," as she pulled and smoothed the sheets into submission.

"Well, aye, I am, indeed!" I replied. "Ahmad has devised a fine brace for my foot, and I feel certain that I shall be more mobile and have a far better day for it." I announced.

"Let me see." Galynda waited for me to sit beside her on our bunk. She reached out and began to explore the details of the magnificent brace our friend had made.

"'Tis very well made. Do you find it comfortable? Does it bind anywhere?" She asked with concern.

"Aye, I find it very comfortable and supportive. Nay, I haven't found any place that it binds yet. I only just put it on. I am very excited to get on with my duties today!"

"Willow, Magda anticipated this. She knew that you would devise something, or that you and Ahmad would. She has asked me to keep you off your foot as much as possible. You shall still be on restricted duties until your foot heals."

I could see that it hurt her to tell me this. She did not like being the bearer of bad news nor did I like being the receiver of bad news. I chose not to react in a negative manner. Nothing could stand in the way of the glorious day I knew was in store for us.

"I should have known that you would all be looking out for my welfare." I said, nodding my head. "I appreciate that."

"Oh," Galynda breathed, "That is good news. I rather thought you were going to make hard work of these next two moons." With this she began to brush her long dark hair.

"Not me." I jested. "I shall be a most compliant patient." And I meant it. I realized that two agonizing moons of light duties was much easier to endure than a lifetime of infirmity. I had witnessed far too many people living off scraps and begging in the streets of their own villages because their clansmen were not as supportive as my own. I shook my head at this. It truly was a shame that the villagers felt nomads were barbaric people.

I pulled my dress over my head and tied on a clean pinafore. I quickly wrestled a brush through the tangled brambles I called hair and tied it up in a lopsided braid.

"Are you ready to go and get some tea, bright eyes?" I teased.

"Aye, that would be lovely," she said, as she put the finishing touches to her sleek, smooth plait. "I should love some."

I enjoyed the newfound freedom that improved mobility afforded me. I was able to do more than I had without it, but the uneven gait made my hip and back ache before the day was through.

I decided that I would endure the pain. It was a small price to pay for the freedom that I had gained. Ahmad had put a lot of thought and hard work into making the brace for me. I certainly did not wish to hurt him by complaining about something that was undoubtedly my fault. I was, perhaps, over working I convinced myself.

When our families began to gather around the central fire that evening, Ahmad eagerly approached me. "Well, little Willow, I am seeing a problem." He said, stroking his mustache.

"A problem?" I asked with furrowed brow.

"Aye, I am seeing a problem with the brace. It is causing one leg to be longer than the other. It is making your walking a bit catawampus. I am not liking this problem, so I am fixing it." He said rubbing his callused hands together.

"How do we fix it?" I asked, now pulled into another of his ingenious ideas.

"I am thinking that we are traveling north." He said looking skyward. "And I am noticing the air is getting colder at night." He stalled for effect. "I am thinking, what you are needing is new boots." He said with a broad white smile.

I realized that he was a very handsome man despite the tragic loss of his family to a camp raid.

As I had lost my family to a camp raid too, Ahmad had elected himself as my surrogate father and protector. He had a profound interest in my whereabouts and my activities. He took special care of me by making specialized herb digging tools and sharp tools for cutting and preparing them as well. He lovingly made my otter skin medicine bag, explaining that the playful and inquisitive otter was my animal protector. He took special care to make comfortable winter shoes for me since he knew that was the only season I would wear them.

Looking into his leathery brown face, I could see the remnants of a lifetime of smiles and laughter. I had made it my job to keep him laughing, which was not a difficult task.

"You have a very busy mind do you not?" I answered with a smile.

"Aye! That, I have." He agreed with a smile. "Now let us measure your other foot for a winter boot," he said, withdrawing a piece of leather thong from his pocket.

I extended my bare foot and he set about measuring my instep and arch, heel and toes. He traced the outline of my foot onto a piece of stiff leather, which I took to be the sole of the boot he would make.

After a hearty meal of lamb and vegetable stew and flat bread, I helped Galynda with the dishes and promptly went to bed.

I was awakened by a knock on the door of our wagon. I recognized the knock and invited Magda in.

"Are you well, Willow?" There was concern in her voice.

"Aye, why do you ask?" I blinked sleepily.

"Everyone has eaten breakfast and put away dishes and still you have not come out for your meal. This is not in your character. You are usually the earliest bird."

I was surprised to hear that I had overslept. "But I went

to bed early!" I said as I sat up.

"And you are still in your clothes from yesterday!" Magda exclaimed. "Are you certain that you do not have an infection in that wound?"

"It does not feel feverish and it is not weeping." I answered. "Perhaps I overworked yesterday."

"That is a very good possibility." She nodded with a thoughtful frown. "I watched you scuttling about all day on that brace." She flicked an accusatory finger toward my foot. "If you are not more watchful, I shall have to take it away from you so that you will rest and allow your foot to heal."

I felt ashamed of myself and hung my head. "I am sorry Magda. You are the best healer I know, and I have insulted you by ignoring your orders."

"I do not want apologies. I want to see you mend. We need your help and you are not much help to us when you are sleeping in and going to bed early. You may do a little without tiring or injuring yourself.

You did not say so, but yesterday you had more pain than just the pain of your foot. I saw by the end of the day that you could scarcely move. This helps no one." She turned to leave the wagon.

"Magda," I began. "I shall do better. Your advice is sage, and I have made a fool of myself by not following your orders. You are a great and wise teacher and I have proven myself to be a poor student."

"Willow, I am not here to punish you. I came out of concern for you." My guardian replied.

"Aye, I know this, but I also know that your medicine is the finest in all the lands we have traveled. I feel I have insulted you by not respecting your orders and by doing more than I should and..."

"Willow," Magda halted my babbling with an upraised hand. "I understand your sentiment. I know that you understand what it is to be a student and a healer. Now you are learning what it is to be a patient. Perhaps they are called 'patients' because they must be patient while they heal.

There is no better way for you to understand the needs of your patients than to be one yourself. We must have patience and compassion for even the most difficult patient. Every one of them has a reason for not taking the powders or not resting. As you can see now, it is not always easy to surrender to your healing process without a struggle first." Magda always seemed to understand me better than I understood myself.

"Now," she continued. Shall we see about your breakfast? We shall have a long day on the road. We must be moving along soon."

That day, I followed her advice and only permitted myself to help with a few light chores. That evening, I felt much better than I had the night before.

I was helping to prepare the fire and was just setting out a large pot for evening tea when I heard familiar footsteps approaching me from behind.

"There you are, Willow! How did your day go?" It was Ahmad. He had a ready smile for me. One hand was hidden behind his back.

"I had a wonderful day Ahmad. Thank you for asking. This brace is really giving me a great deal of freedom."

"I am happy to see that you are not abusing that freedom as I noticed the first day." He shook his finger at me. "I was thinking to myself that maybe I had done a bad thing when I saw how much pain you were in." He brushed his great moustache with his palm. "Today was a better day for you. Aye?"

"Aye." I acknowledged with a nod. "Thank you." I poured two cups of tea and offered him one. "I am keeping my enthusiasm on a shorter tether now that I know what trouble I can cause for myself." I answered honestly.

"This is good to know," He began. "Because I would hate to think you would cause a great scuffing to this new boot before I can fit you for its mate!" he said with a broad white smile. He produced a boot from behind his back and presented it to me.

"'Tis beautiful, Ahmad!" I was breathless. I set my cup of tea on a neighboring log and embraced his neck. I found a place to perch myself beside my teacup while I tried the boot on.

He set his own tea aside and stood proudly over me with his thumbs hitched under his leather suspenders while I slid my bare foot into the sheepskin-lined boot. It was a beautiful mid-calf boot in fine pebble grained leather. It fit perfectly. I laced it and stood.

"Oh, it has a bit of a heel!" I observed, feeling taller. I turned this way and that, moving my skirts back and forth in an attempt to see the lovely boot from every angle.

"Aye, to keep your legs more level." He extended both of his arms in front of himself drawing his hands even with each other.

"My back feels better already." I said honestly. "This boot is gorgeous, Ahmad and so comfortable. I feel so grown up! I love it! And I love you!" I embraced him again and he gave a hearty chuckle.

"So much fuss about a boot...from a wild pony who does not like shoes." He said with a cocked eyebrow and a smug grin that told me he was pleased that I liked it. He took up his cup of tea and seated himself beside me on the log. We sipped the steaming liquid in companionable silence.

When his cup was drained, he patted me on the knee and rose to his feet. "Tomorrow shall be another long day on the trail, my little Pony. We need to sleep. I am pleased that you like your boot. Wear it in good health." He added with a wink.

"Oh, Ahmad, I love it!" I said over my mug. "I appreciate you more than you will ever know! Thank you for the brace and the boot. They are lovely."

A Change of Plans

The air was still warm, but autumn had added just a pinch of briskness to the air. Dread was weighing on me like a stone in my belly as the last of the warm days died away. We all felt the bitter sting of loss as, beloved families from our clan chose villages to settle in and we had to leave them behind. The void in our caravan was filled with the dust of the few remaining wagons. Our circle around the fire dwindled as the emptiness grew.

We had whittled our caravan down to the final three wagons now. These were the core members of my family. Galynda and I shared a wagon, Magda and her sister, Ahnja shared a wagon and Ahmad followed behind in his.

The burden of chores was shared by all. Now there were fewer of us to share the same number of chores. 'Twas a true sacrifice I made, allowing the others to do a portion of my share.

As we bumped along on the road, I was deeply tangled in the thought of having lost so many families in recent days when Galynda interrupted my thoughts. "What are you thinking?"

I had forgotten even that I was driving the wagon. "Oh, I am sorry. Did I leave you sitting here all alone?" I asked.

"I have been sitting here listening to the creak of the wagon for what seems like hours." She replied. "You have been very quiet. Are you well?" concern crept into my companion's voice.

"I am thinking of the families we have lost along the trail. Some, we have lost to illness and death. So many families have been destroyed by villagers who hate nomads and burn our vardos as we sleep!" These numbers included my parents and Ahmad's family. "I cannot make any sense of it. Others have fled to avoid persecution. I do not wish to lose any more people! Everyone who is left is my family." I finished sadly.

"I agree." Galynda nodded "We have lost more to hate than we have to illness or accident. I am glad that so many that have left have been able to find villages to live in where they shall be safe. Other bands of nomads have been killed in plain sight of villages. On the trail, we are no longer safe. 'Tis clear that we are nomads, as we travel in a caravan. We are easy prey to a band of angry villagers." Galynda brought all my tangled thoughts and fears out into the brazen light of day.

"I feel frightened. I am tired of so much loss." I confessed. "I don't like it!"

"I am frustrated by the changes too, Willow." She shared openly. "I pray every day that our remaining families shall be safe." She interrupted herself, "Willow, what is it?" she stiffened in her seat listening strenuously. "What is wrong? Why are we stopping?"

We were traveling along a stretch of gently rolling hills. The grasses were turning yellow in the early autumn heat. Great V's of geese honked overhead as they made their migration to warmer climes for winter. The sky, stretched broad and scattered with thin white clouds, was made jagged along the northern horizon by craggy mountains. Oak trees dotted the landscape, offering shade for the weary traveler.

On the trail ahead of us, a plume of dust was growing as it approached us. "Riders, Lynd," I explained. They are approaching us from the North. They are coming upon us very fast."

With growing apprehension, I willed my eyes to find clarity. "I see riders. They have raised flags or banners. I cannot recognize anything from this a distance.

"Willow," Galynda reached out and placed her hand upon my knee. "I want you to know that no matter what, everything shall work out as it should. All will be well. I feel it." She assured me tapping herself on the chest with her fingertips.

After the conversation that we were having, I feared the worst. My heart silently screamed out in fear. Like a trapped animal, it beat itself brutally against the bars of its prison that was my ribcage. Sweat burned its way down my spine. A heavy stone settled in my gut. My legs and face went numb in anticipation of the unknowable, the unthinkable.

As the riders drew nearer, I could see the crest with greater clarity, but could not identify it. Something disturbed me about that emblem; something about it was frighteningly familiar. I had seen that insignia somewhere recently and the feeling connected to that memory left me with a knot in the pit of my stomach, which only made me feel worse.

"The riders look very official. They are wearing matching green and gold velvet tunics and leggings." I explained in a whisper. "Their demeanor is quite somber." I observed aloud as they approached our wagons.

The riders stopped the lead wagon, which was Magda and Ahnja's. I held Galynda's hand in silence. I held my breath and strained my ears to hear any stray word or sound that would hint at what was to become of us. Were we going to be burned out? Shot? Raped? Tortured? Murdered?

A horse snorted and nearly sent me running for my life. The knots in my stomach had reached my throat and were strangling me. I watched, breathless, as Magda climbed down from the driver's seat and led the men to the back of her wagon. They remained outside as though they were on guard while she went inside. Moments later, I saw her emerge again, but could not see her clearly because the Kingsmen had her surrounded.

My heart leapt to my throat when they turned to our wagon next. I swallowed several times in attempt to ease the tension in my throat. "They approach our wagon. They have Magda with them." I choked.

"All will be well. I feel no danger." She assured me in a whispered voice.

She leaned in closer and whispered, "Willow, do you remember the vision I have been telling you about? The wagon wheel? I can see now that the wheels are in motion! The journey has begun!" Her hand squeezed my knee lightly before she withdrew it and placed her hands together on her lap.

"Willow, I shall need your assistance." Magda called up to me. "Fetch your medicine bag and come with me."

I climbed gingerly out of the driver's seat and up into the back of the wagon to gather a change of clothes, my medicine bag, herbs and tools. While I was alone in the stillness of the wagon, I also tried to gather my wits.

Who are these men? Where are they taking us? What do they want? My mind was spinning with questions. Then Galynda's whispered message came to me. "I feel no danger." If Lynd felt no danger, I would take strength in that and I would not allow myself to feel fear. I straightened myself and smoothed my hair and adjusted my skirt.

A young Kingsman greeted me at the door and helped me down. He must have only had one or two years on me. Now that I was no longer allowing fear to cloud my vision, I detected an expression of apprehension on his face. "Have you everything you shall need my lady?" He asked politely.

"Aye, thank you." I heard myself reply.

"Then we must make haste to get you on to the carriage." He politely urged.

I had not noticed that they had also brought a spindly carriage with them. It was a fine coach, the likes of which I had never seen before, drawn by a beautifully matched quartet of fine-boned bay colored horses.

My own wagon, constructed of heavy timbers and grey with age and weather, appeared bulky as an ox next to the gazelle-like shiny carriage. My grey fells pony looked stocky and cumbersome beside the fine, sleek bays.

The young Kingsman extended his hand to help Magda into the carriage. Next, it was my turn. I followed Magda's example and soon found myself inside a lavish traveling compartment. The seats were upholstered in leather and the backrests were of a rich silk and velvet tapestry of scrolling leaves. The effect was beautiful.

Inside, we found two women already seated. Their dresses were so rich in color and elaborate decoration, that I was certain that they were fine ladies, though not royalty.

"Good afternoon." The first woman said. "We are glad you are here." She was a beautiful woman who must have seen the passing of 40 years. She had light olivine skin and the soft body of one who might work indoors. Her eyes were a mystifying blend of hazel and grey. Her full lips were outlined with a matching pair of dimples that appeared at the corners of her mouth when she smiled. There was something magnetic about her, for I found myself drawn to her by some powerful unseen force. I could not look away and I had a dizzy, heady feeling just being near her.

"Good afternoon." Magda replied.

Magda had taught me when I was a small girl to speak

only when spoken to. This was not just a lesson taught to young children who must never be heard from, it was a lesson in observation. Magda had taught me that if I remained silent and watched how others spoke and behaved, I could blend in well in all situations. Situations could get awkward or very uncomfortable if an inexperienced person burst out with something inappropriate, especially when working with *Gajikané*, non-Rom people.

I sat silently in the carriage, thanking Magda for her gentle wisdom. I would do my best to avoid making embarrassing statements.

"My name is Madame Rosmerta, I am the personal companion to the Queen regnant, Her Royal Highness, Alyssandra of the High Plains." The first lady spoke. "And this is Miss Constance." She indicated the young woman seated next to her.

Miss Constance was a young woman of the marriageable age. She was exotic to look at, as her skin was a delicious warm brown color. It was darker than the skin of my people and her hair was tied back in many small braids. The free tendrils of hair at her temples and nape were tightly curled like the wood shavings I had seen Ahmad make with his wood plane.

"How do you do?" Magda said with a slight bow of her head. "I am Magdalena, *drabarni* of the Tsigani tribe.

"'Tis lovely to meet you both." I said, also bowing my head. In my busy mind, I was certain that had I been standing, that would have been a curtsy. "I am Rajani, the apprentice *drabarni* of the Tsigani tribe. I am known to all as 'Willow.'"

Outside, the Kingsmen had mounted their refined and agile matching sorrel horses. The carriage had been turned to the north, the direction from which it had just come.

I was surprised at how nimble the fine-boned carriage was, and not near as bone-jarring as our humble, functional wagons. I decided that it must have been designed to carry its passengers swiftly with as little burden to the horses as possible. It seemed to be doing its job. I had never traveled so swiftly by carriage.

Madam Rosmerta addressed Magda and me with a serious expression. "We are here on an errand for our Queen." She said looking from Magda to me.

My breath caught in my throat. I had been to the houses of wealthy people. I had treated the very poor. I had never been in the presence of royalty.

"Our Queen has been ailing for some time. The healers in our Kingdom have tried to help her, but her condition is worsening, she is gravely ill. The Princess, Madeline, sent scouts out to find the best healers. Most of the villages they visited spoke of a traveling band of nomads. The further south the scouts traveled the more specific the villagers were. If our Queen were to get better, we had to search for the caravan whose healer wears the hat of a man. We had to find you and bring you to our Queen.

As she spoke, I realized that it was me that she was speaking of. I wore a man's hat. It had been the only memory I had of my father. It was an indulgence. Magda had allowed me to wear it in his memory. Eventually, that hat had been replaced so that I could preserve the original.

"The further we traveled the more apprehensive we became." Madame Rosmerta continued. "We learned that many nomadic caravans have broken up and disbanded. Our scouts even encountered several encampments that had been burned out where they stood.

We were quite distraught that we would not find you in time." She explained. "We were so relieved when the scouts encountered a family that had caravanned with you at one time. They were very guarded and hesitant to speak to us. Once we convinced them that we meant you no harm, they were able to recall the trading circuit that your family follows at this time of year as well as the markings of some of your wagons." She continued. "They created a map for us, and our scouts went in search of your caravan.

We very nearly missed you," she said pressed the palm of her hand to her chest. "The scouts had watched your caravan for a day or two, but they did not see the healer who wears the hat of a man!" she stopped to take in a breath and then continued on. "The decision had been made that if we could not locate your caravan, we were to return to the north lands." Her eyes brightened slightly with tears she would not allow to form. "Luckily," Madame Rosmerta continued, "they were able to identify you early this morning." She indicated me with an outstretched hand. Once they identified you, they immediately sent word to us that they had located you and here we are."

Listening to her story, I could hear the anguish and concern in her voice. I could sense that her Queen was more than a ruler or employer. She must have been a very beloved figure in her Kingdom.

"I am sorry that your Queen is not well." Magda said bowing her head respectfully.

"As am I." I agreed, following my sage teacher's actions.

The younger woman, Miss Constance, spoke. "Our Queen is a very generous and loving leader. She leads by example and does not expect anyone to put forth more work than she would do in a day."

I was impressed, certain the Queen did not pay them to speak this well of her in her absence.

"If I may," Madame Rosmerta's steady gaze was upon me, "How is it that someone as young as you can be such a revered *drabardi*? Did I say that word correctly?"

I had seen others laugh at failed language attempts. I had seen the spirit smoke of the person who had innocently made the mistake shrivel. I had also seen further attempts at communication weaken and fade away to nothing.

Not wishing to offend our hostess, I bowed my head again and spoke, "You did very well. The words are quite similar. The word you used, *drabardi*, means 'fortune-teller'. The word you were seeking is *drabarni*, which means 'healer'." I carefully explained.

Looking somewhat alarmed, she placed a hand upon her chest. "Oh, do forgive me." She said. "I did not mean to offend." Her spirit smoke diminished noticeably.

Smiling, I replied, "On the contrary, I am honored. My dearest friend is a truly gifted *drabardi*."

Relief flooded her face and she adjusted herself in her seat so she could lean in toward me. "That is incredible! Does that really work? Fortune-telling, I mean." All the formality seemed to fade into the rich upholstery.

The miles rushed past our windows as we picked our way over roads that were foreign to me. The terrain changed from the brown flatlands we had been traveling, to more hilly country dotted with trees dressed in fiery autumn colors and majestic mountains that rose from the horizon to meet the sky. The views were breathtaking.

"Actually, Galynda is more like a 'seer'. She can see future events, but she does not use cards, runes, bones, or a crystal ball." I explained.

"Does she do this for just anyone?" Miss Constance joined in.

"She shares what she sees in other people's lives if it is important." I stated, uncertain how comfortable I was to find myself the center of so much attention. "It is a gift." I stated it as a matter of fact.

"Like healing?" Madame Rosmerta asked pointedly, holding me steadily in her gaze.

This was one woman who did not let much information slide by easily. She seemed to absorb information out of the air around me.

"Well, aye." I said looking at the floor. I could feel myself blushing. It was not our way to speak of our gifts in a prideful manner.

"People would pay good silver to hear their future." Miss Constance said.

"Aye." I admitted. "*Drabardi* tell fortunes for *Gajikané*, non-Rom people only." I explained. "Galynda does not do readings for Romany people. She might warn family and friends of danger, if she chooses, but most do not even wish to know that much and she respects their wishes."

"Is it odd having a friend who can see the future?" Miss Constance suddenly blurted.

It was obvious, to me, that Miss Constance had not been taught the finer skills of silent observation. I felt that her questioning pressed in on me and took away my privacy.

At the same moment, I saw Madame Rosmerta cast a glance toward Miss Constance that would have sent me skulking into a corner. Apparently, her line of questioning was inappropriate in their culture as well.

Miss Constance turned her lips inward, covering her teeth with them and closed her mouth. She looked at the floor and smoothed out her skirt.

"I beg your pardon," Madame Rosmerta apologized.

"You need not apologize, for it was not you who overstepped your boundaries." I replied.

Inwardly I knew I should have said nothing. They could decide at any moment to have the driver stop and deposit me and my belongings on the roadside, leaving me to fend for myself. I decided I had said enough and vowed to keep my opinions to myself.

"I do hope you will forgive me." Miss Constance began. "It is just that I find your culture so, so fascinating!"

Her spirit smoke had shrunken with the admonishment, but it swirled and furtively reached out to me as she apologized.

Miss Constance was youthful and had spoken without

forethought. Watching her spirit smoke, I could see that she was genuine in her efforts at an apology. "I accept your apology." I said with a bow. "I am certain I have quite a lot to learn of your culture as well." I replied. "I am very sensitive where my friend, Galynda, is concerned."

Miss Constance sat awkwardly in her seat with her lips clamped tightly in her teeth, struggling to contain another question, which probably would cost her another freezing glare from her companion.

I could see that we each acted as ambassadors from our respective cultures. It was incumbent upon each of us to teach the others what was taboo and what was acceptable in each of our cultures.

"If you will allow me to explain my sensitivity," I began.

Both women nodded in unison.

"I grew up with Galynda. We are like sisters. I can not imagine my life without her. I do not like to think of her as an 'oddity' or an 'attraction' as they call 'fortune tellers' in the traveling circuses I have seen." I explained.

"I never thought of that. Yes, I can see why that would be a sensitive area for you. I did not mean to imply that your friend was an 'oddity' and it certainly sounded as if that was what I was doing. I really do ask your forgiveness." Miss Constance spoke earnestly. Her spirit smoke hung low as though it were weighted by her shame.

"I have already accepted your apology, you are forgiven. I am pleased that you understand why I would feel as I do. I wish more people could be as easily enlightened." I offered.

Magda bore an almost imperceptible smile. I could sense her silent approval.

Miss Constance's spirit smoke swelled to its original size and I was relieved to see that I had chosen the right words.

We sat silently then. I looked out the window. Birches of brilliant gold and flaming maples of blazing red slid into view and out again. Hills of brown turned to hills of green and then to craggy mountains as the day wore on.

I sat and wondered how far away the Kingdom might be. Or, I wondered, if a Queen was ruler, would the land that she reigned be a Queendom? If not Queendom or Kingdom, what would it be called?

My mind wandered off again. What would become of the caravan? Who would drive the wagon for Galynda? I supposed, they could hitch Lynd's wagon to Ahmad's wagon and tether our pony behind like we did when we had horses to sell or trade.

It was Magda who broke the silence. "How many days' travel is it to your homeland?"

"We are not far now. Perhaps, if we make haste, it is only a day away." Madame Rosmerta answered. "We were fortunate to come upon your caravan on the very road that leads to our homeland. The horses are fleet of foot and the carriage light for speed. Time is of the essence."

"Aye." Magda replied. She was in deep thought about something. "Indeed." She said absently nodding her head.

It occurred to me then what she might be thinking. We had heard of Kingdoms where healers, who were unsuccessful in healing the monarch, were put to immediate death. That was not a pleasant thought.

My mind began to race. How long until we arrived? What could possibly be wrong with the Queen? Would we be able to invoke a cure? How would we meet up with our family? I suddenly realized I was clenching my jaw; my head was pounding, and Madame Rosmerta was studying me in earnest.

"Willow, are you well?" She asked.

"I believe I shall need to get out for a bit of air and to stretch my legs." I replied. Would that be acceptable to your driver?"

I had no sooner made my request and she had opened the window and was knocking on the outside of the door.

"Driver, may we request a small respite?"

"Aye, there is a small waterway in that patch of trees up ahead where I can water the horses and you ladies can sit in the shade and have some lunch." He replied.

I had not realized how exhausting it had been sitting in that carriage all morning. I stretched my arms over my head and stretched my back and legs. My foot was beginning to ache a bit.

The driver had unhitched the horses and led them into the stream to allow them to cool off and get their fill of the cool refreshing water.

I hobbled upstream from the horses and found a convenient rock to perch upon. I removed my boot and brace and plunged my feet into the icy water. My feet felt as if they were being penetrated by millions of tiny needles. It was refreshing and exhilarating.

"Willow, are you well?" It was Magda.

"Aye." I answered. "I was just wondering what was to become of us if we are not successful." I whispered.

"As was I." Magda replied. Her expression was serious. She dipped a kerchief in the water, wrung it out and refreshed her face and neck with the cool, clean water.

"Do you think it advisable for us to simply ask? They have been in search of our caravan for nearly a moon cycle. They must have grave concern for their Queen. We must be their last hope." I stated in hushed tones.

"Indeed, and as such, I do not see that they are in any position to put us to death for giving their dying Queen one last chance." Magda defended.

"Let us have a look at that foot, shall we?" She extended her hand to assist me in swiveling around on my rock-perch.

"'Tis healing quite well." She observed. "Let me apply more herbs to assure that the bones heal up good and strong." I could see she was already extracting boneset from her pouch.

Magda walked over to the carriage driver and requested a cup of the water he was boiling. He was more than happy to oblige and offered that it would taste better once he had added tea leaves to it.

Magda explained that it was for an herbal wrap for my foot, not for drinking. He smiled politely and asked if there was anything he could do to help.

"You are burdened with tending to the horses and building the fire and making the tea. It is I who should extend an offer of assistance to you." Magda replied.

He appeared genuinely puzzled that a guest to the Queen would make him such an offer and mean it. He removed his cap and scratched his head. He straightened up from the fire and watched Magda bandage my foot.

The ladies had unpacked a lunch of cheese and bread and grapes. Such a meal felt like a feast. Seeing the food, I realized I was indeed, famished.

"Your foot, Willow, what happened to it?" Madame Rosmerta gestured toward my foot with her teacup. Her Clear hazel-grey eyes set warmly upon me.

"I am embarrassed to say, I struck it upon a tree root." I said with downcast eyes.

"Embarrassed, why?" her eyes held me as surely as she had cupped my chin in her hands.

I could not look away from her then. "I was running in a storm. Lightening struck and I lost sight of what I was doing for a moment." I replied.

"And for this, you feel embarrassed?" She asked, incredulous.

"Aye, I had others who were relying upon me and I was fearful of letting them down. The thunderclap startled me and that is when I struck my foot upon the exposed tree root."

"You must have a lot of responsibilities in your caravan." Miss Constance observed.

"We all share in the labor. I have no more responsibility than anyone else, but I am frustrated that with my injured foot, I am unable to uphold my share of the work as I would like to."

"Our caravan is more than willing to divide the labor until Willow is well enough to resume her chores. We are all family. We share not only labor but joys and sorrows as well. We are all saddened by her injury and we all want to do what we can to bring her a rapid recovery." Magda said.

"That is a pretty interesting bit of handiwork on that injured foot of yours." The driver observed. "I could use a leather craftsman like that around the stables."

I smiled in my heart. Ahmad. He loved me so much and the feeling was mutual.

"I am afraid 'tis also my fault that you were delayed in locating us." I began.

"Why, Willow? Why ever would you say a thing like that?" Madame Rosmerta asked with genuine concern.

"Because of my injury," I replied. "Since I hurt my foot, I have been out of sight in my wagon for the past few days." I admitted. "Your scouts were looking for the healer in the hat." I placed an invisible hat on my head to show her the gesture that was universally used by townspeople and villagers who were seeking my care.

"Not to worry." Madame Rosmerta soothed. "What is important, is that we have found you and we are on our way back to the Queen."

I felt relieved to know that I was not held culpable for delaying care to the Queen.

After we had eaten our fill and drunk our tea, we took turns voiding in a convenient bush. I thought I would seriously hurt myself fighting back my laughter as the ladies in their finery fussed about trying to preserve their dresses and their dignity whilst trying to find the perfect spot to urinate.

The driver tried to busy himself with the horses, but I could see his shoulders shaking with mirth as he tried to stifle his laughter too. I knew right then I liked the man.

Once we were all settled in the carriage, we were off again. We had traveled a great distance in a short time. I was grateful for the cooling temperatures of autumn. The trip could have been unbearable in the heat of the summer or the dead of winter.

I sat staring out the window lost in a swirl of thought. What would our fate be? Finally, it became more than I could bear.

"Your Queen, she has been ill for a very long time. Your healers feel they are losing ground. What will happen if we find that our medicine is no better help?" I heard myself blurting out the heavy question.

Inwardly, I cringed in a dark corner of my mind waiting for the horrible news that I would be put to some gruesome, slow, painful death.

"We sought you out so that we might offer our beloved Queen regnant and her Kingdom another chance at life. Since our Queen is sovereign ruler, she has the full right and power to govern her Kingdom without interference of any other governing body, including the King, who is a king consort, is king by name and marriage only.

The alternative is not a pleasant one. Our Kingdom needs your help. We have needed hope and finding you will be a great balm to our countrymen." Madame Rosmerta answered.

"I understand that you stand to lose a beloved monarch." I said. "But what is to become of us if we fail?" I persisted.

Again, I huddled down inside myself, expecting doom. My heart was racing and my palms were sweating. Magda, seated next to me, blanched.

"You will be welcomed into our Kingdom as heroines. You carry the gift of hope. If we return to the palace and find that the Queen has already passed on, you are free to return to your people. If the Queen still has fight left in her, then you shall proceed with the healing.

If the Queen is suffering a great deal and her time is near at hand, or she no longer wishes to continue her struggle to live, you will be obligated to see her gently through to the next world. The Queen may pass away while she is in your care.

Our countrymen know that we have been seeking you. They know you are gifted healers with different techniques than ours. We all know how grave the situation is. As long as you are giving our Queen the best care that you can, that is all anyone can hope for. No one can hold you accountable for her death if they know that you are giving her your very best." Madame Rosmerta carefully explained.

"Yours is not a Kingdom that puts the unsuccessful healer to death then." I heard myself saying. I wished in that moment that I could keep my mouth shut.

Madame Rosmerta's gentle eyes sparkled with laughter. "It is no wonder you have been so quiet! I can not imagine sitting with that question weighing so heavily on my mind! No, Willow, of course not! It is our hope that you will heal our Queen. Whether or not she lives, we hope you choose to stay on to help heal our community."

I felt Magda heave a great sigh of relief beside me. "Stay on?" I asked furtively.

"Of course, you are welcome to stay on. If that is what you wish. We have learned how dangerous it can be for nomadic caravans such as yours. We are extending an invitation to your clan to stay and live among us in the High Plains if it suits you to do so." Madame Rosmerta generously offered.

My mind was reeling. My heart leapt for joy. No death penalty was good news. Staying on could mean Galynda would have her little farm. Suddenly, I could not wait to get there.

"Thank you for your kind and generous offer." Magda replied. "Indeed, in recent years, many of our nomadic clansmen have fallen victim to the emotional shift among the permanent villagers. Naturally, our clan would prefer to settle somewhere rather than to risk a dreadful fate. Our Elders would have to determine whether or not settling in your villages is in the best interest of everyone in our clan or not.

Before we hasten to any conclusion in this matter, let us first see how we find your Queen." Magda sagely advised. "Her prognosis may well determine how our clan is received by your people. Once our service to your Queen is at an end, the answer to that invitation may be quite clear to all of us." She concluded.

Madame Rosmerta and Miss Constance both nodded in agreement. "I admire the wisdom and the fortitude with which you speak." Madame Rosmerta commented.

"If I may, I would like to know, in what capacity do you serve the Queen?" Magda queried.

"The Queen has taken me on as a personal assistant and advisor. As her assistant, it is my job to assist and guide you and answer any questions you might have." Madame Rosmerta answered.

"In my many years with the Royal Family, my role has taken many forms. One of my roles is midwife. I delivered the prince and princess when they were born. I have also served the royal family as a courtesan, teaching them the fine art of lovemaking and pleasuring. We simply can not tolerate royalty who are awkward in the royal bedchambers." She ended with a wink and a smile.

Magda gently nodded her head. She had a thoughtful, far-away expression on her face.

My monkey mind was racing. I had heard of teachers of sexual pleasuring before. My ancestors from India had taught about Tantric sex and the Kama Sutra. It was well known that royalty from the eastern countries enjoyed having numerous wives. Some kings had harems full of concubines. In my very limited experience with such things, I concluded that Madame Rosmerta must be the lead concubine.

In my extensive travels, I had met so many different kinds of people in my life. In all that time, never had I met a person like Madame Rosmerta. She was important to her Queen and her Queen was important to her. She had the task of teaching people how to do something that nature should have provided for. Then again, I smiled, perhaps the women of my tribe would have benefited from sending their not-so-skillful men to Madame Rosmerta for some wooing lessons. I wondered how that would work. When my inexperienced mind began to create images, I tried to turn my attention to the scenery outside my window.

"Have you any idea when we might arrive?" I asked, trying to occupy my adolescent mind.

"Perhaps as early as tomorrow afternoon, we are making good time and the landscape is becoming more familiar to me." Rosmerta answered.

We set up camp beside a small stream. Again, I planned to soak my swollen foot and reapply my brace. But the chores must be done first.

"How may I help?" I asked the driver.

"As driver, it is my duty to tend to the horses, erect the tent and light the fire. The scouts have spread themselves out and will keep an eye out for our safety. The women will do the cooking and the dishes." He replied politely.

"I shall gather the wood and make the fire whilst you tend to the horses." I offered.

The driver seemed pleased with my offer and after thinking it over for a moment, nodded his acceptance. With everyone working together, the chores would take less time.

Magda offered to help pitch the tent. It was an enormous

affair with room for all of us. The bright red and white stripes made it appear to be a circus tent. I suddenly felt a craving for freshly roasted peanuts.

As I carried my armload of dry wood into camp, I strode past the driver. "My name is Willow. Please, I cannot continue another mile with you without knowing how I should address you."

"My name's Pieter." He replied, collecting a hand brush from the trunk in which he carried his tackle.

"'Tis good to know you, Pieter." I said as I dropped the armload of wood near an abandoned fire surround. "I know that you are a driver, how else do you serve the Royal Family?"

"I tend to the horses and the stables and the carriages and all the tack. There is always plenty to polish and paint and repair." He answered briskly brushing the horses until they shone.

I was thoughtful for a while. "Are you a farrier as well?" I asked conversationally.

"No, we have an old blacksmith in the village outside the palace walls that comes in to do that sort of thing. He is getting up in age though. Not sure how much longer we will be able to use him." By now he was getting out a bit of burlap sacking and was rubbing down the horses' legs. They waited patiently, seeming to enjoy the attention.

"Ahmad, the man who is like my father, is a blacksmith. He is especially good at making remedial shoes for gait defects. He also makes wagon wheels for all of our carts and wagons." I explained.

"Is that so?" He inquired, rolling up the sacking and putting a halter on the last horse he rubbed down. He led the horse to a clearing that included an area on the water and tethered its lead securely to the ground.

"I know your family comes from a long line of nomads, but he could have a weather-tight cottage and a good paying job if he was interested in settling down." Pieter offered.

"How shall we meet up with our clan when our business with the Queen is done?" I asked. I had decided I liked Pieter and I felt I could trust him.

"We left four of our men with your family. They will travel at the pace that your caravan can travel. Our Kingsmen and flags show anyone who sees them that your family is on official business for our Kingdom and no harm shall befall them." He explained.

Relieved by this bit of news, I felt some of the tension in my shoulders relax. "So, they are coming to your village as well?" I asked, filling my pinafore with kindling for our fire.

"Yes, to the palace." He said. "We plan to board your horses and store your wagons under cover in the stables until your family has had the time they need to make a decision about what they would like to do. In the meantime, your family will be guests of the Queen, and the Princess...and the Prince, if he has returned by the time we arrive." He answered gathering larger bits of wood for the fire.

"Has he been away? Does he know his mother is so very ill?" I asked putting bits of kindling into the fire pit.

"Yes, he has been away in search of a bride." Pieter explained.

"Has he only the one sister?" I asked repositioning several rocks that had been displaced in the circular fire surround.

"Indeed, twins they are. She is the elder. She is acting as monarch while their mother has been ill and her brother is away. Since she is the eldest, she is destined to become the reigning Queen Regnant in the event..." His voice broke and then trailed off.

Not wanting to call attention to his heartbreak, I continued with the task at hand. "That must be a very difficult position to be in, being ruler of an entire Kingdom." I blew on the tiny spark that leapt from my flint into the bed of moss and leaves.

"Yes, I suppose it is." He responded, pleased that I appeared to not notice his moment of weakness. "Our whole Kingdom loves the Royal Family. All of them except Edward, the renegade King." Pieter added with a look of utter disgust. He stopped himself and took a deep breath in order to compose himself.

I didn't pursue the issue but made a mental note to keep my ears open for more news about this renegade King. I blew hard once more into the tiny flames and breathed life into the fire.

"What are their names? The Prince and Princess, I mean." I began to feed the fledgling fire.

"Prince Phillip and Princess Madeline of the High Plains." He answered as proudly as if they were his own children.

Miss Constance appeared with a pot of water for tea. "And the Queen's name is Alyssandra. She is a very wise and compassionate leader."

"And such a lovely name too." Magda, who had accompanied Miss Constance, commented.

I showed my agreement by nodding my head. I rose to my feet dusting off my skirts and then my hands. "How else may I help prepare the camp?"

"What do you know about hunting and gathering?" Pieter asked hanging his head, half- ashamed. "It's my duty to provide sustenance for this party and I'm a bit of a green horn. I grew up in a village with everything so handy, I never took to hunting."

"'Tis grand news to know that I might be useful after all." I said. "I shall catch us some fish." I stated.

"And I shall gather some vegetables and herbs for the meal." Magda offered. With that, she revisited the carriage and returned carrying her medicine bag. "Now that I have the tools I need, I shall return soon enough with the vegetables." She said with a small smile.

"May I accompany you?" It was Madame Rosmerta. "I know a bit about the plants around here, but I have a feeling that I could learn a lot from you. Would that be acceptable to you?"

"Aye." Magda nodded and lead the way out of camp.

As they departed, I could hear Magda asking Madame Rosmerta about the appropriateness of wearing such fine clothing to go poking about in the earth in search of herbs.

I shook my head and laughed inside my heart. It was rather comical to think of such a fancy lady with soil under her nails and the edges of her skirts torn to ribbons.

I hobbled over to the carriage for my medicine bag. I carried it to the water's edge and cut a willow branch, which I bent and formed into a hoop. I secured it with a bit of sinew from my bag.

"I have an idea that I think might be helpful," offered Miss Constance. "My father would go fishing once in a while and he often fashioned my mother's old stockings into nets to fish with."

"'Tis a brilliant idea. That should work splendidly." I replied.

Pleased that she had a good idea and that she could help, Constance strode to the carriage and returned with the hosiery in hand.

"Would it be acceptable to stretch your hose to fit this hoop?" I asked. "It may destroy the stocking."

"Oh, yes, 'tis the very way my father would do it!" Miss Constance replied excitedly.

"So much time you have saved us." I exclaimed as I stretched the stocking around the edge of my willow hoop. "We shall be able to get to the cooking and eating more quickly this way." I said with a smile.

I bent down and drew the back edge of my skirts between my legs and tucked it into my waistband.

"This way, I shall stay as dry as possible." I explained to the two blank faces that stood watching me. The quizzical expressions melted, in unison, to an expression of relieved understanding.

I wandered off to the stream, finding an ideal rock on which to remove my boot and brace. I slid gingerly into the water and began to watch for fish.

I could see immediately that we had found a good spot. Just below the surface, I could see the undulating shadows of several brook trout.

I carefully positioned myself so that I would not cast a shadow upon the small school of fish. Slowly, I bent down and slid the makeshift net into the water. Almost immediately, I had a fish in the net.

In her excitement to see that first fish tossed onto the grassy bank, Miss Constance clapped only the palms of her hands, clapping silently, so as not to frighten away the other fish.

Before long, I had netted enough fish to feed everyone in the group.

I turned to climb out of the water and took a misstep onto a sharp stone in the sandy streambed. I must have made some sort of face because before I knew it, both Pieter and Miss Constance were in the water beside me.

"Did you hurt your foot? Are you all right?" They asked in unison.

Their faces were pale with concern and yet, I had to laugh in spite of myself. "I am fine! I merely trod upon a stone." I gestured toward the water. "With my sound foot no less!"

Soon we were all laughing aloud. It was a comical scene. I, the commoner, with my humble cotton dress tucked up to protect it from the wet while the refined folk, stood knee-deep in the icy water with their fine clothing clinging to them in a sodden mess.

"Let us help you out of the water." Miss Constance said. "We can ill-afford to have anything happen to you, the healer of our beloved Queen."

I could see the frankness in her demeanor and decided it just might be a good idea to accept their help after all.

Once we were out of the water, I thanked them for their concern and their help. When they were assured of my safety, they went off to the tent and carriage to change out of their wet clothing. They went eagerly as the water was quite cold and the sun was beginning to set.

I adjusted my skirt, put my brace and boot back on and began to scale and clean the fish.

By the time I had cleaned the first three fish, Magda and Madame Rosmerta had returned to camp. They were carrying wild rice, wild onions, and starchy wild yam tubers. We would have a feast tonight.

They strode to the water's edge together, talking in hushed tones while they worked. The feeling in the air was one of quiet harmony. There was something that had happened between Magda and Madame Rosmerta while they foraged for food. It may have been something they said to each other or something they had done that had changed them both. I could see the change. They were closer for the secret they shared. If it was good news, they shared the joy. If it was bad news, they did not have to shoulder the burden alone. Time would reveal the truth. I could wait.

As we ate and laughed and enjoyed our meal and each others' company, I reflected upon a simple truth that resounded in my spirit. Even though we were from different worlds, we all had the same need to eat and sleep and void. Our cultures felt differently about some things, but we all had the same basic human needs.

After dinner, we all gathered the dishes and washed and put them away together. It was decided that it would be best to turn in early, for tomorrow, we would meet the Queen.

Polish

When I awoke, the air outside the tent was crisp and full of the promise of autumn, my favorite time of year. Autumn was for me, the season of gathering of harvest and family. It was a time of renewal and a time of cleansing and quietude.

Magda joined me in the quiet, predawn, mist. Together, we celebrated the new day with a small ceremony. We prayed to the four directions and asked the gods to guide us safely along our journey.

I placed bits of moss and lichen in the fire pit and breathed life into the dying embers. I added small twigs and then larger ones until our fire was large enough to make tea.

"Willow," Magda spoke softly. "Willow, my child, this will be our last journey together. Our family has come to the end of its travels. Now is the time for us to settle down in a colony. These people offer us an excellent opportunity. I believe we would do well to accept their offer to stay on."

"I agree." I said nodding my head. I fed the fire a large branch and watched the flames lick at it and then feast upon it.

Magda seated herself on a large log and patted it indicating I should seat myself next to her. "How do you feel about settling?" she asked.

"My mind is of two roads, Magda. I have always traveled. 'Tis all I truly know. I have itchy feet to keep traveling but I know 'tis no longer safe to continue. I feel making a settlement is a good idea for safety, and for Galynda."

"I am happy to see that you are not fighting this idea. You have learned to make mature and sage decisions."

"You raised me to think as a sage woman." I said, leaning into to her with a smile. "I am thankful everyday that my life has been blessed by you."

"And mine by you." Magda replied. She placed her arm around my shoulder and gave me a warm one-armed hug. She held me close for a moment and leaned into me.

"Really? How?" I asked, bending to pour water into the teapot.

"A child's love is absolute, Willow. They give and receive love as readily and freely as they breathe. Were it not for you, I never would have had such a profound, first-hand experience with it.

"As a *drabarni* I chose to live the solitary life of a healer. I had chosen a life path with no marriage and because I had chosen not to marry, I expected no children of my own to raise. I am sorry for the loss of your parents. You have missed much by not knowing them personally. But I am truly thankful every day that the elders allowed me to care for you. Since I was destined to be your teacher, it seemed a natural choice. But 'tis so much more than that for me, I have loved you from the depths of my soul as though I had birthed you myself." She explained.

I had never heard her speak to me with such depth of emotion. Hearing her now, I felt it was important to give her my undivided attention. I set the pot on to boil and listened intently.

"Since we shall become settlers, I feel 'tis important for you to consider your future. You shall want to seek companionship and a home of your own."

"But, Magda," I puzzled. "As *drabarni,* it is my destiny to live a life of solitude as you, my teacher, have done." I stated.

"No Willow, my daughter. You deserve so much more than that. I believe with that big, loving heart of yours, you shall experience a great love. 'Twill be a love to last you ten lifetimes." She said stroking my hair. She gently kissed my head.

"As a *drabarni* I can not take a husband." I replied.

"That is not your destiny. That is not the way of our people. As a *drabarni,* I have chosen to commit myself wholly to the task of healing with plants and minerals and right living. I have always had a very full and busy life committed to you and the medicine. My interpretation of right living meant I did not have time to commit my life to you, my daughter and apprentice, the medicine and a husband." Magda patiently explained.

"I am confused. Are you telling me now that I am marriageable?" I was uncertain where this conversation was leading, and I was so utterly confused my head began to ache.

"Willow, you are confusing love and marriage. One does not have to be married to know love. Nor does one always know love in a marriage." Steam was streaming from the spout of the tea pot. Magda bent and removed the tea pot from the flame and positioned it so that it was near enough to the fire to stay hot.

"Are you telling me I should take a paramour?" I queried. By this time, I realized my brow was knit tightly and could very well be the source of my headache. "As a holy woman and healer, I am not forbidden, is it acceptable for me to take a paramour?" My throat was beginning to constrict and my voice was fading and rising in pitch.

"Magda, I want very much to do the right thing. I want to be like you. If you do not need a husband, then neither shall I need one!" I could feel anxiety beginning to rise from the pit of my stomach. Where was this conversation leading?

"If you wish to be like me then you must know some things about me. Even though I have never married, this does not mean I have lived a loveless life.

There has only ever been one love in my life. We have given each other love, comfort and companionship for many years." Magda smiled warmly as she told me this, her gaze softened and drifted far away.

"You will do what feels right for you, Willow. For me, loving another on the profound level that I do is an extension of my deep and boundless love of the Universe. I feel nearer to the gods when I am most intimate and vulnerable with my partner. It nourishes me deeply and gives me strength.

"However, 'tis forbidden to take many lovers." She continued. "With many lovers, the relations are only superficial and sexual. There is no profound love shared and instead of feeding your soul, it will drain your energy." She explained. As she finished this statement, Magda took two cups and poured steaming water into each of them. Handing me one of them, she withdrew a small bundle of cloth from her medicine pouch and sprinkled a small pinch of tea leaves into each cup.

I sat watching the steam rise and join the mist of the morning for a moment while the tea steeped. It had never entered my mind that Magda might have sexual feelings or needs or that she might have ever had a paramour. These thoughts were as foreign to me as Madame Rosmerta and her unique set of skills. It occurred to me then that this discussion might well have been the result of Magda and Madame Rosmerta's conversation while gathering food. Aye, I decided, that seemed the logical course of things to me.

"In affairs of the heart," Magda's voice broke into my thoughts. "We must sometimes surrender to our heart. At other times, we must listen to reason to avoid getting hurt or hurting others. It is never a good idea to take up with a lover who is already spoken for."

All these new ideas were unexpected and foreign to me. I took a small thoughtful sip of the steaming liquid. "I believe I may have more to think about than I can process all at once."

"Quite so," Magda agreed nodding slowly. She, too, took a small sip of her tea and then continued. "I am happy to see that you are not entirely at odds with the idea of finding love in your life. I was afraid we would have more of a fight on our hands. I do worry about you Willow, for I can see that you are willing to sacrifice your heart in order to fulfill your destiny as a healer.

You have such a good and kind heart. You are capable of giving such great love and showing tremendous compassion. I felt it was tragic for such a loving person to never experience receiving love. Remember, as healers, it is our duty to take care of ourselves so that we have the strength to continue to give to others. Allowing ourselves to be loved, is how we fill ourselves up again when we exhaust ourselves by reaching out and giving to those in need."

"Do you mean that having someone to love is important for my health, just as eating the right foods and meditating are?" I asked.

"Aye," she nodded with raised eyebrows. "When you consider all that one needs to remain healthy, you will see what I mean by this." She drew another sip from her cup as if she were gathering her thoughts.

"You need good, clean food to keep up your body's strength. Without it, you grow weak and tired. You enjoy your studies, which feed your busy monkey mind, and which also answer your endless hungry questions. You need to meditate and pray every day to strengthen your spirit without it; your medicine is not as potent or as affective.

You are doing all these things that are right and healthy for you, but I feel your life is incomplete. You also need someone to support you when you are faced with obstacles in your life, someone besides a mother or a teacher. I can not be everything to you, nor should you want me to be. You need someone who loves you differently and more profoundly than a friend can. The kind of love that will nourish your soul like no food or drink ever can."

"I think I understand what you are saying." I said, nodding. "I do have a lot to think about." I heard my voice croak weakly. My entire world has just been turned inside out and I felt very tired all the sudden.

Magda wrapped her arm around my shoulder again and drew me to her. "Growing is almost never easy and 'tis almost always exhausting!"

I sat silently staring into the fire. I took a sip of tea and held it in my mouth, tasting it, and feeling the astringent nature of it under my tongue.

"Magda," I began again. "Why would the Queen wish to be represented by a couple of her husband's concubines?" My monkey mind returned quickly with its endless stream of questions.

"That is an honest question." She replied. "It is important that you understand that these women are not concubines." She explained. "There is a world of difference between concubines and courtesans. These women are courtesans. As courtesans, they are educated women, who are trusted supporters, or let us use the word from which it is derived, "partisans", to the Queen. Rosmerta serves her Queen as a member of the Royal Court. When these words are combined, you have a par*tisan*, to the Royal *Court*, thus, *courtesan*."

In patriarchal kingdoms, a king will often employ a courtesan who will serve her king loyally as a second wife, or concubine. He may have many such concubines, but for this instance, let us just use one as an example." Magda said.

I nodded my head silently, intrigued by this fascinating bit of new information.

Magda drank some tea to moisten her throat and continued. "The courtesan will often be employed by the king to bed with his enemies and allies alike. Men, you see, often share useful information with women when they are liquored up and feeling amorous. By engaging his trusted courtesan as his emissary, the king can gain greater insight into the minds of other statesmen before he makes any decisions that might endanger his kingdom or his throne.

Because they are often in the company of political minds and important world leaders, they are trained in politics, literature, world religions and the social graces of the highest societies. And because so many of these leaders happen to be men, they are also highly trained in the art of love. The art of loving as these women are trained goes far beyond the primitive sexual act. As I now understand it, courtesans have far more to offer their kingdom than just carnal services. Certainly, if that is what a statesman desires, a lesser concubine or a common street wench may be dispatched for such services."

"Madame Rosmerta is the teacher for the other courtesans." I said, thinking out loud. "Then, she must be very wise indeed." I was in awe. "But how do you suppose it is to teach others about...about conjugation?" I asked, utterly mystified.

"I teach all of the courtesans and the concubines, it is true." Madame Rosmerta said as she joined us at the fire. "First, it is important that all of my girls are polished socially. I work on poise, social skills and etiquette." She counted off on her fingers as she spoke. "I teach them how to walk and talk and laugh with the wealthiest, most highly bred people. I teach them how to care for and serve others with compassion. When they are servicing someone, they must serve with the appearance of love. I have also taught them, when necessary, how to defend themselves." She said rubbing her arms and wrapping her shawl more tightly around her shoulders. To Magda's offering of tea, "yes, please."

"Good morning, Madame Rosmerta." I stammered, embarrassed that she should overhear me speaking about her.

"Good morning Willow." She replied pleasantly. Her countenance was relaxed as she wrapped her hands around her teacup and sipped from its steaming contents.

I was relieved that she did not appear offended by my questions.

"Willow," Madame Rosmerta addressed me. Why don't you and I go for a little walk and gather more wood for the fire?"

"I shall stay here and brew some more tea for breakfast." Magda volunteered.

Before I had a chance to respond, Madame Rosmerta had cupped my elbow in her palm, and was gently guiding me away from camp.

"I am glad you are asking these questions now," she said. "It tells me what you do know and what it is I might teach you. If you want to know, that is." She said over her cup of tea.

"Oh." I said, suddenly without a single thing to say. I looked down at my feet feeling stupid.

"I understand that customarily *drabarni* do not marry. Did I say that right this time?" She interrupted herself.

I nodded in the affirmative.

"You would be married by now if you were not a sacred healer dedicated to her work, is that right?"

"Aye." I responded. I still felt awkward, but far less resistant, since I had recently learned the importance of love in my life and since I could see that she had genuine respect for my position in the clan.

"What you do is very important to you and the people you care for. What I do is very important to me and to my kingdom. In my years of service, I have stopped corrupt men from infiltrating the Kingdom by observing and listening. I have had the opportunity to save many young girls from a terrible life in the streets. I have cleaned them up, educated them and taught them how to behave as proper ladies should."

"Educated them?" I caught myself asking.

"Yes, I teach them how to read and write. It is important that they know the cultures and traditions of the noblemen that visit our homeland. Many can speak several languages."

I was fascinated by this. The street wenches I had treated generally had no education but had to rely on their instincts and savvy to stay alive.

"Not all of these young ladies are concubines. Many of them have become wives with very satisfied statesman husbands." She said with pride. "Some of the women provide service to visiting dignitaries as escorts only. It is a matter of matching the woman with the service that she may be called upon to provide. Everything she does, she must do with the highest respect to the crown she serves." She said decisively.

"I sense that you may have questions for me. I want you to know that I wish to answer each of them, in turn, when you are ready." She said with warmth. "It is important that you understand who I am, and what my role is. It is far better to know the truth about something than to live in fear and ignorance. I tell the girls that every day. I want them to be comfortable enough to ask any questions of me they wish as long as it is done with respect, just the way you ask your teacher."

I nodded an indication that I was listening and that I understood her point.

"You seem to have a question. Do you want to ask it?" Madame Rosmerta stopped herself. She drained her teacup to allow me a chance to catch up and ask questions.

"I understand the process of courting, coupling and pregnancy and pregnancy preventatives, and assisted abortion, self-pleasuring and childbirth. Why, suddenly, has the topic of courting and coupling come up so often?" There! I had asked the question that was most on my mind.

"Magda, in all her wisdom about medicine, felt that she might not be the most qualified person to teach you about that particular subject.

That is where I can help out. I can teach about such things without judgment, and without being offended." She offered.

"Oh," I faltered. "Do you ever feel embarrassed by or feel awkward about the subject matter that you teach?" I asked with one eye shut.

"No," she shook her head. "Some of the girls do. When that happens, I allow them to giggle and laugh as they are learning, to relieve their tension, but it must never happen when they are in the service of others. It could cost someone their life." She said seriously.

I nodded my head. I could see how that might, potentially happen.

"I have a question for you." Madame Rosmerta said. "Since you are nomads, how do your people have the occasion to court and marry?"

"Some, court others from another clan or band. Others meet in the marketplace or town square of the village we are visiting." I replied.

"And you, Willow? Have you had the occasion to step out on the town with someone?"

The question struck me like a blow to the side of my head. My ears began to ring and my cheeks flushed as if I had been slapped there. "Nay," I shook my head as much to answer her question as to clear my head. "I have not had the time or the inclination. There is so much to do from sunup until sundown as the apprentice of a great shaman." I explained.

"So, you have not ever stepped out or courted?" She was puzzled, or maybe incredulous. I couldn't be certain.

"It has never been my destiny to do so. Magda has raised me since I was very young. She is a very gifted healer. Her life has been dedicated to healing others and to training me. She has never married. As her student, and a Chosen One, that is also my path." I stated.

"Is that so? Has this always been true in your culture?"

I found myself furrowing my brow. Was it a cultural expectation, or was it self-imposed? I was uncertain how I had come to that conclusion.

"I-I do not know." I heard myself answer. I was unaccustomed to not knowing. I was not used to doubting myself, especially about my own culture. Only moments ago, I had learned that Magda, even though she never married, had always had a paramour and it was her wish for me to find love as well.

I was ashamed of myself. As a healer, I prided myself in my ability to observe others. How did I allow such important information to slip by undetected?

Learning that Magda had found love and support in another was at first shocking. As I allowed myself to think about it, 'twas a great comfort to me to know that she had someone she could turn to.

My inert mind had been stretched beyond the point of no return. I had learned things and thought things I could not unlearn or unthink. Questions began to rush to the forefront of my brain and I was powerless to choose even one to ask. My mind was becoming so full that all my thoughts seemed to melt together.

"I think you have had quite enough education for one day. We should join the others." With that, she gently cupped my elbow and turned us back toward camp.

The sky was painted in soft pink as the sun broke over the horizon, warmly caressing the gentle curves of the hills along the edge of the earth.

"But," I began, halting in my tracks.

"Yes, have you a question?" Rosmerta asked.

"Aye!" I replied. "We haven't gathered any wood!"

Madame Rosmerta smiled warmly at me and softly squeezed my elbow. "That is because gathering wood was just an excuse to wander out of earshot of the others for this talk." She said. "We have plenty of wood for the fire." She guided me back toward the campfire.

"Oh." I said, feeling like a child. "I have so much to learn!" I heard myself say.

"Don't we all?" Rosmerta said with a genuine smile. "Come along, Willow, I need some more tea."

"Good morning everyone, it looks as though I was the last to wake up." It was Miss Constance.

Looking beyond the ever-growing circle of women, I could see that Pieter had already risen and had begun to curry and tether the horses to the carriage. Inwardly, I heaved a deep sigh of relief. For now, I would not have to deal with the embarrassing and uncomfortable new topic that seemed to be at the top of everyone's list of things to be discussed with Willow. Somehow, I knew that we would get back to it, sooner or later.

Together, we ate a light breakfast of freshly made pan bread and sweet wild strawberry preserves, which had been sent with them from the palace. We broke camp except for the tent which we would need for changing after bathing.

There was much fussing as we all took turns bathing in the stream in preparation for the Queen. I volunteered to be the last in the stream since I was fairly fast and did not have a complicated dressing ritual.

Madame Rosmerta and Miss Constance took their turn together. It was my job to soak my foot and keep an eye out for Pieter.

As I sat on my stone perch, a furtive glance afforded me hints of the voluptuous curves of Madame Rosmerta's nude body through the rushes as she bathed. She was smooth and soft and curvaceous. I had never met a woman quite like her. She had a magnetic way about her, I wanted to get to know her better, but it was intimidating just being near her. Glimpsing her nude body in the sun, I felt a flutter somewhere deep inside me.

From my vantage point, I could not see everything, rather, fleeting intimations of her, which somehow left me desirous of more. I froze suddenly, mortified, when I realized that I might be a voyeur.

I shifted, uncomfortably, on my perch to avert my wandering eyes. Inwardly, I felt a knot of shame in my stomach. Never had I spied on another in the bath. There was nowhere inside of me that I could run away to and hide from my feeling of shame. I felt I had been dishonorable for watching. I felt embarrassed and ashamed for enjoying the fluttery sensation in my stomach.

I was awhirl inside my head when I heard my name somewhere far away.

"Willow, you're next." It was Miss Constance. She was bundled in a large cloth towel. Water was still dripping from her hair. I could feel the droplets of icy water as she walked past me on her way to the tent.

I wandered down stream, careful not to place myself in a position to see Madame Rosmerta, or to be seen by her. I found a spot amongst some rushes and began to disrobe.

I had removed my pinafore, skirt and bodice and left them on the grassy riverbank. I gingerly stepped into the icy water and dipped my entire body under. When I returned to the surface, I had planned to remove my chemise and wash it and myself. Suddenly, I heard something move in the water behind me.

I turned to find Madame Rosmerta standing behind me clad only in toweling. I gasped, more out of shock than fright, although just being near her was a bit terrifying.

"I promised Magda yesterday that I would prepare you to meet the Queen." She explained.

"I have been bathing myself for years. I think I have a knack for it. Thank you, just the same." I deflected her offer nervously.

"You will need additional help, special preparation, to meet the royal family. It is of the utmost importance that you make a positive first impression, especially if the Queen does not make it. We can not have the family believing it is because you were careless or haphazard. You must appear impeccable and beyond reproach."

I recognized the logic in what she said immediately. It made perfect sense. But all the logic in the world could not take the embarrassment out of my situation at that moment.

I wished Magda had warned me, but then, on second thought, I would have argued the point with her. She usually knew best. She was wise and I should trust her. I could usually trust my instincts too, but right at that moment, my instincts were not standing on stable ground.

"What are you going to do to me?" I asked, sounding just a little too frantic.

"Just relax and trust me. I am only going to wash your hair with a special soap, to bring out the shine. Then, I am going to massage out some of the kinks in your back. Magda tells me you have had a bit of a rough time with your foot. She felt it would do you good to get a little bit of attention."

"I shan't have anything to say in my defense about this shall I?" I said giving in to Magda's request.

"Come on, it is not so bad being cared for. You healer

types have the most difficult time surrendering your caring role to another." She said placing a large cake of soap and a small scrubbing brush upon a nearby stone.

I could see her point, but the smell of her skin and nearness of her body made me all confused inside again.

"I have not had anyone wash my hair since I was quite small." I said, feeling a little small.

"The water is shallow here. Are you able to sit or kneel? Here, sit here upon this smooth rock." She indicated with her gaze.

I obediently seated myself upon the stone, in my now sodden chemise. It clung to me in ways that I was certain may have revealed more than my nudity would have, but it was the only shred of dignity I had left.

Madame Rosmerta scrubbed her hands on the bar of soap until it made a rich lather. She gently began to work it through my hair. It smelled fresh and clean of mint, rosemary and lavender. The soap made my scalp feel tingly and refreshed.

The gentle massaging motion of Madame Rosmerta's fingers on my scalp helped me to relax. Bit by bit the resistance I held in my body broke up and melted away. I no longer felt afraid or ashamed, I merely felt safe and relaxed.

Her movements were gentle but with purpose. She spoke softly to me so that I could anticipate where she would place her hands next. She made no sudden movements and she transitioned so smoothly from my head to my back that I hardly noticed she was bathing me. She slid me into deeper water and continued to speak gently to me as she directed me to move this way and that. She paid especial attention to my fingernails and employed a small scrubbing brush to remove any evidence of herb gathering or mushroom digging.

I was a baby again. She was the mother I could not remember. She was there, tenderly caring for me. I was the only concern she had in the world. I was safe and well attended to.

"Are you ready to get out? Are you not cold, Willow?" She asked.

"Hmmm?" I asked, lost in my reverie. "Oh," I slowly realized the bath had ended and that she had been asking if I was ready to get out of the icy water. "Aye," I exclaimed. "I am ready to get out." I made ready to stand, realizing suddenly, that I was sitting neck-deep in icy water without a stitch of clothes on and no towel in sight.

"Wait here. I have a towel for you on the grass." She turned away and was back immediately with a large towel. She held it out for me, and I rose from the water. She embraced me in the towel and I was transported back to my childhood. I was being coddled.

We walked to the tent where we found Miss Constance and Magda going through the same process. Miss Constance was seated behind Magda, bestriding her. The younger woman was brushing Magda's beautiful silver streaked hair in long, smooth strokes.

Magda's face was more tranquil than I had seen it in a long while. Her forehead was relaxed and the corners of her mouth were slightly upturned. I thought I heard her humming tunelessly to the rhythm of the brush.

Madame Rosmerta provided me with a smaller, dry towel and had me lie down, on my stomach, on the mattress where I had slept. She began to massage my neck and shoulders. I was surprised to find so many tender places on my back.

She used oil to help reduce the friction of rubbing my knotted muscles. She worked her way down my back in such a methodical and predictable manner that again, I did not feel frightened and I could predict the next placement of her hands. She left the towel over my buttocks and avoided any contact with them. She continued with the massage down my thighs and legs and finished with my injured foot.

The massage was somewhat painful, and at the same time, it was comforting and relaxing. When she announced that she was done, I was certain that my face must have looked as Magda's had.

The experience had made my body and my spirit feel more relaxed. I felt closer to Madame Rosmerta than most people I knew. Her gentle, predictable touch had tamed my wild spirit and earned my trust. This, I decided must be what she meant by the art of loving.

She pulled the towel up around my shoulders as if to tuck me in. "If you will sit up, we can get you dressed." Madame Rosmerta's voice quietly announced the end of the massage.

I wrapped the towel around myself and dutifully sat up, sorry to see the massage come to an end.

Madame Rosmerta dropped a long, white chemise over my head. I put my arms through the sleeves and stood up, allowing the toweling to drop to my feet as the chemise dropped to my ankles.

She then handed me a pair of pantalets. These were made of starchy, thin cotton muslin. They extended to my knees and tied securely at my waist.

Next, I donned the farthingale, a petticoat with hoops sewn into it to give the skirt fullness. At the waist she tied a bumroll to give my body the appearance of fullness where there was none. Above this, she wrapped a corset, which squeezed my waist mercilessly and pressed my breasts so firmly together that they bulged a bit at the top, looking something like dough rising over the edge of a bread pan.

With all the layering and complicated trappings, I could see why I might need help dressing for the Queen.

Next, Madame Rosmerta brought a beautiful dress over to me and helped me wriggle into it head-first. The dress was a rich burgundy with the tiniest pattern of berries and vines running through it in pink. The bodice was of burgundy velvet. The effect was stunning.

The dress fit rather well. The tailor, who had made the dress, had put lacing closures at the waist and chest to adjust for size.

"If you will have a seat, I shall help you brush your hair." Madame Rosmerta offered.

I was in no state of mind to disagree and sat obediently on a nearby stool. The smooth rhythm of the brush was hypnotizing. I could feel my eyes closing. I could not keep them open. I felt too many sensations. Adding sight to what I was already experiencing was more sentient information than I could process.

"If you will turn this way, you can see what you look like in the mirror." It was Madame Rosmerta. She had finished braiding my hair. She had managed to duplicate Magda's braid wrap on my head.

"Madame Rosmerta, 'tis beautiful." I said turning my head this way and that so I could take in the full view of my hair in the reflection. "I never manage to get my braids even and they never lay straight!" I said lovingly touching the tight, shining grown-up braids upon my head.

"A woman's pride is often her hair." She replied. "You and Magda both have such beautiful hair. I love how Magda braids hers. I wanted to see how it would look on you. I wouldn't dream of doing anything to your hair that was not appropriate to your culture. I did not do anything to offend you did I?" she asked with concern.

"Nay, you did a beautiful job with Willow's hair." Magda replied. "She looks so mature, all dressed up with her hair done so neatly, I feel compelled to address her as 'Rajani'." She said with a placid smile.

I blushed. I had never heard such words of flattery from Magda. She was genuine, which made it even harder to accept.

"I hardly recognized myself in the mirror just now." I admitted shyly.

Lessons in Etiquette

Since we were dressed in our finery, we had to sit and wait for Pieter to take down the tent and tuck it away inside a trunk that he stowed on the roof of the carriage. After he had put the tent and all of our camping equipment away, it was his turn to bathe himself and dress.

As we waited beneath the shade of the tree, it was all I could do to keep from popping up to help with something. I decided that being a lady of fine breeding was a task far too difficult for me. My clothes were too fine to do anything useful in. Having stiff, new underclothes was a miserable proposition at best. I had only worn the corset for a short time and I was already convinced that it was a torture device.

Pieter finished with his ablutions quickly and soon we were tucked neatly inside the carriage, whisking along the road toward the castle again.

Once we were on the road, Madame Rosmerta began our etiquette lessons. "It is important to teach you a few things about how to behave in the presence of royalty."

"You must not speak unless you are addressed first. You must curtsy before speaking. Be mindful that you are invited to sit before you seat yourself. You are in the employ of the Royal Family and as such, you are to respect their wishes without question.

Sit up straight Willow. Hold your head up high. You are an ambassador for your people. Be proud." Madame Rosmerta instructed.

"Begging your pardon, but these stiff new clothes and this suffocating corset make it difficult for me to either feel Rom or proud. Although I look quite lovely and sophisticated, I feel stiff, artificial and itchy."

I thought I saw a fleeting smile scamper mischievously across Magda's face. Maybe her corset was strangling the life out of her too.

I wondered if we would have to wear these miserable contraptions every day or if we would be allowed to wear our native dress once we met the Royal Family. My sigh of resignation was cut short by the corset and I vowed to myself that I would find a way to represent my people in native dress.

"There is a hierarchy in the palace. Those in direct service of the royal family are of a higher caste. Those who work on the grounds or in the kitchen, for example, are usually identified by their uniform dress. They are considered to be of a lower caste and are accountable to those of us who work directly with the Royal Family.

So, what this means is that as the Royal Physicians, you will be granted entrance into the Queen's private chambers. The other servants are to show you respect and are there to serve you while you are in service of the Queen."

"Am I to understand," Magda began, "that there are servants who have servants?"

"Well, there are servants who do work which requires little or no special training, such as washing dishes, mucking barn stalls or plucking chickens. They are at the beck and call of others who are more skilled, such as someone like Pieter, he knows all about horses and is given more responsibility to oversee the care of the stables."

"Does everyone have a fair chance to become head cook or stable manager? Or Must they remain at the lowest level of the caste system all of their lives?" Magda asked.

"Yes," Madame Rosmerta replied. "Yes, everyone has a chance to apprentice and learn. Everyone has a chance to become a leader in his or her chosen skill."

"Madame Rosmerta, we are strong, independent people. Everyone shares in the work that must be done. Each has his or her part that must be done. No one is looked upon as less than anyone else, although, 'tis true there is some division of work based on what each individual is capable of."

"Our cultures are very different." Magda persisted. "I shall suffer greatly if I am made to order others to do work that I can readily do myself."

"Magda, we want you to feel comfortable. This is why the Queen sent me. I am here to tell you about our culture so that you will be prepared, and you will know what to expect."

"Does this mean that after we have had our formal introductions with the royal family, I shall be permitted to wear my native dress?" this thought blurted out before I could refine it through sifters.

All eyes were on me. Madame Rosmerta's eyes held my gaze and I felt cornered and looked away.

"Yes, Willow, if you wish to represent your people by wearing your native dress, we shall see to it that there is ample cloth for you to make many new dresses in the style that you are accustomed to."

I furrowed my brow. "Many? I only need two. I wear one while the other is washed and drying. What would I do with many? Where would I store them?"

Madame Rosmerta had an expression I could not quite interpret. She was quiet for a moment and then she spoke.

"You are guests from far away places. You represent your tribe. You shall be introduced to many people and it is a point of pride for the Queen and Princess that they and their guests are dressed in fresh, new finery for each occasion."

I squirmed in my seat trying to escape the confines of my corset as well as the tremendous burden of being a spectacle.

"Who chooses the wardrobe, the guest, or the Queen and Princess?" I found myself asking.

"Both, I would have to say. The Queen and Princess will often choose the colors and the textures. I would think it would be acceptable to them if you were to incorporate their fabric choices into your native garb."

"If I am required to don corsets daily, then *I* shall suffer greatly." I said with a grimace.

We all laughed then.

"Willow, I have not met a woman yet who likes to wear a corset!" laughed Miss Constance.

"I wear a bodice laced in the front, but I usually inhale deeply before I tie it so it does not cut off my wind." I confessed. "It is still somewhat confining but not nearly as uncomfortable."

"Aye, that is the truth!" Magda agreed. "I find I do not much care for corsets either, but I do see the value in holding the body erect. I have never seen Willow sit so straight and tall." She said with a gesture directing attention to my constrained posture.

I cast Magda a look of exasperation, in jest. We all began to laugh again. I was glad to see the tension had dissolved and was forgotten.

Once it had been established that we were all miserably beautiful, we rode a while in silence.

Trees dressed in brilliant hues of gold and red whisked

past my window. Trees, I thought, were always in fashion. There was no fuss of inappropriateness or unacceptable styling or cultural differences. Trees were all different and yet, they lived together in the forest in perfect harmony. There was no caste system, no servants and no rulers, just trees and flowers and rocks and grasses. The further we rode, the deeper I felt my commitment to accept my role as ambassador and healer. I began to realize that I was probably as new to them as they were going to be to me. We would all have some adjusting to do. I hoped they would allow me to wear my customary clothes.

The air in the carriage seemed to be flat as no one spoke. Each woman sat silently enrapt in her own thoughts.

It was some time after our lunch break that outside my window, I noticed a man dressed in clothing similar to Pieter's riding toward us. He waved to Pieter and turned at a full gallop back in the direction from which he had come.

We must be near the palace now, I thought. He must be the messenger who will alert the Queen and Princess of our arrival.

The Queen

Not long after I spotted the messenger, our carriage rounded a long, steady bend in the road. There were no gates to the Kingdom but tall, natural rock outcroppings that were staggered. The effect was quite amazing, for there appeared to be only a wandering road that ended at a wall.

The entire village was enclosed inside the safety of the great stone walls. Most homes were tucked into the foot of the great craggy bluffs. No sooner had the village come into view, there was a great fanfare with cheering and music. People of all ages had turned out to welcome us to their kingdom.

As for the castle itself, there was not much of the edifice to see, the masons who designed the castle had carved it out of the surrounding cliff walls, making it difficult to locate and nearly impervious to invasion.

I reasoned that this design marvel would have been a strategic plan to safeguard the villagers and the castle from invaders.

"Oh thank heavens," Madame Rosmerta whispered. She

placed a hand upon her chest. "The flag is still flying." She pointed out the window to a single green pennant flying high above the courtyard. "That means our Queen is still with us." She brought both hands to her face and wept silently.

My heart leaped inside my chest. I felt a lump in my throat that made it hard to swallow and would have made speech impossible all together. What a lot of responsibility we had. Each of the people cheering in the streets knew we were here and each of them knew why we were here. There was a lot of hope and expectation. I sent up a prayer that we would be successful in helping to bring their beloved Queen back to health.

I glanced around the faces in the carriage. Madame Rosmerta and Miss Constance both had tears streaming down their faces. Magda, too, had a tear coursing its way down her cheek.

I looked out the window and realized we had entered the castle keep. There had been no way to identify the presence of the castle from the distance. From my seat in the carriage, I could not see traditional castle-like structures. There had been no curtain walls or towers that I had seen. We had ridden through a second gateway, which had been cleverly carved from the face of the mountain itself. Here, we found ourselves in a very large courtyard. The carriage rolled under a great portico and here, we were greeted by more people, this time in the royal colors.

Each of us stepped down in turn, helped by a gentleman who guided us to the doorway. When it was my turn, I put my otter skin medicine bag over my neck and shoulder so that I would be ready to meet the Queen.

As I stepped down, I realized how fatigued I was from the ride. The stiffness of the confining corset was no help. I stretched a little without extending my arms in an obvious way. It felt good to know the journey was over.

Madame Rosmerta hurried over to a velvet-clad

gentleman. He bent his ear to her. "How is the Queen?" She whispered

He bent to her ear and replied. "She is still with us, but she is fevered and has not spoken in several days, Ma'am."

"We must make haste to her then." She replied.

We were ushered into the castle. My eyes had to adjust from the bright, midday autumnal sunshine to the muted lighting inside the castle. In my semi-blind state, I noted that the room was voluminous as there was a wind caused by opening the heavy wooden doors. Sounds were slightly displaced as we moved from the out of doors into this room. Banners which hung upon the wall on either side of the door rippled on the breeze as we entered.

In my heart, I sent a prayer of thanksgiving to Galynda for teaching me to see with all of my senses.

Vast windows permitted sunlight to pour in great radiant streams into the ante room, forming geometric puddles of light upon the stone floor. Tiny dust motes were made luminescent as they wafted quietly into the light streams.

Our footsteps echoed in the stone hallways as we were led, in utter silence, straight away to the Queen's private quarters. Tension was building with every step. I was grateful to be with others who knew the way, for I was certain that, had I been left to my own wits, I would certainly have gotten lost in the labyrinthine complex of passageways and rooms.

The Queen's quarters were darkened with heavy velvet curtains at her windows. The bed was a huge four-poster affair with draperies hanging from the ceiling. These too, were drawn.

There, on the bed was our patient, the Queen. She appeared quite small in the enormous bed, covered with pillows and comforters and bolsters. She had hair the color of honey. It was spread out over the pillow that her head rested upon. Her eyes were closed and sunken from her lengthy illness. Her lips were withered, chapped and cracked from the fevers. Her breathing was shallow but steady, a small sign of hope.

Madame Rosmerta stood in the doorway wringing her hands. She bit the right corner of her lower lip. She was the picture of apprehension, not at all the self-confident teacher she had been on the trip here.

"Please, let us have the curtains drawn away from the windows." Magda requested.

"May we wash up before we get started? I should like to be clean before I touch your Queen." I requested of Madame Rosmerta.

"Oh, of course, certainly." She turned to a woman in a plain grey dress and white pinafore, "Martha, will you send for some towels, please."

"If you will come this way, I will show you to a washroom." Madame Rosmerta seemed more in control and at ease when she was called upon to do something.

The washroom was enormous. The entire room was made of brown and white marble. A large pot-bellied stove was the source of heat as well as hot water, which was evidenced by a steaming kettle.

Madame Rosmerta busied herself by pointing out the amenities of this room. "This low marble wash basin on the floor is for washing or soaking the feet. That reminds me, we must remember to revisit this and get your foot tended to." She said, almost absently.

"And," She continued. "Martha has left a nice stack of towels here for you on the sideboard next to the wash basin."

The wash basin was a huge, waist-high trough like affair. A large matching marble bathtub, in which to bathe the entire body, took pride of place near the stove.

"Oh, and this is the garderobe." She indicated a small room set off to the side. Inside was a smooth wooden ring over a knee-high stone basin.

I noted that all the basins that Madame Rosmerta had pointed out had holes in the bottom. The garderobe was no different.

Peering into the washbasin, Magda asked the very question that I was about to ask. "How does one go about containing water in such basins?"

"We place a cork inside the hole as a stopple." Madame Rosmerta replied as she guided our attention to the corks that were placed nearby each of the basins.

"And the garderobe? I am not familiar..." I began.

"That is an indoor privy." Madame Rosmerta explained.

"Indoors?" Magda asked, somewhat appalled.

Madame Rosmerta patiently explained, "The men who built this castle built it so that water will come indoors with a hand pump such as this." She grasped the handle on the pump and gave it a bit of work and there was water in the basin. I was amazed.

"There is a small rivulet that has been directed beneath the garderobe to wash away waste."

Again, I was amazed. The people who lived in this castle went to the bathroom in their own living quarters! It did not smell as outhouses tended to. There were no flies, so I figured it might not be as ghastly as I first thought. Although, it might take some getting used to.

"Where does your waste go?" I queried as I reached into my medicine bag and fished out a special bar of soap. It was not my customary sage-scented soap, but a bar of soap I used to wash my hands with before and after I touched a patient. It was made of marigolds, chrysanthemums, and burdock, many of the same herbs I would prepare to treat infection.

"I would assume that it simply flows downstream and meets with a larger river, but I can't say for certain." Madame Rosmerta answered.

I used the pump over the basin to produce water enough

to wash my face and then again, to wash my hands. Madame Rosmerta produced a folded, crisp white linen towel for me to dry my hands on.

Magda washed her hands next, using the same type of soap I had. When we had prepared ourselves, Madame Rosmerta directed us toward the Queen's quarters.

"We would like to examine the Queen alone please." Magda requested.

The woman that Madame Rosmerta had addressed earlier as Martha spoke, "Begging your pardon, ma'am," she said with a curtsy, "Madame Rosmerta has given me strict orders, not to leave anyone alone with our Queen."

"That's correct. And I thank you for your help. It shall be all right to take your leave now, Martha. I shall stay with them myself." Madame Rosmerta replied returning hastily from the washroom.

With that, Martha and the rest of the Queen's attending staff surrendered their Queen into our care.

"Magda, where do we begin?" I whispered.

"Where do we always begin, Willow?" she whispered back.

"We look at the patient and her spirit smoke." I evaluated.

"What do you see?" She encouraged.

"The smoke is very weak. It hovers very near the body, but it is still rooted to the body. This is a good sign." I breathed.

"Aye, it is hopeful to see that the spirit smoke is still attached to her. She has not entered the death process. This is good. What do we look for next, Willow?"

"We observe the patient's skin color. She is pale with sunken eyes, signs that she has been ill for a long time and has had blood loss. Her skin is dry, and her hair is dry with no luster, signs that there is dehydration and possibly bleeding.

If she were conscious, we would look at her tongue body and tongue coat, to identify possible internal disease.

We can also observe the internal body functions by observing and smelling her urine and solid waste." I continued.

"Since she is unconscious, what do you suggest we do to diagnose this case?" Magda guided.

"I would suggest we take her pulses." I answered.

"From what you have observed, what do you expect to find?"

"I expect that because she has been sick for so long, her pulses will be weak. She is reported to have fevers so the pulse may be rapid. If the disease is deep at the blood level, we could see bruising and, if she were conscious, vexation."

"Check her pulses and see how accurately you have observed your patient." She nodded for me to continue.

'My patient,' I noted. Magda was taking a hands-off approach. Why had she chosen now to let me take on such an important case by myself?

Dutifully, I stood beside the bed and felt the pulses on each the Queen's wrists. Despite being tucked in under many quilts, her hands were cold.

"As I predicted, the pulses feel slightly rapid, but they do not feel full. Rather, they feel weak. I can feel tension in the pulses indicating that there is physical pain. It could also indicate that the illness may be affecting her spirit or there may be an emotional aspect to her illness."

"My findings will be incomplete without an interview with someone about how she has been sleeping, if she has had chills, fever, thirst, appetite..."

Madame Rosmerta left the room and returned with Martha. "Martha has been caring for the Queen in my absence you may ask her anything you wish."

Martha gave me a curtsy and seated herself on a small stool near the bed. Madame Rosmerta brought a chair for me, and a second one for Magda, who stood silently at the foot of the bed.

I began my long, detailed interview with Martha.

With all of the information I had compiled, I concluded that the Queen had lost blood as a result of uterine hemorrhage that had been left unreported until it was too late. She had lost so much blood and body fluid that she was experiencing fevers in the afternoons and severe sweats at night, requiring a change of bedclothes.

I discovered upon a physical examination that, while she was no longer hemorrhaging, she was still losing blood.

I could understand why Madame Rosmerta had taken this whole illness personally. As midwife, she might have felt she could help the Queen without help from the village healers.

"Madame Rosmerta, I shall need to wash my hands again. Will you please show me to the washroom?" I asked.

"Yes, follow me." She replied as she led the way out of the room.

Once we were alone in the washroom, I had a few more questions to ask.

A Time to Mend

I bent over the basin to wash the Queen's blood off my hands. Madame Rosmerta was there, beside me to work the water pump for me. I rinsed my hands thoroughly before I picked up my soap to wash my hands.

While I did this, I thought about how I might ask the questions that were weighing so heavily on my mind.

"Will this be the washroom I shall always use when caring for the Queen?" I asked.

"Why, yes, yes of course." Madame Rosmerta was uncharacteristically nervous.

"May I leave my soap here on the basin without disturbing others?"

"Yes, I shall see to it personally." She said nodding nervously. She picked at a loose tendril of her hair and began to twirl it on her index finger.

I noticed a small stack of fresh towels exactly like the one I had used previously. I picked up the top one with my index finger and thumb. I shook it out and began to dry my hands,

"Madame Rosmerta," I began. "How long did your Queen hemorrhage before she enlisted your aid?" How long had she hesitated before it became apparent that she was too ill to care for herself?"

"She kept her illness hidden. She never enlisted my help; we had a meeting with a visiting dignitary and Her Highness did not appear for the meeting. I know some royalty like to keep their guests waiting but not Queen Alyssandra. She is known and respected for her timeliness and swift justice.

When she did not appear, I arranged for tea to be served to our guest and I excused myself. I ran all the way here and found the Queen unconscious in a pool of her own blood.

"How long has your Queen been ill?"

"One full moon and half of a second one." She said in a small voice.

"What was happening in the Queen's life when she fell ill?" I asked.

"There was a great deal of turmoil here in the castle, which sent ripples out to the kingdom. We had much to grieve and much to be angry about."

"Will you tell me about this turmoil? Please give me as much detail as you feel I will need to help heal your Queen."

The King, Edward, and the Queen, Alyssandra, had found a prince for Princess Madeline a year ago. She was wed to Prince Alexander only six months ago. Everyone thought 'twas great fortune to find a prince who was so agreeable to the King and whose name complimented that of the Queen.

Because of the wedding, there was much celebration in the land. In the castle however, the King was restless, for the Prince, his only son, had not found a woman suitable to marry. Because the Kingdom was the Queen's birthright, the Princess could well inherit and rule it as Matriarch. The King could not stand to relinquish power to any woman and therefore, vowed never to let this happen.

As it happens, Alexander was a corrupt and brutish man himself. He began to puff himself up as the next Monarch of the Kingdom. He insulted the King, saying he was impotent as a man and a ruler. He accused Prince Phillip of the same, or worse, perhaps, Prince Phillip, who had not settled on a bride, might be doing so because he was fond of the boys. Alexander boasted that, as the only real man in the castle, he should rightfully rule our Kingdom.

Edward drank heavily before the princess married, but he began to drink even more once Alexander began to voice his desire to overthrow the throne. Edward became unruly and abusive to everyone he encountered.

One night, when most of the castle was asleep, Edward, in a drunken rage, went into Alexander's private bedchambers. Edward stabbed Alexander several times in the chest and left his dagger there, in Alexander's chest, for all to see and for all to know it was he, who had killed the new Prince.

The Queen, seeing that her beloved son could become the next target of the King's abuse, sent him away to seek a suitable bride.

When Edward learned of this, he turned his rage on the Queen. He struck her and cursed at her. He attempted to rape her, but she was able to call for the servants.

When he could not defile the Queen, he came to the harem wanting to abuse my girls. I refused to allow any of them to service him. In his rage, he was becoming murderous.

He left the castle in pursuit of common street wenches. He had to travel a distance out of the kingdom to find such women. As was expected, he was brutal with them and we heard several horrific stories about him. One tragic story of a woman who tried to fight him off stays in my mind. They struggled and he killed her. He broke her neck with his bare hands. Our messenger raced back to the castle to alert the Queen.

This kingdom has been in the Queen's family for centuries and she was determined not to allow it to fall into the hands of such an evil ruler. When the news of the murder had arrived here before he did, she had drawn up a notice for his arrest.

The servants were afraid to arrest him as he was still the King consort. He managed to intimidate his way past the night watch and managed to isolate the Queen. He had heard that she was going to have him arrested and that meant that he would surely be put to death. He intended to have no part of it. He beat her brutally and still he could not satisfy himself with that. His desire was to humiliate her and to strip her of her power. He raped her brutally and repeatedly." Madame Rosmerta sobbed.

"Was there any possibility that Queen Alyssandra was with child?" I asked as sensitively as I could.

"Oh my, I-I don't think so." She answered, shocked and appalled at the thought.

"It appears that Edward may have used a foreign object to either abort a pregnancy or simply to destroy her ability to bear children. Was she seeing someone, other than Edward, that may have made a child with her?"

"She has taken herbs to prevent fertilization since the twins were born. There was no possibility of her being with child."

"Could he have learned about a lover? Was she seeing someone?"

"Yes, but she could not have been with child." Madame Rosmerta shook her head.

"You sound fairly certain of that. Did Edward know the identity of Queen Alyssandra's lover?"

"Yes, yes he caught them together and made threats to kill the Queen's paramour. Perhaps killing the Queen slowly is a painful way to kill her lover inside too."

"Madame Rosmerta, I know you understand the pain and politics of love and lovers far better than I. How does it happen that your Queen could find a lover and hide her affair within the walls of this castle; unless, her lover lived in the castle?" I answered my own question, without meaning to.

Madame Rosmerta stood silent for a moment, trying to decide whether she should share the information she was privy to or if she should keep it to herself.

"Do you arrange place and time for trysts as part of your services? Have you a part in this affair? If you have something for me that might help your Queen, I do wish you would help me." I beseeched.

I bowed my head before addressing her again. "I seek only the truth so that I may help your Queen recover. I do not seek to cause more injury or discomfort. Please help me." I pleaded.

Her voice was small. Her head was bowed. She was wringing her hands. "'Twas me Edward found the Queen bedded with." She uttered almost inaudibly.

"Then you are in danger as long as Edward lives." I stated with concern, hoping that my utter surprise had not appeared as an expression of judgement or ignorance.

"Yes, but I am not concerned for myself, only for Alyss." Madame Rosmerta sobbed.

"Does anyone else know about your intimate relationship with the Queen?"

"No, no one. Everyone knows I am her courtier. It is known that I help her to dress for occasions and that I am her travelling companion. Since I am her assistant, no one questions my closeness to her Highness.

Although," she paused, "The King may simply assume I was in the service of the Queen."

"This means no one knows that you shall require protection? No one knows you are in danger?"

"No, I don't suppose they do." She replied absently.

"I thought, at first, that you felt the burden of not being able to care for your Queen with the tools of midwifery alone was the cause of your feelings of helplessness. I can see you have that pain, but now it becomes clear that you have the greater burden of pain from watching helplessly as someone you have deep feelings for slips further away."

She nodded her head. Tears streamed down her cheeks. 'Twas difficult to see such a powerful woman cry.

"'Tis my job to see that she recovers, and to see that you are safe and well enough to help me do that." I said, hoping that I sounded reassuring.

"We should take a break and get something to eat. I shall send for a kitchen maid. What would you like to eat?"

"I have not stopped to think of food." I admitted. "Now that I think of it, I am growing hungry. A nice soup and some tea would be lovely."

"Very well, soup and tea it shall be." Madame Rosmerta brightened again knowing that she would be included in her Queen's care and that her secret, would be safe in mine.

"I should like to write a report on my findings so that I can present it to the Prince and the Princess so that I may have their permission to treat their mother before I proceed."

"That is a wonderful idea. The other healers just locked us out and did what they would. We never really knew what was wrong or how she should be treated other than the standard bed rest and constant vigil, for which we did not require instruction.

In no time at all, Madame Rosmerta had me seated at a writing desk in a well-appointed office just off of Queen Alyssandra's quarters. She excused herself to see about our meal.

The walls, I noted, were lined with fine leather-bound texts of every size and color. The hand carved desk was decorated in ornate thistle and ivy vine patterns. It was tastefully delicate and ornate; the matching chair was upholstered in fine soft green velveteen. This, I decided, was definitely a woman's library. I wondered, then what great thoughts and words had been written or read within these beautiful walls.

I poised my quill above the inkwell, willing myself to write the most detailed and accurate report and treatment proposal of my life for the Prince and Princess.

Magda had taught me to read and write, from the time I was very young. These skills were useful in recording modifications to herbal formulas and for writing our findings in a case.

She told me that if we wished to be compensated fairly for our work, we needed to be thorough. Writing a report often helped me to tease out the intricate details of a case before I engaged in treatment. It was a tool that helped to recall which formulas worked and which had not. It was also a tool that separated us from the charlatans and witchdoctors who took people's money without providing care.

The families of wealthy patients were usually trained to read and write. They were often so impressed with the eloquence and precision in our reports that they paid us handsomely for our services.

It was reputed that the husband of one such wealthy patient spoke out in our support. He took his parchment to the village plaza the evening of an anticipated wagon burning. Our caravan was the target. He showed his parchment to the angry lynch mob gathering there. He told of our gentle methodical care. He told his fellow villagers that we were not dirty, illiterate savages. He explained that while he could not read the paper himself, he found local men who could, and that the parchment was precise and well written.

Most of the men in the mob could not read either. In their shame, they backed down, unable to claim that we were less intelligent than they were. It was the power of the written word alone that kept our clan from being burned out in our sleep that night.

I dipped the tip of my quill in the jar of ink and began to pen my report:

On initial examination of HRH Queen Alyssandra of the High Plains, I have found her in a state of dehydration with signs and symptoms of profound blood loss and internal infection, which are the result of brutal and deliberate trauma.

It is my opinion that while her condition is grave, and the current prognosis is also grave, the Queen, under intensive medical and dietary care, could make a full recovery.

My recommended treatment protocol would include treatment to staunch bleeding, followed by herbal packing of the womb to rid and prevent infection. The packing, to be continued until there is no further sign of infection, shall be replaced with freshly washed and boiled cloth soaked in antiseptic herbs every four hours.

Her Highness must be fed the broth of blood-rich organ meats and long bones of cows and chickens. These meats are to include livers, hearts and spleens. The meat shall be killed humanely with a sincere prayer of thanksgiving for the healing gifts bestowed upon the meats of which she shall partake.

These meats shall be cleaned in freshly boiled and cooled water three times to remove clots. Then, the meat shall be boiled until tender with long bones, dates, ginseng root, thyme, onions and garlic to make a broth.

When fully cooked these meats shall be finely ground to release as much nourishment as possible and added back to the bone broth.

This broth shall be spoon-fed to HRH every hour until she is strong enough to eat on her own. When she is strong enough to chew, she shall be fed this same broth with the addition of root vegetables including carrots, turnips, yams, and potatoes to rebuild her strength.

In the event that internal herbal treatment is required, formulas specific to her signs and symptoms at that time shall be prescribed and prepared for her specific needs.

Signed by Rajani, Drabarni,
Master healer of the Tsigani Tribe.

As soon as I placed the pen on the blotter, there was a familiar knock on the door.

"I am so happy that you are here with me, Magda!" I sighed deeply and realized I had been holding my breath.

"We have always talked about 'one day,' in the future, when you felt I was ready to treat patients on my own, you would step back. One day is here, today, isn't it! I can feel the shift in you, but I am not so certain that I am as ready as you believe me to be. I am frightened and I feel so uncertain of myself."

"Willow," She cradled me in her arms and I was enveloped by her warmth and her scent. "As your teacher, I find that you know nearly as much as I do. The only thing you lack, is experience working alone. As your mother, I see that you no longer need me to coddle you. You are a grown woman with a vardo if your own. There is little else I can offer,

save, for my love and support, and you have them both always. You are ready for this rite of passage. Do what must be done, Willow, even if you tremble inside as you do it." With this, she kissed my hair and unfolded her arms and took a small step back.

The chasm felt infinite. The room was silent. Nothing stirred. I could hear my broken heart pounding in my ears. The salty taste of the bitter tears I would not allow myself to cry, slid down my knotted throat. I felt my childhood fall silently into the abyss. I obediently but reluctantly assumed the new mantle of adulthood and that of lead shaman.

This was an enormous time of growth for me. It was my time to prove myself. But what of my mother and teacher? What was this like for Magda? She had just surrendered her role as mother, teacher and shaman. I vowed to accept my new role with little resistance, as I realized that it was possibly a very difficult transition for both of us.

Magda, I have drafted the proposal for the Princess and I would very much appreciate your advice. Have I inadvertently omitted anything, or shall I add anything before I present this proposal? When I am alone in audience with the Royal Family, I shan't have the luxury of consulting with you, my loving mother and most revered teacher." Saying this, I bowed my head in genuine humility and presented her with my parchment.

She read in silence. Her brows were furrowed in thought. Occasionally she would purse her lips and nod.

She handed the paper back to me and said, "My dearest little Willow, how did you become so grown up? I am so very proud of you. You have done well and I anticipate great things from you."

Having said this, she held me in a warm, loving embrace. I felt stronger knowing she felt I had been thorough. I felt better knowing that even if she would no longer be guiding me, she would be here if I needed her. I hoped this would be true always.

Madame Rosmerta came back into the room. "The kitchen has prepared our meal. I have taken the liberty of setting it up on the balcony. We can take advantage of the last of the warm autumn days." Seeing the ink on my fingers, she added, "Do you wish to wash up before we eat? You shall have just enough time to eat a good meal before your audience with the Princess."

I gathered the parchment, rolled it and tucked it under my arm. "Yes, please." I replied.

Madame Rosmerta, Magda and I were seated around a small round table. From the balcony, the view was breathtaking. I could see rugged mountains beyond the castle in one direction and I could see a green valley dotted with the rooftops of the nearby village off in another.

Our meal was not the simple broth and tea I had anticipated. The kitchen had baked fresh bread and had a large loaf for us to share. There was butter and cheese to eat with it. The soup was savory chicken soup with a variety of different vegetables to enjoy. The broth was slightly thickened by wild rice. I could smell sage and thyme.

I had not realized how long ago we had eaten our last meal until I smelled the food. Everything smelled so delicious. I wanted to abandon all etiquette and eat with my hands. Instead, I sat carefully in my confining corset and chafing bloomers and ate with as much courtesy as my ravenous appetite would allow.

The soup was so delicious I could have eaten an entire caldron of it by myself. The bread was made of white flour instead of the course, brown flour I was accustomed to. It too, was wonderful. I enjoyed nibbling on the cheeses that were sliced for us. For dessert, I enjoyed two varieties of grapes.

There was another knock at the door. Madame Rosmerta rose and answered the knock. She returned with a tray bearing three thick slices of apple pie. It was still hot from the oven.

Already stuffed, I indulged in the pastry. The crust, rich and buttery, melted on my tongue. The apples were firm and delightfully sour, while the thick filling was sweet and spicy with cinnamon.

"That, my friend, was an incredible experience! Please tell me there won't be another knock at the door. I shall eat myself sick!" I said smiling over the table at Madame Rosmerta.

"I am glad you enjoyed it. We want you to feel welcome here. We want to take care of you so you shall be well and strong. The fate of our Queen, nay our entire Kingdom rests upon your shoulders."

I nodded my agreement at the enormity of the task at hand. "If I do not stop eating now, I shall burst this corset at the seams and someone may get hurt!" I said, rising gingerly to my feet.

I was going to regret the quantity of food I had consumed. For now, the corset felt even tighter and I was beginning to feel sleepy.

"What can I do to help tend to these dishes?" I asked.

"You shall do nothing about these dishes. You are here in the capacity of healer and that is all you shall be allowed to tend to." Rosmerta scolded. "We have people who work in the kitchen who shall come and gather the dishes. You would not want to deprive someone of her job, would you?"

"Nay, you are right, that would not do." I agreed. "When you put it that way, it puts things into perspective for me."

"When am I to meet with the Prince and Princess?" I asked.

"I shall take you straight away." Turning to Magda she asked, "Are you coming as well?"

Magda answered, "Nay, I shall act as a second in this case and shall consult with Willow as she wishes. This is her destiny."

That seemed a rather odd thing to say. I felt my brows begin to furrow in puzzlement. I made a conscious effort to smooth my countenance.

"I shall send Miss Constance for you." Rosmerta said to

Magda. "She has had your bags taken to your rooms and she shall help you to settle in."

Rosmerta turned to me and said, "Shall we go then?"

"Am I presentable?" I asked plucking at my skirt. "The Queen did not object to my appearance but having a conscious audience may be different."

Madame Rosmerta led me back to the washroom. She set about primping and combing back wild tendrils of my hair that had escaped the braiding.

"You look beautiful. Now, when we meet the Princess, I shall introduce you and you shall produce your report. Come along, the inner chambers are a bit of a walk from here."

We walked down a long corridor of closed doors; each door was flanked on either side by a suit of armor. "Along this hall are the private quarters of the royal family. Down this corridor to our right are the guestrooms where we shall house your family. There is a dining hall where meals will be served.

Our kitchen staff has been informed as to how many guests are arriving. They look forward to serving you and your family for as long as you choose to remain with us. We all do."

The architecture was stunning. Almost every room and corridor were made of marble as the washroom had been. There was beautiful white marble and bronze statuary in common areas and colorful tapestries and painted frescos reflecting the idyllic landscapes I had seen during my journey here. Intricately woven carpets covered the floors and helped to dampen the echoes of our voices and footfalls.

I made the entire trip swiveling my head about wildly, taking in the sights, sounds, colors and smells of this new and fascinating place. Surprisingly, I made the journey through the castle without bodily harm.

"Here we are," My guide announced as we stepped into

an arched alcove and stopped before a large wooden door. "Wait here for a moment, I will be right back."

Madame Rosmerta took a deep breath, straightened her shoulders and stepped forward to engage the large metal knocker, which hung in the middle of the door. She entered the room closing the door behind herself and leaving me alone in the alcove.

Alone, I suddenly felt small. The room was dimly lit, heavily draped in golden velvet curtains. A small settee with gold silk brocade upholstery rested against one wall with a beautiful floral arrangement on the small occasion table flanking it. The wan flicker of lantern light did little to brighten the sense that I could suffocate in this stifling room. A large ornate mirror was on the wall opposite this. In it, I saw the reflection of a woman I hardly recognized.

I stood before the heavy wooden doors which lead to the throne room. I could hear Magda's parting words in my head. "It is Willow's destiny." I tried to swallow.

The Princess

Madame Rosmerta returned quickly and ushered me inside. As she closed the great wooden doors behind me, I found myself in an antechamber. A narrow pathway of brightly colored tiles in patterns of thistle leaves and flowers led the way, I assumed, to the throne room.

I hesitantly followed the twisted thistle path toward the inner chamber, which was bathed in rich sunlight. I had to avert my eyes to the floor while they adjusted to the brilliance.

My foot was aching, so I carefully metered my footfalls with a cadence that would appear reverent, and hopefully, mask my irregular gait.

The thistle pathway divided and formed a circle around a large, beautiful compass rose in the center of the floor of this great room. It was crafted of many tiny, brightly colored tiles carefully pieced together. It was stunning and I wanted to remember every detail so I could retell it all to Galynda.

I was stung by a sharp longing for my sister as I, alone,

made my way across the floor that was pointing north toward the dais.

Daylight streamed in through high windows above the tall, ethereal figure seated regally upon the throne. Her hair shone in the sunlight like spun copper giving her the appearance of having not only a crown, but a glowing halo as well.

Dust motes sparkled in the sunlight like tiny gems, lending to the magical moment.

Dumbfounded, I stood frozen to the spot. I suddenly felt uncertain of what I was here for and what I was supposed to do next. A lump formed in my dry throat. I tried to swallow it, but it would move.

The Princess, I observed, was breathtaking. She was much younger than I had imagined. She could not have had more than one or two years on me.

"Come inside and let us have a look at you." She made a gesture with her delicate, graceful hand indicating I should come nearer to her.

The majestic woman had a slender, graceful neck that curved gently into the slopes of her strong shoulders. These were the shoulders, I realized, upon which an entire nation depended.

With tremendous effort, I dragged my wandering monkey-mind back to the room, wondering what had gotten into me lately.

Remembering my brief etiquette lessons, I bowed gently before moving toward this woman, who would, some day, be Queen regnant. When I was standing at the edge of her dais, I curtsied.

"I am Princess Madeline, of the kingdom of the High Plains. How do you do?" she stated in a very powerful, forthright manner. Her striking features and fine nose were a startling contrast to my own common features and aquiline nose.

Dizzily, I heard my own voice engaged in an exchange with the Princess. "I am Rajani, *Drabarni*, healer to the Tsigani Tribe, pleased to make your acquaintance Your Highness, and honored to be at your service." With this, I curtsied again.

"Have you anything for me?" she asked. There was little sparkle in her wide-set eyes. She had met other healers before me. She had seen their hokum tried and fail. She had been through all of this before.

"Aye," I replied with a curtsy. "I have conducted a preliminary examination of the Queen's condition and have recorded my findings, proposed a treatment protocol and the prognosis for her recovery." Speaking about medicine helped me to recover a strand of confidence.

For a brief moment, I saw an almost imperceptible flicker of hope cross the Princess's royal countenance. It was gone even before it had fully developed. She was able to maintain her composure, save for her eyes, which changed from the dull grey of despair to clear green with hope. Her striking, changeable eyes belied her calm surface.

"May I examine the document please?" With this, the Princess extended an exquisite arm. Her palm was upturned, awaiting the document I had drafted only moments ago. I had never come upon skin so smooth and unblemished. From the moment I saw it, I wanted to reach out and touch it. The color was lighter than my own olivine skin, but not so fair as to be freckled by the sun.

Her fingers were delicate and beautiful. I became shy and nervous, what if I dropped the parchment? What if she thought me a fool? I felt I was a jester at her feet. Everything I did was slow, as if I were made of clay. Why did I suddenly feel so awkward?

My humble peasant's fingers, only a hair's breadth from her regal, slender fingers presented the Princess with the scroll. My gaze rested upon her fingers as she curled them gently around the parchment. I was thankful in that moment for all the care Madame Rosmerta had taken in bathing me and scrubbing my nails.

The Princess unrolled the proposal slowly.

It was as though she were revealing my vulnerable underbelly, and I felt naked, exposed to her scrutiny. I could feel her eyes panning the proposal in a profoundly probative manner. I felt at once frightened and exhilarated.

I worried that this might have been the way Madame Rosmerta felt, had she known my eyes were upon her in the rushes. Inwardly, I squirmed, feeling my shame rekindled.

A single bead of sweat escaped my underarm and ran down my ribs, stopping short at the corset.

The Princess read my proposal slowly and deliberately. I watched in silence as she almost imperceptibly raised an eyebrow and subtly stiffened her back just the slightest bit as she read. When she had finished, she slowly rolled the scroll up again and rested her hands upon it in her lap.

The scroll, freshly exposed to the eyes of the Princess, and coiled upon itself once more, rested there, in her delicate hands, upon her lap. I stared at it, wondering, agonizing. Had she liked it? What had she made of it? What did she make of me?

I felt light-headed and realized I had been holding my breath. I stood before her in the thickness of the silence, reminding myself not to stare and to remember to breathe and not to fidget or pick at my clothing. My mind began to wander and to toy with me. "What if I had drafted the document so quickly that I left a misspelling? What if she found my ideas preposterous? What if I had misdiagnosed the Queen?"

I consciously shifted the focus of my mind from myself to the Princess. As I observed her initially, she was lovely. So lovely, in fact, that she nearly took my breath away. Closer observation told me that she was under tremendous pressure. The dark circles under her eyes told me she was tired and probably had not been sleeping well. Her eyes appeared deeply set and her cheeks, slightly gaunt as though she had lost weight recently, which led me to conclude that she was probably not eating as she should either.

"You shall treat her then?" The voice of the Princess broke the suffocating silence. A remote glimmer of hope arose in her voice. Her grey-green eyes searched for answers in mine.

Bowing my head slightly, I breathed a deep sigh of relief. She liked it! I nodded my head in response. Remembering my voice, I replied, "Aye, if what I have proposed is acceptable to you."

"With your permission," I began hesitantly. "I should like to begin her treatment straight away." I breathed a sigh of relief; I could get myself through this. 'Twas routine, just another treatment, like any other.

"Permission is granted." She said with an authoritative nod of her coppery head. "I should like to be kept abreast of her progress and included in her treatment whenever possible."

"It shall be done." I replied. Realizing I had spoken without a curtsy first, I bowed to hide my embarrassment.

Without appearing to have noticed my awkwardness, the Princess continued. "I shall have the food preparation portion of this parchment transliterated by our scribe and it shall be delivered to your kitchen staff straight away."

"Of course," I replied, bowing again. "Thank you." My heart was beating so vigorously in my ears I was in fear of missing the details.

"Your document is very eloquently written." She observed, reviewing the script on the page. "I trust your care for my mother shall be equally as thorough." She continued with authority; the last statement punctuated by raised eyebrows.

"Aye, Your Highness, it shall." I felt the lump in my throat growing. She had understood and approved of my proposal! She had said it was eloquent!

"Madame Rosmerta speaks highly of you." The Princess continued. "Since Mother thinks so highly of Rosmerta, I shall take her at her word."

"Thank you, Your Highness." I said with a bow. My mind was still working on the compliment. She had said my proposal was eloquent! I was so overwhelmed with relief that I was prepared to turn on my heel and bolt for the door. I was eager to set about the comforting familiarity of treating my patient.

"Before you take your leave, we have other business to discuss." It seemed the Princess realized my sense of urgency and yet, she detained me, speaking with a slow and deliberate pace.

My heart stopped. What more could there be? I agonized.

Before I could speak, the Princess elaborated. "I understand that your people do not dress as our people do. I would very much like to learn about your people and your traditions. I would consider it an honor to have your people grace us by wearing more traditional garments and teach us of your customs."

What was she saying? I dragged my wandering mind back to the present. She wanted me to dress in my own garments, not in the torturous corsets and chafing linens.

"I would be honored, Your Highness." I replied. Words stopped coming to me. I was so thrilled to think I would not have to wear the corset anymore that it was all I could do to remain composed.

"I also understand that in your culture, your people often have two names. Madame Rosmerta tells me this is so, for you." She began. "May I enquire as to your second name?" she asked almost hesitantly, and finished with, "by which name am I to address you?"

Fortunately, I managed to find my voice and my manners at the same moment. "Aye, Your Highness, that is correct. My people often have two names." I said with a bow. "One is the formal name and the other is the familiar name."

The Princess gently cocked her head to one side and formed a small, thoughtful pout as she mulled this over. She gave me a gentle nod, inviting me to proceed.

"Rajani is my formal, given name. If Your Highness wishes, that is the formal way to address me."

"And your familiar name?" she queried. "What is your familiar name?"

"I am known to most as Willow." I responded honestly.

Her brow furrowed and the corners of her mouth formed the tiny almost imperceptible pout again. "How is it you came to be known as Willow?" She leaned in toward me slightly with her head gently cocked to one side in thought.

"I was born to be a healer, Your Highness." I replied, hoping my explanation would be succinct and satisfactory. I took in a breath and continued. "The bark of the Willow is an invaluable medicine. It is curative for fevers. When I was born, it was foreseen that I would be as healing as the bark of the Willow." I responded.

"Let it be so." the Princess breathed softly. Her eyes grew clearer as if a cloud had lifted, and the green of them, became a softer hue.

She pressed a hand against her breast and allowed herself the indulgence of looking heavenward. I knew in that moment that this powerful woman had sent up a prayer and placed her mother, the Queen, completely into my care.

Regaining her public persona, the Princess stated "I like the power and the meaning behind your beautiful name. I rather prefer to call you Willow" she replied. "If that is agreeable to you." She leaned toward me slightly and requested with a warm smile. The smile reached her eyes with a small sparkle of hope.

In that moment, I thanked the gods that my parents had shown the good sense not to name me after the heal-all spike, for this magical moment might certainly have worked out differently if I had been faced with the humiliating misfortune of granting this beautiful woman permission to call me Prunella.

In that moment, I felt perhaps, most enchanting of all her exquisite features, were the delightful dimples that framed her full lips when she smiled.

"As you wish, Your Highness." I answered with a bow before my monkey mind could dart off in a new misdirection.

"Since we shall be seeing a lot of one another, it would be much more comfortable for us both if you were to address me simply as Princess Madeline."

"It is as you wish, Princess Madeline." I shyly replied with a bow of my head. So intoxicated was I in that moment, that I could no longer allow myself to look upon her; for fear that my gaze might become a fixed stare.

In the few short moments I had spent with her, the Princess had won me over utterly. She had called my proposal eloquent and had accepted it in totality. She had freed me from the suffocating shackles of the corset, and she had shown a genuine desire to break down the barriers of the oppressive caste system.

The Care and Treatment of a Queen

Madame Rosmerta was anxiously awaiting my return in the outer antechamber. She was to act as my guide around the castle. She linked her hand into my elbow, much the way Galynda had done for so many years, and I suddenly realized how much I truly missed Galynda and the rest of my family.

My guide pulled me along at a rapid pace. Once again, we were scurrying down cavernous corridors, this time, on our way back to the Queen's quarters.

"How was it? How did your meeting go? What did Princess Madeline say?"

If this was how Magda felt with my many, monkey-minded questions all the time, I felt I definitely owed her a debt of apologies.

"It went well, I think. She liked my proposal; she said 'twas eloquent. She has granted me permission to begin treatment straight away. Her scribe will deliver a copy of the food preparation notes to the kitchen staff in the guest wing just as soon as it has been transcribed. The Princess is lovely, really.

I am certain you had something to do with this, and thank you very much, she has invited me to dress in more traditional clothing.

She wants to be kept abreast of everything that goes on with the Queen's treatment. She would like to be included in the treatments whenever possible.

Oh, and one more thing," I hesitated, noting that it was too late to stop myself from sharing this detail. "She wants to address me by my familiar name." This last bit seemed to go unnoticed by Madame Rosmerta, who was busy guiding me through hallways and human obstacles.

We returned to the Queen's quarters unscathed but definitely out of breath. With Madame Rosmerta as my guide, she had made short work of the trip. I was glad to have her with me. So elated was I to have my initial meeting with the head of the country successfully behind me, that I was more than happy to allow my mind some empty time.

"It went far better than I had anticipated. I wish to begin treatment at once." I stated

"Very well, what shall I send for?" asked Madame Rosmerta, eager to see treatment underway.

"I shall require several strips of clean cloth, cloth that does not unravel or fray. I like the cloth that the towels in the washroom are made of." I thought aloud.

"We shall need strips of this cloth no wider than half the breadth of your hand. These shall be boiled in fresh water. While the cloth is boiling, I shall decoct a tea that we shall soak the boiled rags in." I said.

Madame Rosmerta followed along on my mental journey as I listed off the items I would need. "We shall use the kitchen here in the guest wing." She interjected. "This way, you can prepare your medicines and store your herbs without having them disturbed."

I nodded my agreement. Aye, that made sense.

"I shall enlist some of your kitchen staff so that you may train them to prepare the medicated meals and teas." She continued, adding to the list of things we needed to do. I appreciated her co-operative efforts.

As we made our way down the hall, I realized how tired I was. I had not stopped to prop my foot up or to soak it all day. I could feel that it was swollen inside my brace. It was beginning to throb. I tried to walk as if there were no pain, but that only slowed our pace.

Madame Rosmerta brought me into the guest kitchen. On the back wall was a huge inglenook with heavy iron hooks from which great, black cast iron cauldrons hung at the ready for stewing or soup preparation. This was flanked to the right, by a large brick oven for baking, which was operated by two women. One was kneading dough and the other withdrawing freshly baked bread from the oven. On the opposite side was the well-stocked pantry.

In the center of the room was a flat-topped wood stove which was used as a cooking surface. Along the side walls there were long wooden sideboards laden with baskets of fresh produce, above these, dried herbs hung in bundles. In every corner of the kitchen, women were employed in various stages of food preparation.

Beside one sideboard was a large wooden wash tub which was conveniently located near a hand pump for water. On the far wall was a grand wooden table decorated with baskets of flowers and fruits meant to be inviting for guests. In the opposite corner was a humble table with long benches. A handful of native flowers in a clay jar graced the center of the table. This, I assumed was the table for the kitchen help.

"Emily, your head cook, was here earlier and lit the fire in the stove and put the kettle on to boil. Should you require it, any pot you might need will be hanging along the wall. If you will excuse me, I will gather the kitchen staff and the cloth for you." She gave me a little curtsy and backed out of the room.

I found a cast iron kettle hanging among many of various sizes along the wall where she had indicated. I set it on the stovetop to boil for medicinal tea. The Queen, I thought, would benefit from the iron in the kettle.

Next, I located a large, clay crock in which to prepare my herbal decoction. Then, I remembered that I had left my medicine bag in the Queen's quarters when I had my audience with Princess Madeline.

Before I had time to chastise myself for forgetting it, Magda and Miss Constance came into the kitchen.

I was relieved to see that Magda had brought both medicine bags with her. "I thought you might need this." She said as she held my medicine bag out to me.

"I am so glad to know someone is thinking clearly today!" I said as I stepped forward to take it from her.

"Your foot, Willow. How is it?" Magda asked with concern on her face.

"I had quite forgotten about it until we were walking back from the meeting with the Princess.

Oh, Magda, you would love her. She has accepted my proposed treatment. And she actually wants us to dress in our native clothing! She is so beautiful. Her hair is made of spun copper and her eyes are green and grey. Her voice is soft and gentle, and she has dimples when she smiles." I ran out of breath before I ran out of things to say.

"I look forward to meeting her. I have heard much about her. I am sure she is a lovely young woman. She is not much older than you from what I understand.

Now, we should see about your foot. You will be of no help to the Princess or the Queen if you cannot stand or walk about."

Turning to Miss Constance she asked, "Is there a basin or tub we can use to soak her foot for a while?"

"Why yes, of course, there is a wash tub in the pantry

that we can use. Let me fetch it for you and we can fill it."

Miss Constance turned to me and pointed toward the servant's table. "You can sit there and supervise the kitchen staff while you rest a bit and soak your foot. I am sorry we did not stop to think about this before now."

"Before I sit and soak, let me at least prepare the herbs and put them on to boil. It will take them a good half-hour to soak and another to cook and come to full strength. That should allow plenty of time to soak my foot."

Magda and I worked together, just as we had since my early childhood. Carefully, we selected and measured several herbs that we would use to stop the bleeding and pain, clear the heat and inflammation of the infection, and promote healing and tissue regeneration.

When I was satisfied with the combination of herbs that we had selected, I placed them into a large cheesecloth bag. I pulled the drawstring tight and placed it in the clay pot, added the appropriate amount of water, and set it aside to soak.

Magda poured some of the hot water from the teakettle into the tub I would soak my foot in. She carried it over to the humble table, where I had seated myself, and placed it on the floor before me.

She reached into her medicine pouch and produced a folded bit of parchment. From it, she poured a small measure of sea salt into the palm of her hand. This, she added to the steaming water in the tub.

Miss Constance went to the sink and pumped water into an earthen pitcher and carried it over to the table and poured it into the small washtub before me.

Magda bent down to feel the temperature of the water. She swirled her hand in the water to help mix in the dissolving salt crystals.

When the temperature pleased her, she took my foot in her hands and examined it.

Most of the bruising had been resolved with herbal soaks. The flesh wound was healing over nicely and would probably not leave a scar. Magda felt the edges of the break and when she was finished, she placed my foot gently in the tub of steaming water.

The water was delightfully warm. As the salt dissolved into the water, so did the pain in my foot. As the pain began to subside, I began to relax and drift off to sleep.

I awakened with a start. I hoped no one had seen me asleep on my first day on the job.

Moments later, Madame Rosmerta arrived with cloth to tear into strips and a staff to do the tearing.

"Willow, I have brought Emily to help you with any special kitchen requests. She has selected a staff to help her with anything you may need.

Here are the towels you requested. They are clean from our laundry. We boil and bleach all the white clothing. Will that be sufficient, or would you like for us to boil them again?"

"Why don't we tear them into strips first? We can add them to the tea and boil them again there." I answered.

"If you please, set the towels here on the table and I shall be able to help tear them." I directed. "We may need enough for more than one treatment."

There was a sense of hopefulness in the air. The room was filled with the sounds of cloth ripping, friendly chatter, fresh baked goods and the pungent smell of boiling herbs that Magda had seen to while I slept.

"We can add the cloth strips now. Stir them in well. We want to soak them in the decoction." I said.

"While this cools, I shall dry my foot, put my brace on and be ready to proceed."

Emily was at my feet with a towel. "I am glad you are here to help our Queen ma'am."

She was a round woman with rosy cheeks. Her hair was

greying at the temples and drawn back in a tired bun. The lines around her mouth and eyes bore witness to her kind nature and healthy sense of humor.

"I am honored to be here, Emily. Please, call me Willow. We are all working together to help save the Queen. No great thing can be accomplished without all of the parts fitting together and working smoothly. I can not take on this incredible task without help from each one of you. With all of us working together, I believe we shall help the Queen to recover."

I could see Emily's face brighten with a smile. She began to gingerly pat my foot dry with the towel.

When she had finished, she spread the towel on the floor and set my foot carefully on it. "Thank you, Emily. My foot should be quite ready." Having said this, I bent down and put it back into the brace, laced it, and rose to my feet. I put a little weight on the brace to test it out. Yes, the pain had subsided, for now.

"Let us hasten to the Queen's chambers so that we can begin treatment at once." I said.

Madame Rosmerta hurried ahead of me carrying the clay pot containing the medicinal decoction and rags.

"Be careful you do not hurry so much that you spill that tea and spoil your beautiful dress! The healing herbs can leave a nasty yellow stain." I warned.

"I am not worried about the dress, I am excited about getting started on the healing process!" came the answer over her shoulder.

I followed behind Madame Rosmerta, but I found that having spent all day without putting my foot up was beginning to slow me down.

Madame Rosmerta scuttled through the anteroom to the Queen's quarters in a hurry, then, hesitated.

She set down the still steaming pot of herbal decoction and began shaking her hands. At first, I thought she had burned herself. I watched her pace in a tight circle, she wanted to start the healing process, but she seemed to be working out some sort of inner struggle.

"I shall be right back!" She said. She left the room, running and was back in a matter of minutes. She returned a bit disheveled and out of breath, carrying a large piece of canvas.

"We will want to cover the Queen's bed linens or we shall stain her sheets yellow too. I have a cloth used for childbirth that we might use to protect the sheets. Will this do?" She asked between gasps for air.

"That is beautiful. 'Tis just the thing we need. Here, let us remove the quilts and coverlets so we can get this under the Queen."

We worked in tandem to turn down the quilts. Together, we rolled the unconscious Queen onto her side, toward the edge of the bed. While I held her there, Madame Rosmerta spread out the protective canvas, smoothing away any wrinkles that might cause her Queen discomfort.

I gently rolled the Queen onto her back and covered her again. "Now we should go to the washroom and wash our hands. We may wish to bring a tub of water in here to wash with as well."

Madame Rosmerta led the way to the washroom. I went directly to the hand basin and began to draw water. She walked to the large stove in the corner near the bathing tub. She took the kettle from the stove and poured boiling water into a small ceramic basin. She returned the pot to the stove and carried the basin to the sink, where I stood, and slid it under the pump. I obliged and helped to fill it.

"This way, your hands will not be cold. And you shan't burn them either." She explained thoughtfully.

I nodded my head with a smile. I had to agree that this woman was good with the details. She found ways to show her Queen that she loved her even when the Queen was no longer able to notice. She had dedicated her life to "the art of loving," as she called it. I decided that the Queen must, indeed, be a wonderful woman to be so loved by someone as dedicated as Madame Rosmerta was.

We washed and dried our hands and then Madame Rosmerta refilled the little basin with fresh boiling water to take with us.

"Have you ever done an internal pack on a woman before?" I asked.

"Yes, but only after a difficult birth. I have never seen it done on a woman who was not giving birth." She began to sound nervous.

"We shall do just fine." I assured her. For a moment, I felt Galynda seated on the wagon beside me. That was what she had said as we parted. "All will be well." I repeated. I felt it in my marrow. Everything was going to be all right.

"We shall require plenty of light. I am glad we still have abundant daylight coming in the windows."

I examined the Queen again. "Madame Rosmerta, do you see this? This area, just inside here," I said, placing her hand on a purple swollen area just inside her birth canal. "'Tis swollen and discolored. I shall need to open it to release the fluids gathering there. That should relieve some pressure and pain.

"Wait for me here" I said. "I just need to fetch my knife from my bag, run it under the boiling water in the washroom, and then, when I return, we shall begin.

"Allow me to do that for you. Your foot must be quite painful by now." Without hesitation, she took her leave and in only an instant, she returned.

"You are looking rather pale. Will you be alright to assist me or shall we summon Magda?" I offered.

"No, I," Rosmerta began shakily. "I shall be fine." She nodded her head as much to assure herself as to convince me. 'Tis difficult to see the damage done to her beautiful body."

"Aye, 'tis a whole new world when you are caring for a loved one." I agreed. "If you will hold this skin back, I indicated the tender and bruised labia, I shall be able to see what I am doing." I requested.

As Madame Rosmerta shifted the fold of skin that I had indicated, the large, purple hematoma slid out into plain sight. I swiftly flicked the sharp point of my knife into it. Thick brownish purple clots of stagnant blood oozed out. I quickly surrounded the fresh wound with a clean towel and squeezed. More dark sticky drainage sluggishly flowed out. I worked at this for several minutes until finally, bright red blood began to trickle in earnest.

I took another towel, soaked it in the water basin, wrung it out and cleaned the area. "You may release the fold of skin now." I directed. "You are certain you will be all right? You do look pale." I observed.

"Yes, I am fine. I want to be here." Changing the subject, she asked, "That releasing that you just did there, how are you certain when to stop squeezing?"

"When I opened it, the drainage was very dark. 'Twas not moving. 'Twas old, stagnant blood that she was no longer able to use. I cleared all the stagnant blood out of the way so that the Queen's body does not have to. Once I saw bright red blood, I knew to stop. Her Majesty needs that fresh, healthy blood to nourish her body."

"But now she is bleeding more." Madame Rosmerta protested. Her eyes began to brim with moisture.

"Aye, for the moment. But the herbs in her decoction will stop the bleeding." I said with confidence.

"Will you please bunch up several clean towels and place them just there, between her thighs. Way up close to her body."

Madame Rosmerta did as she was instructed.

I placed my right hand on the Queen's lower abdomen and massaged the area deeply.

As I pressed on her uterus, I was also applying pressure to her urinary bladder. The pressure caused her to void pungent, dark yellow urine onto the toweling.

I met Rosmerta's quizzical gaze and offered, "I want to be certain that we break up any wounds that may be harboring infection. 'Tis also important to help her void in this way. Martha informed me she has not passed water in two days. Passing all that concentrated waste will reduce her Majesty's pain and help eliminate toxins.

We mopped up the urine that escaped the towels. "Now that that is done, let's cover the area that may have gotten wet with another clean towel."

"Do you mind bathing your Queen while I go to the washroom and wash my hands?" I asked.

"I would be happy to." She said as she gathered a clean towel and dipped it in the basin. As I left the room, I thought I heard her humming.

When I returned from the washroom, Madame Rosmerta was still humming but her task was done. The room smelled less like urine and more like soap.

Excellent, you are ready. If you will hand me a strip of cloth, please, we shall begin."

I began the process of packing the strips inside the Queen's injured womb. Madame Rosmerta's brows seemed to writhe in torment. She was chewing her lower lip mercilessly.

I had her sit in a nearby chair and set her to the task of counting the strips as I used them.

"We must pay close attention to the number of strips we use." I said, "What we put in must come back out."

"Very well," she said. She watched silently as she shook her hands and opened and closed them as if to restore circulation to her fingers.

"Are you breathing, Madame Rosmerta?

"Yes, yes I am." She answered.

Sweat beads had begun to form on her upper lip and her forehead shone with perspiration.

"Very well, we are finished here. This packing may need to be retained in place until tomorrow or the next day."

"How, how do you decide how long?" Rosmerta stammered.

"The Queen will decide that. Let us remove that canvas and get her covered so she does not get a chill."

We carefully rolled her toward the edge of the bed again and Madame Rosmerta rolled the canvas up and removed it from the bed. She ran her hand over the sheet and nodded her satisfaction. The sheets were clean and dry. She smoothed them with her hands until they were wrinkle free.

Together we gingerly rolled the Queen onto her back again. Madame Rosmerta tucked a pillow under her Majesty's knees and straightened her chemise. We placed her hands upon her abdomen and then we pulled the coverlets up to her chin.

"She should sleep very deeply tonight." I said.

"But she is already unconscious, how will this be any different?" Madame Rosmerta asked.

"She has been unconscious because of the pain and the infection and general weakness due to blood and fluid loss.

Today, we drained a gathering of stagnant blood, which has relieved both pain and pressure. We massaged her uterus to break up pockets of infection. We massaged her urinary bladder and helped her to void two days' urine. That will also relieve pain and pressure. We packed her uterus with cloth soaked in herbal tea to stop the bleeding, fight infection, reduce swelling and because the cloth was wet, it restores some fluid to her body.

She will be in less pain now which means she will be able to rest more comfortably. When the body can rest comfortably, it can take over the healing process. Does that make sense to you?" I asked.

"Yes, thank you." She replied tucking a stray tendril of hair behind her ear. She seemed small and meek somehow.

What you just said, you really did a lot just in one treatment today. I am amazed." Madame Rosmerta said thoughtfully.

We gathered the dirty linens into a pile, which Madame Rosmerta assured me, would be taken care of without any help from me.

The sun was setting into deep oranges and bold reds outside the window. I had not realized how much time we had spent in the Queen's chambers.

As we crossed the hallway to the washroom Emily popped her head in. "Are you finished?"

"Aye." I replied.

"Did all go well?" she asked, almost afraid to hear the answer.

Madame Rosmerta answered for me. "Oh yes, you should see Willow work. She is so confident. She has such a skilled hand."

Emily smiled a warm smile. "Oh, I am happy to hear it went well. Are you hungry?"

Madame Rosmerta and I exchanged looks. We had been so busy we had forgotten to think about food.

I said. Aye, now that my work is done, I suddenly feel tremendously hungry."

"Grand!" Emily said. "I have prepared baked chicken stuffed with..." her voice faded off as she saw Madame Rosmerta and I exchanged another meaningful look, one of exhaustion.

"No stuffed chicken then?" she asked, without fully understanding our hesitance. She offered, "I also prepared a chicken pie for the kitchen staff, if you would rather..."

"Emily," I said. "I hope that we have not put you out. I

would be honored if you would trade meals with us. Today, I am very tired and finding my meal all in one place would be a nice gift." I had not lied. Finishing the treatment and washing up for dinner, I could feel the miles and days of anticipation unraveling inside me quickly.

Emily had a warm smile of understanding. "That is just grand, Willow." She said, patting my shoulder. "No imposition at all. Come along now and let's get you two fed."

Walking down the hall behind her, I drifted into a kind of trance. I could smell a faint scent of vanilla and cinnamon. I was lulled into warm, happy memories of Emily's apple pie. I was hooked. I knew that every time I saw her, I would begin to salivate spontaneously.

Magda, Miss Constance, and the cooking staff that had helped us shred the towels, greeted us eagerly in the guest wing kitchen.

"What is your assessment?" Magda asked quietly.

"I am confident that the Queen will rest much better tonight. We helped to eliminate several pain causing factors and have administered herbs to help stop the bleeding and infection." I said.

"Oh, this is good news!" Emily said. "I am so happy to hear this. I am sure we all are. Won't you please sit down so we can serve your meal?"

"I shall, but only if you and the staff join us at our table. We work together and we eat together." I said.

The staff quickly gathered their dishes from the far corner and brought them to the big table, near the hearth, where our meal was being laid out for us.

Our meal was delicious. The chicken pie was covered with a flaky tender crust. It was salty and sweet and buttery all at once and melted on my tongue, almost before I could chew it. The savory filling was thick and filled with tender chunks of chicken, carrots, tiny peas and diced potatoes. I could taste sage and thyme with a hint of onion.

My head was filled with the delightful smells of the freshly prepared meal and growing scent of the dessert that was still to come. The flavors of the chicken pie possessed me entirely. I found little room left in my head for conversation, so I ate my meal in silence.

All around me, there was a feeling of joy and growing hope. The voices of the women sitting around the great table were more cheerful and light than I had heard them since our arrival. I sent up a silent prayer of thanksgiving.

After our meal, I had planned to return to the Queen's quarters to check on Her Royal Highness.

"Thank you, Emily, for another lovely meal. Your meals nourish me and give me the strength I need to attend to the Queen."

"Yes, thank you Emily." Magda and Madame Rosmerta agreed.

"If you will excuse me, I would like to return to the Queen's quarters to make sure that she is resting well."

Madame Rosmerta rose from her chair. "I shall take you there straight away. Excuse us everyone."

The sound of dinner dishes being gathered and water being drawn from the pump at the sink receded as we moved down the hallway toward the royal chambers.

"Just by being here, you have given our people hope. I have been fortunate to watch you work. I have faith in your medicine, but, more than that, Willow, I have faith in you. That says a lot. I have been independent most of my life. I have not had much reason to depend on or trust in others, until now. You have given me a gift beyond my greatest expectations. I do not know how I will ever repay you."

She finished her statement as we entered the Queen's bedchamber. The room was growing dark.

Madame Rosmerta lighted a lantern and set it upon the bedside table and left the room to light lanterns in the anteroom and washroom.

I sat at the bedside and took the Queen's wrist in my hand to take her pulse. The rate was already slowing and the quality of the flow was just perceptibly stronger.

I smiled a small, personal smile of satisfaction.

"You are smiling, Willow, this must be good news." It was the Princess. She had entered the room and was standing so near to me that I could smell the delicate perfume of her skin.

"Aye, there is a small sign of promise. Your mother's pulses have slowed down but only by a fraction. They were more rapid before, indicating fever. Now, they are becoming steadier and slightly stronger too. Please understand that these changes are nearly imperceptible. These are positive changes however minute. 'Tis not by much, and would not be measurable by anyone else's account." I warned.

The princess stood silently, studying me and absorbing every word I said.

"Oh, but it is very good to hear that there is progress, no matter how slight. It has been so long. I am tiring of my solitary voice in the throne room. I think I am forgetting the sound of hers. She is such a powerful speaker. I admire that about her." She trailed off, feeling self-conscious that she might be confiding too much.

"I am confident that she now has the right tools to fight her way back to you. She has been greatly weakened by this trauma and it will take some time for her body and spirit to mend. 'Tis a wonderful thing that she is loved by so many. Your love will help her to heal.

I shall replace her packing and remain by her bedside through the night so that you might rest easy, Your Highness." I said.

"Please, call me Princess Madeline." She replied with a gentle smile.

"As you wish." I conceded with a bow. "If you would like to have a bit of supper, we shall finish up here in less than an hour's time." I offered.

"Very well," the Princess agreed. "I shall await your instruction in the ante chamber."

She gathered her skirts and turned for the door.

"Princess," I called after her. "Please make certain that you eat something to keep up your strength."

When we were alone, Madame Rosmerta and I set about removing the packing. Each strip I withdrew had the distinct, fetid odor of infection and necrosis. We collected the fetid strips in a basin.

Madame Rosmerta carefully counted each one and once she had assured me that we had removed all of the strips, I carried the fetid strips to the washroom and dumped them in the fire.

I washed my hands with calendula soap and returned to Rosmerta, who was preparing the fresh strips.

We worked together seamlessly packing fresh disinfecting strips inside the Queen's traumatized womb. This time, knowing what to expect, Madame Rosmerta appeared to be more at ease with the process.

After cleaning the room and straightening the bedding Madame Rosmerta and I opened the doors to the ante room.

True to her word, the Princess had stationed herself outside of her mother's chambers. Evidence of a meal sat on a small side table.

"I am pleased to see that you were able to eat something." I observed.

"Yes, thank you." The Princess flushed. "I have been so concerned for Mother. I sometimes forget to tend to myself." She confessed, unable to make eye contact.

"We have finished up treatment for the evening." I stated with a bow. "I shall stay at her bedside so that I might monitor her progress.

Turning to Madame Rosmerta, Princess Madeline said, "I shall stay with Mother tonight, Rosmerta, please take Willow to your quarters and see to her foot. If anything arises, I shall know where to find you both."

"Very well, we shall be back at first light to relieve you. Goodnight Princess Madeline." Madame Rosmerta said with a curtsy.

Uncertain how I should feel, having just been relieved of my duties for the night, I curtsied too. "Good night Princess Madeline."

Before I could say more, Madame Rosmerta had hooked her hand into my elbow and had spun me on my heel so that I was facing the door. Out we went. This time, we walked down a corridor I had not seen before.

The Harem

As it grew darker outside, the natural lighting in the castle faded as well. A candle lighter busied himself, scuttling from lantern to torch to chandelier, chasing darkness from the corners of corridors and great halls.

He rather reminded me of a bee as it flits from flower to flower, gathering pollen to make honey.

"This is us," Madame Rosmerta indicated with a sweep of her hand.

It was indistinguishable from any of the other doors I had seen along this and the other hallways I had traversed today.

I had never been inside a harem before. I was a bit nervous. Would I see men and women, strewn naked, across couches fornicating?

Madame Rosmerta turned the large ring knob and the door unlatched with a small click. Just inside the door was as lovely a sitting room as I had ever seen.

The air was perfumed with incense and flowers. The couches and chaises were upholstered in beautiful shades of green and gold with burgundy and pink accents. These matched the large bouquets of roses and peonies that were placed on the occasion tables on each side of the large, pillow laden, overstuffed couches. All furnishings rested upon a marble floor covered in richly colored rugs from the orient.

One wall was dominated by a large fireplace, which was flanked by a window on either side. The fire flickered merrily behind the great, nude-woman-shaped andirons. The windows were dressed in heavy burgundy draperies, which were drawn back to reveal filmy pink sheers. The light of the setting sun was muted and made the decadent room more inviting.

Looking at the window dressings, I smiled. The effect was sensual, akin to a woman drawing up the hem of her skirt to reveal the gauzy chemise underneath. It left me with a giddy feeling.

"Willow, follow me."

I must have stopped to look at the room. Madame Rosmerta was talking to me and I was not hearing her.

"I am sorry, too many new things to take in all at once. You were saying?"

"I was saying that you have had a long day of work. We should get you out of that corset and into something more comfortable."

"Oh, that does sound lovely." I replied, rejoining the conversation.

"Your belongings from the carriage were delivered to your room in the guest wing. I sent someone to fetch them, but they won't be here until morning. You may borrow something of mine in the meantime. We will go to my quarters to get what we need. Won't you follow me please?"

I was following a courtesan into her private quarters, quarters that she had only shared with the Queen. These walls must have housed countless hours of passion and secret lovemaking. I was exploring uncharted territory and the butterflies in my stomach made it hard for me to think.

Why was I so nervous? Why was I not this nervous meeting the Queen?

I rolled my eyes at myself for being so stupid. The Queen had been easy to care for, she was not a threat because she was unconscious and I knew how to care for her. Madame Rosmerta, on the other hand, was awake and had a way about her that made me feel ignorant and naked and curious and afraid.

She led me through the sitting room down a corridor and to the door of her private quarters. She withdrew a key from her between her breasts and inserted it into a keyhole beneath the ring knob. Watching her insert the key into the lock gave me a flutter in my chest that I could not explain.

Here, in the harem, in her presence I felt truly foreign, even to myself. Before my mind could swim away with me, she cupped my elbow in her hand and herded me inside. I watched as she gently inserted the key into the inside latch and secured the door behind us. She withdrew the key from the lock and hung it on a hook next to the door.

I stood and stared dumbly at the key as it swung gently on its hook.

"Do come in, Willow." Madame Rosmerta said from far away.

Her quarters were beautiful. A large ornate fireplace stood at the end of the room. A small loveseat, flanked by twin matching chairs faced the fire. A small desk was positioned in front of a great oriel to the left of the fireplace. The oriel was draped in rich red velvet over gauzy golden sheers. A window seat, upholstered in red and gold fabric, was nestled at the foot of the large bay window.

"Are you all right Willow? You seem to be far away. Not at all the powerful medicine woman I worked with this afternoon." Rosmerta observed.

"Well," I began, "When we were treating the Queen, I

knew what I was doing and what to expect. I was strong in my conviction and assured in my actions. But here, I am lost and uncertain. Much the way you were in the Queen's quarters when you had to await the diagnosis and prognosis. I see the two of us as very powerful and wise in our chosen work, but when we are not in control of our situation, we become mere mortals."

"A very wise observation. You are right." She said wagging her index finger in the air and nodding her agreement.

"Now, let us see about getting something more comfortable for you to wear." She walked to the end of the room and stepped behind a heavy drapery. "Come along, Willow." She outstretched a hand for me to take.

I felt like a child who could not keep up with her mother at the market. The only way for me to keep up was for me to hold on.

She led me into another room. It was her bedchamber. I stiffened and drew in a deep breath through my gaping mouth. I was in a courtesan's bedchamber.

A large four-poster bed draped in sheer curtains of red and gold dominated the wall before me. Beside the bed was another oriel, which matched the one in the sitting room. It too, had a matching cushioned window seat.

Rosmerta was moving along, and I was being pulled along with her. At the end of the room, she pulled back another drapery, revealing her wardrobe. I had never seen so many colors and textures in one place.

She pulled a chemise from one end of her closet. "I have many newer and nicer, but my heart tells me you would prefer comfort. This is one I wear for comfort."

"How lovely." I exclaimed. "Aye, comfort suits me best." I nodded numbly.

"Come along then," she said, pulling me back into the bedchamber by the hand.

"If you will just turn around and lift your arms" She began.

Turn around? My mind began to race. Turn around, what for?

"Come on, Silly! If you don't turn around and raise your arms, how shall I help you out of your dress or that corset?" Saying this, she dropped the fresh chemise on the foot of the bed.

I felt as if my mind were moving at the speed of molasses in wintertime.

I obediently turned and raised my arms out to the sides. Madame Rosmerta unlaced the dress at the bodice and helped lift the dress off over my head. I knew I should say something or offer to help her with hers, but freedom was only moments away and I could not wait.

I grasped the post of the bed and she stood behind me and unlaced the corset. As soon as I felt the confining corset release its grasp on me, I filled my lungs with air. My skin turned to gooseflesh and I felt my nipples harden. It was so liberating! My mind shifted to horses. I had witnessed them roll on their backs at the end of the day, as soon as the harness was removed. I suddenly felt a closer kinship to our ponies.

"Now, will you help me with mine?" Madame Rosmerta asked.

I had seen a rabbit freeze in mid-chase, unsure of which way to run. Suddenly, I was that rabbit. My heart was beating so hard I was sure Madame Rosmerta could hear it.

I fumbled with the laces on her dress. My hands felt like paws. I seemed to have no thumbs and my fingers would not bend as they should.

"Your hands are trembling, are you quite alright?" She asked. I thought I saw the hint of an arched eyebrow.

"Umm, aye, 'tis just that I have never..." the words lodged in my throat.

I felt so incompetent at that moment I was not at all sure what I should do next.

"Here, take this lace and untie it." she said, indicating a lace at her waist.

I made another attempt to untie it and actually managed to finish the job. I moved to her other side and clumsily untied that lace as well.

"Now, we will lift the dress over my head, just as we did yours."

I was shaking so badly that I managed to get her beautiful hair tangled up in her dress.

She was more than patient with me.

"That's all right. Can you see where it is tangled?" She asked.

"Aye," I answered, feeling humiliated. "'Tis tangled in your brooch."

"Let us see if you can free me of the brooch." she suggested. Her arms were in the air. She was half disrobed. I could see the crest of her breasts above the top edge of her corset.

I dragged my mind back to the task at hand. I managed to remove the brooch and extract her from the dress with badly shaking hands. When her head emerged from the depths of her skirts, her neatly coifed hair was rather disheveled.

"I...I ruined your beautiful hair." I said, feeling stupid.

With the sweep of her hand, Madame Rosmerta pulled the pin that had been holding her hair. It cascaded down her back in shiny chestnut ripples. She shook her hair for good measure and ran her fingers through it at the scalp.

"Not to worry, no harm done, Willow. We are not going out again this evening anyway. It feels so good to have it down. She shook her hair again and crossed the room, putting out torches as she went.

Watching her hair undulate over her back made me feel

weak in the knees.

"Won't you please help me out of this corset?" she asked. She tipped her head forward and tucked both hands into her hair at the nape of her neck and raised it up to the top of her head.

The scent of her soap wafted up from her smooth skin. I felt a wave of heat flash through my body as she stood before me, silhouetted by the firelight. I felt my nipples grow tight and I could feel my heart beating hard between my legs.

What was wrong with me? I had never experienced anything like this. Maybe it was the rich foods I had eaten today. Maybe I was sick.

"Willow? Are you there?" Rosmerta asked patiently.

I blinked hard and silently told myself to concentrate. What was the matter with me anyway?

With shaking hands, I managed to unlace the confining corset for Rosmerta.

"Oh, it is good to breathe naturally again. Thank you for that." She said, seating herself heavily upon the bed.

"Come and sit with me. She said, patting the bed. I want to take your hair down."

I moved slowly, as if I was in a dream. I found myself beside the bed and then she was pulling me down next to her. Another wave of panic shot through me and I felt another searing chill scamper up my spine and dart out through my nipples.

I silently stared down upon my breasts, wondering what could be causing them to betray me in such a manner.

Madame Rosmerta removed my hat. As she withdrew the pins that she had used to secure my hair up, she put them between her teeth. My freed braids dropped down over my shoulders. She skillfully removed the thong from my left plait first and unbraided it, then, she moved on to the right one.

I sat stock-still and stared down upon my hands. They were smallish and the nails were short. The palms of my hands were rough and callused compared to Madame Rosmerta's.

She stood and moved to her dressing table beside the window. She returned with a hairbrush and began gently brushing my hair, first at the tips and then higher up, until she could brush from roots to tips in one smooth stroke.

I felt myself begin to relax. Madame Rosmerta began to hum. It felt awkward at first, but once I allowed myself to loosen up and relax, it was lovely having someone care for me.

If I closed my eyes, I could imagine Magda brushing my hair as she had done when I was a child. I could imagine Galynda brushing my hair as she sometimes did. When I imagined Madame Rosmerta, with her full-bodied bosom, brushing my hair, I began to stiffen up again. I vowed to keep my eyes open and I tried to keep my mind on Magda.

"Is everything all right Willow? You are awfully quite this evening." Rosmerta said around the hair pins in her mouth.

"I think," I began unsteadily. "I have had so many new experiences today that I must just sit quietly and process them." I answered honestly.

My companion began to loosely braid first one side of my hair and then the other.

"You are trembling," she observed. "Are you cold?" she asked as stroked my arms, in an effort to warm me.

"I am hot and cold" I told her. "I do not know what the matter is with me tonight." I confessed honestly.

"I shall make some tea to take the chill out and to help you relax that busy mind of yours." She said as she moved to the fireplace. She placed the teapot on a hook and swung it closer to the flames.

"I shall be right back." She said plucking the hair pins from her lips.

Moments later, she returned carrying a tub of water. "Magda will never forgive me if I do not attend to your foot properly. Come over here and let's get your brace off." She said, setting the tub before the loveseat near the fire.

I hobbled over to the sofa and seated myself. Before I could bend to unlace it, Madame Rosmerta was at my feet loosening the lacing of the brace and the boot.

"I'm sorry it is so cold. Magda told me it should be cold to take the swelling down." She apologized with warm, soulful hazel eyes.

"Aye, it should be." I agreed. I instinctually gritted my teeth when she put my foot in the water. The water was so cold that it felt as if it had gripped me about the ankle and was sucking the life out of me.

"Here, this ought to warm the rest of you." She offered apologetically.

I accepted the steaming cup of tea and cradled it in both hands. I carefully sipped from the surface to draw off only the coolest portion of the tea.

"You are smiling, that is a good sign." Madame Rosmerta commented.

"Aye, I was just reminded of Magda. When I was very small, she taught me to 'give the tea a little kiss' so that I would not burn myself."

My companion smiled. "She is a wise and loving person. I enjoyed getting to talk with her the other day when we gathered herbs for our meal. Was that only yesterday?"

"Aye, 'twas." I responded, nodding. "Difficult to believe." I agreed, taking another sip from my tea.

The cold of the water slowly crept up my leg to the knee. My knee began to ache and I could no longer sit still.

"Is it too much?" she asked, indicating the water.

"Aye, when the bones start to ache, 'tis time to stop." I said, taking my foot from the water.

Madame Rosmerta took the teakettle from its hook and poured boiling water into the tub. To this, she added lavender flowers and sea salt.

"Go ahead and put both feet in." She said.

I obeyed, enjoying the warmth of the water this time.

"What's on your mind, Willow?"

"I was just thinking about the day's work. I am glad that I decided to change the packing early, because I noticed that after only a short time, the Queen was already showing positive response to the treatment. I made the decision to change out the toxic dressing and apply fresh packing to speed her healing. I noted that the strips we removed were nearly dry. The added moisture from the second application of the decoction is very important to her recovery as well." I was beginning to feel the effects of the tea and the foot soak.

"I noticed that too." Rosmerta commented. Placing her cup on a nearby occasion table, she slid from her seat and knelt before me taking each foot, in turn she dried and then massaged them.

I had not realized how sore they were until she began to ferret out the tender spots with her talented fingers.

She began to work her hands up my shins and calves. She found more tender areas and gave them her undivided attention.

"Let's go to the bed where I can see to your back." She offered.

I raised a hand to attempt an objection, which was immediately overruled.

"I shan't take 'no' for an answer!" she scolded with her fists upon her ample hips. A towel dangled limply from one fist. "I made a promise to your mother, and I intend to keep it!" She said warmly, wagging the index finger of her empty hand at me. Now, get up to that bed!" She said with a wink of her twinkling eye.

I hobbled over to the bed. Madame Rosmerta stood behind me and instructed me to raise my hands over my head. When I did, she deftly removed my scratchy chemise and laid me face down on the bed, leaving me wearing nothing but my bloomers.

She climbed upon the bed, sat beside me, and began to scratch my back. I felt a chill that shot up my spine and burst from my skin as goose flesh. I was glad I was lying face down or Rosmerta may have seen that my nipples were hard again.

She did not seem to notice anything out of the ordinary. "I have always found that there is very little else that feels quite as good as a back scratching after a day in a corset."

I thought of the ponies rolling in the grass again and I had to agree. It did feel especially nice.

I could smell the essence of cinnamon, cloves and mint in the massage oil as she began to rub my back. The sensation was warming and cooling at the same time.

As Rosmerta's hands worked on my body, I was amazed at the way she was able to discover tender spots I had no idea were there.

"It is easy to find them, the muscles are drawn up tight like a rope here," she indicated, pressing on a spot near my spine. "And here," she squeezed the muscle between my neck and shoulder, "here, it is more like a rock."

I could definitely feel an increase in pain when she pressed or squeezed a place she had indicated was knotted up.

She worked from my neck to my shoulders, to my back and then began on my thighs. First, she massaged my right leg, and worked her way to the left, where she finished with my injured foot.

The massage hurt, the way bruises hurt, while she was working on a particular sore spot. When she was done, I could feel the area heat up as the circulation was restored.

"Willow, you have an awful lot of tension in your body." She observed casually as she worked.

"I do?"

"Yes, you need a physical outlet for all this tension. You should allow yourself to be touched and cared for more often." She said matter-of-factly.

Casually, she asked, "Have you ever taken a lover?"

"A lover?" My ears began to burn. I was glad they were hidden from view by my hair. I was certain they were glowing red.

"Nay, I am not marriageable. So, I live a life of celibacy." I dismissed the issue.

"I seem to recall your discussion with Magda." Rosmerta said, as she dug into a particularly tight muscle. "Magda said that it was her choice to have no husband. Does that not mean that you have a choice as well?"

"I ...I have not given any thought to it." I defended. "All this talk of me taking a lover!" I exclaimed with a scowl. 'Tis a foreign concept to me! All my life I believed I could never marry. I never had reason or opportunity to consider having lovers. Now, I..." my voice faded.

"Now that your mind has been opened to the possibility, perhaps, you could find interest in sharing yourself with someone else." She finished my statement for me.

"Aye," I nodded, relieved that she understood. "Aye, I think 'tis true." I replied. My brow was furrowed again.

"You seem to be confused about something. Is it something I can answer for you?" she asked, leaning into my line of sight.

"I ...I do not know much about this subject. I feel so ignorant! I do not even know what to ask!"

"Well, I do not know much about medicine and herbs." She began.

"That is not true." I defended. "You are a midwife. You must know many herbs and healing techniques."

"True," She conceded. "But I have seen you work. I feel as though I know nothing compared to you. Do you understand what I mean?"

I nodded that I understood.

"You have far more experience with your medicine than I

do with mine, and I am many years your senior." She said. "I have far more experience and training than you do on the subject of love and pleasuring. Just as Magda has taught you about healing and herbs. I could teach you about love and desire." She offered.

She handed me the soft chemise and turned the comforter back and patted the bed.

I froze. Now? Was she going to teach me about carnal pleasuring now?

"Come on Silly, I don't want your muscles to get cold. They will knot up worse if they do."

I slithered into the chemise, careful to keep my back to her. I slid into the bed beside her and lay as stiff as a board.

She slid her hand under the sheet and tucked a pillow under my left leg and then crawled into bed beside me and pulled the comforter up to our chins.

"Have you ever shared your bed with a friend?" She asked.

"Aye, I share a wagon with Galynda. She is the *drabardi* I told you about in the carriage. We have only the one bed on our wagon. We share everything with each other." I was beginning to think however, that my conversations with Madame Rosmerta might be the one thing I would not share with Galynda.

"You have your own wagon?" Madame Rosmerta broke into my thoughts. "That must be a sign that your people feel you are old enough to make your own decisions, right?"

"Aye and nay," I responded. "Galynda and I were the only two unmarried people left in our clan and we are both unmarriageable. Since, the caravan was breaking up and neither of us was going to move away from our families, they decided we could try living in our own wagon."

"No single young men in your camp?" She asked.

"Not anymore. Not for many years now. We marry our marriageable girls to other caravans and more recently, to men in the villages we trade with."

"Have you ever liked to play with boys?"

"Nay, I spent most of my days studying." I said shaking my head. "In my free time, I would play with Galynda. We have been best friends all my life."

"Best friends?" She asked with an arched eyebrow.

"Aye, she is my cousin, but we grew up together, like sisters." She looked disappointed when I said this.

"Why is Galynda not eligible for marriage? Is that a question I can ask?"

"I think 'tis a senseless rule." I scowled. "The elders said she should not marry because she can not see with her eyes." I felt myself becoming angry just thinking about it.

"Can not see with her eyes." Rosmerta repeated to herself. "That is an interesting way to say that." She said with her brow furrowed in thought.

"'Tis true." I replied. "She can not see with her eyes, but she can see things no one else can see. She saw into my foot and told me I had broken two bones!"

"So, she has a true gift. She is not like the charlatans we have all seen at the circus. That explains why you became so protective of her." She was far away in thought.

"Do you spend much of your time as her protector?" She continued.

"Aye. I would never want anything bad to happen to her."

"That is a lot of responsibility."

"But she is not a burden." I defended. "She does everything everyone else does. She can cook and wash clothes and sew, and find herbs, she just can not see with her eyes." I was beginning to feel frustrated and was wondering where she was headed with this conversation.

"I am so looking forward to meeting Galynda, Willow. She sounds like a very lovely young lady. Your family should be arriving tomorrow or the next day."

I had been so busy with my duties to the Queen and

Princess that I had forgotten that my family would be joining us soon. I did miss them all.

"Are you quite comfortable?" my bedmate asked.

"Aye." I said and 'twas true.

"Good, she replied. Then we should get some sleep. Tomorrow will be another busy day." With that she blew out the lamp at the bedside and kissed me gently on the forehead.

Awakening

I awoke in the early morning with a start. Unaccustomed to sleeping in such a cavernous space, I felt small, insignificant and lost. I had heard that some people who were trapped in small places felt that they could not breathe. In this huge room, I felt that my breath was lost to the space and I could not catch it.

I sat bolt upright, gasping for air, waking Madame Rosmerta. "Willow? Are you all right?" she asked with a voice that was filled with concern and numb with sleep.

I felt small and frightened. I could not find my voice at first and only nodded, as a diminutive child does. I sat silent for a moment gathering my thoughts and trying to catch my breath.

When at last, I found my voice, I explained. "My entire home fits in a wagon that is the size of your bed!" I sat blinking, still feeling dazed. "When I awoke, I had quite forgotten where I was. I could not see the ceiling above me, and it felt as if the roof of my tiny wagon had been torn off, but I could see no sky or stars! Nothing about my surroundings felt familiar." I blurted.

"Oh my, that does make this room seem huge." Rosmerta replied, looking about and seeing her quarters with new eyes. "You are sure you will be all right?" She asked again, tucking a loose wisp of hair behind her ear and rubbing my back with the flat of her palm. "I had never realized that a space could feel too big before. I am sorry for the oversight she stated leaning in close to me.

Her kindness and proximity comforted me. I liked Madame Rosmerta, but she liked to talk about things I would rather have forgotten all about.

"We had better get up. We will need to give the Princess a respite." I said.

She scurried behind the closet curtain. When she returned, she was in a fresh chemise and was holding her corset on for me to tie.

I obliged and tightened the laces as gently as I could until she told me that I needed to pull harder.

Someone was to deliver your things to the harem last night. You shall wear your own things today if you wish. She strode to the closet and returned with a dark green dress on.

The thought of not having to wear that corset again made me smile.

"Would you mind lacing me up, please?" She asked with her arms outstretched. "Did I mention that I have a private washroom? It is back this way." She led me into a much smaller washroom than I had used the day before. It was made of the same brown and white marble I had seen in the other one and it had all of the same amenities.

I went into the washroom alone, while Madame Rosmerta unbraided her hair and began to brush it.

I reluctantly used the garderobe and then set about washing my hands, face and body.

When I had returned to the dressing room, Madame

Rosmerta, putting her hair up, had a mouthful of hairpins. She pointed with her hairbrush, indicating my bedroll and clothing had arrived.

Putting the finishing touches to her hair she said, "I had your clothing laundered, mended and ironed. I felt you might want to show the castle what beautiful colors your clothing is made with.

Just keep the chemise you have on; it is thicker than the one you brought and should keep you warmer in this drafty castle." She said as she drew the coverlets up over the mattress and placed the plump pillows back on the head of the bed.

I hugged the chemise to my body; it was very soft and I realized she was right. It was thicker than mine.

"Oh, thank you! I exclaimed, pulling it away from my body so I could examine the fine embroidery. "'Tis so lovely!" I twirled in it like a child in a new dress. I meant it. This undergarment was, without a doubt, the nicest vestment I had ever owned.

I dressed myself quickly, noticing that my clothing never looked so fine.

"How did they do it?" I asked.

"Do what?" Rosmerta asked, pulling on her stockings.

I had found my hairbrush among my things and began raking the brush through my hair briskly.

"Make my clothing like new," I said between strokes of the brush. "I can't even see my awkward stitching along the bottom." I said holding my skirt up to examine the places I was certain I had mended.

"Everyone has a job that they are good at. We have some of the finest seamstresses and tailors working here."

"Are your clothes to your satisfaction?" She asked.

"Aye, they are like new, so clean and crisp and fresh. And your soft chemise, 'tis as white as snow!" I twirled around looking at myself in her large full-length mirror.

"It is yours now." She smiled.

"'Tis lovely. Thank you, Madame Rosmerta. I shall treasure it." I said, hugging it to my body.

"Please, after all that we have experienced together, I feel we are friends, you may call me Rosmerta.

"Very well," I said. "I like that. Rosmerta it is."

I began to braid my hair in the haphazard manner to which I had grown accustomed.

"Stop! Stop! Willow, you are such a lovely young lady, but you must learn to spend more time grooming yourself. Here, let me help you." With that, Rosmerta began to smooth my hair with the brush again and then she braided it tightly into two braids of equal size and shape. She carefully wound these around my head and tucked it all neatly under an ornate hat.

"There! That is much better, now I believe we are both fit to tend to the Queen and Princess."

"Do you think Her Highness will like my dress? Do you think she will find it acceptable?" I asked.

"Well, Honey, if you are asking about the Queen, I do not see how she can object." She nudged me with an elbow and flashed me a wry smile.

"Nay, Rosmerta!" I cast a scowl from beneath furrowed brows. "I was speaking of the Princess, Madeline."

"I should expect that your exotic beauty pleases her. You will only be more beautiful and exotic in your native garb, don't you agree?"

"You think I am beautiful, even with my wild hair and torn skirts?" I asked for reassurance.

"Even so." She nodded, smiling. "Yes, you are very beautiful and exotic." She said stroking my cheeks in her soft hands.

"Come; let us continue our discussion as we make our way to the Queen's chamber." She said, tucking her hand into my elbow and herding me toward her washroom.

"What are we doing in your lavatory?" I asked, uncertain what to think.

"No one is to know about this passageway but you and I. Agreed?" She whispered confidentially.

"Aye." I looked questioningly at her.

"Come on." She urged. "Let's take a lantern."

She pulled open a panel behind her garderobe and we stepped into a dark corridor.

We were in a tunnel between the broad sweeping corridors and inner walls of the castle.

"This is very like the tunnels field mice make in grassy meadows and under snow so they can travel about without being seen by predators." I observed out loud.

"Yes?" She asked, mildly interested. "Willow," She began, "I wish you could see yourself as others do. You have lovely, unblemished olivine skin, you are so fortunate to have naturally wavy hair. I spend all day working with mine to make mine do what yours does naturally. You have the most beautiful clear green eyes, when I look at them; it is like looking into a fresh, clear pond on a hot day. And your body, you are young and wiry. You have no need to draw your waist in with a corset."

It never occurred to me that others might find me attractive. I had never had occasion to think about it before. Now that I was thinking about it, I began to realize that I found Rosmerta to be alluring. I was fascinated with her and intimidated by her at the same time. She thought I was lovely.

"We turn here." My companion directed. "See this chink in the marble?" she raised the lantern to illuminate it. "That is our sign that we should turn."

We arrived in the anteroom to the Queen's chambers. We were able to check that the room was empty before we made our entrance.

"Close the door behind us," Rosmerta whispered to me.

The 'door' turned out to be a bookshelf. It swung closed easily and latched with a soft click.

Madame Rosmerta opened and closed the main door into the Chamber to make it appear as though we had only just arrived by that door.

"Good morning, Your Highness." Madame Rosmerta addressed the Princess.

The Princess rose to her feet. Tears were streaming down her face. She turned to address me.

My mind was racing. Had the Queen's condition worsened? Had she passed in the night?

"Willow, you have exceeded my expectations." She said. "Mother awoke last night."

The Prince Is Coming

"This is good news." I agreed. "I requested to be informed if there was any change in her condition. Why was I not awakened?" I demanded.

Madame Rosmerta stood with her mouth agape, looking rather like a fish out of water.

"Willow." Rosmerta called.

"Aye?" I said turning from the Princess to her.

Rosmerta, standing out of sight of the princess, cast me a wild-eyed look and shook her head mouthing hugely the word "No!"

The Princess interrupted Rosmerta's nonverbal admonitions. "She is quite right Rosmerta, she did request that she was to be apprised of any change and I sent no one to seek her out."

Turning to me, the Princess said, "I do apologize, as Royal Physician, you had every right to be informed. I took it upon myself to monitor Mother. I felt it was important that you rest. How is your injured foot?"

"The foot is mending well enough, thank you for asking." I replied respectfully, realizing, too late, that I had just brazenly questioned the Princess's authority.

Changing the subject, I asked, "Please tell me how it happened, when your mother awakened, I mean, and what did you do?"

"'Twas nearly two hours after the moon had reached her zenith this morning." She answered. "Mother awakened and saw me here." Saying this, she rested both hands on the back of the chair, indicating that she had been seated in it.

"Mother spoke very softly, requiring me to lean in to hear her. She said she was thirsty and requested something to drink.

I went to the door and asked the sentry to fetch someone from the kitchen. I filled a pitcher with fresh water and tried to help her to drink from her cup. She could not and began to choke.

When the woman from the kitchen came, I turned her away. Mother had fallen back to sleep and I no longer needed her assistance."

I was saddened to think that I could have been so much help to Her Majesty if someone had summoned me.

"Madame Rosmerta," I assumed my role as medicine woman. "Would you please go to the kitchen and ask them to prepare the broth as prescribed in the parchment?"

"Very well," she replied. "And I shall see about breakfast as well." She curtsied as she backed from the room.

"Princess Madeline, have you had your breakfast?" I enquired, gathering the sleeping Queen's limp wrist into my hands to take her pulse.

"I have not. I did not realize it was time until you arrived." She admitted.

"You should go and have something to eat." The caretaker in me ordered. I suddenly realized I had undoubtedly broken protocol and anticipated that I would again with my next breath.

I am sorry, Your Highness," I began. "I am certain I am completely making a mess of your protocol, for that I do apologize. Your ways are quite foreign to me." I begged forgiveness.

"What do you mean?" The Princess puzzled.

"Your people have a hierarchy system. There are different levels of mankind. Each level has its own separate set of rules. There are so many things to remember to do and not to do that I am quite afraid I shall forget that I am talking to a person and only think of the rules that should or should not apply to them.

My people treat everyone as equals. While it is important to respect the elders of our community, what is disrespectful to the elders is disrespectful to the children as well. What is polite is polite for all. No group has special rules which estrange them from the others." I explained.

"I can see where our lifestyle would be confusing for you. I have lived my life isolated from the others in our community. I have been estranged, as you say, from everyone, save for those select few who visit and those who serve us."

The pulses were steady, but still thin. The rate was moderate, indicating she was winning the battle against the infection. Her spirit smoke hovered feebly above her body, but it was still firmly rooted.

When I had read the pulses on both wrists, I placed both of her hands upon her abdomen.

"What did you learn?" The princess's face was eager.

"The pulses are steady but weak, the rate has returned to normal, indicating that your mother's body is defeating the infection."

"This is good news!" She said with elation.

"Aye, there is promise when there is fight." I agreed. "If you will excuse me, I shall be right back with some water for your mother." I retrieved the water pitcher from the bedside table and made a small curtsy and left the room.

Someone had kept the fireplace in the washroom lit throughout the night. The kettle for hot water was kept at the boil as well. I emptied the pitcher in the hand basin and poured boiling water from the teakettle into it. From my medicine bag, I removed a bit of dried gingerroot and sliced off a few bits and left them floating in the water. I then added enough water at the pump to make it tepid. I returned to the queen's chambers with the pitcher.

"I have thought about what you said," the Princess began. "I have hated being isolated. Father would not allow Phillip and I to play with other children. We were to play only with each other and with our nursemaid. I would look out our windows into the village. I would see children playing together and laughing. I could see that I was missing something wonderful."

"Have you ever left the castle?" I asked.

"Mother and I visited the village, once. Father heard about it and beat Mother mercilessly. It was the last time I was allowed out, save for my wedding day. That day, I was carried by royal carriage to the large church in the village. You can just see the steeple down there above the rooftops." She said, indicating with an outstretched hand toward the window.

"When the ceremony was over, we were returned here to the palace. I have not set foot outside since."

"You have not been outdoors? Or did you mean you have not been outside the castle walls?" I was incredulous.

"I have not been outside these castle walls and certainly never beyond the village walls, to my recollection. I do feel as though I am imprisoned here." The Princess admitted sadly.

"I am sorry." I said, genuinely feeling pity for her. "I have never lived in a house, and yet, I am at home everywhere I go. The world is my home."

"I should love to visit the world some time." She said with a faint smile. "It is just that I am afraid Father will know and he will punish me by hurting Mother or Phillip."

"And what of your husband?" I asked, allowing her to tell me the story from her perspective.

"Father chose him for me when he was out in search of ...in search of women who would have him, for a price." She said this with a look of deep dislike.

"Alexander was handsome enough, but he did not have a good spirit, which is perhaps the reason Father liked him so." Her focus was no longer in the room as she recalled her dead husband.

"And you, Princess Madeline, Madeline the person, did you like him?" I enquired, quite demolishing anything that resembled protocol.

"He was cut from the same evil cloth as my father." Her reply seemed distant. "He liked to imbibe in alcohol as much as Father does.

One day, he decided that if Father was no longer living, and if Phillip was not married, he might be next in line for the throne. He had a plan, he decided to get my father drunk and help him have an accident. Unfortunately, Father is hardheaded. When Alexander tried to smash Father's skull, he only managed to smash his nose and knock him unconscious.

It was when Father awakened that he found Alexander asleep with, what we assume was a celebratory cask of wine, Father killed him while he slept and then he proceeded through the castle breaking things and hurting people. He did a thorough job on Mother." She ended her story with a sad look on her face.

"What would you change about your life if you could?" I asked.

"It would be lovely not to be afraid of Father. I would love to travel and to learn about other people and places. I would love to have friends who loved me as Madeline, and not as Princess Madeline..." There was a stirring in the bed that stopped her speech suddenly.

"Mother, how are you feeling? Are you well?" She asked anxiously.

Queen Alyssandra nodded her head to indicate that she could hear and that she was recovering.

I leaned near her ear and spoke softly. "I have some water here for you, Your Majesty, would you like some?"

Again, she responded with a weak nod.

I poured some water into a swallow bowl on the bedside table. Some of the gingerroot followed the water into the dish.

"What is that?" Princess Madeline asked.

"That is gingerroot. It is soothing for the stomach. Your mother has not eaten anything in a long while. This will help to warm her stomach so that her digestion process can commence with as little discomfort as possible. Plain, cold water might chill her stomach and cause cramping."

I laid a small, clean hand towel on the Queen's shoulder and then I dipped a bit of sea sponge in the water and spoke softly to the Queen. "I will give you a bit of water. You shall help to swallow it. Are you ready?" I asked, making eye contact with the nearly unconscious monarch.

Nodding.

"Take this bit of sea sponge between your lips. I will squeeze it and you will suckle the water." I explained.

I placed the sponge between her lips and squeezed gently.

She was able to drink only a small amount, but she was drinking on her own without choking. We repeated this several times before the water began to run out of the side of her mouth. I quickly dabbed the water from her cheek with the towel on her shoulder.

"Are you finished for now, Your Majesty?" I asked.

Nodding.

"Very well, we shall let you rest and then we shall try again later." I offered.

She nodded even more faintly and then her breathing became heavy with sleep.

"Madeline, I should like to request your presence at breakfast." I said.

Astounded at hearing her name without the title, she stopped breathing for a moment.

During that moment of silence, I wondered if I had finally over run my boundaries. What had I done? Had I insulted her? Had I angered her?

"Willow, I ...I ...would like that." She said with a smile.

Just then, Madame Rosmerta entered the room, closing the door behind herself more loudly than usual.

"I have arranged for the kitchen to prepare the Queen's lunch and our breakfast is awaiting our presence." To the Princess she said, "I am sure you are tired from sitting up all night, I have someone coming to sit with your mother for a while."

"Thank you, Rosmerta" the Princess said. "Mother just drank a bit of water. It is so nice to see her awake."

There was a soft knock at the door. It was Miss Constance, who would look after the Queen in our absence. Madame Rosmerta gave her the information regarding where we would be and when we would be returning.

After the door had closed behind us, I addressed Madame Rosmerta, "I invited Princess Madeline to have breakfast with us this morning."

Madame Rosmerta was unflinching. "Welcome. We would love to have you join us." She said with a large, genuine smile upon her face.

The kitchen staff members froze collectively when they saw the princess in their midst.

Emily hastily made her way to the Princess drying her hands upon her apron. "Good morning, Your Highness," she said with a curtsy. "Welcome. Would you care for some tea?" She gestured toward the table where other kitchen staffers had begun to gather.

Breakfast was a polite affair, with everyone trying to be on her best behavior. Only Magda appeared to be comfortable and genuine in her conversation with the Princess.

I was embarrassed. I realized, belatedly, that while they loved her, the staff members could only ever be indentured servants. I would try again another time to find a more comfortable way for her to enjoy a meal in the company of friends.

Thankfully, our strained meal was interrupted by a great deal of commotion in the castle. Prince Phillip was arriving later today. The kitchen buzzed with gossip like a honey-filled beehive. No. There was no sign of a new Princess, he was spotted riding alone.

There were meals to prepare, things to be done. The kitchen staff that was not engaged in preparing the broth for the Queen was immediately dispatched to the main kitchen to assist with the feast.

The Princess thanked me for the invitation and excused herself. There was much that she would be required to do as well, in preparation of the return of her brother.

Rosmerta and I departed the kitchen destined for the Queen's Chambers.

It was she who broke the silence. "It was kind of you to want to include the Princess at our breakfast table. As you can see, royalty and commoners mix about as well as water and oil."

"I am embarrassed that I did not realize that these people do not know the Princess as a person, they only know her as royalty. In their minds, she will always be untouchable. You found the human part of your Queen. You have given your heart to her, and not just in service, but in life.

The Princess is a prisoner of her life here. 'Tis sad that she is so lonely. Would it not be lovely for her to know true friendship?" I spoke from my heart, a place deep in my chest, where hollowness ached with sadness for the lonely, untouchable Princess.

"I can help you with that, Willow. No one understands that situation better than I do. Tonight, we shall begin to work on how you can befriend the Princess."

The thought of more harem lessons sent a shudder through my soul. I decided to change the subject. "First things first, Rosmerta, we have plenty of work ahead of us today.

Would you please go and fetch that bit of canvas we used yesterday?"

I went to the Queen's washroom and washed my hands with the chrysanthemum soap and then I went in to check on the Queen.

Miss Constance rose from her chair near the Queen's bed and quietly took her leave.

It was amazing to me how very many people were in service of the Royal Family and how easily they all blended into the surroundings, becoming little more than an extraneous piece of furniture.

They rarely spoke, unless addressed. They never offered ideas or opinions, accepting completely what they were told by the Queen's family. Inwardly, I was grateful to see, thus far, that this family was respectful and kind to everyone in their employ.

I approached the bedside and leaned in toward the Queen's ear.

"Your Majesty?" I said quietly.

Her grey eyes opened and sought mine.

"Good morning Your Majesty, I am Rajani, I am a healer, and I was commissioned by your daughter, Princess Madeline, to help you recover. Everyone calls me Willow, so if you hear someone using that name, you shall know, they mean me.

Your Majesty, you have had a terrible trauma. You have been very sick, and you have had an infection inside your womb. I have put medicated packing inside of you to help heal the infection. The infection and the fevers are gone, which is very good. I need your permission to remove the packing."

She looked deeply into my eyes as though she was trying her best to find the strength to tell me something.

"You need not speak. We can communicate with aye and nay questions. Is that acceptable to you?"

She nodded. Her face relaxed with relief.

"Madame Rosmerta has been here with me to help with every detail. I shan't begin until she is here with us. Is that acceptable to you?"

She nodded again, more relaxed.

Madame Rosmerta came in carrying the canvas. "Oh my heavens, Alyss, it is so good to see you awake!" she breathed, hugging the canvas to her chest.

She handed me the canvas and sat on the bed and rested her head on the Queen's chest and wept.

The Queen wept too, tears rolled silently off her cheeks and into her ears.

I set the canvas on a nearby table and went to the washroom to allow the two women some time alone.

I refilled the teakettle and set it on the hook over the fire to boil.

It was only an instant before the water was ready and I poured some in a ceramic washbasin. I pulled a gauze drawstring bag from my medicine pouch. To this, I added marigolds and lavender. I dropped the bag into the boiling water, gathered several towels and was prepared to return to the Queen.

Madame Rosmerta came into the washroom dabbing her

eyes on the corner of her pinafore. "Oh Willow, I had no idea I would react like that! I am sorry if it made you feel uncomfortable."

"Not to worry. I was not uncomfortable. I merely left to prepare the wash we shall need and to gather some towels. I hope my presence did not make you or your Queen uncomfortable." I offered.

Madame Rosmerta leaned in toward me and whispered. "I explained everything to Alyss. She understands that you know about our unique relationship. I told her that you are a healer and a holy woman and that you did not judge us." She continued.

"Judge you?" I was incredulous "Why ever would I judge you? Love is the greatest gift that we can share. It is indeed rare and we should rejoice in it when we can find it! Where is there room for judgement in that?" I was truly puzzled.

"Where, indeed!" She said shrugging her shoulders and shaking her head.

"Now, Rosmerta, if you are going to help me, you will need to wash your hands." I said, carrying the basin and stack of towels toward the Queen's chamber.

I could hear Rosmerta working the pump as the door closed behind me.

I set the steaming basin on the bedside table and the towels beside it.

"Your Majesty," I said softly. "We are just about to start. I do not want there to be any surprises so I shall tell you what to expect before I do anything. Is that acceptable to you?"

She nodded her head.

Madame Rosmerta came into the room silently and stood near the foot of the bed as I spoke to the Queen.

"Rosmerta is here now, so we shall begin, all right?"

She nodded.

"First, we need to put this canvas over your bed sheets so that we shan't soil them. I shall roll you onto your side so that Madame Rosmerta can put the cloth on the bed. Then we shall roll you on to your back. With your permission?" I raised my eyebrows in anticipation of an affirmative response.

Nodding.

"Very well," I said. Turning, I addressed the midwife. "Rosmerta, are you ready?" I asked.

"I am." She said with a nod. She tucked a bit of loose hair behind her ear and pushed her sleeves up.

We worked together seamlessly.

"I am sorry, Your Majesty, but we are removing the infection with the cloth, which is why it has the strong odor. I promise that you and Rosmerta can have some time alone after we are finished here for a nice bath before your son arrives."

Another silent tear slid across her face.

"With your permission, I shall continue."

I withdrew strip after strip of toweling until Madame Rosmerta assured me I had removed them all.

"Now, I shall leave you two to the ablutions. Rosmerta, I have a basin of fresh warm water for her bath here." I indicated by lifting the rim gently. "I have made a wash to help fight infection. It is here, in this basin." I specified by testing the temperature of the herbed decoction with my hand. "You will want to cleanse the tender areas with this wash." I said, drying my hands on clean toweling.

"Is this an internal wash?" Rosmerta asked.

I shook my head vigorously to the negative. "This is an external wash only." I emphasized. "An internal wash may seem to be a good idea, but I want her blood to congeal over the wounded areas. If we cleansed her womb now, it might wash the clots away and she would begin to bleed again."

"Understood" Rosmerta said, nodding.

The Queen may become thirsty while I am away. This is her drinking water. You will want to wash the decoction off your hands, as it shall be quite bitter. You may soak the sponge you see there and place it between her lips and gently squeeze it into her mouth. We have already done this once and the Queen knows how to drink in this manner."

Turning to the Queen I said, "I shall return shortly with your lunch, Your Majesty."

With that, I removed the offending basin of cloth and carried it with me to the washroom. There, I burned the cloth in the fireplace, rinsed the basin with boiling water, and washed my hands.

I made my way to the kitchen alone, for the first time since coming here. It was a lonely walk, with only my solitary, uneven cadence echoing in the cavernous corridors.

In the kitchen, I greeted Magda.

She was happy to hear that the Queen was awake. "'Tis good news." She said with a nod. This small nod let me know that Magda held out hope for a positive prognosis.

"Aye, 'tis, but I have a concern as well." I agreed. "She wishes to be presentable for the arrival of her son, the Prince. She is so very weak. I do not wish for her to over do."

I walked across the kitchen to Emily and shared the good news with her. She was delighted to hear it.

"How is the broth progressing?" I asked.

"Quite well. We only have need for you to add the herbs."

"Excellent, let me think... infection, bleeding, weakness, blood loss..."

"Are bleeding and blood loss the not the same?" Emily asked with concern.

"In words, they sound the same, but in treating a person, they are quite different. Bleeding is a condition that must be treated as soon as possible. A condition with much bleeding must be staunched because it drains the body and weakens the organs and muscles. Once the bleeding has stopped, we have a new condition, malnourishment of organs and muscles that was caused by bleeding."

"That does make quite a difference doesn't it? She said, wiping her hands on her apron.

I went to my medicine pouch and brought forth the herbs I would need. I put these into a gauze pull-string bag and dropped the bag into the cauldron of boiling broth.

"This shall be done in half an hour's time and then, I shall take some to the Queen." I told Emily.

While the herbs cooked, I seated myself at the table against the far wall. Magda joined me.

"How is your foot?" Magda asked.

"'Tis doing fairly well. I thought I could use this occasion to raise it up a bit to prevent swelling."

"I agree." Magda said. With this, she stood up and walked across the room and returned with a small three-legged stool. "Try this." She said placing it on the floor in front of me.

"Madame Rosmerta tells me that our family will be arriving today or tomorrow." I began.

"Aye, that is what Constance tells me as well." She agreed.

"It would seem that we are all having a grand reunion." I said. "I do miss everyone and there is so much to tell them."

Magda smiled and shook her head.

"Am I talking too much all at once again?" I asked, knowing the answer. "I shall stop." I said. "Sorry." I apologized hanging my head.

"Oh, Willow, you need not apologize." Magda said, cradling my chin in her hand. "'Tis always refreshing to see you behave as a young person should. So often, I see you behaving as an elder does because you grew up in the care of an old crone."

"But I am so glad I grew up with you. I can not imagine my life any other way." I defended.

"Nor can I." My mother agreed. "Living with you has changed the way I look at life." Magda admitted with a faraway gleam in her eyes.

"Really? How?" I leaned into the conversation, resting my chin on the heels of my hands.

"Well, in order to teach something, one must know that thing very well. When I teach you, I must think and rethink what it is I know. And then, there are always questions, which I can neither predict nor ignore." She smiled as she wagged a weary finger in my direction.

I realized I had always had an inquisitive nature and that my incessant questions may well have been exhausting for Magda, who had to be both teacher and mother and was never free of me.

"I wonder what my life would have been like without you." I pondered aloud. "It would probably be frightfully dull. I would undoubtedly be married by now and up to my elbows in children." I said with a frown.

"Children are a blessing, Willow." Magda admonished mildly.

"Aye, but so many? I am happy to have none. Perhaps, I shall adopt a student as you did."

"I have been thinking about something since we arrived here. I would like to hear what you think of my idea" Magda said.

"Aye, what is it?" I asked, genuinely interested.

"I have been thinking about settling in this village." She said gesturing over her head and all around.

I nodded showing her I was listening.

"I have been thinking about remaining in one place and allowing the sick to come to me. I should like to have a house large enough to tend to more than one patient at a time." She said looking far away into her thoughts. "I am also thinking about taking on more than one student. I can teach them the same things at the same time. They can assist me in caring for the patients in the infirmary."

"That is a good idea. When we are done here..." I began

enthusiastically.

"Willow," she held up a hand to stop my interruption. "You are a grown woman. Have you forgotten that you have moved into your own wagon?" She responded calmly.

"Aye, but I still have so much to learn from you." I argued feeling abandoned.

"Willow, you are the very brightest pupil I have ever encountered. I do not anticipate ever finding another student who will be as intelligent or as advanced as you are. Surely none will possess my heart as you have, my daughter." She stroked a loose bit of my hair back, away from my face. "But even you must see that you have finished your studies with me."

I was shocked to hear her say this. I had never imagined this day would come. I had not seen this coming. My mind reeled with so many new ideas that needed my attention.

Not wanting to react too suddenly to what I had just heard, I said to Magda, "Oh, what a lot of things I need to think about. My head feels quite full and my heart feels quite sad." It was difficult for me to breathe.

I stood slowly and walked to the cauldron of boiling broth. I took a ladle and dipped a small quantity of the soup into a bowl.

I walked back to where she was seated and embraced her, from behind. "I love you so much. It never occurred to me that we would part ways. Please allow me some time to process what you have told me."

"I shall give you that, Willow. 'Tis not been an easy thing for me either, and I have had more time to think about it than you have."

I took the bowl of steaming broth and began the journey down empty corridors toward the Queen's chambers.

Tears began to blur my vision. I found a small settee tucked away in a niche along one wall and sat down. I placed the bowl on a small, neighboring table.

I wept silently. The waves of grief that swept through me shook my body. My breathing was ragged as though someone had torn my chest open and left a jagged wound.

I had not realized that I had graduated. I had not realized that I was emancipated. How had I missed it? Did the whole rest of the world see this and I was the only soul who had not? How could I be so bright and miss the thing in front of me?

Life had changed for me the night I injured my foot. It was as if when I struck that root, a giant wheel began to turn, setting others in motion. Everything was so changed for me now. I wondered if Lynd would even recognize me when next I saw her.

I did not wish to keep Her Majesty waiting. I dug my palms into my eyes and dried my tears. I picked up the cooling bowl of broth and continued to the Queen's Chambers.

I entered the washroom first and washed my hands and face. I added just a bit of boiling water from the teakettle to the broth and proceeded to the Queen's Quarters.

I knocked lightly as I entered the room. I set the bowl on the table near the water basin. I could see that Madame Rosmerta had managed to coax her to drink nearly half of what I had poured for her. That was a good sign.

The Queen was bathed and dressed. Her hair had been washed and was fanned out on her pillow drying. On her head she wore an intricate circlet of gold. Instead of a simple chemise, she wore a beautiful red bed jacket outlined in ermine.

"Your Majesty, I have brought some broth for you. It may have a bit of a bitter taste because there are strong healing herbs in it. I have included these herbs to help your body fight the infection from the inside.

With your permission, I shall allow Madame Rosmerta to feed this to you using a sponge, as she did with the water.

'Tis important that you take as much of this broth as you can. 'twill help you regain your strength. When you are finished eating, we shall allow you time to rest before your son, Prince Phillip arrives."

The Queen nodded her head slowly.

Not knowing what to do with myself, I went to the washroom where I made myself a comforting cup of tea. I drew water in the footbath and removed my brace and began to soak my foot.

I drifted away in a swirl of thoughts about my past, present, and future.

Homecoming

"You look far away, are you all right?" It was Madame Rosmerta, with concern on her face.

"Aye? Did I not respond to you? I am sorry." I said.

"I came in and began to speak to you. When I got no response, I became quite concerned. You are certain you are quite well?"

"Aye, I am well. I just have a great many things on my mind." I said, flustered.

"Alyss is asleep, so I thought it might be a good time to slip out and get a bit to eat for lunch."

"I am afraid I have so very many new ideas to digest, that I have very little appetite. I am certain I would make poor company just now."

"I have an idea." She said, holding an index finger aloft. "I shall be back in just a few moments." With this, she took the front of her skirt in both hands, raising it just enough to allow her to maneuver the labyrinth of corridors at top speed leaving me alone with my thoughts.

My mind was awhirl with all the new concepts inside my head. Magda was moving on with her life. She wanted me to move on with mine.

Thinking back, I realized this whole trip to the palace had been a series of good-byes. Magda had begun to fade away from me when the royal carriage picked us up. This case was to be my first big case without her guidance. Now I understood her silence.

I was not the only soul who was suffering from growing pains. Magda had indeed had more time than I, to think about how to make this separation complete, but as gradually and painlessly as possible.

It was ingenious, really, having me start my new life by treating a queen. I was sure to get all the work I would ever need. Magda would have my success to her credit and she would have no difficulty finding qualified students and patients for her infirmary.

Magda had said she wished to settle in the village. I felt confident that she would do well here. I hoped that when my work in the palace was complete that I would be able to find a place in her infirmary.

I pulled my numb foot from the water and dried it with a towel. I put my brace on and began to pull the laces tight when Rosmerta reappeared in the washroom.

"I have arranged for a quiet luncheon for two in the conservatory. Come along and we shall get you a bit of something to eat."

We walked down another new corridor. It opened into a great glass room filled with autumn sunshine and green plants and colorful birds of all kinds. It was breathtaking! I was suddenly reminded that I had not been outdoors in days. I missed my family and I was very tired.

"Lunch will be here shortly, there is a small table over here, just beyond the large palm tree." My guide said, indicating with an outstretched hand, which way I should go to find the table.

I wandered around the tree and found someone already seated at the table.

"Oh! Lynd!" I was stunned. 'Tis you! 'Tis so wonderful to see you! I have missed you so." I bent to embrace her where she sat.

"Oh Willow, it is so good to finally be here with you! I have missed you too." my beloved sister replied, squeezing me just as hard in return. "How is the Queen?" She asked.

"Madame Rosmerta, the lady that was just here, she is the Queen's assistant, she has dressed the Queen to greet the Prince. He is returning home today. The whole palace is buzzing with excitement."

"Madame Rosmerta knew I was blind. She knew what to do to guide me and she was very good to explain the layout of the palace." Galynda puzzled aloud.

"Oh, aye, she has a talent for making others feel comfortable. 'Tis her ...she practices...she teaches the art of loving." I finally blurted out.

"So, she is not an assistant, she is a courtesan?" Galynda's judgmental eyebrow began to arch ever so slightly. It never ceased to amaze me how quickly Galynda could get to the heart of the matter.

I felt myself squirm in my seat. "Well, aye, she is that, but she does many things for the royal family. She is the Royal Midwife as well." I said hoping to put this part of the conversation at an end.

This luncheon with you was her way of showing me a kindness for caring for her Queen. Can you not see how that is a way of giving me pleasure? She made a surprise lunch for me with you because she knows how important you are in my life. She knows I have had a difficult time here and she wanted to show me she cares."

"Surely you have not..." Galynda stopped herself before she said something she might regret.

"I have not what?" I asked, confused by her reaction.

"You have not...had too much time to miss us." She smoothed her question and returned her brow to neutral.

"Aye, I have had time to miss all of you. Magda is thinking about teaching new students and opening an infirmary in the village. There may be a place here at the palace for Ahmad's leather, wood and metal works. That leaves only your mama and she is one of the finest seamstresses I know. She might have her own shop, or she might work here in the palace if she wishes.

I have kept my eyes and ears open for places for all of us. When I am finished with my work here, perhaps Magda will allow me to work with her in the infirmary. For now, she wants me to be independent. I am treating the Queen by myself."

Galynda sat silently in thought.

"So very much has happened since I left Lynd, I was worried you would not know me anymore." I said.

"Aye, much has happened. You are being called upon to do a great deal of growing in a very short span of time. How are you doing?" She asked with genuine regard.

"I find that I am tired a lot. No wonder babies sleep so much!" I exclaimed.

"Indeed! She said with a smile"

"Oh, Lynd! You should meet the Princess! She is so beautiful, she takes my breath away. She has lovely coppery hair. 'Tis a warm color, not cold like the metal, 'tis warm like the sun. Her eyes are the clearest green, fresh, like a lily pond. Her skin is fair, but not transparent and freckled."

Galynda stiffened and her expression became pinched. "Madame Rosmerta has returned with our lunch." she reported briskly.

Madame Rosmerta appeared from behind the large palm carrying a tray with enough food for two people.

"How did you know I had returned? And more

specifically, how did you know it was me?" She asked setting the tray down on a nearby buffet table.

"I heard you approaching; I recognized your footsteps, which are unique to you. You have a smell like incense and jasmine that gives you away as well." Galynda revealed.

Madame Rosmerta was amazed that Galynda had been so observant. "Now I understand what you meant, Willow, when you said, 'she does not see with her eyes.' Galynda, you are amazing." She scurried about setting out our lunch for us. "You see so much, even without your sight." She poured tea for us, made a small curtsy and left saying dessert would arrive shortly.

"I told her that you are a *drabardi*." I said. "When I introduced myself, I included the title *drabarni* with my name. She was the only *Gajikané* who had tried to speak our words. She tried to repeat it and called me '*drabardi*' instead. I explained what it meant and I told her that while I was not one, my best friend, and sister was."

"Shall we see what there is to eat?" Galynda asked.

"Aye. Now that you are here, I feel that my absent appetite has returned." I commented.

I lifted the lids from each platter in turn. "Let me see, we have small fowl stuffed with rice. Here is a dish of carrots, peas and potatoes. Lifting another lid, I announced "and here, we have biscuits and honey." I interrupted myself. "Have you met Emily yet? She is an amazing cook." I served two plates with a bit of everything from the tray.

"We only just arrived and were told to wait for Madame Rosmerta, she was to come and show us to our quarters."

"She must have been planning this for a while. I had no idea you had arrived. I am glad you are here." I placed a plate in front of her and handed her a delicate fork. "The biscuits are between us."

I was so happy to see Galynda, and yet she seemed to be somewhat cool toward me. I was puzzled and a bit hurt by her behavior.

"Is everything well with you?" I asked.

"Aye," she said sullenly. "Why ever do you ask?" her eyebrow, although not arched, was poised to do so.

I put a mouthful of fowl into my mouth to allow myself time to decide how to approach the subject.

I looked at her spirit smoke. It appeared spiked and short, much the same as her attitude felt. I was perplexed to find it was slightly green. Was it possible that Galynda was jealous? It appeared so, but what did she have to be jealous of, I wondered?

"I have been speaking so much about what is new with me." I stammered "perhaps 'tis time we spoke of what is new with you. How did you fare when I was gone?"

"We did well. We are all quite well. We had no mishaps. We were escorted here by the King's men."

"What was that like? Did you feel safe then?" I tried to show my interest and support.

"'Twas rather like being treated as though I was a child. I rode with Mama and one of the Kings men drove our wagon."

"I am sorry, Lynd." I meant it. After our experience in the cave, I realized that being blind would always have its disadvantages for her.

"Aye, me too." She conceded, stirring her vegetables idly with her fork. She was slowly letting her guard down.

I closed my eyes and enjoyed the flavors of the meal. The biscuits melted on my tongue. The butter ran down my fingers.

Outside, a fanfare of hornpipes could be heard.

"His Highness Prince Phillip must have just arrived." I announced.

Prince Phillip

After lunch, Madame Rosmerta returned and brought dessert for three.

"I wanted you to know what to expect this evening." Rosmerta said.

"Since the Prince has arrived, the Royal Family has extended an invitation to you and your families to join them in a feast of homecoming for the Prince and a celebration of the Queen's recovery."

"How shall we dress?" I asked, remembering my personal discomfort at having to wear a corset.

"Unfortunately, Willow, this is one of those occasions when you will be required to wear that corset." Madame Rosmerta responded with a frown.

I hung my head and looked up at her through my furrowed brows. To Galynda, I explained the horrors of wearing a corset.

"It made me forget the pain in my foot for a while." I said with a smile.

"Who shall help Galynda prepare for the festivities?" I asked.

"I would love to, Willow, but I must return to the Queen to see that her hair is put up."

"I will help her with the washroom, if someone will help us with all the fancy under things." I volunteered.

"And her hair!" Madame Rosmerta said with her brows raised. "I shall see to it that you do not help with that." She said with a wink and a smile.

She lifted the cover from the dessert tray and presented us each with a decadent slice of chocolate cake.

"Why do I need help bathing and grooming myself?" Galynda asked defensively.

Before I could answer, Madame Rosmerta answered, "Because, Prince Phillip has never met a young lady as lovely as you. He has searched far and near and has not had the pleasure of meeting anyone of your talents or beauty. If he had, he would most certainly be wed by now."

I sat back in my seat, amazed. How this woman could put an answer like that together without thinking on it all day made my head spin.

Galynda sat silently too. Was she shocked, amazed, put off?

"What ever do you mean?" Galynda began.

I did not like the path this conversation was taking. I took a bite of cake to engage my mind elsewhere.

"May I call you Galynda?" Madame Rosmerta asked.

Galynda nodded. "Aye, you may." She answered.

The cake was so moist and the icing so light, my eyes rolled back with the sheer pleasure of it. I hoped no one had taken notice of me.

Rosmerta put her elbow on the table and rested her chin upon her hand and leaned in toward Galynda. "There are different kinds of beauty, Galynda. Some beauty can be seen and some you must feel when you are with someone. You have both. You have the exotic beauty of olivine skin and jet-black hair. Your eyes are the most amazing shade of blue. It reminds me of the deep blue of the sea. Sitting with you, I feel that you have the poise, wisdom and patience of someone far beyond your years.

I am certain that you understand the importance of the Queen's recovery. And now, with the arrival of the Prince, it becomes our responsibility to put forth our best effort to show him and the rest of the Kingdom, that thanks to your family, and to Willow, all is as it should be."

I was impressed by what Rosmerta had said. Galynda seemed to visibly straighten herself in her seat. She did look beautiful.

"Aye," Galynda responded. "I do see the importance. I will do whatever it is that I can to help."

I had known Galynda and her fiery temper all my life and I had never seen anything stop her fury in its tracks before today. I sent Rosmerta loving thoughts of thanksgiving. The more I got to know her, the more there was to appreciate.

"Well, then," Rosmerta said. "We must make haste if we are to be ready in time for this evening's festivities."

"Aye," I agreed. "I would like to be certain that the Queen is well rested and fed before she is presented to the Prince this evening."

"And I must see to the Queen's hair and dress." Rosmerta added.

"Is there a washroom where Lynd can get started? When I am finished with the Queen, I can join her and help with whatever I can." I offered.

"An excellent idea," Rosmerta agreed with a nod. To Galynda she said, "I shall have your things laid out for you in the guest wing washroom."

We had finished our dessert. Madame Rosmerta rose to show us the way. "I shall send someone for these dishes. First, we shall take Galynda to the washroom, and then you and I shall see to the Queen."

Galynda hooked her left hand inside the crook of my right elbow. It felt as if something had been missing there for days and had only now been returned to me.

The three of us made our way up the corridor. When I hesitated, Galynda sensed that I was disoriented and urged me to turn to my right at the next intersection. Madame Rosmerta confirmed this and we continued in silence.

"I'm going to step into the kitchen and tell someone about those dishes." She said.

I waited in the hall with Galynda. "I could become lost in here. I whispered."

"You almost did, Silly." She whispered back.

Embarrassed, I smiled inwardly. That was the most natural and comfortable thing she had said to me all day.

"I am so glad you are finally here, Lynd." I meant it. I gave her left hand a squeeze in my elbow.

"The guest wing washroom is down this way." Madame Rosmerta directed.

It was another brown and white marble washroom with all the amenities of the others. I would have to explain to Galynda about the garderobe when no one could hear me.

"I shall have Emily draw you a bath." Madame Rosmerta began.

"Has no one told you?" Our people only bathe in moving water. We are not considered to be clean if the water does not carry the dirt away."

"Well, that makes sense." She replied. "It is rather odd how our people find it perfectly acceptable to sit in their own soup." She said with a look of disgust on her face. "That is not a problem. Galynda, there is a stool right here," she said, patting the stool. "Have a seat while we work out a bathing plan."

To me she said, "There is a dressing screen in one of the nearby vacant guest rooms. We can set that up in here." She said gesturing with both hands toward the corner where she envisioned the screen would be. "Galynda can stand behind it, and you can pour water over her."

"That sounds like a splendid solution." I said. "I can help Lynd in here while you find someone to fetch that screen."

Rosmerta stepped out of the room, leaving me alone with Galynda.

"So, you have met the Princess, but not the Prince?" Galynda asked while I helped to unbraid her hair.

"Aye, the Prince was sent away by his mother to seek a bride. His father, the King, has designs to take the throne from the Queen. He went mad and killed the Princess' husband in his sleep because the younger man wanted to take over the Kingdom. The Queen felt that the King might also try to harm their son, the Prince, since he had no bride and is next in line for the throne."

"Willow, do remember to breathe," Galynda said with a smile.

"The Prince, Phillip and the Princess, Madeline are twins. They are four years older than me, so they are two years older than you. Madame Rosmerta was the midwife who helped the Queen. She and the Queen are dear friends."

"Tell me again why 'tis I am subjecting myself to the humiliation of being bathed and dressed by others." Galynda requested.

"They did it to me too." I confessed. "I thought I would die of embarrassment, but I was fine. Madame Rosmerta has a way of making you forget that you are being bathed and embarrassed."

"She bathed you?" Galynda was incredulous. "And you let her?" she leaned away from me as if I had leprosy.

"Aye, Rosmerta helped me to bathe and dress and Miss Constance helped Magda." I explained.

"Oh, I can not imagine Aunt Magda allowing anyone to disrobe and bathe her!

What has happened to you since you left us? I do not believe what I am hearing!" by this time, Galynda had raised her voice so that it echoed in the hollow room.

She was no longer the calm Galynda I knew so well. As her voice rose, I felt smaller and smaller.

"Galynda is everything all right? What has caused you to become so upset?" It was Madame Rosmerta returning with the screen.

I stood with my head lowered. I was trying to understand what had just happened, myself.

I studied my fingertips as I spoke. "She wanted to know why she needed help bathing since she is capable of caring for herself."

"Galynda, of course you can bathe yourself. Of that, there is no doubt. You have a pair of the most beautifully matched braids I have ever seen." Rosmerta said as she set down the screen.

"Why then, did you and Miss...Miss..." She stumbled, having forgotten the name.

"Constance." I volunteered dumbly.

"Aye," Galynda snapped. "Why did you and she bathe Willow and Aunt Magda?"

Madame Rosmerta nodded in understanding. "It is our job to see to it that our guests represent themselves and their people in the best possible light.

As you know, Willow is handling this entire case by herself. Magda knew before we arrived at the palace that she would turn the case over to Willow. Magda asked me to guide Willow in the ways of social graces. Appearance is an important part of that in our society."

Galynda was silent. She slowly shook her head. "Nay, I did not know. Willow, why did you not tell me?" Her anger was smoldering under the surface.

"So much has happened in so little time." I began. It was the truth, but it felt like a poor excuse.

Madame Rosmerta began again. "I would like to help you, Galynda, but only if you will accept my help. Otherwise, you are free to tend to your own grooming." Her words were kind, but they somehow sounded firm, like the scolding words of a disappointed mother.

Galynda stood dazed. I did nothing. I stood and looked from Madame Rosmerta to Galynda. In my mind, 'twas up to Lynd to decide whether to concede to a bathing and grooming session or to turn it down and risk insulting the Queen's greatest partisan.

I busied myself by pumping water and adding it to the teakettle. I swung the hook closer to the fire. I set the screen up in the corner Madame Rosmerta had designated.

Galynda still chose to say nothing. I had never seen her behave in such a manner.

Turning to me, Madame Rosmerta said, "I shall be in the Queen's chambers tending to her hair. If you need me, you shall find me there." Madame Rosmerta was as composed as ever, but her spirit smoke was every bit as bristled as Galynda's.

"Very well," I acknowledged. "I shall join you momentarily. I should like to see how Her Majesty is progressing having taken water and broth."

Madame Rosmerta left the room with a rustle of her skirt. The silence she left behind was suffocating.

"Lynd," I began.

"What!" She defended.

"Lynd, I know everything is new and scary. I do a lot of things wrong. I forget to curtsy. I insulted the cook when I turned down an exquisite meal. And, I even scolded the Princess!

Madame Rosmerta really is a lovely woman. She is only trying to do her job. Until this very minute, I did not know Magda had asked her to help me. Rosmerta has taken that promise very seriously. She has not left me alone, save for a few moments while I visited with the Princess, and only now, when I had lunch with you." I was careful not to recount the times I had been alone with the Princess.

"You scolded the Princess?" She had a small smile. More importantly, she arched her playful eyebrow.

I hung my head. "Aye, you know me, when I am thinking like a healer, I tell folks the way I see things."

"You did not!" Her mouth was open in shock.

"Oh, but I did. I think this is why Rosmerta is afraid to let me alone, even for a minute. Surely, she can tell just by looking at you, that you are far more refined than I shall ever hope to be.

Perhaps she is afraid that since you are my dearest friend that I shall have been a negative influence on you!" We both began to giggle and laugh. It was soothing balm for the hurt that had come between us.

"I have plenty of water heated, if you will just step this way, you will find everything you will require for your bathing needs."

I poured the water for her as she lathered and rinsed and helped her find a towel.

The dressmakers had laid out a dress of the most stunning blue. "Oh, Lynd, this dress is gorgeous. 'Tis the most enchanting blue. I just know Rosmerta had it made for you, to match your eyes. She has an eye for details."

"Let me see if I can remember how all of these under things work. The pantalets I have figured out." I handed them to her.

She stepped into the pantalets while keeping herself wrapped in the toweling.

"Then you put on the chemise." She raised her hands to allow the chemise over her head. The toweling dropped to the floor.

Now, I think you put on the corset. I was telling you about them. You tighten them until you cannot breathe, and you are certain your ribs will crack. Your breasts will squeeze out the top like yeast dough rolls in the bakery."

"Oh, my, now that does put a horrific picture in my head." It was Miss Constance. "Before this child scares you half to death, may I offer my assistance? I am Miss Constance, Madame Rosmerta sent me to see if I could help you out in any way."

Galynda graciously accepted the offer.

"You must be Galynda. It is nice to finally meet you." Miss Constance said brightly.

"If you no longer need me," I said, "I do need to attend to the Queen."

"I can manage from here," Miss Constance soothed.

"Will you be all right Lynd?" I asked.

"Aye, go on ahead and tend to your business." She said. She seemed much more relaxed after her bath.

I found my way down the corridor to the Queen's Chambers.

Madame Rosmerta was placing the gold circlet over the Queen's hair, which was swept up in a graceful mass of golden curl. The transformation was astonishing.

"Your Majesty, you look positively enchanting!" I said.

She smiled weakly.

"Have they been feeding you throughout the day?"

She nodded, careful not to muss her beautiful hair.

"I would like to take your pulses, with your permission."

She nodded again, lifting her eyes toward her hair.

"Alyss, your hair is fine. I have secured it very well. It shan't fall." Madame Rosmerta reassured her.

"Your Majesty is improving beautifully. Your pulses are back to a normal rate, which means you are defeating the infection. They are still weak, but they are getting stronger each time I check them. Just as you are still feeling weak, but you are a little stronger each time I see you." I explained.

Just then, the door opened. It was the Princess, Madeline.

She was beautiful.

She was dressed in the finest dress I had ever seen. It was made of rich leaf-green silk brocade with an embossed golden feathery pattern. The colors brought out the light in her lovely green eyes.

The bodice was outlined in gold twist and was laced in the front, very much like the bodices I wore. Her breasts nestled warmly in the neckline of her bodice, rather like two kittens snuggling in a basket. Her waistline was trim and then, the skirt blossomed at the hip and flowed down to the floor. She seemed to float above the ground. The effect was both pleasant and dizzying.

Madame Rosmerta rose to her feet, "How do you do, your Highness." She cast me another one of her not-so-subtle frantic looks. I must have stomped on another rule or protocol.

I dragged my eyes from her beauty, long enough to bow slightly, "Your Highness, you are positively stunning. You have absolutely taken my breath away." I admitted honestly.

She smiled shyly and bowed her head. "Thank you." Her cheeks flushed slightly. The effect made her all the more beautiful. I could not take my eyes away from her.

Madame Rosmerta looked from Queen Alyssandra to Princess Madeline and then, to me. She arched an eyebrow.

"How is Mother doing?" the Princess addressed me.

"She is regaining her strength. It may be a slow process but 'tis always a positive sign when a lady regains her sense of presentation. She has taken medicated broth and has drunk gingerroot water throughout the day. I expect she will be eating solid foods before too long." I reported.

"Willow," the Princess turned to me. "You have not changed. Does this mean that you wish to decline our invitation to join in our celebratory feast?" Her cheeks flushed again. This time the effect was not so pleasing to see and I was reminded of the bristly mood Galynda was in.

"My first priority is to tend to your Mother." I defended. "When I am satisfied that she shall be stable and comfortable enough to allow for my absence, then and only then, shall I tend to my own devices." I stated.

Madame Rosmerta and the silent Queen cast each other furtive glances.

The Queen made a subtle shooing gesture to Madame Rosmerta with one hand. I knew we had been dismissed and felt concerned that I may have insulted the Princess and the Queen in the process.

Madame Rosmerta addressed the Princess. "Your Highness, it is my fault. I wanted to assist your mother with her hair. I was so carried away, I quite lost track of the time. It is I who is assigned to act as Willow's valet, and I have delayed her much too long. If you will excuse us, we do not wish to be late to your celebration." With this, she picked up the edge of her skirt in one hand, grabbed my wrist with the other, curtsied, and backed us out of the room.

We were in the anteroom bookcase and scurrying behind walls like mice before I could say 'good day' to the Princess.

"I did something wrong again ..." I began.

"You, my dear, have left quite an impression on our Princess! She is more than a little used to getting her way. What you did in there just now was to set yourself a nice, firm boundary. You spanked her soundly on the behind by making it clear to her that you are here to tend to her mother first and foremost."

"Aye," I began with my brows furrowed. "That is the only reason that I am here. I am not here to attend grand feasts and to be dressed in finery and put on display." I was really confused now.

"Of course this is true." Rosmerta soothed. "But our little Princess has found you to be interesting company. By setting her straight about your priorities, you have proven yourself to be a person of morals and honor."

I furrowed my brow further. Apparently, I was the only player in this game who did not know the rules.

"Willow, you have not ruined your chances of friendship with the Princess, you have only proven yourself more worthy. She will want to get to know you more because you are going about your business and not wildly pursuing her attentions."

"I am confused. Why does this feel like a dance everyone knows but me? I feel I am out of step."

"That, my dear, is why you have me." She poked herself in the chest with her free index finger. "I can teach you the dance." She said with a smile.

"Is it a dance I want to learn?" I asked hesitantly.

"Most definitely!" Madame Rosmerta said with a broad and satisfied smile.

"Let me see if I can explain this to you in straight forward terms. The Princess is Royalty. She is given preferential treatment everywhere she goes. People are either nice to her because they are employed by her or because they want something from her."

"Would I not fit into the 'employed by her' category?" I queried, trying to keep up with her rapid thought processes as much as her trotting pace.

"You would, but you are not serving her, you are serving her mother and you have made that clear to her." Rosmerta stated with some satisfaction.

"So, what you are saying is that I have showed her friendship without expectations?" I paraphrased for confirmation. "But I have also shown her that her mother takes precedence?"

"Indeed. Come along quickly, we are at the harem. We must make haste and change."

"Rosmerta," I began. "I always give friendship without expectation. And, what kind of physician would I be if my patients did not take first priority?" My brow was wrinkled again.

"I know, Bunny, but Princess Madeline is not accustomed to such loyalty, nor is she accustomed to taking second position to anyone."

'Bunny,' it had such a warm, loving and soft feeling to it. I felt something inside me melt. She had called me Bunny.

"You have expressed an interest in her and you have also made it clear that you will give her your time when you are not otherwise occupied. Most people in her life have spent themselves trying to get her attention and keep it." Rosmerta was short of breath in her efforts to explain all of this and gather her things.

"You are a difficult fish to catch, so you will be far more delicious when she catches you." She explained, somewhat out of breath.

"Catches me? Am I running away?" Madame Rosmerta seated me on the edge of her bed and had begun to unbraid my hair.

I cocked and eyebrow. "Should I be running?" I asked, genuinely confused.

"Why don't you take your dress off and freshen up a bit." Rosmerta suggested.

"I think that Princess Madeline and Galynda might be an awful lot alike. I said sliding my skirt off and stepping out of it."

"How do you mean?" I had her attention now.

"Well, when we were small children, our clan was much larger. We traveled greater distances and everywhere we went, the Romany people would gather around Galynda. She was our 'Little Princess'. Everyone called her that. Even people from other clans called her that. They would travel for days to see her and bring her gifts." I said unlacing my bodice.

"She was very angry with me today." I explained. "She is jealous about you for some reason. She behaves an awful lot like Princess Madeline, don't you think?" I went to the washroom clad only in my chemise and drew water into a basin. To this, I added water from the teakettle.

I washed myself quickly but thoroughly and returned to Rosmerta's bedchamber to find her dressed in a red dress. She held out a dress for me. It was sage green brocade with silver leaves and vines winding their way throughout the skirt. The bodice was similar to that of Princess Madeline's dress. It laced in front.

"No corset?" I asked.

"The boning is in the bodice. This dress was designed to fit you more like the clothes you normally wear. Princess Madeline had her dress made in the same fashion. She flatters you by emulating your culture."

I put the dress on and it was, indeed, far more comfortable than the corset had been.

Madame Rosmerta began to brush my hair. I thought I could get spoiled with all the hair brushing and massaging.

"Willow," she began, when you said that Galynda was called 'Little Princess,' do you think there was any truth to that?"

"Truth? Everyone wanted to help her. Her Papa died before she was born. There is a famous legend about it. I guess everyone knows that legend. She is a very famous *drabardi*. She is a Chosen One."

"What does that mean to your people, to be a Chosen One?" She asked braiding my hair.

"It means that she has special gifts. She is a *drabardi* the likes of which are very rare indeed." I explained honestly.

"You are a Chosen One too, aren't you? We heard many amazing stories about you and Magda along the road.

"Aye." I said, embarrassed to admit it out loud. I hung my head.

"That is amazing, Bunny! Why do you hang your head?" she said, cupping my chin in her hand.

"'Tis not good to fill the spirit with prideful boasting. I have a job to do and I do it." I admitted.

"You do it phenomenally well, Missy! You are famous." She said tapping the tip of my nose with her index finger.

"We were talking about Lynd." I firmly changed the subject.

"Yes, we were." My companion said with an exaggerated nod. "Does this legend about Galynda tell much about her parents?"

"Aye, something about her father, he was to die the day after her mother became pregnant with Galynda. Rom gathered from all around, including other caravans, to send her papa to the afterlife. He was a very important man to our people and the people we traded with."

She finished my hair by tucking my braids neatly under a very ornate pill hat that had been made of the same cloth as my dress.

"We had better make haste my dear; we don't want to keep the Prince and Princesses waiting."

I thought this was an odd statement for her to make. Was she being sarcastic, or was she honoring my people by accepting Galynda's honorary title?

For Blood and Honor

We scurried like mice through the walls to save time. Rosmerta carried the lamp in one hand and held my hand with the other.

"Where shall we end up?" I asked.

"The main dining hall is down one level. We shall find a staircase at the end of this corridor."

We left the wall space and appeared at the end of a quiet hallway. The last brilliant rays of the magnificent red and orange sunset shone through the great leaded windows along the marble hallway.

Lanterns were lighted along both sides of this hall. Suits of armor glistened in the light. Great floral arrangements flanked the doorway to the great hall, which was outstretched before us.

The great hall was awash with candles and lantern light. The balconies that overlooked the hall were swathed in silk and velvet bunting. The hand-hewn wooden table ran nearly the length of the room was swathed with yards of green and purple silk and velvet runners. Between the highly polished candelabras, there were bountiful crystal bowls brimming with colorful and exotic fruits, floral arrangements, woven baskets of breads, and platters of cheeses. It was surfeit for the senses. I could not possibly see more color or smell anything more delectable, nor experience more variety of textures than I did in this room. The whole experience was quite dizzying.

I could see that most everyone had already begun congregating in the great hall. Many people were taking their seats.

The Prince and Princess were seated side by side at the head of the table. The prince was to the right, the Princess to his left. Rosmerta led me along by the hand toward the head of the table. I was to be seated to the Princess's left. Galynda was seated directly across from me at the Prince's right. Magda was seated next to me, Ahnja was next to Galynda and Ahmad was beside Magda.

Galynda was dressed in the amazing blue dress I had seen laid out for her in the washroom. It complimented the blue of her eyes. Today, instead of a simple three-point scarf, she wore a regal blue veil upon her head. It was secured with a small silver circlet.

After everyone had taken their places, the Princess rose from her seat. Everyone stood, out of respect for her. She made a gesture indicating that we should remain seated.

Princess Madeline was even more stunning than I had remembered. She had an ornate circlet of gold about her head. It was set with a large, oval cut, red cabochon in the center that rested upon her forehead. The light of the lanterns and candles danced off her crown and played lightly on her face. My, but she was lovely.

"Ladies and gentlemen," The Princess addressed the group. "I would like to thank all of you for attending our celebration.

We are celebrating the safe return of my beloved brother, Prince Phillip." She gestured with a sweeping motion with both hands to her right where her brother sat. He stood and everyone joined him by rising. He gestured for all to sit.

He was a handsome man. He had the same red hair as his sister, although his was receding a bit at the temples. His neatly trimmed moustache and beard were the same delightful shade of red. His features were small and delicate for a man of such great power. He had his mother's grey eyes and gentle demeanor. I knew I liked him already.

Everyone cheered and clapped. Many raised glasses to toast the Prince. "Long live Prince Phillip!" They cheered.

The room was electric with excitement and anticipation.

When the applause died down, the Princess continued. "We are also celebrating the recovery of our dear mother, Queen Alyssandra." There was a great cheering for the Queen. Everyone raised glasses to salute the Queen.

"Long live Queen Alyssandra!' everyone cheered.

When the cheering quieted, the Princess continued. "We are pleased to be joined here tonight by some much honored guests.

Seated to my left, is Rajani, healer to the Tsigani tribe of the Rom people. She is the Royal Physician to the Queen. It is to her credit that our Queen is making such a fine recovery. I would like to present Rajani, or Willow, as she is called, with this small token of our appreciation."

Willow, will you please rise and come forward." She summoned me with a motion of her exquisite, graceful hand.

I slid my chair back, suddenly aware of the silence in the room and the pressure of many eyes upon me.

Before I was even out of my seat, everyone was cheering. I was amazed that such a fuss should be made over a job that needed to be done.

I stood beside the Princess, embarrassed and wishing I could disappear.

"We wish to extend our thanks to you for providing excellent care to our Queen. As a token of our appreciation, we award you with this chest of gold." She gestured toward a silver chest that was inlaid with numerous brightly colored gems. It was nearly double the size of a loaf of bread.

At first, I was confused. The box was of silver, not of gold. Then, it occurred to me, it was not the chest she referred to, but its contents. I was astonished. The chest alone was a great treasure. I had never had money of my own and I was certain that this must be a fortune.

"Willow, I wish to thank you personally. I present you with this brooch." It was beautiful. It was an oval brooch crafted of gold and encrusted with gemstones in the shape of the family crest, a lion rearing in the foreground and a golden castle in the background on a field of green.

The Princess embraced me, and gently gave me a clandestine kiss upon my right cheek. As she pinned the brooch upon the chest of my bodice, I was fearful that she would be able to feel my heart as it pounded inside my ribs. I was not certain what had happened for a moment. My belly tingled and a chill slid up my spine. When I regained my senses, the people at the table were cheering and encouraging me to speak.

I hoped I had not hesitated too unnaturally long. "I bowed my head and prayed for the right words to say and that they might come out intelligently. I waited for silence to come. When the room was silent, I began.

"I am humbled by the powerful company that I keep today. I look around this room and find that I am in the midst of great and wonderful people. Every one of us is extraordinary, either by our training in a chosen craft or by our birthright.

Ordinarily, I would decline such an offer of gold. Today, however, I have been given the greatest reason to accept it. I would not be here if it had not been for my beloved mother and teacher, Magdalena, *drabarni*, healer of the Tsigani tribe of the Rom people.

Only today, she chose to share her plans for an infirmary where she can teach others the healing arts. She wishes to build such a school here in this village. I would like to honor her by donating whatever money she needs to build and operate her infirmary. Thank you for this opportunity, Your Majesties, and thank you, Magda for loving me and teaching me."

The applause that followed was the heartiest I had heard all night. I was glad I had not offended anyone. I bowed my head, curtsied to the royal siblings and returned to my seat on wobbly legs.

The Princess rose to her feet again. Again, the audience rose and she gestured for them to be seated. "Ladies and Gentlemen, we are most pleased and honored to share our table with royalty from another land. Before we eat, I would like to recognize and welcome Her Royal Highness, Ra Ahnan, Princess of the Tsigani Tribe of the Rom people."

My mind was reeling. Ra Ahnan. Princess Ra Ahnan, my brain rolled this over and over trying to form a complete thought. That is the formal name for...

Galynda slowly rose to her feet before me.

I was bewildered. How could this be? Galynda? Why did I not know she was royalty? I consciously tried to keep my brow smooth and my mouth shut.

Everyone at the table stood and cheered for Galynda.

"Love live Princess Ra Ahnan!"

She bowed to the royal twins and then turned to bow to everyone at the table. She then sat silently and everyone joined her.

Princess Madeline said, "Thank you so much for sharing this evening with us. Enjoy the festivities."

Everyone clapped and raised glasses again. "Long Live Princess Madeline!"

I was grateful for the food service. With my mouth full, I would not have to try to speak or make sense.

Growing Pains

After the festivities ended, I picked my way through the crowd and found Madame Rosmerta.

"Please, I would like to see to the Queen before I retire." I said.

"Certainly," she said. "First, I shall see to it that the infirmary fund is put away for safe keeping." She summoned a gentleman in a green velvet tunic and spoke instructions directly into his ear so she would be heard over the din of the festive crowd.

To me she said, "Very well, are you ready?"

"Aye." I said.

She led me to another hidden passageway. She borrowed a lantern from a neighboring table and held the door open for me.

When we were alone in the wall corridor, where we would not be overheard, she said, "I was awfully proud of you tonight. You did well. I was afraid you would turn the Princess's gift down. I am glad you chose to accept it."

I was silent. My head was full from the day's activities and my foot was beginning to ache.

"Bunny, you're awfully quiet. Is everything all right?" She asked, reaching out and placing her hand lightly on my back.

"I have had quite a long day. I would like very much to tend to the Queen. When I have done that, I..." I very much wished to be alone with my thoughts and feelings.

"When we have done that, you and I are going back to the harem to soak that foot and discuss what is so heavy in your heart." She said.

There was no point in arguing. The thought of having time alone with Rosmerta to myself sounded like the very best medicine for me. "I would like that very much." I said, feeling a large lump beginning to constrict my throat.

We walked on in silence. I could not have spoken if I had wanted to. I tried to think about the Queen and what progress she had made.

I do not remember how it was we got there, but I soon found myself in the Queen's Chambers. The draperies were drawn. The lighting was muted. A lone lantern glowed on the bedside table. The flames in the fireplace danced merrily. The room was very serene in contrast to the festivities in the dining hall.

The Queen was awake when I approached the bed.

I bowed "Good evening Your Majesty." I said. "How do you feel this evening?"

"Stronger. Thank you." Came the whispered answer.

"I am most pleased for you. Will you allow me to feel you pulses?"

She nodded her head.

I took her wrists, each in turn.

"Your Majesty, have you any pain? There is an edge to the pulses that feels like you might."

For a brief moment she appeared puzzled by what I said. Then she nodded.

"Can you take your hand and show me where your pain is?" I asked.

She pressed her hand to her lower abdomen, just above the pelvic bone.

"I am sorry it hurts, Your Majesty. I need to know what kind of pain it is so I will know how to treat it. I will ask aye and nay questions until we can identify the source and type of pain. Are you ready?"

She nodded.

"Does it burn?"

She shook her head, no.

"Is it twisting?"

Again, she shook her head, no.

"Is it sharp and stabbing?"

She nodded.

"Does it hurt all over down in this region?" I asked using my own body as reference.

She shook her head and pointed to the same spot she had indicated before.

"It is in one specific location." I stated.

Nodding.

"No one likes pain your Majesty, but in this case, I am happy to hear that it is localized. The type of pain that you have is a positive sign.

When pain is in one place only, it is specific to the site of the trauma. That is the place where you were injured. That is the place where there is much bruising inside.

I will boil a tea for you, which will help move the stagnant blood out of the area. That will relieve swelling and inflammation as well. You should sleep quite comfortably tonight and feel much better in the morning. If you will excuse me, I shall see about your tea." I grasped the front of my skirt, and curtsied.

She caught my hand before I could leave.

"What is it Your Majesty?" I asked.

Her grey eyes held mine. She looked deeply into my eyes, first one and then the other. Her brows were furrowed and raised in the middle. Tears began to well in her eyes.

"You are welcome, Your Majesty, I am honored to be in your service." I said, covering the hand that held mine with my free hand. I gave her hand a gentle squeeze and held it there for a moment.

"With your permission, I shall see to that tea." I stood, holding her hand and waited to be dismissed.

She nodded her head and relaxed her grasp of my hand. I carefully placed her hand on her abdomen, curtsied, turned and left.

I entered the washroom and checked the teakettle. It was full. I found my medicine pouch hanging on a hook on the wall. I took it down and pulled from it the herbs I would need to move the Queen's blood and relieve pain.

The formula would be a small one and would not taste terribly bad because one of the main ingredients was cinnamon bark.

I placed the herbs in a small clay pot. I poured boiling water over these and placed the pot on the top of the stove. They would need half an hour's time to boil.

I decided that while the herbs boiled, I would tend to my foot, which was swollen and beginning to throb.

I pumped cold water into the foot bath and added some hot water from the teakettle warming it enough to melt the sea salt crystals. I then added lavender to the water, refilled the kettle and set it back on the stove.

A stool stood at the ready near the foot basin. I seated myself and removed my brace and then my boot.

I plunged both feet into the water. It was cold, but not icy enough to feel sharp.

I closed my eyes in an effort to gather my thoughts in some sort of orderly fashion. I had never seen Galynda as angry as she had been today. Nor had I seen her look so beautiful. She had been stunning. Why had I not known that she was a true and real Princess before today? I had upset Princess, Madeline too. She seemed to have felt better about it at the feast. She had embraced me. And that kiss! She had indeed kissed me upon the right cheek, shielded from view by my body. I began to feel tingly again.

I sat with my eyes closed, remembering the feel of her arms around me and the moist warmth of her light kiss on my cheek. I began to feel better as I sat there. I smiled, warm with happy memories.

"You are feeling a little better?" It was Madame Rosmerta.

"I was attempting to put myself in a better frame of mind." I replied. "Queen Alyssandra is looking well."

"Yes, she is, thanks to you." She said with a smile. "I am so relieved." She said placing a hand over her heart.

"She shall also be relieved when she gets her tea. 'Twill only be a few minutes more. 'Tis beginning to smell as if it is ready."

"Stay as you are," Rosmerta said extending her arm in a gesture to halt any movement from me. "I shall remove it from the heat and let it cool as you soak your feet." Saying this she grabbed a towel from the neat stack beside the hand basin and slid the bowl of boiling liquid off the heated surface of the stove. You seem to have forgotten to fetch a towel for yourself before you sat down. Here." She said, offering me the one she used to handle the hot bowl with.

"Oh, thank you, it would seem that I did forget. You have been indispensable to me these few days. I do not know how to thank you."

"I shall think of something." She said with a sparkle in her eye.

I took my feet from the water and dried them. I hated the thought of putting my brace back on. I was tired and wanted nothing more than to leave it off. Grudgingly, I tugged my boot and brace into place and dutifully laced them up.

I washed my hands and took another bit of sea sponge from my pouch, which I replaced on its hook.

"Now, let us get this pain-relieving tea to the Queen." I said, carrying the small bowl on a clean towel." Madame Rosmerta made no move toward the door. "Are you coming, or shall I expect to see you later?" I called over my shoulder.

"I shall be right here. I have some tidying up to do." She said.

Rosmerta was not a woman to clean washrooms. Puzzled by this, I left the room shaking my head.

I entered the darkened room. I could see that Rosmerta had turned down the lanterns and had made her Alyss more comfortable.

"Your Majesty," I whispered. "I have that tea I promised you. It shan't be terribly nasty, I have added a bit of cinnamon for you."

The Queen smiled.

"Good evening, Willow." Princess Madeline, who had been seated in the darkness in a tall, wing-backed chair, leaned forward, into the light to be seen.

I was so involved in what I was doing I nearly leapt from my own skin when she spoke. "Begging your pardon, Your Highness." I said, turning to the Princess. "I was not aware that you were here." I was grateful for the muted lighting, for I was certain my hot cheeks meant they were flushed.

"That is quite all right. Please, go about what you were doing. I shall stay here, out of your way."

I turned back to the Queen, her circlet and velvet cloak were gone. Rosmerta had, doubtless, put them away for safe keeping.

"The tea is still quite warm; it should sit better in your stomach. I shall place this towel under your chin to avoid spills, if that is acceptable to you."

The Queen nodded her head.

"I shall give you a bit of the tea as I did with the water and broth. Are you ready?"

Nodding.

I squeezed some tea into her mouth and allowed her time to swallow. I asked, "Did you have a nice visit with your son?"

She nodded and smiled.

"I am happy for you. You were lovely today. I am sure he was very pleased to find you looking so well."

She smiled.

I gave her nearly half of the tea. "You should rest much more comfortably tonight. I am going to leave this tea here for you. If you need more there is enough to help you through the night until morning."

She nodded.

I turned to the Princess. "Your Highness, will you be staying with her tonight?"

"I came to tell mother how the feast went and to tell her goodnight. Someone shall be along shortly."

"Very well," I said. I turned to the Queen and asked, "Will you require anything further?"

She shook her head no.

"May I offer you a bit of water to rinse the taste of the tea from your mouth?"

She nodded.

I gave her as much water as she wanted and then removed the towel from her chest.

"I have made some salve that should help your lips heal. Do they hurt you?"

She thought for a moment and then nodded.

"I have some in my pouch. If you will excuse me for a moment, I shall be right back."

I made a small bow and left the room.

Rosmerta was not in the washroom when I retrieved the

small clay unguent jar from my bag.

I washed the tea from my hands and returned to the Queen's Chambers with the ointment.

"Your Majesty," I whispered. "I am back. With your permission, I shall put some ointment on your lips."

She nodded, more weakly.

The tea was beginning to work. I could see her face visibly begin to relax.

I dipped the tip of my little finger in the unguent jar and spread a thin film of it over the Queen's lips.

"This should help. The bees wax helps to seal your own moisture in to help keep them from drying further. The comfrey will help your lips heal and the mint helps to cool them and ease the pain.

Does that feel better?" I asked.

She nodded. This time, her head scarcely moved.

"I shall say good night to you, Your Majesty. Rest well." Turning to the Princess, I said, "Good night to you, Princess Madeline. Thank you for inviting me to your table. I am honored. Thank you for your help establishing Magda's infirmary."

"Mother is sleeping. I shall walk with you to the door." She rose from her chair to accompany me to the anteroom.

A lantern on the wall cast more light there, reflecting beautifully in her eyes and dancing in her hair.

"Willow," she began, "You are an amazing woman. I do not know how to communicate that to you. I do not know how to tell you how much I appreciate you." She said wringing her hands and biting her lower lip.

"Did I offend you by giving your gift away?" I interrupted, fearing the answer.

"No." She shook her head. "Quite the contrary. You never cease to impress me. I can not name many people who would do what you did. In sharing your gift, you are giving so much to our community. You sacrifice a lot to the people by giving them your own mother. I can not imagine that is easy for you. You give them a great teacher, a great physician, and a safe place to come to when they become ill. It is as if you took the gift I gave and made it so much greater."

I was stunned. I had not realized I had done all of that. I had only wanted to help Magda realize her dream.

"'Tis not so very different from what you do, Your Highness." I discovered another pesky lump had found its way into my throat. "You have sacrificed your mother to the people of your kingdom every day of your life." I croaked. Why was my voice failing me now?

The Princess was standing quite near me now. The lantern light danced in her eyes. There was something different about the way she looked at me. Her eyes were bright, but they appeared misty somehow. There was a soft flush in her cheeks and her lips seemed fuller and rosier too.

I began to feel a tingling inside my belly, way down below my umbilicus, deep inside. I could hear my heart beating in my ears and I could feel it beating in waves between my legs.

I thought I might faint. I was beginning to feel giddy and light-headed. It was a good feeling, but I did not understand it. Nothing in my life before this moment had equipped me with tools to deal with these new symptoms.

I could smell the clean light scent of her skin. We were standing so close. I could feel the warmth of her body next to mine.

Her spirit smoke was very full and pink. It was wafting serenely about her and mingling with mine.

I felt burning hot sweat slide down my back. It found its way past the waist of my pantalets and burned a path down the crevice that separated my buttocks.

Why there? Why now? How odd it was to be standing in the presence of such great beauty, thinking about sweat in my nether creases!

The Princess pressed in closer to me. I was backed against the wall. I tried to swallow, only to discover, the knot that was there would not budge. My vision became blurry and I was aware of nothing else but the throb of my heart and my rising temperature.

I was beginning to suspect I was truly ill. Aye, perhaps that was my problem. I was sweating, I had a fever, my vision was blurry, I had a lump in my throat the size of a small pomegranate and I was having palpitations...

She leaned in just then and kissed me gently upon the lips.

Something inside me melted and trickled down the inside of my right thigh.

The door swung open. Madame Rosmerta stood speechless for only a moment. "Good evening, Your Highness." She said with a curtsy, as if nothing out of the ordinary had just happened.

The Princess flushed and nodded a silent greeting to Madame Rosmerta.

Rosmerta briskly turned to me and said, "There you are Willow! I was beginning to wonder what had happened to you."

I felt like a child that had gotten free in the marketplace and had found her way into mischief.

Madame Rosmerta took me by the wrist. "Begging your pardon Your Highness, but Willow and I have an appointment to keep this evening."

The Princess had regained enough composure to reply with a bow of her head. "Yes, of course, do not let me keep you."

Madame Rosmerta was curtsying and backing out the door.

"Will you please tell Miss Constance or Martha about the tea?" I said over my shoulder as Rosmerta pulled me away. "Sleep well Your Highness."

"I shall, and I wish you pleasant dreams as well." She replied. A soft smile played upon the rosy full lips that had just grazed mine.

Rosmerta and I were trotting down the hall before my mind could mist over into dizzy memories of what had just taken place.

"We must go the long way since the Princess is in the doorway to the Queen's Chambers." Rosmerta explained, out of breath.

I agreed. That made sense.

She was pulling me quickly down the corridor. So quickly, I nearly could not keep my footing.

Tapestries, paintings and lanterns whisked by. I thought I spotted a candle-lighter extinguishing some of the lamps nearby.

"Rosmerta," I croaked.

"Yes?"

"My foot." I said through a grimace. "I can not keep up at this pace."

"Oh dear, I am sorry." She replied. She slowed to a walk. "We can not speak here."

"I only want to know if you are upset." I said.

"No, no, I am not upset," she replied, waving her free index finger in negation. "We just have so very much to talk about."

I agreed. We did.

We found our way to the harem with no interruptions.

Once the door was closed behind us Rosmerta locked it and hung the key on its hook.

"Oh, Bunny!" Madame Rosmerta exclaimed. "Oh, my! Have you ever caught the Princess's attention!"

"Aye, I guess I have." I nodded dumbly. That was fairly evident. "You saw what happened then?"

"I saw that the Princess had you against the wall and that she was just pulling away when I came through the door. I assume she kissed you." Rosmerta hesitated, leaving space for my reply.

"Aye. That she did." I agreed, nodding vigorously.

"Was that your first kiss?" Rosmerta asked warmly.

"Aye." I answered. I could feel my face flush.

"How was it? Did you like it?" She pressed for details.

"Aye, but..." I hesitated.

"But, what? Is it that she is a woman?" She asked cautiously.

"Nay! I was just concerned that I have been feeling feverish and dizzy these past few days. I only hope I do not make Her Highness ill."

"Has your heart been bounding?" She asked patting her chest.

"Aye, are there others who are also ill?" I asked, genuinely concerned.

"Oh, Bunny, you really have no idea, have you?" She shook her head side to side. She sounded almost as if she pitied me.

"I really have no idea, about what, Rosmerta?" I asked, feeling more nervous with every second.

"Willow, honey, I think you are in love."

"Me? In love? What makes you think that?" I stammered.

"Bunny, do you feel dizzy and hot all the time or only when Madeline is in the room?"

I began to process what she was asking. Suddenly, it was as if someone had turned up the wick on a lantern. Slowly everything came into brilliant focus.

When I realized what she said could be possible, I hung my head to hide my flushed cheeks.

"It's nothing to be ashamed of. It should happen to everyone. Love is a beautiful thing." She said cupping my face in her hands.

"I am not so sure I am supposed to be in love." I felt shame rush into every corner of my being. There was no place to hide from it.

"Of course you are! It would not have happened if it was not meant to be." She soothed. "Are you concerned about being a *drabarni* and being in love?"

I nodded my head.

"Do you remember what Magda said? She said she chose to have no husband. She also told you that she has shared love with someone for many years. She just is not married to her him.

"Come over here and sit with me on the bed." She invited. She walked to her dressing table and picked up her brush.

I sat next to her and she began to unbraid my hair.

"Willow, the day that Magda and I went in search of herbs, Magda asked me to teach you social graces. Do you suppose you know what she meant?"

"She wanted you to show me how to behave according to the palace's caste system."

"Indeed, you are correct, but that is only part of it. Magda felt that she was depriving you of living a full life. Because she chose to live a life without a spouse, she felt she was not the person to teach you how to behave with a partner." She brushed my hair steadily with long soothing strokes.

"Why is that?" I puzzled. "She has had someone for years. She knows how to love."

"Perhaps," she began, "She did not feel she could model the kind of love she felt should be meant for you." She put my hair into one loose braid that ran down my spine.

I furrowed my brow. "I am confused now. The *kind* of love that should be meant for me?"

"Yes," she said, picking up the hairbrush. "There is the kind of love where a woman wants to be with a man and only a man. That is one kind of love. That is the kind of love people engage in to produce children. It is most generally accepted.

There is another kind of love where a woman loves both men and women. She enjoys a wider variety of sexual pleasures. Sometimes the woman chooses not to have children because she enjoys her freedom.

Then there are those women who enjoy the closeness they can only achieve with other women. Women have a kind of tribal closeness. They share many things in common and they understand one another on a much deeper level than a man and woman ever could."

I was silent for a moment. "Essentially, what you are telling me is that there are man to woman, woman to man and woman, and woman to woman relationships. Are there not also man to man relationships?"

"Yes, that is true. Since we were discussing you and Magda, I omitted that possibility. As you can see, there are basically three sexes. Males; who are attracted to females, females; who are attracted to males; and males and females who are attracted to members of their own gender."

"I have heard some of this before" I said "But not in the detail in which you describe it. Why do people not talk about it?" I puzzled.

"Do you remember meeting me for the first time? You were frightened and you did not trust me. Just by meeting me, you opened yourself up and allowed yourself to think about things you had previously been able to ignore about yourself.

Most people are, like you, afraid to trust their own sexual drive. It is a powerful force within us. Sex is intoxicating like alcohol. A person can become as dependent on sex as they can on wine. Some people will do just about anything to get it. Others avoid the subject because they like to feel that they are in control. They are frightened to surrender to the power of love and sex.

Most people have the capacity to enjoy companionship with both men and women. We can see a beautiful woman and enjoy her beauty. We can see a handsome man and enjoy his good looks. Given the right circumstances, most could have a sexual relationship with someone of the same sex. That frightens a lot of people to the point of violence. A man would kill a male lover to prove he did not love him. A woman would shun her lady love in order to be accepted by the other women in her community."

"But I see you and how much you love your Queen. She must love you as well or you would not be here." I reasoned.

"That is true, but my lover is the monarch of a Kingdom. She makes the rules. There is no greater ruler in this land." Rosmerta replied.

"Is your love a secret?" I asked. "Or do the Prince and Princess know?"

"We have been together since the beginning. I was here before the Queen took Edward as her husband. It was the acceptable thing to do. She did what was expected, she bore his children. As far as she is concerned, he has served his purpose. He was just a drone; he fertilized the Queen Bee she has heirs to her throne and now she is done with him. As I told you before, he has seen us together in bed, but it is not certain what conclusion he has come to.

"Alyss has not told the children because she wanted them to make their own choices in life. She was relieved when Madeline accepted Alexander, but she is very concerned that Phillip has not found a bride. She knows Edward would target him and kill him if he suspected Phillip was not attracted to women."

"I can not imagine such a thing." I was aghast.

"Magda is a very wise woman. She recognized that you were of the third sex since you were very small. Since it was not her experience, she did not know how to teach you about love and sex as a person of the third sex. This is why she came to me." Rosmerta said as she shuffled to the wardrobe to remove her dress.

"Are we very rare?" I asked. "People of the third sex, I mean." I unlaced the bodice of my dress and lifted it off over my head.

"True people of the third sex are fairly rare, yes. Ancient civilizations believed that citizens of the third sex were harbingers of good luck and they were sought for their great talents in art and music and healing, which was one of the first clear signs for Magda." She interjected, returning to the bed chamber in her chemise.

"First clear signs?" I puzzled. "Because of the prophecies and because I am a Chosen One?" I said, perplexed. "Were those the signs that I was of the third sex?"

"They might have been some of the first clear signs Magda was talking about." Rosmerta responded thoughtfully.

"I think I just figured something else out." I said slowly.

"What is that?' She asked through a mouth full of hair pins.

"I am a Chosen One. That is part of our tribal history. Our *darbardi* is also a Chosen One." I spoke slowly to keep my thoughts clear.

"She is also a Princess." Rosmerta interrupted, brushing her own hair now.

"Yes, but hold that thought for a moment." I said, holding an index finger aloft.

"Very well." She conceded, nodding. "I am sorry, go on." She made a forward movement with both hands to urge me to continue and returned to brushing her hair.

"If our tribe has a Chosen healer and a Chosen seer, do you suppose they thought that we were unmarriageable because they believed we would both be of the third sex?"

My friend stopped brushing and sat, thoughtful, for a moment. "That is a possibility." She agreed through hair pins. "But, not every Chosen One is of the third sex, and not everyone who is of the third sex is a Chosen One." She clarified.

"Since Lynd was blind, the elders believed Lynd was unmarriageable. And since I was identified as being of the third sex, I was also considered unmarriageable. 'Tis interesting that eventually we were given a wagon to share. Do you think that they assumed that Lynd and I were already lovers?" I concluded slowly. I was incredulous.

"It is possible." Rosmerta said. "But if they observed you as I have," she pointed at me with her hairbrush, "They would know how truly innocent you are." She walked to her dressing table and deposited her brush and hairpins in their respective places. She returned and seated herself on the bed next to me again.

"Let's have your foot," Rosmerta swiveled onto the bed, in the tailor position, with both feet crossed in front of her. She invited me by patting her lap. I obliged by turning myself on the bed and lying with my injured foot in the hollow of her lap made by her crossed legs.

"That could explain Lynd's jealous behavior toward me!" I exclaimed. "As *drabardi*, she has made many prophesies about me. Perhaps she knew that I would be of the third sex. This would explain why she has been wary of all of my friendships with other women. She becomes possessive, not because she is in love with me, but because if I have a paramour, she will be alone." I had never thought of any of this before now.

"That, my dear, is a very real possibility!" Rosmerta stated. "I believe that could be a real likelihood." She nodded as if confirming something in her own mind.

Her strong thumbs worked out the tension in my foot, while we talked and puzzled out the tension in my confused mind.

"I would never want Galynda to feel abandoned." I said sadly.

"Of course not." Rosmerta replied. "But her behavior does seem to indicate that she may believe that could happen to her."

"I had better talk with Galynda and get this worked out before one of us says or does something she might regret." I muttered.

I agree Bunny, but right now, you are my priority and I say we can not resolve all of this tonight. You have had a very full day. I suggest we get some sleep. Tomorrow, we shall tend to the Queen, you shall breakfast with Princess Galynda, and then we shall begin your education."

"Good night Rosmerta. Thank you for helping me to sort through everything and thank you for the wonderful care." I said gratefully.

"You are most welcome, Bunny. It has been my pleasure. I think a good night's sleep might just be the perfect remedy to help put things in perspective. Goodnight, Willow." With that, she settled my injured foot upon a pillow, climbed into bed, blew out the lamp, and kissed me lightly on the forehead. Pulling the coverlets up under our chins, Rosmerta settled back on her pillow.

I was so exhausted from my emotional day that the moisture of Rosmerta's kiss still lingered on my forehead as I faded into sleep.

A Thief in the Night

It felt as if I had only just drifted off to sleep when suddenly, I was being awakened by a very frantic Madame Rosmerta.

"Willow, Willow, Honey, wake up!"

"Hmmm?" I remember that I was having a very pleasant dream. I felt slow and disoriented.

"Oh, Willow, do wake up! Edward has returned and has made his way into the castle!"

My thick mind ambled along slowly, Edward...Edward...castle. The pieces fell together quickly then and I was wide awake instantly.

"The Queen!" I exclaimed, awake now. "Is someone keeping watch over the Queen?"

"Yes, I was just there." Rosmerta answered frantically tucking loose hair behind her left ear. "Come on Honey, we've got to get back to her!"

I was pulling on my dress and hopping into my boot and lacing my brace all in the period of one breath for there was not time to do all three.

"Do you know where Edward is? Has he gotten to any of the royal family?"

We were hurrying through the mouse hole in her lavatory, Rosmerta explaining what she knew as we went.

"Edward has an insider, someone who is feeding him information about activities inside these walls. I had no idea he had any sympathizers left! I feel so exposed! He has a spy!"

"And if we knew who the spy was, we could seal the leak. I understand. Right now, we have got to get the royal family into hiding! Have you a hidden room to take them to?"

"There are a few places Edward does not know about. I have an idea, but I have not gotten it all worked out yet. Give me a little time and I will tell you what I know."

We were already at the Queen's door. Rosmerta peeked through a tiny hidden peep hole in the bookshelf to be certain we would not be seen. When the path was clear, she summoned me to follow.

A worried Emily was sitting with Princess Madeline as they kept vigil over the Queen.

I hurried to the bedside and bowed to the Princess and Emily. Turning to the Queen I bowed and said, out of breath, "Your Majesty, how are you feeling?"

"Edward has entered the castle and is in hiding somewhere." She spoke softly. This was the first time I had heard her speak aloud.

I leaned in close and spoke softly to the Queen. "Your Majesty, I understand that this is your family's castle. Am I correct in assuming that no one knows your castle as well as you?" I asked.

She smiled and nodded gesturing with one hand toward her daughter. "Madeline knows the passageways nearly as well as I do, she always was more adventurous than Phillip."

The Princess nodded agreement. "How can I help?" She

asked.

"We must enlist the help of two strong men that you know are loyal to the Queen." I heard myself say to no one in particular.

"Rosmerta," I spoke softly. "We shall need two stout poles. The tall candlesticks in the hallway will do nicely. I know I need not tell you this, but try not to talk to anyone you are not certain is loyal to the Queen."

Rosmerta nodded and ducked out the main door into the corridor.

My head was filled with scattered thoughts. I needed to protect both royal families.

I would have to find a way to get word to my family as well. "Emily, please go and waken the Princess, Ra Anan and her guests. Apprise them of what has transpired. Inform them that I shall join them as soon as it is safe for me to do so."

"Right away." She replied. She curtsied and backed from the room.

Turning back to Princess Madeline, I began, "Madeline, I pray that your childhood adventures yielded a safe place large enough for two families to hide."

She hesitated for a moment upon hearing her name stripped of its title, but she was quick to recover. "I believe I may know of just such a place." She said. "We will need to carry lanterns to find our way along the passageway."

It was only when she said this, that I was suddenly aware of time. It was still quite dark outside. I do not believe it could have been much after midnight. I gathered two lanterns from the Queen's bedchamber.

"I do not wish to offend Your Highness, but I must ask. Are you willing to trust your life to Emily?"

"I take no offense; I can see that you have my best interest at heart. Yes, I would say that I trust her. She has been with Mother since before Mother was married."

The Queen nodded agreement. "She is one person I would never doubt."

"Is there anyone new or peculiar on the staff that may sympathize with Edward?" I asked. "Has there been any angry rumblings? Any hint this was coming?"

"I am not thinking very clearly at the moment," the Queen answered, massaging her forehead with her left hand, "but I will let you know if I think of anyone." She replied.

"Madeline, you and I must make haste to remove all evidence of medicine and illness from this room. We want it to appear as though the information the King has been given by his informant was misleading." We scurried about removing bowls of tea and broth and straightening out the pillows on the chairs.

Madame Rosmerta returned, out of breath, with Prince Phillip, Pieter and Ahmad. Each man carried a tall, ornate candle stick that was easily a full foot taller than he was. I was thrilled to see Ahmad and to know at least he was safe.

"Was there anyone suspicious in the corridors?" I asked.

Rosmerta shook her head "I only met the candle lighter. He helped me find these three candlesticks."

"Princess Madeline, what do you know of this candle lighter?" I asked. "I have seen him wandering up and down all of these corridors including the private family hallways."

"I do not know him well. He is an old man who has been with us for a long while, but I have not made his acquaintance." She said, deep in thought.

"Rosmerta, what do you know of him?" I asked. The suspicion in my mind growing stronger.

"He seems to have access to all the corridors and rooms in the house. He is everywhere, and yet he is almost invisible." The message was clear. Everyone had gone about life without a thought for who was hidden in the shadows, gathering unknown volumes of information about the Royal Family.

I summoned Rosmerta and the Princess to step in nearer to the Queen and me. "I would suggest that we find some way of feeding him inaccurate information about where we will be keeping the royal families and see if we can guide Edward away from the vulnerable ones and into the waiting arms of the strong ones. We will need to devise a plan. That is where your knowledge of the hidden rooms and corridors will certainly help us, Princess Madeline. First, we must transport the Queen away from here."

Did we have that bit of canvas laundered and returned to this room?" I asked Rosmerta.

"Yes, it is there on the chest." she indicated with a glance.

"What we need to do is make a litter on which to carry the Queen. Let us place the two tallest candle sticks on the floor next to the bed. Lay them side by side and lay the canvas over them. It is large enough to lay it in a diamond pattern with a point at the top and bottom. Wrap the side tips over and around the candle sticks, rolling away from the middle so that the canvas will support the Queen and tighten under her weight. Leave enough space for Her Majesty to fit comfortably.

Pieter, if you will come to the head of the bed and Ahmad, if you will move to the foot, grasp the sheets and on the count of three, you shall pick the Queen up, bedding and all, and place her gently upon the litter.

Each man took his position near the bed and gathered a corner of bedding in each hand. All eyes were on me as they awaited my next command.

Ready?" I asked, looking from one to the other. They both nodded.

"Are you ready Your Majesty?" I asked.

"Yes." she said softly.

"One, two, three." The men lifted the bedding from the corners, carrying the most precious cargo either of them had ever encountered, in a hammock of sheets and blankets. In one smooth pivot, they gingerly set the Queen on the litter as though it was something they did every day.

"Was that all right, Majesty?" I asked the Queen as I tucked her into the bedding both to keep her warm and to prevent possible hang ups.

"Oh, Yes. You needn't worry about me." She said.

"When we are prepared to go, each man shall bear an end of the litter. Prince Phillip, if you please," I tried my best to maintain a modicum of etiquette. "You shall carry a lantern to light the way. If we have far to travel, you may spell the men when they grow weary."

Prince Phillip's expression was one of concern for his mother and determination. He nodded agreement and took up a lantern.

"Princess Madeline, do we have far to travel?" I enquired.

"Not so very far." She replied. "I am confident that we shall make a clean escape. However, the passage is narrow. We shan't be able to move very quickly."

"Getting the Royal Family out of here safely is our primary concern. It is absolutely vital that you all make haste and take your leave now." I said looking from one concerned face to the next.

Each acknowledged agreement with a small nod.

"Since the passage we are to take is narrow, I shall go to help the others prepare and we shall await your return." I stated to the Princess.

An expression of disappointment crossed her face, but she seemed to find logic in my decision and offered no argument.

"Come then, we must make haste." She called to the others. The men smoothly bent in unison to pick up the litter.

"Hold tight to the ends of the canvas to prevent it from unrolling." I called after them.

I watched them file from the room, Princess Madeline in

the lead with a lantern and Madame Rosmerta following the litter, carrying a large candle in a glass chimney that I suspected had come from one of the candlesticks. Prince Phillip was bringing up the rear with his lantern held high. I was mildly surprised to see them exit through a panel in the entryway, opposite the bookcase Rosmerta and I had used.

I straightened what was left of the bedding and found a decorative spread which had been tossed aside. I used this and made the bed up. I gathered decorative pillows from various corners of the room and placed them upon the bed making it appear as if it had been unoccupied for some time. One by one, I extinguished the remaining lanterns, save for the one I was carrying.

I hastened from the royal bedchamber in search of my own family. Who by now, I was certain, were all dressed and assembled in the guest kitchen.

My heart raced as I bumped along the dark corridors. In the darkness, the shadows grew and shrunk with my every foot fall, appearing to be dangerous dark beings jumping out of niches. Each, I was certain would be the King, whom everyone in the Royal Family feared.

My mind was reeling. Somewhere in the back of my head I could hear the screams of horses and humans. I could see the night brighten as a wagon, with all its occupants trapped inside, burned to the ground. I could smell the unforgettable odor of burning hair and wood and I could taste the bitterness of scorched flesh. And then there was the thundering of hoof beats as the culprits rode away under cover of darkness.

My heart was pounding in my ears keeping time with the hoof beats. I wanted to run with fear. I needed to remain calm to avoid losing my way in the dark. I needed to keep my wits, to think. I felt I could trust no one outside of the families.

Shadows stretched and slithered like striking snakes,

licking at my feet as the light in my lantern flickered with my haste. As I hobbled along in the corridor, I would occasionally stop to listen for footsteps or the rustling of tapestries. My ears strained to hear beyond the pounding of my heart.

I hastened down the darkened corridor, suddenly, I saw him, standing there before me. He was a giant of a man, standing silently with his back against the wall, watching me. My eyes pressed against the viscous darkness straining through the velvet obscurity to see him with more clarity. A scream had formed in my throat, ready in the event I should need it.

I held my breath and made my way closer to him. Why hadn't he made a move? When I felt I could no longer endure life without air, I realized, he would not move from that spot. I recognized him as a suit of armor that I had walked past every day since we had arrived.

It wasn't Edward or his men! I felt giddy then. It took all of my effort not to laugh and cry out maniacally with relief.

Silently, I willed myself forward. The kitchen seemed to be so much further away than I remembered. My mind began to gnaw at me. Maybe I had missed the kitchen. Maybe I was wandering, lost. What if I were lost...where was Edward? What if I were to encounter him here, in the corridor?

I was flooded with relief when my straining eyes spotted the soft glow of lamp light coming from a familiar doorway. The guest kitchen was just ahead. I had made it! I sent up a prayer of thanksgiving that I had not missed it in the dark. I finally allowed myself to breathe.

The kitchen was unnaturally silent. The air was heavy with anxiety. When I rounded the doorway, I found everyone huddled together before the cooktop stove. Each was holding a knife or cleaver. The faces I had known all my life were masked in terror and foreign to me.

"Tis me, Willow!" I whispered roughly, raising the lantern, to identify myself.

The room sighed collectively as each woman lowered her weapon and let down her guard.

"I am so glad to have found you all well" I breathed. I could feel my bounding heart regulating itself and relief flooding my veins. My legs felt as if they suddenly had no bones at all. I sat heavily upon a nearby bench, grateful it was there for I surely would have fallen upon the floor.

"Is there anything here that needs my attention?" I asked out of breath.

I could see that Emily was the only kitchen staff member present. She, Magda and Ahnja had begun to gather baskets and crates to fill with food and other provisions that she felt might be needed in the event of an extended absence.

Magda came to me with Galynda on her arm. "Willow," Magda said softly. "Your face is ashen. Sit here a while and allow yourself to recover a bit. Allow the others to help as much as they can."

Still out of breath, I nodded my agreement. 'Twas true, now that I was safe in the arms of my family again; I began to feel my strength dissolving as quickly as salt will in boiling water.

"I shall rest a while, Magda." I said. "Go ahead and help the others, I shall be all right."

"I am leaving Galynda here with you to be certain that happens." My concerned mother said.

She quickly turned to rejoin the others. "Emily, how may I assist you?" Magda offered.

"Let us make haste in filling these baskets with as much food as we can." Emily answered over her shoulder without stopping to converse.

It was clear that the situation was far too urgent to concern oneself with etiquette.

Galynda sat beside me on the bench. "Willow," she

stroked my arm. "I am concerned for you. Your breathing is so ragged and uneven are you well?" my sister asked.

"Aye." I responded with a nod of my head. "Do you understand what is happening?"

"Aye," she replied, holding space for me to continue.

"Because it is dark, everything takes on a different shape in lamp light. Since I have never traversed these corridors alone in the darkness, I was afraid I had lost my way. I saw shadows move and stretch. Harmless armchairs and occasion tables seem to become villains crouching in every shadow. I had a start or two in the dark corridors." I explained.

My companion, never having seen light or dark offered no words but squeezed my arm to assure me that she had heard me and that we were safely together now.

"Willow," Galynda began in a low voice. "Their King is a very bad man." She warned.

"Aye, Lynd, that he is." I agreed, trying to catch my breath.

"No," she exclaimed in a voice just above a whisper. She applied pressure with her hand upon my arm. "Listen to me!"

"You have my attention." I said, feeling the hairs on my neck bristle. "I am listening." I said inviting her to continue.

Desperation had begun to creep into her voice as she struggled for the words that would help me understand. "He is the kind of bad that is pure evil." She corrected.

"The King has hurt and killed many people unjustly. He has been among the angry ones who have killed Rom people." Her eyes brightened with tears.

Her voice dropped an octave as she continued. "He has tasted blood and means to kill again." She said in a slow, steady monotone. A tear broke free of her lashes and silently glided down her cheek.

"I have a very strong impression that our tribe has suffered at the hands of this man before. He is a hateful, vengeful man who will not stop until he gets what he has come for. He may be here in search of our people. There is something about 'unfinished business.'" She said with a look of deep concern on her face.

I had never seen Galynda behave this way. She had my full attention. In fact, her revelation had my senses on full alert. An icy chill rushed through me.

"What you just told me gave me goose flesh!" I exclaimed, rubbing my arms vigorously both to ward off the evil chill as much as to comfort myself.

"Lynd," I spoke quietly in her ear. "Just now when I was in the corridor making my way here, I had a memory or a vision or something. I witnessed one of our wagons being burned. I was small, but I must have gotten out of bed for some reason. I saw everything as it happened. I smelled everything, burning wood, burning hair. I heard the people inside the wagon screaming! Lynd, the family inside the wagon knew they were about to die and there was nothing I could do! I saw men riding away from our camp. I feel that what is happening now might, somehow, be related to what happened then. This is why I was so very frightened when I felt I would not be able to find you all." I remarked.

"Do you think this might also have something to do with the vision you have had about the wagon wheel?" I continued, urgently trying to fit shattered fragments of a puzzle together without having seen the entire picture.

"Aye, Willow." Galynda said. Her face reflected recognition. "But," She shook her head. "'tis only a piece of it." She narrowed her eyes, as if to bring them into clearer focus. "The wheels of change have begun to turn, but there is more change to come." She said with finality.

"Lynd," I began. "We suspect that the King has sympathizers inside the palace and that they are the ones who brought him back into the castle! We must not make a sound and we must not draw attention to ourselves." I said squeezing her hand.

Magda returned to the bench where we sat. "The color is returning to your cheeks. Are you feeling stronger now, Willow?"

"Aye," I replied. "I have caught my breath and have my legs back underneath me." I said rubbing the remnants of gooseflesh out of my thighs.

"What is to happen now?" Magda asked. "Have the others devised a plan?"

I realized in my state of panic, I had neglected to inform my family of the plans that had been set in motion.

"Let us all gather around so that I can tell you what I know." I said softly gesturing a small circle with my arms indicating that the others should form a small huddle around me.

Magda quietly went to each person and had them stop what they were doing. Everyone silently assembled around me. All eyes were on me. A heavy silence made space for me to impart my knowledge of the plan thus far.

"The Princess, Madeline has taken her family to the safety of a hidden room somewhere in the castle. She is hiding her family there now and shall return for us as soon as it is safe to do so. We are to prepare food and provisions to take with us. And we are to wait here for her return. When she returns, we are to follow her to a safe location."

"We have not seen Ahmad." Ahnja's voice wavered with emotion. "Someone should go to him and bring him here!" her features were pinched with worry and her eyes bright with tears.

"He is sleeping in the stables where he can tend to our horses and wagons as he has done since we came here." Magda answered. Her face, while calm and controlled, was creased with anxiety.

"Aye," I nodded. "He has been in the stables, but he was

enlisted by Madame Rosmerta to help carry the Queen's litter. He has gone ahead with the others to safety and shall be waiting for us in the hidden room." I replied.

Everyone seemed to let out her breath at once. Magda's face visibly relaxed and she heaved a ragged sigh of relief.

In seeing her despair, I was overcome with a sudden revelation. It should have been so clear to me before now. I must have been blinded by the selfishness of youth! Of course! Magda would know where Ahmad was at all times! And he would know where to find her! Of course, it was all beginning to make sense now.

Magda and Ahmad, my foster parents, were united not only by their love for me, but by their mutual love for each other! I felt foolish and selfish for thinking that I might be the sole reason they associated with each other. I flushed with shame for holding such a selfish belief.

"Willow," Magda interrupted my thoughts. "Perhaps I should go now and fetch your medicine pouch. If the Princess, Madeline returns, do not wait for me." She offered.

"Nay." I responded. "I shall go at once. Do not wait for *me*. 'Tis far better that you are all safely together. I shall go and fetch my pouch. I would not want anything to happen to you while you were waiting for me." Before anyone could protest, I was out the door, bound for the Queen's private washroom.

"I shall leave word for you." Magda called after me.

"I shall just have to make haste!" I said to no one but myself as I scuttled into the dark, sleeping corridor.

My mind was filled with ten thousand thoughts at once. Where was Madeline? Where was Edward? Who was the informant? Why did this corridor seem so much longer when I was so frightened and in such a hurry? Would I return in time to join my family or would I be forced to scurry through dark and strange hallways in fear of an unknown man?

While worrying kept my mind off my foot, it did little for

my confidence.

I limped into the Royal bedchambers through the main doorway and slipped silently into the washroom. My medicine pouch hung on the wooden peg on the wall just as I had left it. I plucked it from its hook and as I reached for the soap, I halted abruptly.

I thought I detected sounds coming from within the walls. My heart bounded for joy. The Princess, she has returned for us, I thought. In the very next moment, I felt my heart plummet to my belly. What if it was Edward, coming to get me? No one would know. No one would hear me...

I swallowed hard to dislodge the lump of fear that had formed in my throat. I shouldered my medicine pouch, turned the flame on my lantern down to a scarce flicker, and ducked down low inside the doorway of the washroom. I waited silently as I listened for further scrambling noises in the wall.

I could hear my own heart as it pounded out a savage beat in my ears and throat. It was so loud, in fact, that I quite feared I would be detected. I feared it would be so loud I would not be able to hear anything else.

There 'twas again! This time, there was no denying that I had heard shuffling and thudding sounds between the walls.

My already bounding heart began to pound wildly. I was very much alone and I had to devise a plan.

I heard the bookcase open in the anteroom. I was overcome with relief. It must be Madame Rosmerta, for this was her favorite entrance to the Queen's private chambers! Before I could make a move to leave the sanctuary of my darkened doorway to greet her, I realized that the sounds could not possibly have been made by the Princess, Madeline or Madame Rosmerta. I froze on the spot and listened.

As children, Galynda and I would often play a game wherein we would listen and identify members of our clan and others by the sound of their footsteps. I had become just as adept at this game, as Lynd had at identifying herbs with her sense of smell.

I stood in total silence, listening with my entire being. My heart pounded so hard in my ears that I feared I might not be able to hear anything else. I was certain that I did not recognize the heavy, unsteady gait.

I sent up a silent prayer of thanksgiving for my sister and the providence of her second sight which had equipped me with such a useful tool.

I remained still, squatting near the floor, listening to the unstable gait and the weighty footfalls. This person was too large and heavy to be a woman. Even Ahmad with his round, full, belly did not have footfalls as substantial as this. I suspected this was a bulky man who was either injured or drunk or perhaps, both.

I could hear him muttering angrily under his breath. He was walking away from me into the Queen's bed chamber.

I crept to the doorway of the washroom where I could make out the anteroom and the bed chamber beyond that. I saw the stranger in silhouette, for he was standing in his own lantern light. He appeared to be a large man. His body was fleshy and soft. It was a body of excess and leisure. I watched him to be certain I would not be seen. I silently eased myself around the doorway and into the nearest shadow in the anteroom.

I quietly breathed a sigh of relief. I had not been seen. I could hear the bear-sized man pawing through the Queen's belongings and overturning furniture noisily. He blundered about recklessly, leaving a trail of destruction in his wake.

I rose slowly and soundlessly to my feet. I kept my back against the bookshelf to hold myself erect and to avoid being taken by surprise from behind. I was very near the anteroom doorway, the threshold of which would lead me to the corridor, and to freedom.

The movement was so subtle in the dim lighting, I very

nearly missed it. The tapestry, opposite me and the bookcase, rippled ever so slightly. My heart stopped cold. I froze in the nearest shadow.

My chest became a cage filled with bats yearning to free themselves. It was too late to flee. I couldn't hide anywhere. I was afraid to attempt to find my way in the passage the large man had just traversed. What if his men were lying in wait in that passageway?

A fair-skinned, elegant hand, which I immediately recognized as Madeline's, folded the tapestry back away from the wall. Her other hand appeared clutching the candle I had seen Rosmerta with earlier. I quietly sprang from my hiding place in the shadows. Reaching around her shoulder from behind, I covered her mouth with one hand, wrapped my other hand firmly about her waist, and leaned over her shoulder to blow out the flame of her candle.

I could feel her body stiffen against mine. Her breath was hot against my palm.

I leaned in close to her and whispered in her ear. "'Tis Willow, Your Highness. 'Tis me! Shh, shhh. "tis only me." I soothed, still covering her mouth.

She let out a long, silent breath that I am certain was originally intended to be a scream. As she began to relax her muscles, her body leaned heavily into mine. She nodded her head to acknowledge that she believed it was, indeed, me and that she was no longer a screaming risk.

I removed my hand from her mouth but held her waist for a moment longer. I leaned against her body and whispered in her ear. "Your Highness, there is a very large, drunk man smashing through the Queen's quarters."

She nodded her head and took me by the hand, pulling me into the main corridor. We had only gone a short distance when she pulled me across the hall and into another hidden passageway.

In the relative safety of the isolated passage, I turned up

the flame of my lantern. Madeline's regal countenance was pinched with worry and looked wan in the yellow lamplight.

"Please forgive the intrusion on your personage, Your Royal Highness." I whispered.

"Do not apologize, Willow, what you did just now may well have saved the entire Kingdom!"

I was relieved that she was not offended that I had grabbed her so savagely.

With no warning, she embraced me hard, taking my breath away. She pressed her body fully against mine and held me there. She kissed me passionately and urgently. I returned the embrace, and this time I was ready for her and I returned the kiss.

She held me at arms' length for a moment, studying my face, searching first one eye and then the other. Her eyes had brightened with tears she had resolved not to shed. Her jaw was set in a determined pout.

She nodded at me and without a word; she took up my free hand and led me hastily along the foreign passage. We wordlessly scurried between the walls toward the guest wing and my waiting family.

In the silence, I had several minutes to mull over the events that had just unfolded. I was happy to have been able to avert her from the angry intruder. I was sorry to have frightened her so, but it was thrilling to be so close to her, to feel her body against mine to embrace her, to be embraced, to have her kiss me, to kiss her back. My mind swirled and swam, lost in thoughts and emotions I had never experienced before.

We found ourselves in the guest wing pantry without further incident.

The air in the kitchen was so still when we entered, it was as though everyone was frozen in place and holding her breath.

Madeline was well composed and in complete control of

the situation as she spoke to everyone in the kitchen. "Edward is here. We discovered him in the Queen's private quarters. It shall not be long before he is upon us. Quickly now, we must make haste!"

"How shall we get six women down the corridor unnoticed?" Ahnja asked.

"We shall travel by another route, since Edward is hindering the first." The Princess replied with a gesture toward the pantry. She moved aside a wine cask and a flour sack. Behind these, was a concealed doorway to yet another of the hidden passageways.

Princess Madeline instructed us to move ahead and wait for her where the passage widened. Once the crates and baskets were gathered up and carried away, we left behind a spotless kitchen.

We entered the narrow opening single file. Madeline then retraced her steps and covered the doorway of the mouse hole to keep our whereabouts undetectable.

When she was satisfied that the pantry appeared to be as unremarkable as possible, she rejoined the group.

Princess Madeline led the group carrying a lighted lantern high above her head. Emily followed, bearing one end of a heavily laden basket. Magda followed behind Emily, helping to bear her basket in one hand, and in her other hand, she shared the burden of a second basket with her sister, Ahnja.

In my mind, I felt we might look like a family of elephants, each linked trunk-to-tail, shuffling slowly in single file.

It was my job to bring up the rear. I carried a lantern in my right hand and Galynda's hand was tucked safely in my left elbow. I described the elephant image in my head and all that I saw along the way as we scurried through the walls.

Galynda, I knew, was putting all the pieces together between what she felt in the environment and observed with her sensitive fingers and nose as we went along. She had become adept at adjusting to an ever-changing environment.

We walked for what seemed like hours but had probably only been a matter of minutes. Finally, we came upon a wooden door at the end of the passageway.

"Willow, is everything all right? I smell dampness. The path beneath our feet is softer and the air here feels cooler." Galynda observed.

"You are quite right, Princess Ra Ahnan. We are no longer in the confines of the castle. It is not safe to stay there when Edward is about." Princess Madeline answered.

"We have only a few minutes more. Are you all able to continue?" Our leader asked, wiping a loose bit of hair and perspiration away from her forehead with the back of her hand.

"I am able to continue until I am certain we are safe." Ahnja replied.

"I agree," replied Magda.

"Indeed," added Emily.

"And you, Princess Ra Ahnan?" Madeline asked, are you ready to continue?

"Aye. Of course, Your Highness." Galynda's reply was just a trifle too curt.

I stood silently cringing inwardly when I realized that Galynda had an angry edge to her voice. No doubt, I thought, she could sense a change in me. Maybe she could smell the Princess on me. I felt a heavy knot forming in my stomach.

I promised myself that if I would have to live with both Princesses in a small space, I would have to resolve this whole issue of jealousy and insecurity once and for all and that sooner would be better for everyone than later.

The path began to climb uphill, so I suspected that we were nearer the surface now. I could feel the air in the tunnel growing cool with dampness. The air seemed especially frigid immediately between Galynda and me. This was going to be a challenging time for us all.

Mouse Holes and Pack Rats

Our journey through the bowels of the palace brought us outside the castle walls and into a stone outbuilding in an apple orchard.

"I smell apples." Galynda observed.

"As do I." I replied.

"That is correct." Princess Madeline answered.

"This is a sentry post. The residents here watch over the forest and the grounds outside of the castle walls. It was they who informed us that Father was more of a threat to our Kingdom than any enemy outside our walls. It was their vigilance that brought us warning of Father's return. Come, it is late and they are waiting for us inside the cottage." She pointed with her candle in the direction of the cottage.

Under the cloak of darkness and shadow, we quietly filed out of the small outbuilding and followed the flagstone pavers, by candlelight and the light of moon, we silently made our way the short distance to the sentry's cabin. It was a modest stone dwelling. In the dim light, I could just make out its shape and size. It seemed to share its architecture and materials with the stone barn that we had just left.

I realized in that short, brisk walk out of doors that I had not seen the open sky for days. I halted and stood gazing up at the dark blue, predawn sky. A light breeze played at a loose bit of my hair.

"Willow, is everything all right?" Galynda asked.

"Aye, I was just looking up at the sky. I have not seen it for many days and I just suddenly comprehended how much I have been missing that too." I replied.

Galynda squeezed my arm gently. "Tell me about the sky."

"'Tis a beautiful riding cloak of blue-black velvet with diamond dust scattered over the whole of it." I painted a picture with my words.

"It sounds lovely," Galynda responded with a smile.

I lightly squeezed her hand inside the crook of my elbow to indicate that I would begin walking and continued along the path into the cabin.

The women bearing baskets were happy to unload their burdens once they were in the safety of the cottage kitchen.

The entrance to the kitchen was a small corridor that was used as a mud room and pantry area where braids of onion and garlic hung from the ceiling along with clusters of dried herbs. A runner of faded handwoven rags led the way to the kitchen. Once inside, the kitchen had a long wooden counter for food preparation and a copper tub for washing dishes. To the right was an inglenook and beside it, a flattop stove and oven. The floorboards were bleached and worn with age.

The chimney of the inglenook must have been shared by the fireplace in the sitting room. The hearth was raised and provided seating. The mantle, created from a thick hand-hewn timber, was lighted with lanterns. Immediately to the right of the fireplace, was a wooden staircase. The stones of the fireplace made up the left-side wall that led up to the rooms upstairs.

The eating area consisted of a long wooden table and two long benches just off the kitchen to the left and was only separated from the sitting room by arrangement of furniture. The conversation area in the sitting room consisted of a settee and two chairs that faced the fireplace and the staircase. Another longer couch and two wingback chairs faced the front door, which was flanked on either side by two leaded glass windows.

The Princess introduced us to our hosts. "This is Augustus, and his wife Enid. They are the keepers of the watch."

To our hosts she said, these are our distinguished guests, Her Royal Highness Princess Ra Ahnan, and the Queen Mother, Ahnja, the Royal Physicians, Rajani and Magdalena, you have just met Ahmad, I hear he is the finest sword craftsman in many lands. You already know Emily."

The lady of the house was a short, stout woman with greying hair, who was no stranger to hard work. The experience lines running from her round, button nose to the corners of her mouth bore evidence that she had found much joy in her life. She was busying herself in the kitchen, finding places to store the provisions that we had ferried over from the castle.

Her husband was a tall, barrel-chested gentleman with a large, grey bushy mustache that covered his upper lip. He was nearly an elder now, but I could see that he was a hard worker and that his labors had kept him strong. He stepped forward and said to the crowd, "Most folks just call me Gus. I can't stand for none of them fancy titles. We are just plain folks who love our Queen and her lovely children. Nearly raised this one up since she was no more than a pup," he said embracing Princess Madeline in a one-armed hug.

The Princess smiled demurely. I thought I saw her cheeks flush. It was lovely to see her as a person instead of as a ruler. I felt comforted to know she did have some fun and adventures as a child.

Inwardly, I smiled. I liked Gus, the way he lovingly spoke of Madeline and how he showed her warmth and affection, he reminded me of Ahmad and how he openly displayed his deep affection for me.

I stepped forward and introduced myself. "Most folks call me Willow." I offered my hand with a smile. "I am one of the healers in service of the Queen. I am not one for cumbersome titles either."

Gus took my hand in his enormous callused paws. "Pleased to make your acquaintance, Willow. I hope that you find everything that you need to give our Queen the best care possible." He was genuine. Everything he said was reflected in his warm, brown eyes.

"I am confident that the Queen, who is making a steady recovery, shall now have the greatest chance to flourish thanks to your vigilance." I replied.

"I like this one!" Gus smiled broadly. "Are we going to keep her?" Emotion stopped him from saying more. The smile was present in his eyes, which glistened with tears only I could see. He pulled me into his burly arms in a bear hug.

"Thank you." He whispered into my hair. "Long live the Queen."

It was good to be out of harm's way and amongst friends after the terrifying night we had all experienced. I felt I had forgotten to breathe since I was awakened. I wondered how long it had been.

Turning to Princess Madeline, I said, "I would like very much to see how the Queen is faring after everything we have experienced tonight."

"Yes, I would as well. I shall join you." she replied.

"Where shall we find the Queen?" I asked the room.

Enid, who had joined Emily in unpacking the baskets, wiped her hands on her apron and offered to take us to the

Queen. "She is in the cellar. We thought it best that she be well hidden lest Edward happened upon this place in his search."

I agreed, hiding Her Majesty in the cellar sounded like a clever idea.

Princess Madeline and I followed Enid through the kitchen and into the pantry. Enid lifted the handmade rag rug to reveal a cleverly hidden trapdoor in the floor. It was ingenious how the pattern of the flooring was uninterrupted in the making of the door. Even without the rug, the hatch would have remained hidden in plain sight. She pulled up on the door to open it. Just inside was a set of stairs leading down to the cellar below.

Enid shone her lantern into the cellar. I could make out barrels with root vegetables in them and baskets filled with apples. The temperature down here was appreciably cooler than the rooms over head.

We picked our way through the bountiful barrels and baskets. I could see they would be well prepared for the cold weather ahead, but I still could not see the Queen.

"Her Majesty is right through here," Enid indicated with the lantern. I saw a shelf loaded with crocks of preserved fruits and vegetables.

Enid set the lantern on the floor and slid the shelf aside to reveal a hidden room beyond. "If you promise to close up behind yourselves, I shall leave you to visit with the Queen." With this, Enid left the lantern for us and retraced her steps back to the main floor.

The room was well appointed with a bedstead, chest of drawers and a wardrobe. On the far wall, there was a large fireplace with a warm fire glowing behind the andirons.

The Queen was propped up on the bed with several pillows supporting her back and head.

"Hello," She greeted. "I am happy to see that you are both here, this means we have all escaped from the castle unharmed." Her tired eyes looked relieved.

"Aye, 'tis true, we have all made it safely." I replied. "How are you doing after such an eventful night?" I asked. "May I take your pulses?"

"I believe I am faring quite well, and yes, you may certainly take my pulses." She answered softly.

I gathered her wrist in my hand and prepared to listen to the inner secrets of her body with the tips of my fingers. This, I knew Galynda would be able to do with very little training. She was an astute student with great instinct and extremely keen senses. The great masters taught that one must take thousands of pulses to truly begin to understand the body's inner workings. The great masters, I thought, had not met Galynda.

The Queen's pulses felt stronger than they had before we retired earlier. I felt certain it would not be much longer before she would be able to get up and walk a bit.

"Is there any pain your Majesty?" I asked.

"Some," she replied. "But it is bearable. I believe I shall be able to sleep without the tea."

"I can make more if you would like me to." I offered.

"I do not believe I shall need it. I believe I shall sleep comfortably in the safety of this hidden place. Thanks to you, I feel my strength is returning."

"'Tis an honor to serve you, Your Majesty." I humbly replied. "I shall remove some of these pillows and help you to lie back, if you are ready to sleep."

"Yes, I believe that would be a grand idea. Tomorrow shall be upon us soon enough."

I began to remove pillows from the bed and helped the Queen to recline more comfortably. "Will there be anything else?"

"No, thank you. Willow, I shall be fine until morning."

"Very well." I said with a curtsy. "Good night, Your Majesty. Rest well."

Princess Madeline took her mother's hand in her own. To me she said, "I believe I shall stay and visit with Mother for a moment."

"Very well." I replied. Try to keep your visit brief, this has been a long night for all of us. I shall leave you with the lantern. Sleep well, Princess."

I wandered cautiously through the dark, wending my way through crates and barrels, following the light that shone through the trapdoor.

I approached our hostess, Enid. "I do not wish to be ungrateful, but I am quite exhausted. This has been a most trying day and I feel a tremendous need to sleep. Where might I sleep tonight?"

She and Emily had finished with the baskets and were serving hot tea.

Enid wiped her hands on her apron and scuttled over to me, "Oh, I am sorry dear, let me show you to your room."

From the kitchen, we walked through the sitting room and up the stairs to the bedrooms.

"Thank you for welcoming us into your home." I said.

"Oh, it is our pleasure, we do so love visits from the Prince and Princess, and we see so little of them anymore. Maddy has been so busy attending to the needs of the Kingdom since the Queen took ill."

Enid led me into the room I would sleep in. It had a small fireplace on one wall, a bedstead and a wardrobe. It was a small, cozy room. I loved it at once and at the same moment, I realized how much I missed my wagon and the horses.

My mind wandered to the wagon I had grown up in. It was weathered grey from so many years on the trail. Inside it smelled of clean wood, wood smoke and herbs. It was practical and cozy. To the left of the door was the kitchen and to the right a small bench for sitting, the bed, at the head of the wagon, was tucked neatly under a well-worn patchwork quilt. Herbs hung from the ceiling, drying in clusters. The tiny woodstove was both the heat source and a place for cooking. The teapot was always full and at the ready. Every nook and cranny had a purpose, everything had its place and was stored away as soon as we had finished using it for the day.

I missed the familiarity and quietude of my humble vardo home and the enormous, ever-changing world I could see from my tiny window.

Here, in the orchard cottage, I pulled my boot off and unlaced the brace and inspected my foot. It looked as though it would heal nicely. I was too tired to concern myself with it at this ridiculous hour. I unlaced my bodice and stepped out of my skirt and carefully hung my clothes in the wardrobe. I crawled between the covers in my chemise and fell more deeply asleep than I had since my arrival here.

I only wakened to semi-consciousness when someone slid into bed behind me. Was it Galynda? I wondered. No, I was not in the wagon. It might be Rosmerta. I allowed myself to drift off to sleep again.

My bedmate could not seem to settle in. Her tossing and turning disturbed my sleep. I began to feel quite irritable. "Would you like me to make you some tea so that you can sleep?" I offered in self defense.

"Oh, Willow? Is that you? I am sorry. I did not know anyone was in here! Have I awakened you?"

It was Princess Madeline! In bed with me! I was suddenly very much awake. My heart started pounding in places I certainly would rather not have thought about at a time like this.

"Your Highness! I should lie on the floor and give you the bed! I did not know this was your room! I am terribly sorry!" I apologized.

"Willow, if you lie on the floor, I shall only lie with you there." Came her reply.

"But," I argued. "It is not right. You are royalty..." I

began.

There in the dark, she silenced me, mid-sentence with a kiss. It was cool and moist and ever so delicate. I could taste her breath. Without any thought, I returned the kiss. I kissed her gently.

Her lips were tender and juicy, like freshly washed fruit. They were the rare, exotic kind of fruit that my body had been starving for all my life. I knew in that instant I would never get enough; I would always be starving for the nourishment I could only get from her kisses.

She leaned into me, kissing me with more urgency. I could feel her desire but was not sure what she wanted or how to give it to her. Her lips sought mine, and then I felt the tip of her tongue as her kisses grew more urgent.

She must be starving too, I thought. How do I nourish her?

Oh, how I did wish I had already had my lessons with Madame Rosmerta. It was difficult to think about Madame Rosmerta when Madeline was hungrily pressing her warm body against me. 'Twas difficult to think at all.

My heart began to beat with such passion, below my umbilicus. I thought for certain Madeline could feel my heart beating. She must have sensed it, for she laid the whole of her body upon mine. I could feel her breasts, full and warm against mine. Her nipples had grown as hard as mine. Her skin, what I could touch of it, was soft and smooth. I could smell the scent of her skin mixing with my own. She was kissing me, gently, passionately, tentatively, then fervently. I wanted all she could offer me. My heart was calling her.

I wanted to feel all of her against all of me, free of inhibitions, free of clothing. I began to help her out of her chemise. She helped me out of mine and then, she lay on top of me again. I felt something melt and run down the inside of my thigh. This time it was not mine, it was hers. She was melting too.

My heart was beating, beckoning, yearning for her to find it. "Come and find me. Catch me if you can." It seemed to be saying.

The feel of her against me was powerful. She pressed her pelvis into mine. She stroked my body with gentle hands. She caressed my arms and legs. I returned the caresses in kind, learning by shadowing.

I was overwhelmed with sensory information. I was learning what it was to be touched. I was learning how to touch. Every experience was exquisite. To touch her was almost too much. To feel her touching me was both frightening and invigorating. I wanted her to stop so I could experience what it was to touch her, but I could not bear to imagine the loss I would feel if she did.

I was lost in a confluence of limbs. Which were mine? I could feel her skin with my fingers. I could feel her fingers with my skin. I felt the weight of her pressing against me. I could not get close enough.

My heart pounded. The more she touched me and stroked me, the more I wanted. As we danced together, I felt the supple muscles of her graceful body grow tauter and more sinewy.

The air around us became scented with the delicate aroma of freshly baked bread and the exotic, pungent scent of grapefruit rind.

Slowly, I felt a tremendous ripple that started somewhere below my umbilicus. It rippled up deep inside me. Ripple after ripple, wave after wave, I felt as if she were the mighty goddess of the sea. Surely she could control the ocean, for she had set it free inside me.

Our breathing matched the waves of the ocean crashing inside my body. She was beautiful. Her cheeks were flushed in the rising sun. Her eyes were glazed and out-of- focus. Her lovely lips were swollen and rosy. She was breathing with her mouth open and struggling to refrain from screaming.

Her lovely red hair was quite disheveled. At that moment, I had never seen a more beautiful woman. I knew I wanted to spend my life with her always.

She took my heart and she took my breath away, and yet, I felt she gave me life.

Unity

When I awakened, I was lying alone in bed. I was chilled and then realized the bedding was in some disarray and that I was without clothing.

Last night had not been a dream after all. My nudity bore witness to that. I was naked and my bare skin still smelled of her.

I pulled my chemise from the wreckage and put it on over my head. I rose to make the bed. I was surprised to find that my usually strong body was quite fatigued. As I stood, my legs trembled and I felt as wobbly as a newborn foal.

Slowly I made the bed. As I did, I thought of Madeline, her flushed cheeks and disheveled hair. When I made a move to straighten the bed sheets, I moved in just such a way as to reawaken the dormant sea. The thundering waves of last night sent ripples up my middle. I could still feel her touch commanding the seas inside me.

I had to sit on the edge of the bed for a moment while I gathered my strength.

Princess Madeline came into the room fully dressed but looking pale and weak.

I forgot about my own fatigue and rose quickly to my feet. It was a regrettable choice and I promptly found myself back on the bed, feeling lightheaded.

From my position on the bed I asked, "Are you well Maddy? You look quite pale."

The Princess seemed to struggle with an answer. My mind immediately took me down a frightening path. Had we committed a great crime? Was she in trouble? Was I to blame? Was I in trouble? What would become of her? What would become of me?

"Was it last night that makes you feel ill?" I asked, cringing deep inside myself, afraid to hear the answer.

Her expression softened and she strode over to the bed and sat beside me. She put her arm around me and said, "No, never Willow, last night was the most beautiful experience in my life! Could you not tell?"

"Is it your mother? Has Edward done something?" I could feel panic rising quickly to the surface.

She gently placed her free hand over my lips. I could smell my scent on her fingers, and I felt the ripples again. "I did not wish to alarm anyone," she began. "I, too, have been ill for a while."

"Why did you not say something?" I felt protective and possessive and hurt all at the same time. My emotions seemed far more potent when I was around her.

"I did not wish to draw attention away from Mother. It is she we brought you here to heal. She is our Queen, not I." She answered honestly.

"You are important as well. You have tended to the needs of the Kingdom in your mother's absence. That makes you an important asset to this country as well! Do not make less of yourself because you are not 'Queen,' Madeline, you are so very important to your people!" I realized too late that my tone was harsher than I had intended. I was feeling agitated and did not understand why.

Madeline had folded her hands in her lap and now she looked down and studied her fingers. She looked as if she wanted to cry. I felt my heart breaking because I knew it was my doing. Why was I so agitated?

"How long have you been ill?" I asked, trying to see clear of my emotions.

"I can not speak to you if you are going to be cross with me." She said.

She was right. I was cross and I did not know why. I was learning so much and the more I learned in life, the more I found I had yet to learn.

"I am sorry. I have so many emotions taking hold of me today. I am not certain whether I should laugh or cry or run from the room screaming." I confessed.

"Do you regret what we did last night?" She asked.

"Nay! As you said, 'twas the most beautiful experience I have ever had in my life. I can not imagine sharing such an experience with anyone other than you. Only with you." I said wrapping my arm around her shoulders in a one-arm embrace.

"What seems to be causing all the emotions then?" She asked. Her lower lip formed into a small pout. I felt she was being defensive, but then again, 'twas probably me.

"I do not know." I answered. I suspected that perhaps Madame Rosmerta would understand it. "I just know that all my emotions seem to be swollen larger than they should be, and they are all very near the surface."

"That is how I feel as well." She conceded with a nod. "Perhaps we are both feeling a little vulnerable after sharing so much of ourselves so intimately last night."

"I believe you could be right. I have never experienced anything so intimate and emotional as I did with you last night." I replied thoughtfully.

"Nor have I." She stated matter-of-factly.

"Never?" I was incredulous. "But what about Prince Alexander..." I could feel myself going down a path I was not certain I wanted to venture down. I stopped myself mid-sentence.

"Never." She stated again more firmly. She held my gaze with her green eyes. "I want you to hear me. I was married..."

I dropped my gaze, not wanting to pursue the subject of her dead husband.

She reached out and cupped my chin in her hand and lovingly rested her forehead upon mine. Keeping my head down, I looked up at her through my upper lashes.

"Willow listen to me," she begged. She sat up and I lifted my head a fraction and her eyes sought mine. She appeared to be searching for something, as one does when peering in windows at the marketplace. She seemed to find it and held my gaze, peering first in one eye and then the other. "Now, then," she began, sounding as though she had found her strength again. "Please, just listen."

"I am listening." I said, willing myself to be open to what she had to say.

"I was married. That is true. My marriage was purely political. I did it for Mother's sake, and for Phillip. I knew Father was becoming restless and that he would kill someone soon if I did not do as he wished. He chose Alexander and I was forced to accept him. It took the pressure off of Phillip long enough for Mother to send him away to safety.

So, you see Willow, I was married, but not with my heart and surely not with my soul. I take you into my heart and soul. Alexander never got past the flesh."

I dropped my gaze again. I did not wish to have my eyes betray me.

"Willow, what is it?" she asked.

"He touched you. Everywhere I touched you, he has

already been!"

"Willow, he left smudges and grimy fingerprints on my flesh. When he touched me, it was only for his pleasure. Your caresses and gentle kisses washed away his grimy paw prints! Your kind and gentle spirit has been balm for my wounds. He is gone from my life. He was never in my heart."

I could say nothing. There were no words. I was left with only raw, naked emotions. I felt my eyes well with tears. I did not wish to cry. I would fight it.

The first tear freed itself of my lower lashes and paved a trail for the other tears to follow. I wept until I shook. Madeline held me in her arms and rocked me.

"Your Highness," I began.

"It was so lovely when you just called me Madeline. Please, I prefer it." She spoke softly into my hair. I could feel her breath on my skin.

"Madeline, I've never experienced any of this before." I confessed.

"None of it?" It was her turn to be incredulous. "Really? Loving seems to come so naturally for you. I fell in love with you while watching how you tended to Mother."

"The closest relationships I have had, have been with Magda, who has been both mother and teacher to me, Galynda, my best friend and sister, Ahmad, who has been a father to me, and Aunt Ahnja, Magda's sister."

"Galynda? Why have I not heard mention of her?" Madeline asked.

"I am sorry to have confused you. Has no one informed you?"

"Of what? She asked.

"Princess Ra Ahnan, her familiar name is Galynda. She is my cousin and best friend. We grew up together, so she is more like a sister to me. When we were old enough, the Elders arranged for us to share a wagon."

"And were you intimate with her?" she asked cautiously.

It seemed it was her turn to feel the bitter bite of jealousy. "I have noticed that she has been very cool toward you since her arrival here."

"It would appear that a lot of people thought that we had an intimate relationship." I admitted. "I believe that is one of the reasons our elders decided that we should share a wagon.

In answer to your question, nay, we were never lovers. We were intimate with our hearts, Aye. We told each other everything. We had no secrets.

"Now your Princess, Galynda, really does have something to be upset about." How are we going to deal with that?" Madeline asked me.

She had said 'we' I rather liked the sound of that. I was not certain what should be done about it, but more pressing things demanded our attention at the moment.

That reminds me, Your Highness..." I raised my hand to wave off her protestations about my formal use of her title. "It would seem that you have come to the Royal Physician with an illness. How long have you been feeling ill?"

"Right." She nodded. "It started when Father hurt mother this last time. I thought, perhaps, that it was brought on by worry," she said, standing and pacing. She was wringing her hands.

"Tell me what this illness has been like for you." I requested.

"I have no desire to eat. My stomach is so nervous that each time I eat, I feel nauseated."

"Do you retch and vomit?" I asked.

Her face turned a mild shade of green and she covered her mouth with one hand and her stomach with the other.

"That would be 'aye' then."

"Yes, she said nodding. I have also felt faint at times."

"Have you been able to stomach tea?"

"Yes, a little," she said nodding. "And I was able to drink a bit of the gingerroot water you prepared for Mother."

"I should like to take your pulses if that is acceptable to you." I said.

"It is," she said seating herself on the bed and extending her arm to me.

"Rest it in your lap and let me come to you." I instructed.

I seated myself beside her and took her feminine wrist in my hand. It was my turn to listen to the pulses that coursed through her body.

My thoughts were interrupted by a knock at the door.

I recognized it as Magda's knock. "Come in Magda," I invited. "Would you please come in and close the door."

"You are taking pulses." Turning to the Princess, Magda asked, "Are you feeling ill, child?"

"Her Highness has been feeling somewhat ill since the time of the Queen's attack." I explained.

Looking back to the Princess I asked, "Did you find that you felt better with the water?"

"Yes, I did." She answered, looking thoughtful.

"Your Highness, do you awaken feeling sick and tired but find that you feel better as the day goes on?" I continued.

"Yes, there are some days that I do feel better in the evenings, she answered, nodding. Oh, but there are others, when I feel I shall not make it through. It has been hard to keep this illness hidden. I must admit that I have been terrified I might lose my dignity while I am tending to the Royal duties. So far, I have been able to maintain my composure but I have had some very near misses."

"Your Highness," I said gravely, "I believe that I know what has been causing you to feel ill." I said.

"You do?" she asked. "Can you cure it?"

"You Highness," I smiled and shook my head. "You will have to deal with this 'illness,' as you call it, for the rest of your life."

"What is it?" She asked, looking panicked.

"When was your last moon cycle?" I pressed her.

"With all that is happening with my family, I do not recall, I am late this month. I may have missed last month all together, why?"

"Your Highness is soon to make the Queen a grandmother." I said.

Her face was at once paler and then flushed. She was stunned silent for a short time. Just as suddenly, she snapped out of her stupor. "I must go to Mother at once!"

"I am certain she could use the happy news. I will tend to her after you have had your visit. Would you like me to send for Prince Phillip as well?"

"Oh, yes, that is a wonderful idea. Thank you." She hugged me and then Magda as she left the room.

"That, I believe, is good news for this Kingdom," I said.

"I quite agree. Emily and Constance have told me terrifying stories of the wicked King Edward. This Kingdom could use a bit of light after all the darkness and trouble he has brought to this place.

I came to see if you would care to take a walk with me in the orchard today. It seems so long since I have been outdoors." Magda said.

"That is a delightful idea. We have been so busy since we arrived. I had quite forgotten that I had not been outdoors until last night. Let me grab my brace and boot...what am I saying! Let us make haste! I look forward to feeling the grass between my toes!"

"Willow," she began. "Your hair might benefit from a good brushing."

It occurred to me that she might be quite right. I could still see the vision of Madeline in my arms, with her hair in great disarray. I wondered if mine was equally as mussed and assumed that it must be. I wondered, too, if Magda knew what the Princess and I had done all night.

"I was so tired last night. I tended to the Queen and went to bed straight away without brushing my hair." I confessed.

This was true, I had brushed it the first time I had gone to bed, in the castle, but I had not done so here in the cabin. "It must look frightful." I finished abruptly, for fear of prattling on nervously.

I hobbled to the wardrobe for my clothing.

"Not frightful, but certainly not very dignified when you are in the service of royalty." Magda stated.

"Enid showed me to this room last night after I saw the Queen. I was asleep when the Princess came in and went to bed." I confessed as I clambered into my clothing

"You mean the Princess slept here, with you?" She asked.

I froze inside. I frantically undid the thong on my braid. Perhaps she knew what we had done. Had we made too much noise? Had we disturbed the others? "Aye." I answered, averting my eyes as I fumbled to undo the braid.

"That explains where you and she slept, and if Emily was in with Enid, and Ahnja and Rosmerta were in with me, where was Galynda all night?" she puzzled, counting out beds and rooms on her fingers. "By my count, she should have been here with you and Princess Madeline."

"You mean she was not with you?" I asked. I sighed, relieved for the moment that the focus was not on me and my merry making. I raked viciously through my hair with my brush.

"Nay," my concerned mother shook her head. "I was hoping you could account for her whereabouts." She continued, seemingly oblivious to the nervous ferocity with which I brushed my hair.

"Galynda was with me through the tunnels." I offered. "When we arrived here, I visited with the Queen before retiring. I have not seen her since." I stated thoughtfully while I rapidly braided my hair into two plaits. I secured each with a tie and tucked them both snuggly under my hat.

We descended the stairs single file. Magda followed behind to watch my gait. I gingerly took the stairs one at a time leaning heavily on the rail as much to protect my foot as to support my wobbly legs.

As we crossed the sitting room, I could smell tea steeping already and knew the rest of the group would be awake soon.

"Magda, I am worried about what you said. Do you feel we should be concerned?" I asked. "Do you think Edward could have discovered our refuge?" The anxiety in me was growing with every new thought that seeped into my brain. "I think we should forgo our walk and search for Galynda instead." I whispered.

In the semi-darkness of the room Ahmad's head appeared over the back of the sofa. "What is this? Our own little Princess is missing? Do you want that I should help with the searching?" He asked in a sleepy voice.

He was such a good and loving man. I adored him. Now, more than ever, I appreciated his gentle and protective nature. I knew in my heart that he was Magda's soul mate and it made me glad to know they had each other.

"Willow," Magda said gently. "We know that she made it here safely with the rest of us. It simply does not make sense that she would venture on her own." She said shaking her head. "Nearly every time we could not find her as a child, it was because she had gone somewhere with you. Since we know where you are, but have not found Galynda, we have reason to be concerned."

It was uncharacteristic of my blind sister to go anywhere unaccompanied. After my revelation in the cave, I understood Galynda's vulnerability more deeply and fully shared their concern.

My learned sense of obligation battled with my innate sense of family. I was torn by this inner conflict, which made my thought processes obscure and muddy. I took a deep breath and a moment to calm myself. The sage voice of reason advised me. "Everyone can search for Galynda, but only you can attend to the Queen."

I agreed with this logic. "I really must attend to the Queen. I shall tend to my duties here, and then I shall be able to concentrate on the search. I fear we have all gotten off to a late start today because of all the commotion last night." I reasoned.

"That is a wise decision, Willow. It is also wise to keep your foot bound and warm." Magda prudently advised. "Ahmad and I shall have a look around the orchard and grounds. We shall return in about an hour's time to see if you have learned anything about Galynda."

Having decided to forgo the barefoot frolic in the orchard, I decided I would appear more dignified in the service of the Queen if I were shod. I stumped up the stairs in lopsided fashion to fetch my boot and brace. As I was descending the stairs to the sitting room, I encountered Princess Madeline. She grasped my arm and steered me back up the stairs toward the room we shared.

"Something is bothering you?" I asked, puzzled.

"You are not going to believe this!" she began with an enormous smile. I went down to visit Mother, to share the news about the baby. When I entered her room, she was there visiting with Phillip." My companion gushed with excitement.

"What were they visiting about?" I blinked, dizzy with the fast pace at which topics of conversation and their accompanying moods were changing.

"Phillip has found a bride!" she exclaimed.

"He has?" I blinked again, stunned. "That is wonderful! That is more good news for your family. I am so happy for you!" I embraced her. I meant what I said. Her family had suffered enough. It was time they had good news.

"Willow, it is very good news! It is good news for your family as well! Phillip has asked Princess Ra Ahnan to be his wife and she has conceded to marry him!"

My head was a little foggy. My brain was moving just a

bit too slowly. Prince Phillip of the High Plains had asked Princess Ra Ahnan, Galynda, to marry him. She had accepted his offer and she would be living in this very Kingdom in the castle. My beloved Lynd was no longer a nomad! She had a home!

"Willow, say something!" Madeline pleaded.

"Oh Maddy, that is wonderful!" I exclaimed. "It took me a moment to process what you just said. That is great news. I am just having a bit of a focusing problem this morning."

"You too?" She asked with a smile.

I smiled back and continued, "Magda and Ahmad just left to search for Lynd. Apparently, she has been missing all night. I guess we know who she was with last night."

"I wonder if they had as much fun as we did." She mused with raised eyebrows.

"I have my doubts about that." I said matter-of-factly. "Coupling is forbidden before marriage in our clan and Galynda is far too proper to succumb to passion before marriage."

"That is truly sad," she said with a pout. "Looks as though I found the rebel in your clan, did I not?" She teased.

"Has anyone spoken to Ahnja? Does she know yet?" I asked

"Princess Ra Ahnan or Princess Galynda, would like to meet with her mother and then with mine!" Madeline said placing both hands upon her chest and then offering her arms to me in a tight embrace.

"We have a very big day in front of us." I said. "I shall attend to your mother and then we should all have something to eat.

"We can discuss all the plans at breakfast." She said; those of the new couples, and those of the castle."

Solidarity

Enid and Emily were working merrily side by side in the kitchen preparing breakfast. The cottage was filled with the smell of bacon and freshly brewed tea.

With the delicious smell of bacon, I realized how hungry I was. I suspected that Madeline would be famished as well.

The door swung open and Magda and Ahmad entered the small sitting room. They brought the cool, fresh air in with them. Their rosy cheeks and noses bore testimony to the briskness of the day outside.

"Magda, Ahmad," I summoned them with a gesture and guided them to a corner of the sitting room where we would not be overheard.

"Have you found Galynda?" they whispered in unison.

"Galynda is safe." I nodded vigorously. "She has been here in the cottage all along. Princess Madeline has informed me that Galynda has been tending to important business for the Royal Family. We shall be apprised of all that has transpired at breakfast."

"But all is well?" Ahmad questioned. His face was pale, eyebrows were raised. He stroked his moustache with the palms of both hands. I assured him that all, was indeed, well and that I had been so taken in by the morning's events that I still had not been to the Queen's bedside.

When the color had returned to his face, I excused myself and turned to go to the cellar. I walked through the warm kitchen into the pantry and made my way down the stairs. This group of rooms must have required quite a lot of planning. The cellar was not damp and in the daylight, I could see that it was not dark either.

The fireplace, I supposed shared a chimney with the one above in the kitchen. I could see natural light filtering in through the ceiling of the Queen's room, this interested me.

"It is made of thick glass and mortar." The Queen said. Apparently, she had seen me looking at the ceiling with curiosity.

"A very good morning to you, Your Majesty." I curtsied as I entered the room. "I trust your spirits are having a wonderful day. How about your body? How is it feeling today?"

"Willow, Madeline tells me she is to have a child. That is wonderful news. She has requested that I keep you on here to help her through the pregnancy and childbirth."

"As you wish Your Majesty," I said with a bow. "I shall make it so."

"Not so quickly, Willow," the Queen cautioned. "Madeline would like to request that you stay on and help her tend to and raise the baby as well."

"As a nursemaid, Your Majesty?" I began to feel stirrings of anger. I did not wish to stay here if my stay meant I was to be a servant.

"Oh, dear me, no!" She said placing a hand upon her chest. "I felt certain you knew what Madeline's intentions were. Let me clarify. I am sorry for the confusion."

She started again. "Madeline has expressed deep affection for you since your arrival. She tells me that you share her feelings and she has asked if I would invite you to stay on as her consort and help her raise my grandchild as a second parent."

Consort? Parent? Staying on and settling down. My mind reeled. What a great deal I had to think about all at once.

"Begging your pardon, Your Majesty, but the Princess and I have not discussed any of this yet. Before we made this journey to treat you, I was not even aware that my tribe would allow me to take a lover. Now, here I am before you, a great and respected Queen. You are offering me a treasure that I am not certain I have any right to accept."

"Who do I need to meet with? I know I must speak with Ahnja to get her permission for Phillip to marry the Princess Ra Ahnan." She processed aloud, without permitting me space to answer.

"Are you feeling strong enough for all of this Your Majesty?" I asked.

"All of this is what makes me feel stronger." She replied with a soft twinkle in her eye.

"I ask this because Princess Madeline was planning 'to discuss plans for the new couples and the castle' at breakfast this morning." Then it occurred to me, she had said 'couples'. I shall have to learn to pay better attention.

"Do you feel strong enough to join us? You could address our Elders when we are all together. If they feel the need to discuss the matter in private, they shall arrange a time when they can give the matter their full attention."

"That is a splendid idea. I am growing weary of lying about in bed all day."

"How would you feel if I were to have Rosmerta come down and help you dress and put up your hair?" I asked.

"That is a lovely idea." She clapped her hands together and clasped them in happiness.

"I have another idea, Majesty, how would you feel if we surprised everyone. I shan't tell a soul, save for Rosmerta, that you are coming to breakfast."

"Oh, I do love how you think!" she said with a sparkle in her eye.

The transformation I could see before my eyes was amazing. Her chapped lips were healing nicely, the color was returning to her cheeks, and the circles under her eyes, though present, were less prominent.

"Let's feel your pulses then, your Grand Highness." I said with a sly smile.

"Oh, I *am* going to be a Grandmother soon!" she exclaimed. My witticism was not lost on her. I was glad that she understood me and liked the way I thought.

"Your pulses are feeling every bit as improved as you are. Are you having any pain?"

"No pain, only joy." She answered with a smile.

Madeline had said her mother was a powerful speaker. I could tell by her lyrical voice that she would be pleasant to listen to.

"How do you feel when you sit up? Any dizziness or light headedness?"

"I have been testing the waters when no one is looking." She confessed. "I have even walked about a tiny bit."

"That is good news. Begging your pardon, but are you passing your water without pain or blood?" I continued my inquiry.

"Yes. I can pass my water freely and there is no pain or blood." She replied.

"Have you been able to..." How did one ask a queen if she could move her bowels? Even queens have to move their royal bowels for themselves. There is no servant who can do that for them.

"Have I been able to move my bowels? Yes. Has it been painless? A little dry, but yes, painless." The Queen was blissfully indulging in the reverie of all the good news her children had blessed her with.

I quietly offered a prayer of thanksgiving that that awkward moment had passed with little difficulty. "The dryness is due to the blood loss; I shall add something to your stew to help with that. Have you had any more bleeding?"

"No, none." She said proudly.

"With your permission, I would like to examine the tissue that was injured. I would prefer to have Madame Rosmerta here for that. As your personal midwife, she is familiar with the unique structures of your body and she shall know if you have mended properly. Would that be acceptable to you?"

"Yes." She said.

"Then, if you will excuse me, I shall summon Madame Rosmerta and order up your breakfast."

"Permission granted, dear." She answered with a smile.

I found Madame Rosmerta, barely awake, near the hearth in the sitting room huddled over her cup of tea.

"Good morning, Bunny, how are you?" She asked, smiling and reaching out to hold my hand.

"I am doing very well, thank you. May I speak with you for a moment, please?"

"Do I have to abandon my tea?" She asked with only one eye open.

"Nay, you may bring your tea along with you." I replied offering my hand to help her to her feet.

As we passed through the kitchen, I asked Emily if she had brought provisions for the Queen's stew. "Yes ma'am, I have the stew over the fire in the sitting room. Why do you think Rosmerta was sitting so close to the fire? She is worse than a cat in the fish market that one!"

"I would like you to add these herbs a half hour before the stew is finished cooking." I said. I had placed a small handful of herbs in a small gauze bag and handed it to Emily.

Emily took the herbs in one hand and gave Rosmerta a friendly swat on the behind with the other, as we left the room for the pantry. Over her shoulder the cook said, "Aye, just so you know, the kitchen staff made you a fresh batch of the gauze bags in different sizes as we have been using so many."

"Oh, thank you!" I replied. I meant it. I suspected my own bags were quite tattered and stained with use. I loved the convenience of the pull string bags but my fondness for sitting still long enough to make them, was not over-much.

Rosmerta closed the pantry trapdoor behind us and pulled me down into a sitting position on the stairs beside her. "Oh, Willow," she whispered. "You could not wait for me, could you? You have the glow of someone who has had a night of passion!"

I clapped my hands to my cheeks. "Have I? Does it show?" I whispered hoarsely.

She shook her head to the negative. "Only because I know what to look for, Bunny." She smiled reassuringly and raised her cup to her lips. "So, how did it go? Tell Madame Rosmerta everything." Even in the semi darkness, I could see the smile twinkling in her eyes.

"Rosmerta!" I blushed.

"Well, maybe not *everything*." She corrected herself. "Was it right for you? Did you feel comfortable with the intimacy? Did you feel awkward? That is the sort of 'everything' I meant." She said with a wink that told me I could reveal as little or much as I was comfortable with.

"You are enjoying this." I accused.

"Pleasure is what I do best," she nodded taking another sip of tea. "Out with it!" she gestured desperately with her free hand. "How was it? Tell me, tell me, tell me," she begged.

Her mirth was contagious. I had to smile in spite of my shyness about the subject matter.

"I was worried about not knowing what to do or how to go about things. I was scared it might hurt, or that I might hurt her, but once we were in the moment, the messages in my head were overshadowed by what I was feeling in my body. I just let my body lead me. I had no idea what to do. I just shadowed what she was doing and I did not feel as awkward as I thought I would. It was very much like dancing to a very primal rhythm. We danced and we swayed until the rhythm took over our hearts and then our bodies in a great crescendo."

"It sounds as though everything went well. You were even able to achieve an orgasm, then." She replied peering over her cup of tea. "The crescendo part." She remarked with a wink.

"Aye." I answered shyly. "When does the pulsating go away?" I asked, beginning to feel stupid.

She spilled some of her tea on herself. "Ay!" she exclaimed, shaking the offended hand. Rosmerta leaned in toward me and whispered. "You are *still* feeling it?" She was incredulous.

"Aye." I replied matter-of-factly.

"That is amazing! Good for you!" She said, lovingly leaning into me. "Enjoy it. There are some people who do not experience that at all." She smiled as she took another sip from her tea.

"It does make focusing on other things rather difficult." I explained.

"Well, yes, I can understand where that might be a bit difficult." She nodded. "They will fade with time. You should be able to achieve orgasm again the next time you couple. I am so happy for you! How do you feel now?"

"I feel a lot of strong emotions all at once." I answered honestly.

"It is perfectly normal for a woman to become emotional after such intimate self-expression." Rosmerta stated sagely over the brim of her cup.

"My whole life may be about to change because of it." I muttered. "We can talk about that later. What we need to do now, is examine the Queen's wounds and get her up and dressed for breakfast."

"I shall hold you to your word, Willow." She said winking and pointing her finger at me.

"I know you shall, but right now our Queen is awaiting her physicians." I smiled, relieved that, for now, the harem lessons were over.

We walked together in silence to the Queen's room. She was resting quietly, tucked neatly under her covers.

"Your Majesty, I have brought the sleepy Lady Rosmerta to help me." I greeted her with a smile.

"Good morning Rosmerta! The Queen opened her eyes and reached out for both of Rosmerta's hands. I have just learned this morning that our Maddy is with child!" she proudly announced.

"Rosmerta looked from the Queen to me." She had a puzzled expression on her face.

"She was not feeling well this morning, and since we shared a room, I could not help but notice it. When I asked her what she was experiencing, her answers and pulses confirmed it. She is with child. She is not much more than two or three moon cycles along.

The Queen addressed her consort. "Rosmerta, I would like your assistance preparing for breakfast. There are some very pressing matters to attend to and I would very much like to be at the table with everyone else this morning." She requested.

"It would be my pleasure, Alyss." Rosmerta beamed

"With your permission, we shall need to examine the injury site, once that is done, I can leave you two alone." I said.

"Your Highness, I am going to ask Rosmerta to do an internal exam to see how well your tissues have healed. It may be a little uncomfortable or even a little painful."

"We are going to wash our hands and then we shall begin." I explained to the Queen.

Madame Rosmerta performed the examination. "Everything is in the correct position and aside from a little swelling; everything appears to be healing beautifully." She announced with a relieved smile.

"Your Highness, in a case such as this, I feel that since Rosmerta has served as your midwife, she understands the natural lay of your internal structures better than I could. I trust Madame Rosmerta's judgment. I do not feel that it is necessary for you to endure this exam again unless you want a second opinion. If that will be all, I shall remove myself so that you may prepare for breakfast." I curtsied and waited to be excused.

"Thank you for your sensitivity, Willow. I appreciate your gentle, compassionate wisdom." The monarch said.

"You are most welcome Your Majesty. I try to imagine myself in my patient's position. I know that I would not wish to endure painful, degrading examinations unnecessarily."

"You are wise beyond your years." Rosmerta commented.

"I have Magda to thank for that." I said with a bow.

"I look forward to seeing you soon. Shall I send someone to assist you with the stairs?"

"I think we can manage, and if we can not, we shall call out," said the Queen.

"As you wish." I curtsied and left the room.

I ascended into the delightful scent of smoked bacon, fried potatoes and freshly baked bread.

I encountered Galynda, engaged in a conversation with her mother, Magda and Ahmad as they huddled in a tight circle at the foot of the stairs. They were speaking in hushed tones. I understood what the meeting might be about and did not approach the group directly but greeted them on my way up the stairs, "Good morning everyone."

"Oh, Willow," Galynda said. "I want very much to speak with you."

"Whenever you wish," I replied. I am free right now."

"May we speak before breakfast?" she requested, rising from her seat near the fire.

"Of course," I nodded, extending my arm for her. "Where would you like for us to go?" I asked.

"We shan't go far, 'tis nearly time to eat." Galynda said. "I shall try to be brief."

I could see Madeline having an animated conversation with her brother at the far end of the sitting room. "How about we go to the room where I slept last night?" I offered. "'Tis not far and it is vacant at the moment."

"Take me there, then." Her hand was in my elbow and I was stumping up the stairs and guiding her into the privacy of the small bedchamber in no time. I helped her find a seat on the bed and I went to close the door.

"Willow," she began. "Willow, are you certain this is the room you were in last night?" she asked with an expression on her face that seemed to be a mix of confusion and distaste.

"Yes, quite, why?" I forged ahead knowing a storm was brewing.

Her face reddened and her brows furrowed. I could see that she was battling some unseen foe in her mind.

"Please tell me you did not couple in here with that Rosmerta woman!" she blurted.

I was stunned. She was so accurate and yet, so wrong. "No, Lynd, I did not couple with Madame Rosmerta." I answered honestly. "She is a friend and a teacher, but she is not my lover."

"I can smell it on you. I know you have lain with someone in this very bed. Do not lie to me Willow, I could not take it if you lied to me." Her voice rumbled in a low and threatening tone as thunder does.

"Lynd, I have never lied to you. We have always shared everything. I have wanted to tell you for so long about everything that I have learned and everything that has happened since Magda and I came here, but everything is happening so fast. I feel as though I have not had any time to process everything, let alone, share it with you!" I wailed.

"I know and I am very sorry for my behavior too." She apologized. Her eyes grew bright with tears and I knew she meant it.

"Lynd," I began. "I came here looking for a home for all of us, but especially for you. I wanted you to find a place that you could memorize and call home. It would be a place you would never have to feel lost in. That is what I wanted to find for you here."

"I know Willow, and you did!" she said. Silent tears broke free of her lashes and trailed down her cheeks. "You found us all a place to live out the rest of our days and for that, I am truly, truly grateful."

"Do you want to hear a story Lynd?"

"You would not be trying to change the subject would you Willow?" she asked. I could tell by the tone in her voice that she had arched a suspicious eyebrow at me.

"Nay, of course not." I answered. "Actually, it is right on the subject, it is relevant and I want you to hear it first." I said, draping an arm around her shoulder.

"Oh, very well, let's hear your fascinating tale then." She said leaning into me. "That feels nice." She smiled. "I have missed you."

"I have missed you as well, Lynd. So much has happened since we arrived here. I know we have not been here so very long, but I feel a great deal has changed for us all.

When I left you, you were just 'Lynd,' my very best friend and sister. Now, you are 'Princess Ra Ahnan'. When did that happen? That is not a small secret to keep from me. That is huge! I nearly fainted when you rose as a distinguished guest of the Royal Family! Someone should have told me!"

"I never told you anything about it because you knew as much as I did. We grew up together you were there with me. You heard the people call me the Little Princess."

"Aye, but I certainly did not know that you were a *real* Princess!"

"Actually, neither did I. Mama brought the crown to me the night of the feast. She gave me a little background on my father and told me that he was known, even to strangers, as the 'Gypsy King'."

"Now I am going to marry a Prince!" she blurted with excitement.

"This is all so very sudden." I said.

"Not so very sudden. While you have been healing the Queen, I have been keeping company with the Prince. It all started, at the big feast. We sat up most of the night and just talked. He asked me who he needed to ask for my hand in marriage. I never thought that would happen to me, not in a million years!" she said shaking her head.

"I am so happy for you!" I said, and I squeezed her against me and leaned into her at the same time. "Congratulations!"

"Phillip loves his mother and his sister very much." Galynda continued. "After their horrible experience with his father, he did not wish to bring any more negative people into the castle. He was under so much pressure to find a wife that he very nearly made a regrettable mistake. Thankfully, someone from the castle sent him a message to return home straight away and that is just what he did."

"Now, may I tell you my story?" I asked.

"You are certain that you will not stray from the subject?" she asked.

"Positive!"

"Very well then," she said in her very best Princess voice, "carry on."

"While I was attending to the Queen, I was staying in the harem with Madame Rosmerta so she could act as my etiquette coach, or so I thought.

On our way out here, we had learned that Rosmerta was a courtesan. When I was otherwise occupied, Magda had told Rosmerta that she suspected that I was 'of the third sex'. She asked if Rosmerta would talk to me about it and encourage me to live a fuller life by considering the possibility of accepting love into my life. The whole idea of accepting love in my life was a foreign concept for me, but Rosmerta can be persistent.

I figured out early on that Madame Rosmerta was more loyal to her Queen than any royal subject. She told me that she has have been with the Queen since before Edward was ever King.

Princess Madeline, a very recent widow, thanks to King Edward, seems to take after her mother. She has taken quite an interest in her mother's physician. That would be me." I paused here to catch a breath. "Anyway, as the days have passed, Princess Madeline has become a more prominent feature in my days and well, as of last night, my nights as well.

This morning, the Princess was not feeling well. I asked her about it and took her pulses to be sure. Lynd, she is pregnant! I swear. I made an 'x' across my heart. "The baby is not mine!" I teased.

Galynda gave me a crooked half-smile and a mildly disapproving arch to her eyebrow.

I continued. "Anyway, Madeline had to run and tell her mother the news. The Queen is going to ask the Elders if they might let us live as a couple!"

"Wow! That is an amazing story. I am getting married. You are starting a family! We are becoming sisters-in-law."

"So you see, 'twas a captivating story and very much on the subject." I said, quite satisfied with myself.

"Congratulations, Willow. I am happy for you." She said. "I only became upset when I thought you were giving yourself away to a common street wench. You definitely deserve better."

"I have two things I have to say about that. First, I cannot do much better than a Princess, and second, Madame Rosmerta is a dear and trusted friend and teacher. She is not common, and she is certainly no wench." I stated matter-of-factly.

"I promise, Willow, I shall try harder to understand this friendship you have with her." We embraced. "Now," Galynda said, "We had better go back out with the others before they begin to miss us, sister-in-law!" She pressed her forehead to mine.

"Or before they forget about us entirely and just start without us." I added.

I was pleased that the day was starting out well and that Galynda and I had been able to share before everything was brought to the table. There would be no secrets and no surprises.

We arrived at the table just as Rosmerta and the Queen ascended the pantry stairs. Rosmerta announced, "Ladies and gentlemen, I present Her Royal Highness Queen Alyssandra of the High Plains." She waved her hands with a flourish in the Queen's direction.

Everyone cheered to see that the Queen was on her feet and dressed in an ermine edged robe. Phillip and Pieter ran to assist her and Ahmad pulled the chair at the head of the table out for her.

When everyone was seated, Emily and Enid began to serve dishes heaping with steaming fried bacon and eggs, and herbed potatoes.

There was pleasant, jocular conversation as we ate our

meal. I knew it was not in keeping with tradition for royalty to dine with the staff, nor was it customary for them to dine with ordinary villagers. Here, we had a mix of everything.

I watched the Royal Family silently as they observed the joy with which common, ordinary folks ate and chatted and joked. I was pleased to see smiles on their faces. This was what I had wanted Madeline to experience that morning in the castle, camaraderie with no preferential treatment. It seemed to be working.

When the meal was ended, the men, including Prince Phillip, cleared the table. The great stack of dishes was given a thorough washing by the women, including Princess Madeline. I taught her how to wash dishes and she only broke one cup. When she did, everyone gave a great whooping cheer.

The men stood by and dried the dishes as quickly as they were washed. Since it was Gus's home, he was in charge of getting everything put away in proper order. He and Ahmad took the stacks of cups and dishes that Pieter and the Prince dried, and they returned everything to its cupboard.

Emily and Enid had prepared tea for the after-breakfast meeting. Cups were passed out to those who wanted tea.

The Queen was beginning to look a bit peaked, as was Madeline. I hoped that this meeting would not take its toll on either of them.

"May we please come to order?" The Queen requested. "We have a great many things to discuss before I retire for the day."

Everyone gathered at the table and gave the Queen his or her undivided attention. Cups were left in their saucers on the table and all talking ceased.

"I know we are all concerned about Edward's return to the castle. It is of the greatest importance that we confront that issue with a well-devised plan as soon as we possibly can.

Before we make plans to overtake Edward, I feel it is important to remind you of what we are fighting for.

To our dear allies of the Tsigani Tribe, I ask your counsel on two very important issues.

First, my only son, Prince Phillip requests your permission to marry your precious Princess Ra Ahnan, sacred seer and advisor to the Tribe, Tsigani, Princess Galynda." She gestured toward Galynda.

There was a profound silence, followed by excited murmurings of joy by everyone seated around the great kitchen table. "To the Prince and Princess!" everyone cheered.

The second bit of news involves my daughter, Princess Madeline. She wishes to announce that she bears the first heir to the throne. She learned only this morning that she is with child.

Everyone cheered and congratulated the Princess and the Queen. "Long live Princess Madeline! Congratulations!"

"Finally, I make one more request of our beloved allies of the Tsigani Tribe. It has come to my recent attention that Princess Madeline has found, among you, the person she wishes to raise my grandchild with. She requests your permission to share her life with your treasured healer, Rajani, healer and holy woman to the Tribe, Tsigani, Willow." She extended a gesture toward me.

Everyone at the table looked from one to the other, at first confused and then everyone cheered. "To the Princess and the healer!"

"I feel we all have a tremendous personal stake in this battle. It is of the utmost importance that you all understand the challenge that is facing us. We must eradicate Edward before he can cause more damage to this family. By destroying our family, he shall succeed in destroying our Kingdom entirely."

Strategy

We all huddled closely together to hear and be heard. It was lovely to see people from such diverse perspectives working so smoothly together for a common cause.

"I would like to take care of this issue with as little violence and bloodshed as possible. Unfortunately, I have received word this morning that Edward, finding the castle devoid of any head of household, has invited several rogues in to drink our wine, eat our stores rape our women and generally destroy the palace.

This activity must stop. We must find a way to stop the destruction and the hatred before it takes root in our homeland." The Queen reported.

I raised my hand slightly so that I would be recognized and acknowledged by the Queen. She saw my hand and addressed me. "Yes, Willow, do you have something you wish to add?"

"Aye. If I may, Your Majesty, you still have staff in the castle. If Edward is the barbarian that he is reputed to be, might he be using your staff to serve his needs and wishes?"

"Yes. I imagine that he is." The Queen Replied. "Tell me, what is it you are thinking?"

"The majority of your staff is loyal to you. They shall do whatever it takes to maintain your leadership. I am fearful that without your directive, they may try to wage war on the interlopers, ill-equipped though they are.

What I am proposing is that we send a messenger into the castle and spread the news of our plan to those that are known to be the most loyal to you.

It is quite clear that Edward either has more sympathizers than was first believed, or he has ruined a lot of lives to get back into the castle. Either way, we must approach him and his partisans with caution.

I believe we ought to welcome your King Edward with open arms." I concluded.

Everyone at the table groaned and mumbled in disbelief.

"Please, time is of the essence, let her speak." The Queen spoke with an upraised hand to silence the room.

I continued. "I believe welcoming him home would be the last thing he would expect. The last time he returned to the castle, he left a trail of Royal blood. I am certain he felt that his life was in peril or he would not have fled. I suspect, now that he has returned, that he has brought in reinforcements and does not plan to give up without violence."

"I agree." Her Majesty responded. What do you propose that we do?"

"I believe we should prepare a feast fit for a King." I said with a wink.

"A feast? Emily asked.

"Aye," I said. "Would it not be grand if you and your most trusted staff prepared the most delicious dishes for the King? I am certain Magda and I could provide an ample supply of herbs and spices to give the meal that extra kick."

"Oh, dear me! Yes!" Emily cried as she clapped her hands

together. I would be honored! But shan't he be suspicious if we are only serving to him and his people?"

"You are a genius in the kitchen, dear Emily. I am certain you and your staff will find a way to serve everyone the appropriate meals with no incidence." I said.

"Willow, do you not think he shall be suspicious of such an offering?" Princess Madeline asked from her esteemed seat to the left of her mother, the Queen.

"Of course he shall, which is precisely the reason why we shall enlist Prince Phillip to propose the feast and to personally test the King's food and wine."

"That is unheard of!" declared Gus in disbelief.

"Of course it is!" Magda agreed. "Which, is precisely the reason I believe Willow's plan will work." My sage teacher nodded her support, picking up on the web I was spinning.

Phillip sat proudly to his mother's right. "I shall do everything that is within my power to keep my homeland safe! What, exactly are you proposing?" he asked.

"First of all, we shall give you the antidote to the toxic herb we shall give to the King and his men. The antidote shall make you immune to the effects of the herb we shall put in the food." I answered.

"Actually," Magda added, "all who sit at the table with the Royal Family must take the antidote except for Princess Madeline; we can not risk poisoning her or the child. We must be certain that her food is seasoned with neither herb."

"Willow, Magda, what you are proposing sounds plausible, however, I do see a certain amount of risk for both the Prince and the Princess." Madame Rosmerta interjected.

"Yes, I was about to address that issue myself," added the Queen.

"If I may," I began. "The particular herb I have in mind is not dangerous. It shall only cause those who take it to become paralyzed temporarily. Fortunately for us, its effects are intensified when it is taken in conjunction with wine. The more wine a person consumes, the faster it will take effect and the longer it shall take for the herb's effect to wear off.

We can protect ourselves by taking the antidote and by avoiding the wine. Edward's men will, doubtless, already be drunk when they sit for the meal. What we can anticipate is a general slowing and drowsiness of those who have taken the herb. To Edward, it should appear that his drunken men are passing out from the great volume of wine they have consumed."

"What shall we do with a castle-full of limp barbarians?" Princess Madeline asked with an expression of disgust.

"Treason is a capital offense." Spoke the Queen. "The customary punishment for such a crime is death. During the course of my rule, I have sought alternative punishment for capital offenders in order to avoid putting anyone to death.

Edward knows that I have taken a nonviolent stand and this policy is, perhaps, the very reason he feels secure enough to return."

"Mother, we must devise a policy to ensure that we shan't have further treasonous encounters." Prince Phillip proposed.

"I agree, we should make an example of Father and his followers. But how?" added Princess Madeline.

"That is for you to decide. I wish to be consulted when you have devised your plan." The Queen said. "I must retire to my quarters with all of the activity and excitement today, I fear I have grown quite weary." She said with a gentle smile.

I rose to offer my assistance to the Queen. "I shall help you to your quarters, Your Majesty."

"Thank you, Willow." She said. "You have been a great comfort to me."

As we descended the stairs I stated, "I noticed that your appetite has improved. Did you get enough to eat? I can request that you are given small meals throughout the day so that you can regain your strength more quickly.

Your wounds have healed sufficiently. They are no longer a concern to me. I am concerned about all the blood you lost. It will require some time for your body to regain its strength and to replace the lost blood."

I helped her to sit on the edge of the bed. When she had rested a bit, I helped her to swing her legs onto the bed and lie back. I pulled the coverlets up to her chest and set about adjusting her pillows.

"Would you care for some water or tea or perhaps a bit more of your stew? Your Majesty."

"No, thank you Willow, I would just like to rest." She replied.

"As you wish, Your Majesty." I said.

"Willow,"

"Aye, Your Majesty?"

Since we are to be family, perhaps you might consider addressing me by something other than 'Your Highness' or 'Your Majesty'."

"Very well, how would you prefer to be addressed?" I asked.

"Perhaps you could address me as Alyssandra or Alyss."

"I have heard Madame Rosmerta call you Alyss. Are you certain 'tis not a personal nickname that she has given you? I do not wish to offend her."

"I am certain. My parents called me Alyss when I was a small child. It is the name I use with my intimate friends. I would like to include you in that group." She said with a wan smile.

"Your Majesty, I am honored that you would consider me among your trusted friends. I will do my best to remain in your good graces. If it is quite all right with you, I prefer to call you "Majesty" because you are so majestic. It is a word that speaks to me of fresh air and mountains and kingdoms and the magical people who live in far away places. I feel I would be terribly sad if I could not honor you with such a lovely name."

"I never thought of it as anything more than an isolating title, until now. Of course, I shall treasure it, now that I know what it means to you."

"Thank you, Majesty." I said with a bow, pleased that I would be allowed to have a familiar name for the Queen.

"How are you feeling about Maddy's proposal?" She asked.

"I feel so many things at once, Majesty. I love Madeline. I know she loves me. I want to spend the rest of my days learning about her and what she likes and dislikes. I want to know what frightens her and what comforts her.

Until we came on this journey to your Kingdom, I was unaware that I was allowed or even capable of loving another in the way that I love your Madeline."

"Why is that?" she asked intently.

"It was my errant understanding, that as a *drabarni,* or healer, I was not considered eligible for marriage and therefore did not pursue potential partners."

"Ever?" She sat up in bed, incredulous. "You are so beautiful! You mean to tell me that you have never even felt an attraction to anyone before Maddy?"

"Never." I answered matter-of-factly.

"I will have to have a little talk with that daughter of mine. I would hate to have her frighten you away!" she mumbled to herself.

"If it were not for Rosmerta she just might have." I confessed. "Rosmerta was observing and explaining what was happening at every corner. I am most grateful to her for her patience and kindness. I am not sure what I would have done without her gentle guidance."

"Rosmerta feels a great affection for you as well. She has learned a great deal from you in return. She tells me she has never met anyone as pure of heart and as innocent as you are. She said she wished more people could be like you. If they were, the world would be a much better place."

I was amazed anyone would say such things about me. I thought about how I had watched Rosmerta bathe in the creek and how I felt when I was looking at her body. I thought about the things I had done with the Princess only last night and thinking about her sent the ripples coursing through me anew. No, I had to disagree with Rosmerta. I did not think I was as pure as she felt I was.

"That is a lovely thing to say." I said looking down at my feet. I felt my cheeks flush.

"But you disagree?" She asked.

"I feel that I am learning new things. I have always been a student. Rosmerta's area of expertise is one of my weaker points. Perhaps this is where she finds me so innocent."

"Perhaps." She smiled.

"You are growing weary. I am enjoying this conversation very much, but I do not wish for you to tire yourself. Perhaps we can speak like this another time?" I offered.

"I should like that." She said. "You are right, I am very tired."

Very well, Majesty, I shall let you rest a bit and then I shall see to it that you have more stew brought to you. Is there anyone in particular you wish to have me send it with?"

"Oh, yes." She said with a smile. "I should like to speak with Ra Ahnan, or, Galynda, rather." she corrected herself.

"Very well." I said with a bow.

As an afterthought, I added, "Majesty, Galynda and I are very similar. I hope that she has the opportunity to visit with Madame Rosmerta. She, like I, never anticipated marriage.

I love her very much and because of that love, I feel it is most important that I tell you that her first encounter with a man was not a positive one. She was not harmed but she was very badly shaken up. If I had not been there to intervene, she could have been badly damaged or even killed. I know that Prince Phillip is a kind and gentle soul or she would not trust him as she does, but as her friend and protector, I worry."

"I shall have a talk with my son as well. I would not want to see him lose his bride when it took him so long to find one." She smiled and smoothed the sheets with her hands.

"Thank you for listening Majesty. I hope I have not offended or said the wrong thing. I am not always the most eloquent person. And," I added, "I can be quite clumsy with the finer points of protocol."

"You did just fine. I appreciate your candor. What you have shared with me is important to you and Galynda. Because it was important enough for you to want to share it with me, I shall do what I can to ensure that Galynda feels in control and secure with Phillip at all times. I would like to think that as his mother, I can do that much!" She smiled.

"I feel much better now" I said. "Thank you for listening."

"You are most welcome Willow, dear." She smiled warmly.

Without thinking, I embraced her. For a moment she seemed startled and then she returned the embrace warmly.

"I think I had better go before I break some other rule of protocol!" I said, biting my lower lip.

"The embrace was lovely, Willow. What a tremendous compliment it is that you can see me as warmly as you would a dear friend, rather than a cold, unapproachable queen."

I was relieved that she did not take offense to my spontaneous fit of affection. Again, I felt a wave of overwhelming emotions. I could not allow myself to stay any longer.

"I shall send Galynda with your stew shortly. Rest well, Majesty."

Taking Action

Upstairs, some of the group were still seated around the table discussing the plan of action. The expression on each face was either of determination or deep contemplation.

"Have you come to any conclusions?" I asked as I joined the group at the table.

Enid rose from her seat, took a clean cup and saucer from the center of the table, placed it before me and poured me a cup of steaming tea. "Emily has gone back to the castle to determine how many men Edward has brought with him." Enid explained. "She will also instruct her staff to prepare a great feast which shall be served for the King and his men tomorrow evening."

Gus slid a platter of freshly baked apple tarts toward me adding, "Pieter and Ahmad have gone to the stables to bring back tools and equipment that we may need. Since your wagons are being stored there, Magda went with them in order to replenish the supplies in her medicine bag, and yours. She shall also bring plenty of the paralyzing herb and the antidote herb as well."

The first bite of the still warm apple tart melted on my tongue in a delicious and soothing Manner. If everyone could taste this pastry, all would be well in the world. It was difficult to think about the serious business at hand when I was experiencing such bliss at the tip of my fork.

Phillip added, "Madame Rosmerta has gone to locate the women of the harem and apprise them of our plan. She shall also assess the damage done to the castle and report back to us."

"What is our plan?" I asked, dipping my fork into the flakey crust of the pastry.

"We shall know more when everyone returns, Willow, but for now, we are going to follow your suggestion to drug the food and capture the traitors. We shall hold them in the dungeons until we find the most fitting punishment for their crimes." Madeline offered.

"Lynd, may I speak with you privately for a moment?" I asked, wiping away any evidence of the tart with my napkin.

"Aye." She replied. "Are you all right?" She asked, concerned.

"Aye," I waved my hand to shoo the concern away. "I just burned my mouth on the hot tea is all." I explained.

She nodded her head in understanding, but the subtle arch of her eyebrow let me know she was not satisfied with my answer.

"I should very much like a walk outside. I have not been outdoors since we arrived here. Can you imagine that?" I pushed my seat back from the table, strode across the room and took her hand, helping her to her feet.

"We shan't be but a moment." I said over my shoulder as we crossed the sitting room floor and exited the door.

As soon as I felt we would not be overheard, I spoke. "Lynd, you were the only person in the room I did not hear from. I am uncomfortable with your silence. Something is wrong. What is it?" I studied her face closely.

"Willow," she began. "Something feels terribly wrong. I do not know what it is. I can almost see it and then, it slips away from me." She snatched at the air, grasping nothing for emphasis.

"Are you worried someone will be hurt or die?" I asked, afraid to hear the answer.

"Aye, of course, but that is not what is concerning me." She formed a claw with her free hand. To punctuate her frustration, she closed that empty hand on nothing. "I am very close to something and it continues to elude me."

"Would it help if I asked you questions about your visions?" I offered. "That sometimes helps."

We strode smoothly together as one. This is how it has always been. I was comforted by the familiarity. I had felt I had been missing a part of myself and had now been reunited and made whole again.

"Aye," She nodded. That often seems to help. Perhaps we can give that a try."

I began my litany of questions. "Do you know if any of our allies will be hurt or killed?"

"I can not be certain." She said. Her brows were tightly knit together.

"Lynd, you can not allow yourself to become so frustrated. You know you can not get your information clearly if you close your mind to the messages."

"Aye, I know." She agreed. "But this information is vital!"

"Would it help you to change the subject?" I offered. "There have been quite a lot of new developments in our lives recently."

"Aye, let's try that. Tell me about this place." She suggested.

"Oh, Lynd! It is a beautiful place. We are on the top of a mountain. The grasses have all turned golden brown. The leaves of the trees in the valley and village below are resplendent in their deep reds and fiery yellows and oranges. From here, we can see a great distance. I can see the tiny rooftops of the houses in the village and a church steeple, which may be the church where Maddy was married. The orchard is a left hand turn from the front door, which we just left through, and the barn that we arrived in last night is opposite that.

The sky is the most vivid shade of blue, with only a scattering of thin white clouds." It was so nice to be outdoors under the embrace of the sky. A light breeze played in my hair and the autumn sun shone on my cheeks, but there was definitely a chill in the breeze and change on the wind.

"Nay," Galynda interrupted my musings, waving her index finger in the air. "Thank you so much for the lay of the land. It sounds so lovely, but nay, I need to stay with this one." Her face was fraught with determination.

"Very well." I conceded. "How may I help?" I asked.

"'Tis nice just to be walking with you while I try to decipher this puzzle." She said rubbing her forehead.

"Are you getting a headache over this?" I asked.

"Aye, a bit of one." She was agitated and began to smack her forehead with the heel of her free hand.

"If you keep that up, you will have a bigger one." I teased. "Do you have bits of a vision or memory that can help you?"

Galynda stopped dead in her tracks pulling me to a jerking halt, leaving me off balance.

"That! Willow! That! You just said it! 'Twas part of a memory. Something about a memory, something familiar, something..." she wiggled her fingers in concentration. She grasped her lower lip between her thumb and index finger, much the same way I had seen men grasp their beards when they were being thoughtful.

"A memory," I repeated. "Is it a memory of an event, a person, or another vision..." I left the threads of my thoughts open-ended in the hopes of enticing her to latch onto them and continue to unravel her tangled message.

She squeezed my arm. Evidently, I had hit upon another thread that she could hold onto.

"I think I am remembering another vision or an event or something." She stopped, seemingly listening to a whisper in the wind.

"Something or someone we have encountered before, Willow. I have strong, negative feelings about this encounter. I cannot see it clearly enough, but I feel warning. I feel as if we are repeating something or we are being warned not to repeat something. Can you make sense of this?" She asked, nearly desperate.

"I understand that you are feeling something in this vision that is similar to or possibly the same as a vision you had before. You are getting some sort of warning, perhaps so that we shan't make the same mistake as we did before?" I puzzled out what she said in an awkward paraphrase.

"You are close," she said with her fingers open at the ready. "But I am just not getting enough pieces of the vision to put it together yet.

"I know this is frustrating for you. We are closer than we were a few moments ago. You will get the rest of the vision when the time is right." I offered.

"I just hope I get it in time to heed the warnings!" She exclaimed. "I do not wish to see anyone get hurt, or worse, because I could not interpret a vision!" She began to cry.

I put my arm around her and pulled her into me. She shook as she sobbed. I stood there silently and held her, allowing her the privacy and time to cry it out. It was not like her to weep. She was experiencing tremendous pressure to succeed. I felt helpless to do anything more than comfort her.

"Thank you." She sobbed. "Everything has been happening so fast. I feel a little overwhelmed." She confessed.

"Overwhelmed is something I understand too." I agreed with a vigorous nod of my head. "Everything has changed so suddenly and so drastically. 'Tis difficult to remain poised and focused." I spoke my truth from the depths of my being. Everything had, indeed, changed so suddenly.

"Oh, but Willow," she spoke, stuffy-nosed through jagged sobs, "the people here all love you. You have won them over completely."

"Thankfully, their Queen is recovering. I believe that is why they like me so much." I humbly offered.

She grasped both of my arms and shook me. "They look to you for answers, Willow, they confide in you, they trust in you. Do you not see that?" She spoke to me as if I were a particularly dim-witted child.

"They seem to find you enchanting as well, Princess Ra Ahnan." I said with a smile. "Do you not see that?" I arched my eyebrow for emphasis. A jibe I realized now she would never see.

She relaxed her furrowed brow and conceded to call it a truce. We were both loved, and we had both found a permanent home. It was a home we could all share in together.

"Lynd," I began.

"Aye?" She invited me to continue.

"We must turn back now. This brisk air, while it is exhilarating for my lungs and refreshing for my spirit, it is causing my foot to ache." It was difficult to keep the tension I was experiencing in my muscles out of my voice.

"Why did you not tell me?" again she took on the role of my scolding mother, and I felt like a disobedient child.

"It has only just begun to ache and I am telling you now." I countered. "I should like to go in and put it up for a while. We should return soon any road, because the Queen is expecting her future daughter-in-law to bring her a bowl of stew." I said with a smile.

"You did not!" she began to scold.

"Oh, but I did." I nodded with a smile. "I promised her

that you would bring some stew down to her. She would like, very much, to get to know you."

"Oh Willow, what am I going to do about you?" she asked in mock exasperation.

"Love me." I said. "I am awfully adorable." I widened my eyes with the innocence of a child no one can resist.

"Oh, I ought to smack you one!" she said, arching an eyebrow and waving a finger in the direction of my face. "I should, but I shan't, you are awfully adorable, after all." She said with a smile.

"I've missed your smile." I commented.

"So have I." She confessed.

"'Twill get better Lynd." I assured.

"I know it shall." She said. "Come along now, so we can get you off that foot!" again, she assumed the mothering role and I was reduced to the reluctant child who needed constant reminding. I figured she would make a great Queen one day.

None of the others had returned from the castle or stables yet. It was too soon, and I was nervous and impatient.

I ladled a bowl of stew for the Queen and guided Galynda down to the Queen's quarters for a visit. I excused myself quickly so I could tend to my aching foot.

I found a basin and filled it with warm water and took it to my bed chamber. I added a small handful of salts from my pouch. I removed my brace and slid my foot into the water.

The water was warm and soothing. I found myself drifting, so I lay back on the bed with my foot hanging over into the tub.

"Willow, are you well?" It was Magda. She was still cool from the fresh outdoors. "They tell me you have been up here alone for hours." Her face was creased with concern.

"Hours?" I asked dumbly. "I only just came up here to soak my foot. 'Twas only for a moment."

"Princess Madeline came up here about an hour after you did and found you asleep with your foot in the basin. She put your foot on the bed and covered you so you would not catch a chill." Magda looked concerned. "As soon as we arrived, she came to tell me."

"I was tired. The water was soothing and it did not take much persuasion to put me to sleep." I admitted.

"As long as you are well," she said, sounding like the mother she was. "We have a lot to do to prepare for the feast tomorrow night."

"I am quite well. Now that I have rested, I feel I can be of more use. Is everyone back?"

"We are concerned, we have not heard from Rosmerta." She said gravely.

"Everyone else is back then?" I asked for reassurance.

"Aye." She nodded. "'Tis a good thing too, the weather has turned from still and calm to blustery and stormy. We could have snow or freezing rain tonight. Come down now, we are preparing to eat supper." She invited.

As I laced my brace, I smiled to myself. It seemed that my own family saw me as a child who needed guidance and the royal family looked to me as an adult with answers. I wondered which of these I truly was.

Return to Power

We ate a hearty meal of flat bread and thick lamb stew. Everyone at the table seemed deep in his or her own thoughts. Tomorrow would be a busy day.

Outside the grey storm clouds blackened and churned. The winds howled and clawed at the doors and rattled windows as if trying to get inside, sending a chill up my spine.

The stormy climate outside reflected the dark, tempest that was brewing inside each of us this day. Each of us sat in silent contemplation, pondering the events of the morrow that would likely change our lives indelibly.

I wondered what could be keeping Rosmerta. I felt that she could be in grave danger because of the nature of her relationship to the Queen. Although I was hungry, the knot of worry in my stomach would not permit me to eat.

I found myself absently pushing bits of carrot and turnip back and forth in my bowl, mentally working out a strategy that might help solve our problems.

After we had finished our solemn meal, we all worked together to wash, dry and put away the dishes.

When they had returned in the afternoon, Ahmad had brought his concertina and Pieter, his fiddle. They had anticipated the change in climate and in mood and decided to try to inject a little levity with music. Together they did their best to brighten our spirits with the comfort of familiar music. Playing folk tunes and soft ballads as the rest of us sat and engaged in quiet conversation.

Magda and Ahnja drifted off to bed. Soon, Enid and Emily made their way to bed too.

I decided to check on the Queen's progress one last time before I turned in for the evening. Lantern in hand, I entered the pantry and was prepared to descend the hidden stairs when I heard a dull thud outside the kitchen door.

For a moment I stood stock-still, frozen by uncertainty. My mind chattered away nervously in my head. What should I do? What could it be? Who could it be?

Somewhere in the midst of my rumination, I thought I heard someone faintly calling my name. Then, I was certain of it. Someone was calling my name. I was not certain where the call was coming from. Was it the cellar, or was it outside?

When I heard someone calling for 'Bunny', I knew it was Madame Rosmerta. Why was she outside? Why did she not come in?

I turned to the backdoor and opened it. I held the lantern high so that I could see into the dark yard. I could barely make out the form of Rosmerta, who was leaning heavily against the wall. Her hair was disheveled and her face was badly bruised and she was bleeding.

"Rosmerta!" I exclaimed. "Come in. What has happened to you? Where is your cloak?" I put my free arm around her waist and supported her down the stairs. "I am taking you to see the Queen." I asserted as I gingerly guided Madame Rosmerta down the stairs.

Before we were in view of the Queen, I announced our arrival. "Majesty, I am coming with Rosmerta, she has been hurt. I thought you might wish for her to be with you. If it is agreeable to you, I shall set her up in the bed next to you."

From the other room the Queen answered, "Yes, yes! Is it serious? What has happened?"

I supported Rosmerta past the crates and barrels toward the Queen's chamber. She leaned more heavily into me with each step.

"Rosmerta," I said. "We need to get you cleaned up. First, let's see about getting you out of that dress." I said, trying to sound cheerful. Inside, my heart was filled with the tears I could not allow myself to cry. I was relieved to see her but dreading the possible prognosis of a loved one who had lost so much blood.

Rosmerta's face was beginning to swell and her lip was split and bleeding. Her hair was disheveled and loose tendrils were sticking to the blood on her face and chest.

The Queen began to help Rosmerta out of her dress.

"Have you any broken teeth?" I asked as I busied myself with the kettle, bowl and pitcher.

Rosmerta shook her head no. Her skin appeared ashen and moist.

"We can be grateful for that." The Queen remarked with a hand over her own mouth.

She busied herself with the task of making the empty side of the bed ready for Rosmerta by turning down the coverings and propping the pillows.

I gently sat Rosmerta on the bed and helped to remove her shoes and stockings.

My blood ran cold and I stopped breathing for a moment. I could see a clear imprint on Rosmerta's cheekbone just below her left eye. Whatever struck her there had left a small cut under her eye.

"Willow, what is it?" The Queen had seen the change in

my expression and was very concerned.

"Majesty," I explained. "I have seen this type of marking somewhere before." I said, pointing to the bruise on Rosmerta's cheek.

"Rosmerta, who did this to you?" I asked.

She was unable to answer. Her eyes had fluttered shut and she had slid back, unconscious, against the pillows the Queen had propped up for her.

"I can not have you tiring yourself, Majesty. You are still quite weak yourself." I admonished.

"I feel I must help. After all, I feel it is my fault that she, and everyone else, is in such danger. If I had never consented to marry that, that wretched man..." Judging by the clenched jaw and fists and the pinpoint pupils, I could tell that she was furious.

"Your Majesty, please, if you would, please lie back next to Rosmerta. She is bleeding and needs our help. I need to remove her chemise so I can see where she is bleeding from."

The Queen, hearing that her dear companion was bleeding, immediately lay back against her pillow so that I could do my job.

"I shall allow you to assist if you promise not to over do." I offered.

"I shan't," she promised.

I was amused to realize that I was giving orders to the Queen and surprised at how compliant she was.

"We need to remove her chemise, but she is laying on it. Since I do not know where she has been hurt or how serious her wound is, I do not want to move her. I suggest that we cut the chemise off."

"What shall I do?" the Queen asked, pale with concern.

"I shall get the knife from my bag. I want you to hold Rosmerta's gown away from her body so that there is no fear of my cutting her." I explained.

I pulled my knife from my pouch and Her Majesty held

the chemise out for me to cut. "I trust you Willow." She said. "But do be careful, won't you?"

"Aye," I said with a smile. "I shall take the utmost care." I nodded as I poised the sharp knife near Rosmerta's décolletage.

"I know you shall," she agreed.

I tucked the tip of my blade into Rosmerta's neckline and ran it the length of her gown without incident.

"Now we need to open the gown and look for the wound." I explained as I conducted my examination.

"There!" she announced. "On her chest!" she clapped a hand to her open mouth.

I could see that someone had been after Rosmerta with a knife. From the location of the wounds, it appeared that her attacker had meant to do her grave harm for it was clear he had been aiming for her heart.

"I need to feel the area with my hands to decide how serious her injuries are," I explained.

She nodded consent and I began to palpate the wounds.

The first wound was a superficial laceration that was situated between Rosmerta's breastbone and her left breast. It appeared as though the attacker had sliced her flesh rather than stabbing her. The second wound, however appeared to be deep. I was relieved to learn that while the blade entered at the chest, it had angled and come out under her left arm.

"Majesty, are you handy with a needle and thread?" I asked.

"I can only do fancy needle work. I was never taught to do anything useful, such as mending and sewing." She admitted offering upturned, empty palms.

"I would like to request that Galynda come down and help us with the needle work. Her stitches are so fine that when Rosmerta is healed, she shall have hardly any scarring."

"Let us have Galynda to do the stitching." The Monarch

agreed.

"If you would, please, hold this towel firmly to this deep wound. 'twill help slow the blood loss."

"I shall." The Queen agreed and anxiously held out her hand for the towel.

I washed my hands in the basin to remove any hint of what was happening. I checked on the Queen's application of pressure. When I was satisfied that she had the task well in hand, I covered Rosmerta's legs and abdomen with the bed quilt.

"I shall only be gone a moment." I said. Without waiting to be dismissed, I took the stairs as quickly as my injured foot would carry me. I turned from the stairs in the pantry and collided smartly with Gus's belly on my way into the kitchen.

"Oh, Gus!" I exclaimed. "Gus, I was wondering, have you any alcohol here, something stronger than wine?" He looked at me questioningly.

Not wishing to engage myself in a conversation or cause anyone alarm, I bent the truth just about as far as a person can, without actually telling a boldfaced lie. "Rosmerta is back and she and the Queen have requested Galynda's immediate presence." I blurted.

"Oh, why did you not say so? I have a fine bottle of..."

"Thank you. If you will get it for me, I will go and get the Princess and meet you back here." I frantically tried to remain calm.

He stood there with his eyebrows knit together, scratching the back of his balding head, as I scurried away to find Galynda.

I found her seated in the sitting room sipping tea and visiting quietly with Phillip.

All this protocol, I thought. I just wanted to grab Lynd and drag her down to the cellar to help me. Instead, I forced myself to go silently to the bed chamber where her things were kept and fetch her sewing bag.

Magda and Ahnja had gone up to bed early so I would have to proceed into the room silently. I was quite surprised to see lantern light coming from beneath the closed door. I knocked politely and agonized while I waited to be admitted. To my surprise, I found Enid and Emily, the other two early-to-bedders visiting with them.

"I just came to get Lynd's sewing bag." I explained politely. "I have a little mending I need help with." I grabbed the bag and backed out of the room quickly. "Please excuse me."

I quickly returned to the sitting room and approached the chatting couple.

"Begging your pardon," I said. "The Queen requests an immediate visit with Galynda."

"Yes, of course," said the Prince, standing at the mention of his mother.

As we scurried through the kitchen, I thanked the still-confused Gus for the bottle of alcohol and hurried down the stairs, with Galynda in tow.

"Willow, what is it? What has happened?" Worry began to rise in her voice.

"Rosmerta has returned." I breathed. My voice was raspy with tension.

"How badly has she been hurt?" Galynda asked.

"She has been beaten and stabbed. I brought your sewing kit. Please tell me you will help her." I pleaded.

"Of course I shall!" She assented.

"I have laid her with the Queen to avoid unnecessary concern." I explained.

"That was smart thinking." She agreed.

"If you will wash your hands, I shall find you a seat."

I led her to the dresser where the soap, towels, bowl and pitcher were. I had worked with Galynda for so many years that I did not concern myself with telling her how everything was laid out. I always spread my work area out the same way so I could find everything easily. Even if I had not been so fastidious, she could just as easily have found the soap by smelling it.

I returned with a small empty barrel and set it near Rosmerta's side of the bed. I joined Galynda at the dresser and poured water for her so that she could scrub both hands at once. She dried her hands and poured for me.

While I scrubbed my hands, I explained Rosmerta's injuries. "I would like for you to stitch the long wound. I shall close the deeper wound. With both of us working together, she shan't lose over much blood." I explained.

I guided her over to her barrel and placed her hand upon Rosmerta's chest.

Galynda quickly withdrew her hand and drew in a sharp breath.

It was that variety of extrasensory reaction that gave me gooseflesh every time she did it.

"What is it?" I asked.

"Does the Queen know that I am a *drabardi*?" Galynda asked.

"Do I know you are a what, exactly?" asked the Queen.

"Majesty, Galynda is a most gifted *drabardi*. That means she has been blessed with the gift of Second Sight. She can see things with her spirit, instead of her eyes. She is a visionary."

"Yes, Rosmerta told me you had a gift, Galynda." The Queen replied. "What is it that has caused you to react so?"

I took the toweling from the Queen and set her pillow at the foot of the bed where she could watch us work. I helped her settle in and covered her with a quilt. "Thank you for your help, Majesty." I said in low tone so as not to interfere with the conversation at hand.

"Of course," she answered absently, awaiting Galynda's answer.

I tipped the alcohol onto a clean towel and cleaned

Rosmerta's laceration. Then, I tipped the bottle over her stab wound and daubed it with the toweling.

"Your Highness, Galynda began, "Rosmerta knew her attacker. She was sought after and targeted. She knew that she was being hunted so she used herself as a decoy to draw her pursuers away from you. She has been running for some time evading them and trying to get back to you.

This was a vengeful attack. Does this mean anything to you?" Galynda asked the Queen for confirmation before continuing.

"Yes. That makes a great deal of sense." The Queen replied, pinching her chin thoughtfully between her thumb and the knuckle of her index finger.

I handed Galynda a needle threaded with a manageable length of thread. Her sensitive fingers delicately palpated the edges of the long wound. It was not bleeding so much now, but the wound was large and the underlying tissues were exposed.

Galynda found a suitable starting point and lovingly began the task of closing the ugly, jagged wound. I knew she put a loving prayer of healing into every stitch, as this is what I had been trained to do as well.

As she stitched, Galynda began to furrow her brow in thought.

I threaded a second needle and began to search the stab wound for the best place to begin.

I decided to begin on the exit wound, where the knife blade had slid out, under Rosmerta's left arm. Carefully, I lifted her arm out of my way and placed it in a natural position on the pillow over her head.

Once I settled on a starting point, I asked Galynda, "You have furrows in your brow that would strand a wagon. What is it that disturbs you so? Is this related to your earlier vision?"

"Aye, 'tis." She said, raising the needle over her head to

draw the thread taut. "There is an important bit of information missing. It still eludes me." She said, shaking her head.

The Queen sat silently, listening to every word. She watched closely so as not to miss a single move we made.

"Galynda," Her Majesty began.

"Aye?" Galynda responded, preoccupied with the task at hand.

"The reaction you had just a moment ago, when you touched the wound. That was quite similar to Willow's reaction when she saw the wound under Rosmerta's right eye. She said the wound looked familiar and it seemed quite disturbing to her. Do you suppose the two are related?"

Galynda stopped her needle in midair and cocked her head slightly as if she were trying to clear her head or to hear more clearly. "Is this true Willow?"

"Aye, 'tis true." I confessed. "When I saw the bruise on her cheek, I felt as if it looked familiar or as if I had seen a marking like it somewhere before. The bruise is unusual. It looks like a wax seal for official letters or an ink chop stamp."

"Let me see," Galynda requested. She extended her hand for me to place it on Rosmerta's bruised cheek.

I guided her hand toward Rosmerta's cheek.

Even before I could lay Galynda's hand on our patient's cheek, Galynda withdrew it as though Rosmerta's face were on fire.

"It gives me gooseflesh every time you do that!" I exclaimed. "What is it, Lynd?"

"I wish I could tell you! I only know that this is part of that warning feeling that I have been getting. You and I have been in this situation before. That mark on Rosmerta's cheek is a reminder to us. 'Remember' it says. 'You have been warned.'

Oh, Willow, I am so close, but I am blocked!" Galynda sighed. "I am stuck in a furrow and I am unable to free myself. Why am I stuck? This has never happened to me before."

"Do you feel you are resisting the message?" The Queen asked.

"What do you mean, Your Majesty?" Galynda asked, cocking her head and furrowing her brows.

"I find that it is often far easier to hear news about others than it is to hear about loved ones." The Queen explained.

Galynda, still furrowed and cocked, closed her eyes tightly in concentration.

I continued to close the wound I was working on. My needle work was sufficient to seal the wound and stop the bleeding, but I was certain it would leave a scar. Galynda's work, on the other hand, was so fastidious that I was just as certain that her stitches would not.

In the time it had taken me to stitch a wound half the width of my hand, Galynda had nearly finished closing a gaping wound more than twice the width of her hand and had done so flawlessly.

A moment had passed before Galynda opened her eyes. "I believe you may well have hit upon something Your Majesty.

In our culture, a *drabardi* does not do readings for people from her tribe. She will only do readings for the *Gajikané,* people who are not Rom. Perhaps this is why this vision is not clear to me. Perhaps, it is just too personal." She sighed with this revelation.

I watched as Galynda's face became visibly smoother and more placid. She appeared to be calmer than I had seen her in a while.

I was pleased that the Queen could understand Lynd's gift and that she was not afraid of it or Galynda. Her Highness seemed to have found a suitable explanation for Galynda's block and this seemed to pacify Lynd in a way that I had not been able to.

Galynda closed the wound she was working on and

extended her hand to monitor my work. "The stitches will scar less if they are smaller." She commented.

"Aye, I know. That is exactly why I enlisted your talented hands to help close these wounds. I am closing the wound that shan't show. I was hoping you would close the entry wound, which is in the front, where it would be more likely to draw attention if it was scarred and unsightly. Here, let me thread another needle for you." I offered.

When Galynda had finished stitching Rosmerta's wounds, the Queen appeared appreciably more sedate.

I admired Galynda's handiwork. In so little time, she had taken an ugly gaping gash and made a tidy row of nearly invisible stitches which closed the wound and all but made it disappear.

I moistened another clean towel with alcohol and handed it to the Queen. "Majesty," I began, "will you please clean the wounds gently with this while I mix up some herbs to keep infection out?"

"Of course, Willow, Dear," she said, extending her hand for the towel.

I went to my pouch for the herbs. I would need something to prevent infection and I would need something for bruising as well. As I rummaged through my pouch, I was so grateful that Magda had restocked everything.

I took a small clay pot from the pouch and added various herbs to fight infection. I took the teakettle from the hook in the fireplace and poured some boiling water into the herb pot. I set this aside to let it steep and returned to my pouch for herbs to dissolve bruising and reduce swelling. I found a second small pot and prepared the herbs for brewing.

Galynda was busy putting her needles away and gathering up her sewing bag when she suddenly became very rigid and still.

"Galynda, what is it dear?" The Queen asked.

"Willow, stop!" Galynda requested. "Stop!"

I froze, teapot in midair, poised and ready to pour. "Why? What has happened?" I queried.

"Oh," she said. Her face had grown pale. She had clapped one hand over her mouth and hugged her bag tightly to her breast with the other. "Bless us with all that is sacred." she swore softly under her breath. She stood silently shaking her head slowly side to side as if in disbelief.

I completed the pour and replaced the teapot on its hook and came to her side. "Lynd, sit here." I moved the barrel so that it was positioned on the Queen's side of the bed and helped her find her seat before she fell down.

"Tell us what is happening. Can you do that?" The Queen gently coaxed.

"Willow, the last time I smelled that combination of herbs..." she had to stop and steady her voice.

"What, what is it?" I asked, feeling desperate now.

"The last time I smelled those very herbs, you were treating me!"

For a moment I was very confused. The last time I had used those herbs, I was treating my foot. Suddenly, the unseen hand of wisdom turned up the wick on the lantern in my mind and I could see what she meant clearly.

I stood silently for a moment and stared at Galynda. Of course she was having difficulty receiving this vision!

She was being warned. There was violence in the air. There was more bloodshed to come. The bitterness, hate and evil that were breeding in surrounding villages had infiltrated the castle walls like a plague.

"Ladies, will you please tell me what this is all about." The concerned Queen requested.

I had already said enough about this issue earlier today. I caught the Queen's eye and pointed to myself, placed an index finger silently to my lips, and shook my head, no.

I returned to the herbs and prepared a poultice. I silently wrapped the infection fighting herbs in toweling. This I gently placed on Rosmerta's knife wounds. I carefully returned Rosmerta's uplifted arm to her side, trapping the poultice firmly under her arm and rested her hand on her abdomen. Then I began to prepare the herbs that I would apply to her bruises.

Galynda broke the silence. "The last time Willow prepared those herbs, in that combination, she was making a tea for me.

Willow and I had sought shelter from a lightning storm in a small cave outside of a village we were to do some trading with." She spoke in a low monotone. "Willow had gone to fetch water in the skin bags before it grew too dark for her to see." She continued.

"A wicked man had followed us to the cave that night. He watched and waited until I was alone and then he trapped me in the cave. He was large, and heavy and awkward. He was drunk, his words were slurred, and he spit in my face when he spoke. His hands were large and rude and invasive. He pawed at me. He reached into the bodice of my dress and his rough hands were groping me everywhere. He said such vile things to me! He lifted my skirts and when I struggled to get away, he crushed me against the wall. He swore at me and struck me in the face." She placed a hand upon the offended cheek and stared into the cave of her memory as she recounted the events of that night.

"Oh, my dear Galynda!" Her Majesty exclaimed. She placed a hand over her own chest and another on Galynda's shoulder.

"I am quite certain that he would have done much worse than that, had Willow not returned as hastily as she did!" Galynda's expression bore witness to her determination to unearth and lay bare all of the events that she had worked so hard to bury these past moons.

"That is when Willow injured her foot so badly!" She ground the heels of her hands into her sightless eyes angrily.

"She was coming to my rescue that night!" my sister exclaimed, taking the burden of responsibility wholly upon herself.

I quietly applied the bruise poultice to Rosmerta's swollen face. Her lower lip had been split badly, so I decided to stitch it as well.

Tears slid silently down Galynda's face as she told her story to her future mother-in-law. It was the first I had heard my sister speak frankly about the attack since it had happened.

Galynda wept bitterly. Queen Alyssandra selflessly put her own need to rest aside for her daughter-in-law. She lovingly reached out and gathered Galynda onto the bed and into her arms and held her closely. She stroked Galynda's hair, rocked her gently and began to hum softly.

Queen Alyssandra's eyes met mine. She profoundly understood what it was to feel trapped and brutalized.

She realized now what it was I had tried to tell her without exposing Galynda's vulnerable underbelly.

Tears were streaming down her cheeks as she nodded slowly to me. It was a nod that said, "I understand. I shall speak of this to my son so that he understands and together, we shall keep Galynda safe. This shan't happen again." Her face took on an expression of deep resolve.

Quietly, I stitched Rosmerta's split lip, mindful to make the stitches small to reduce the chance of scarring. I returned to my pouch and produced some balm for her.

I gently covered Rosmerta's chest, first with dry toweling, and then with the bed coverings. I did not want for her to catch a chill as the herb-moistened toweling cooled.

This was going to be a long night for my dear friend Rosmerta. Realizing this, I opted to make a stout painkilling draught. I included more infection fighting herbs to help her body fight infection from the inside as well as the outside. Her healing process would be as painless as I could possibly make it.

When the tea was finished, I had made enough to last Rosmerta through the night and most of the day.

I awakened Rosmerta with some difficulty and administered a measure of the tea. The Queen watched closely as I did this and asked how often it should be given.

Rosmerta slipped back into a deep sleep immediately. I knew she would rest better, now that she would not be awakened by the pain.

"I shall waken her again in four hours to give her another draught of this decoction." I explained.

"Oh, no you shan't." The Queen scolded mildly from her bed. "I have seen how it is done. I can do that much without taxing myself. You have done so much already. 'Tis time you were off to bed!"

I did not have the strength or desire to argue with the Queen. I could see that she was feeling better and it would do her spirit good to feel useful.

"As you wish, Majesty," I said. "What will you have me do with Galynda?"

Galynda had cried herself out and was breathing deeply, in profound sleep on the bed between Her Majesty and Rosmerta.

"'Tis a large enough bed, you may leave her, and I shall tend to her as well." She said protectively pulling the blankets up over Galynda's shoulder.

"Very well. Good night, Mother Queen." I said with a smile and a bow.

"Sleep well Willow, Dear. And thank you so much for all of your care."

I embraced her warmly and gave her a small kiss on her cheek. "I do it with love, Majesty. Good night."

Marching into Battle

The sun was coming up as I climbed the stairs to go to bed. As I slid into bed beside Madeline she stirred and awoke.

"Your skin is cool. Are you only just now coming to bed?" The sleepy Princess asked.

"Aye," I replied drowsily, snuggling down into my pillow.

"I waited for you for hours. Where were you?" she pouted.

"What is it that you believe I was doing that would keep me away from you all night?" I asked.

"Well, I saw you take Galynda by the hand and take a bottle of liquor from Gus. I saw the two of you go to the cellar and..." she sniffed.

"Listen to me good, Madeline," I said sternly, "because I only intend to endure this conversation once." I was exhausted and this conversation was even more fatiguing.

"I am a healer. That is what I know best. I shall tend to the sick when I am needed, not when it suits me.

You are a monarch. As a ruler you have important

obligations to your people. I know that their needs might often come before yours or mine.

We must both understand that because we serve others, our time is not always our own."

Please, understand me. I love you, Maddy. I have had a very full day and I am exhausted. I am tired and I am hurting. Sleep is the only thing I can think about right now.

"I am so sorry, Willow. Here, let me help you unlace your boot and get that brace off." Madeline tucked me in and told me, "Get some rest, Love, I shall wash up, dress and go and check on Mother." She kissed me tenderly on the temple, closed the draperies and left me drifting off to sleep with a smile upon my lips.

It was early afternoon when Madeline, dressed in finery, kissed my sleeping eyelids to awaken me. I woke up slowly with a smile. I stretched languidly and swung my legs over the side of the bed.

"I brought you a fresh pitcher of hot water so you can freshen yourself before we eat lunch." She said. "I have laid out a towel and some soap for you.

I must have made a deep impression. It was most unlike a princess to surrender control under any circumstance and Madeline had chosen to do so. And she had undertaken the servile task of laying out my toilet things.

"Was the scolding too harsh?" I asked as I undressed.

"No, 'twas just harsh enough to knock some sense into me." She said with a soft smile.

She gathered my dirty clothes and laid out a clean chemise and a kitchen maid's dress as my disguise for the feast.

"You saved Rosmerta's life last night." She said. There was a tone of awe in her voice.

"How is she doing?" I asked, dipping a small towel into the bowl of water I had just poured.

By taking great pains to make the bed, Madeline allowed

me a bit of privacy to tend to my ablutions.

"She is still asleep. Mother told me what you did for Rosmerta and Galynda last night.

I also saw the fine stitching that Galynda did," she continued. "I am in no doubt, that because of you and your dear friend; she shall mend with few scars."

I could hear chatter in the kitchen. I dried myself and dressed hastily.

"How is the emotional climate out there?" I asked.

"Pressure is building. Everyone is feeling tense."

I nodded as I pulled my brace on. I noted that my foot was feeling better.

We joined the others in the kitchen. "Good afternoon everyone," I said. "If you will excuse me, I must see to the Queen and then I shall return for lunch." I said hastily. "Has she had her stew?"

"Willow, we have already taken care to see that the Queen is fed. I know this is difficult for you, but you must allow others who are capable, to help you," said Ahmad. He scooped my face in his large, labor callused hands. "You are no good to anyone, my little Pony, if you are not taking care of yourself. You will wear yourself out working as you have."

Ahmad was handsomely dressed in rich, velvet finery of the deepest blue. He wore a wide leather belt at his waist bearing a scabbard which housed one of his famous ornate, but lethal swords. This costume, though handsome, was a stark contrast to his customary work clothes and leather apron.

Galynda's regal ensemble was of the same rich blue and was of similar cloth and cultural styling.

"May I at least go and see her before I eat?" I acquiesced, tapping my fingertips together in a begging pose.

"Aye, Willow, you may go but make haste, we need you up here." Magda answered. She too was dressed as a kitchen maid.

"Thank you." I said. "Maddy, are you coming?" I invited.

We descended the cellar stairs and found the Queen up and tending to her beloved Rosmerta.

"Majesty? What are you doing up?" I asked.

"Thank you for wisely encouraging me to help you care for Rosmerta and Galynda last night. Reaching out to help others who had also been brutally attacked and ravaged by another was very good medicine for my heart.

I am feeling quite strong today. I can see that I am needed here, and I intend to carry as much of my own responsibilities around here as I can."

I was puzzled, had I really done that intentionally? At any rate, I was very pleased to see her spirits improved.

"How do you find Rosmerta today?" I asked feeling for Rosmerta's wrist under the blankets.

"I have just administered the last of her pain tea so we shall need more before anyone sets off for the palace, please." She requested.

"I shall put the herbs in this pot. When you wish, all you need do is add sufficient water to cover the herbs by this much." I indicated a small distance between my thumb and index finger. "Allow the herbs to steep for half an hour's time." I explained as I measured out the herbs.

I shall need to change Rosmerta's herbal packs." I began.

Maddy interrupted my thought. "When I found Rosmerta and Galynda asleep with mother this morning, I consulted with Magda. She identified the herbs you had used and made fresh ones. She had no more than finished changing these when I woke you."

"I also had Magda make some extra packs for Rosmerta's chest and face so I can tend to her while you are away today." The Queen stated. "You left the balm out on the dresser, so I have been applying that to her lips after I give her the pain tea."

"I do not know what to say. I am grateful to you both for

all your help." I said. "You accomplished a lot while I was asleep."

"You have been doing much more than that for us and you cannot continue as you are or you shall become a casualty yourself. We can not have that happen, Willow dear, we need you." The Queen soothed.

I furrowed my brow. "Did you all have a Meeting of the Royal Elders while I was asleep or something?" I shrugged. "All of you are saying the same thing." I observed shaking my head.

"Perhaps we did, Willow," answered the Queen. "Never you mind about that, you need to get upstairs and join the others for a meal before you set out." The mother in her was more apparent.

"Thank you, Majesty, I shall." I bowed to her and began to take my leave.

"Willow," The Queen caught my arm. "What do Rosmerta's pulses tell you?" Her face was creased with apprehension.

"Rosmerta is fighting back." I assured her. "She has some pain but no infection." I affirmed.

"Oh, thank the heavens for that!" she said, clapping her hand to her chest.

"Now off with you two!" the Queen made a shooing gesture to send us out of the room. "I shall see you when you return." She said with a smile. It was a wan smile that did not reach her eyes.

"We shall see you soon Mother." Madeline assured as she embraced her mother and kissed both of her cheeks. "I love you." She held her mother in her gaze for a moment before surrendering her to me.

I followed suit and embraced and kissed the Queen as well. She surprised me by pulling me in so close.

"Thank you, Willow dear." She said as she tucked a loose tendril of my hair behind my ear.

"You are most welcome, my Queen." I said with a bow. "Please, get some rest."

We left the Queen, to rejoin the others. As I turned to leave, I noted that her eyes were brightening with tears.

The table was set with bowls of broth with small bits of meat with chunks of potatoes and carrots. Cups of tea were lined up in front of every place setting.

"Oh, good," Magda sighed. "You are here." She made a broad gesture beckoning everyone to gather at the table. "Everyone, please, take a seat." She invited. "I have decocted the herbal antidote, which is in the teacups before you.

You will want to drink the tea while your stomach is empty, so drink it first and then we shall eat a light lunch.

Remember, the kitchen staff is preparing a feast this evening and we wish to appear hungry."

Pieter, dressed in the clothing I had met him in, took his cup and raised it in a toast. "To a bloodless victory." He said with a firm and determined smile.

Everyone joined in his toast and drank the tea.

"Prince Phillip," Magda said, "since we are going to use you as the decoy, we shall serve you a second cup of tea at the palace." She explained.

Prince Phillip, who was dressed in great finery, acknowledged her with a nod of his regal head.

"Magda," I questioned, "have they heard about Rosmerta?"

"Aye, child, they have," she said sadly. "This is why we are all determined to continue on with the plan."

We ate silently. While some of us were planning war. I was praying for peace.

With the mundane chores of eating and clearing up lunch dishes out of the way, we each took a lantern or a torch for the journey through the tunnels. With our stealthy plans, they reminded me even more of field mouse holes.

Princess Madeline, having grown accustomed to ruling

the Kingdom during her mother's recovery took charge of the group.

"Enid and Emily will lead Magda, Willow and Phillip through the tunnels to the main kitchen pantry, where Phillip will drink his second dose of antidote," she announced.

"I shall guide Princess Ra Ahnan and her Uncle Ahmad, the 'Grand Sultan', through the tunnels." She stopped herself to explain, "Your family are royal guests; I will introduce during the festivities." To Galynda she whispered, "No one need know you are blind Princess Ra Ahnan. You will always be at my arm or Ahmad's."

Galynda nodded her appreciation.

"Pieter, Gus," Madeline continued, "You will be recognized as palace servants so you shall serve us in that capacity to avoid suspicion.

Both men nodded in acknowledgement.

"Pieter, I need you to stand near the main entrance to the castle. A carriage has been prepared for you to drive if any of us requires a hasty exit.

Gus, I need you standing as a guard at the entry to the grand dining hall, in sight of Pieter. You shall find swords hidden in the plants on either side of the doorways.

Father is aware that Mother has been gravely ill; he has searched the palace for her and has not found her in residence.

Since he saw us the night we moved Mother, the suspicious candle lighter has been informed that the Queen has been transported to a neighboring village to receive treatment, after taking a sudden turn for the worse in the middle of the night. Her false prognosis is not a good one.

This false news has gotten back to Father, so we know two things. First, we were right to suspect the candle lighter. Second, Father shan't expect to see Mother anywhere near the festivities.

We have detained the traitorous candle lighter and have taken him to the dungeon.

In the event that some of our guests do not get enough of the herbs to become incapacitated, Ahmad has hidden a dagger at each of your assigned seats at the dining table. They are there for your protection, use them if you must.

Are there any questions?" the Princess asked.

Everyone understood what he or she was expected to do. No one asked for more information.

"Since there are no questions, this tells me we are prepared to overtake the castle and return order to the Kingdom. Let us make haste." She set her jaw in a determined pout.

I loved her more in that moment than I believed was possible. She was power and beauty all at once. And, she had chosen me. She loved me and that was all the impetus I needed to move forward fearlessly.

I followed Emily and Enid into the storage shed with Magda and Prince Phillip following close behind. Together we made the uncertain journey in stifling silence.

I wished that Galynda were here with me. She always seemed to know what was coming. I had grown accustomed to knowing before I entered into some activity when to feel fear and when to relax into it. Without Galynda, I had no such advantage.

I thought how uncharacteristic it was that she could not predict the upcoming events. It was so unlike her.

The events of last night had been astounding. I had never heard Galynda recall her experience in the cave. I tried to imagine the experience from her perspective; battling an attacker I could not see. The idea terrified me. I understood why she had been profoundly affected by the events that took place in that cave.

After we had walked for nearly half an hour, we came to a door that opened into a stairway. These stairs ended at another door, which Emily slid to the side. It was a false panel in the back of one of the pantry cupboards in a kitchen I had never seen before.

Emily opened the cupboard door a crack and peeked out. When she felt it was safe, she climbed out of the cupboard, leaving the rest of us inside.

Moments later, Emily returned in a flour dusted apron. She opened the cupboard again and allowed us all to exit.

Magda went to the fireplace to retrieve a ladle of boiling water from a large cauldron which hung above the fire. She poured the water into a tankard and added the herbal antidote for Phillip's second dose.

Phillip, feeling out of place in the kitchen, shadowed Magda closely.

The paralyzing herbs had been added to the stuffing and were used as spice in the soups and gravies. More were finely ground and baked in meat pies and dessert dishes.

Everything smelled delicious. I had never seen such a huge production of food. There were roasted fowl stuffed with wild rice, roast pork, and legs of lamb.

I had heard people comment about rich, decadent foods. They often stated that such foods were fit for a king. I smiled at the irony. The unfit food we were preparing was indeed, fit for this king.

"Prince Phillip has taken his second dose of protective herbs. He shall take his leave now to go to the great hall where we shall serve the meal." Magda said.

"Because of your foot, I will not have you serving until most of the men are incapacitated. I shan't have an argument from you on this point, do I make myself clear?" Magda asked searching my eyes for assent.

"Aye," I answered. I could see the logic in her thinking. I could tire myself or I could be trod upon in all the activity.

"The guests are arriving and are being seated." Enid announced to the staff. "Pour everyone wine and keep the glasses filled. Let us begin to prepare the first course. Bring out the soup.

"Magda," I began, "How do we protect Maddy? She has not taken any of the first batch of herbs to protect herself."

"That is a good question. We had to work hard to devise a way to feed her so she would not appear to be suspicious.

Enid will walk in and begin serving the King at the head of the table. Next, she will serve to his right, which will be his son, Prince Phillip.

Emily will begin serving at the head of the table as well. It will not appear suspicious, as royalty is expected to be served first. Emily will begin to the King's left which should be the Queen. In the Queen's absence, the Princess, Madeline, shall take her place. The ladle, containing soup which has not been tainted, shall be held above the level of the drugged soup until Madeline has been served."

"And we are certain we can trust Emily?" I asked.

"Willow, 'tis not like you to be so suspicious." Magda chided. "If it makes you feel better, I have had one of the kitchen maids eat some of the soup from the untainted cauldron when we arrived, I have been monitoring her for signs of weakness or paralysis and she has shown no signs."

"Perhaps it has not been long enough, or the dose was too small." I argued.

"Do you see the big woman sprawling limply on the sack of flour against the wall?" Magda asked. "I had her eat a bit of the other soup. We have had ample time and we know the dosage is strong enough to take down a large woman in a short time."

"But suppose someone has tainted the soup since then?" I worried.

"Prince Phillip assigned himself to watch the pot until he left. Since that time, I have not left sight of it.

The guests have been visiting in the grand ballroom for hours. They have just been served drinks from these casks, which have no herbal additives. The kitchen staff is preparing to carry out the soup.

If you would feel better, you may choose a clean ladle and dip the soup for the Princess. Slide the ladle filled with soup against the side of Emily's cauldron. She will hook her thumb around the ladle and hold it against the side of the pot, suspended above the tainted soup.

When she is ready to serve, Emily will have to do it quickly to avoid detection. I can see almost everything from here. The Princess is nearly at the head of the table, I can not see that from here, but Gus can.

Emily shan't have time to try anything. If she drops the ladle in the soup, I shall signal Gus and he shall signal Madeline not to eat it.

The servers are returning, quickly now, go and dip Madeline's soup."

I carefully did as Magda instructed, as I dipped the soup for my Princess, I realized what a big difference one baby could make. I helplessly watched as the ladle and soup went out the door.

Battle Cries

"How is the feast going?" Magda asked when Emily returned.

Emily wiped a loose bit of hair away from her face with the back of her hand. "It appears to be going quite well. Many of the King's men are quite intoxicated already. That is as you hoped, yes?"

"Aye," Magda replied. "I cannot see if the King has arrived. Is he seated at the table?"

"Oh, yes. He is one of the more intoxicated ones. He is becoming a little too familiar with the servers."

"Is the King eating his soup?" Magda asked.

"I was not able to watch for that. I had to turn away from him in order to serve the others. Looking back upon him might have raised suspicion." Emily answered.

"I did hear him putting up an argument with Prince Phillip about how he did not trust the Queen's intentions in giving him this welcoming feast." Emily said in a conspiratorial tone.

She leaned in toward Magda and continued. "Here is where Phillip became creative; Phillip told the King that he had only just arrived home himself. He was happy to hear that his father had just arrived as well. Phillip told Edward that the feast was his own idea, to reunite father and son after their absences from the palace.

The King was having none of it and told Phillip he felt his son was always something of a girlish man. He did not believe such lies.

Phillip asked why inviting his father, the sovereign of the country, to a party in his own honor was a suspicious event.

Phillip then went on to say that since his mother, who would not have approved, was away and unable to object, he felt he was in charge of the Kingdom and could do as he wished. 'Twas truly inspired." Emily editorialized.

She continued. "The King seemed to warm to the idea of Phillip's rebellious attitude toward his mother. He made a terrible, filthy smile and gave Phillip a heavy-handed slap on the back. He hit the lad so hard the Prince nearly lost his crown in his soup."

"That does sound hopeful," Magda replied.

"I must run." Emily said as we must have the next course ready."

I wondered what it would feel like to sit in the dining hall with so much turmoil and so much drunkenness. Some of the most important people in my life were in that room preparing to fight for their homeland and possibly their lives.

It was difficult for me to stay in the kitchen while my family faced an enemy I was not allowed to look in the eye.

I felt anxious, and powerless to do more. I wondered if this was how Galynda felt that day in the cave. I wondered if Galynda had gotten any more clarity regarding her elusive vision. I had no chance to speak to her today.

I ached to be with them. It frightened me to think of Maddy sitting so close to a man who was capable of causing the kind of harm I had labored for days to mend and would take lifetimes to heal.

Without thinking, I grabbed a tray and headed for the grand dining hall. Behind me I could hear Magda whispering hoarsely to me, "Willow, no!"

It was too late to stop now. I was in the dining hall with an empty tray. I walked boldly toward the head of the table. I would help clear away the dishes as if this was my duty every day.

The dining hall, I observed was not as heavily decorated as it had been from the most recent celebration. The bare wooden table was decorated with candelabras for lighting and the floral arrangements were, undoubtedly some that were relics of another gathering. There were no banners, or flags to celebrate this man's return.

Ahead of me I heard an intoxicated voice say, "What has my Kingdom come to? Look here, we have a crippled servant girl. Maybe we ought to start bringing in one-legged wenches too since we seem to have stooped to the level of employing the crippled and infirm." He laughed too loudly at his own joke, revealing the depth of his mental disease.

Having made his lewd comment, Edward pawed at me with a greasy hand leaving smudges on my dress. I jerked away from him to avoid being subjected to his touch.

Finally, I was able to see the man, the king consort, I had heard so much about.

He was a man whose lifetime of impure habits has aged him well beyond his years. He wore his beard and moustache untrimmed and unkempt. His ruddy face was swollen, pockmarked and scarred, doubtless, as a result of his unclean living habits. His bulbous, red nose bore testimony of his habitual drinking. It was scarred and terribly misshapen at the bridge as though it had been broken more than once. His spirit smoke was a turbid, bilious green that polluted the air in the room around him.

All of my diagnostic tools told me he was the vilest human I had ever had the displeasure of encountering.

I did my best to observe him for goodness, for the kindness that must exist in him somewhere. My eyes rested upon his hair. It was shoulder length and secured behind his head with a leather thong. I noticed in an instant that this was the source of Maddy and Phillip's coppery red hair. His hair, however, was darkened and matted with grease and streaked with yellowing grey hairs.

His grizzled head was adorned with a five-pointed coronet. The center point was the tallest and each of the points that flanked it descended in height. It was a jewel crusted symbol of power. Power he wielded yet did not fully possess.

"You shall allow me to do whatever I wish, you insubordinate cripple!" He spat particles of partially chewed food into his beard and on me as he shouted. He reached for his heavy golden scepter, which he had rested against the table.

At the moment he grasped his scepter, the world slowed to a snail's pace. I caught a glimpse of a ring on his right little finger as it curled around the staff. The ring bore the crest of the castle that had seemed so familiar, and yet, so elusive. I had seen it before, yet the image was blurred, smeared, or smudged in my memory, but it was there and it was real.

In that moment, as I gazed upon that ring, I was transported to another time. I heard families screaming, ponies whinnying helplessly, fires crackling out of control, the thundering of hooves as evil, cowardly men fled the scene in a cloud of fetid smoke.

In that moment of distraction, Edward saw my vulnerability and lifted the tip of his heavy scepter from the floor and drove it forcefully into my injured foot, ending with a twisting flourish.

The room had gone silent. My head began to swirl, and

my vision dimmed. I began to crouch toward my offended foot but thought better of it. I could see this would not end well if I allowed myself to succumb to the pain. I could taste the bitterness of vomit rising in the back of my throat. Nay, I told myself. 'Twas not vomit, 'twas bile. Instead of surrendering to the pain, I willed myself to become angry. I was outraged at the cruelty that so many good people had suffered at this man's hand. I was furious about the pain he had caused Her Majesty and Phillip and my Maddy.

"I may be a cripple, but I shall never be as impotent as you are, you indolent traitor!" In one smooth movement, I sprang unexpectedly to my full height leaning in toward him. I brought my left elbow sharply up under his chin with all of my weight behind the blow. The impact of it caused his teeth to clamp shut on his tongue and sent his crown toppling.

In the silence of the room, the crown made its way over the back of the chair and fell slowly, silently to the floor. It made a metallic clatter at the moment it struck the floor and once again as it rebounded. It rolled in a tight circle on its edge and righted itself, rattling off a series of rapid figure eights as it gyrated to a stop on its base several feet behind the King. It sat silently, free of him.

Outraged at having been insulted in front of his minions, Edward pushed his chair back away from the table. He smashed the tip of his scepter into the floor at his feet and used his ebbing strength to pull himself, hand over hand, to his feet.

Once on his feet, he stood in place for a moment short of breath. He stared at me with venom in his bloodshot eyes. His pinpoint pupils bore holes in me from their vantage point beneath his bushy furrowed brow. His nostrils flared and his pocked cheeks flushed burgundy with rage. Edward curled his lips away from his yellowing teeth in a vicious snarl and set his square jaw in angry determination.

He was infuriated and his wrath was focused solely upon

me. In that moment, I was his quarry and he meant to slaughter me on the spot. He stared me down with the cold, steely glare of the predator poised to strike. He wielded his heavy scepter and swung it overhead with the intention of striking me down with it.

As the scepter reached its zenith above Edward's head, the inner corners of his brows raised almost imperceptibly. The color drained from his cheeks, his clenched jaw slackened, and his eyes widened. In that moment, too late to correct his blunder, he realized his weakened legs were giving out underneath him. The weight of the heavy scepter overhead was more than his weakening arms could bear.

The weight overhead changed his center of gravity, causing him to stumble back, sitting too hard, in his chair. The momentum of his weight and the irresistible force of gravity tipped the heavy King, still grasping his scepter, backward. His scepter clattered to the floor only a blink before his head struck the cold, marble floor with sickening finality. He lay still, his bloody mouth gaping, his eyes wide open with pupils fully dilated.

I went to him to feel for pulses. There were none. I inspected the area about him. A pool of blood began to gather around King Edward's head. I lifted it and found he had fallen upon his crown. The tallest point of the crown had penetrated the base of his skull.

With some force, I freed the crown from his skull and let his head drop lifelessly back to the floor. As I did so, I could not help but observe the irony of this man's life and death. In life, he was willing to kill to keep this crown that was never rightfully his. In his death, it was the crown that ultimately killed him and yet, it was still difficult to convince him to part with it.

It was only by chance, then, that I noticed an almost imperceptible scar on his face. His nose, flattened from having been broken, was also badly scarred. There, on the bridge, was the slightest tinge of blue. I could almost make out the letters I knew had been there.

Without warning, the pain in my foot returned in a great overwhelming wave. I could hear a roaring in my ears that I did not understand. Someone was lifting me, carrying me. The roar subsided and I could see brilliant stars and then everything was black.

Fallen

I awoke in a quiet room. I felt as if my mind and body were quite separate from each other. I was drowsy and wanted to drift off to sleep.

"Willow dear, how are you?" it was the Queen. It was good to see her up. I smiled at her.

"We should allow Willow to rest," I heard Magda say. "You may stay for a moment, Your Majesty, but then we really must allow her to rest."

"Thank you, Magda." I heard Queen Alyssandra say.

The Queen moved to the side of my bed where I could see her. "Willow, dear, what do you have there?"

I could hear her, but I could not respond as readily as I would have liked. Did I have something? Aye, I could feel something in my hands. I had something important that I must give to the Queen.

I heard my voice answering her from far away. Speaking required great focus and effort, "Your Kingdom." I allowed my hand to fall away from the crown I had gripped tightly on my chest.

The Queen slid the bloody crown from my chest and clutched it to her own. Silently she turned her eyes to the heavens and offered up a wordless prayer.

"The King has fallen." I mumbled thickly. Why was I so ponderous?

"So I hear." She said softly bringing her chin down in a bow and gently raising her eyebrows. A solitary tear traced a path down the side of her nose and dripped onto the bed. She fussed with the sheet on my bed, smoothing it over and over with her free hand.

"I find that those who build up their empire by plundering the lives of others tend to fall hard when they fall." Her Majesty said in a whisper.

I silently nodded my agreement.

"Would you like me to send for anyone?" The Queen asked, lightly patting any evidence of her tear away with the finger pads of her free hand.

It was frustrating the amount of time my mind required to process and respond to a simple question. I furrowed my brow and nodded my head slightly. "Lynd."

"I shall send for her at once." she said. "Thank you, Willow, Dear." She said as she bent down and kissed me on the forehead.

I nodded weakly. I must have fallen asleep then, for only a moment later, the Queen was standing beside my bed with Galynda on her arm. "Willow, Dear, I have brought Galynda to you." She spoke softly near my ear.

I opened my eyes. The lids felt thick and heavy. "Lynd," I began.

Slowly I opened my hand to reveal a secret I had kept hidden there. I clumsily dropped it from my hand to my chest. I felt for it, but in my drugged state, I could not find it.

"I have it here, Willow, what would you have me do with it?" The Queen asked holding a ring in her cupped hand.

"For Lynd," I said, raising an index finger.

The Queen placed the ring in the palm of Galynda's sensitive hand.

Galynda's eyes widened and her face paled noticeably. Her free hand shot up to her right cheek as though she had been freshly struck by a fist.

The Queen looked from the ring to Galynda and back to me for answers. "What is it, Dear?" She asked Galynda. That is the very type of reaction you had to Rosmerta's wounds!" She rubbed her arms to ward off the goose flesh.

Galynda's eyes seemed to glaze over. I knew she was looking into the past. I knew she could smell the liquor and she could feel the heat of his breath and spittle on her skin.

"You know then?" I asked.

"Aye." She nodded, still seeing ghosts of the past. "At dinner, he became more and more belligerent. As he became harsher, the voice became ever more familiar. I was absolutely certain of who he was when he began to insult you in front of the guests. It was eerie the way his voice changed as he began to shout. It was if he were two different people.

When you handed me this ring, I was so startled by the negativity on it that I nearly dropped it. I knew immediately whose ring it was." Galynda said holding the ring up as evidence.

"Why, it is Edward's ring, dear, tell me what it is about it?" the Queen queried.

"Your Majesty," Galynda addressed the Queen. "You shall find a contusion upon your Rosmerta's left cheek that bears the impression of this very ring." She said holding it by the shank between her index finger and her thumb as if it were evidence. "It is the very same bruise you had borne upon your own royal countenance not more than a moon cycle and a fortnight ago. I too, have been smote by the same offender. I too, bore the mark of this very ring upon my face.

When I listen to this ring, I hear the cries of the many

women who have suffered at Edward's hand. Some died. Others were ruined for the rest of their lives." Galynda explained.

The Queen pressed her hand against her chest. Her skin was pale. She quietly sat down on the edge of the bed to keep from falling to the floor.

"So, Edward was the one who attacked Rosmerta?" She asked quietly, as if speaking softly could keep the truth from sounding as harsh as it was. "And," she continued, "It was he who attacked you as well, Galynda?"

The Queen asked these questions for confirmation. I have little doubt that she had not already considered this a very real possibility.

"Aye, Your Majesty, that he did." She asserted herself. "I was fortunate to have Willow there to stop him before he could do much to me."

"Yes, you are very fortunate to have such a trusted and beloved sister and friend." The Queen replied taking Galynda in a one-armed hug.

I smiled weakly. "I kept my promise."

"What, honey, what did you promise to Galynda?" The Queen asked.

"Never again." I said feebly shaking my head.

"Never again." Galynda affirmed holding my hand and giving it a squeeze.

"Yes. You kept your promise." The Queen said. A tear rolled down her face. "You are a good friend and protector Willow."

I could no longer speak. I hugged my beloved sister's hand to my chest.

"I love you too Willow." She said as she brushed a tear from her cheek with her middle and ring fingers.

I heard them speaking, but I could no longer pay attention to what they were saying.

In the next instant, Magda was helping me to drink some

tea. It was very bitter. I did not want it, but Magda poured it into my mouth with such skill, that I was swallowing it before I could think to reject it.

"How are you feeling?" Magda asked.

I felt far away. "Separated." I slurred.

"Separated?" She asked.

I nodded my head and patted my chest weakly.

"You feel 'disconnected'?" she asked.

I nodded my head.

"That is the effect of the herbs. Get some rest. You shall feel better in the morning."

I closed my eyes again. Moments later, there was daylight streaming in the window. Madeline was not beside me. I was alone.

I began to wonder where everyone was. What happened after I was taken away?

"You are finally awake! How are you?" Madeline asked.

"Are you well?" I asked weakly.

"Am I well? Yes, of course! Why would I not be?" she asked.

"The traitors?" I asked. I was still feeling muzzy.

"All gone!" she said dusting off her hands as if she had flour on them.

"How?" I puzzled through the haze in my head.

"When Edward fell, the others wanted to rise to protect him. The herbs kept them in their seats and easy to manage. We had them carted off to the dungeon.

"Not angry?" I asked, pointing slightly at her with an index finger.

"Angry? Why would I be angry?" She asked.

"Your father." I wanted to finish my question, but my mind seemed to be at odds with my mouth.

"Yes, he was my father, but he was also my mother's tormenter. And as I hear it, Galynda's and Rosmerta's as well. "He shan't be missed." She ended with a determined pout.

"And Lynd?" I queried.

"She was here asking about you. I can send for her if you wish."

I nodded weakly.

Madeline returned quickly with Galynda on her arm.

"Willow, you are awake. How are you?" She asked seating herself beside me on the bed.

"Disconnected." I said managing a limp gesture with my hand. Why could I not move?

"Aye, Magda has you on some pretty powerful herbs. I was in the kitchen when she was brewing them." She said nodding her head.

Magda came in to check on me. "How are you feeling Willow?"

"Detached." Speaking was an enormous effort for me.

"Aye. I imagine so." She said "I have you on a large dose of herbs for pain.

Oddly, I felt no pain, only the muzzy disconnection.

"Your Highness," Magda requested over her shoulder, "if you would not mind, would you please go and get Ahmad for me?"

"I would not mind in the least" The Princess replied. With that, she lifted the edge of her skirts and took her leave of the room.

Moments later, Madeline returned with Ahmad. His skin was ashen, but he smiled warmly at me. "How is my little Pony this morning?" He asked with concern.

"Drunk." I answered with a stupid smile.

"That is good. The medicine is working as it should then." He said, looking askance at Magda, who nodded solemnly.

"Galynda, would you and Princess Madeline please go and check on Madame Rosmerta's progress, please?" Magda's calm request was terse but polite.

Galynda rose and waited for Madeline to take her arm. Galynda, too looked concerned.

I did not like the mood. It was rarely good news for the patient if Magda cleared the room. Everyone had been too solemn after such an easy victory.

Magda looked at me and spoke slowly. "Willow, your foot has been re-injured. Ahmad and I are going to attempt to put it right the best we can. Do you understand?"

I wanted to cry. My foot had been feeling so much better. Now I would have to start over again. I did not want my shaky voice to betray me, so I simply nodded, yes, I understood.

Turning to Ahmad Magda said, "I know this is hard for you, but you must be strong. It will help her foot to heal. I need help to put it right."

I closed my eyes, anticipating tremendous pain. I felt Ahmad gripping my ankle and heel as Magda instructed him.

I gritted my teeth in preparation for the traumatic moment of reduction. I felt Magda, far away, working on my foot, she massaged and pulled and repositioned her hands and pulled and pushed. I felt the, now familiar, jerking tugs from a distance, as if Magda were working with someone else. I heard several crackling and popping noises throughout the ordeal.

There was very little pain. The herbs had done their job well. I had a suspicion however, that I would feel the effects of Magda's efforts soon enough.

Ahmad released my leg and wiped sweat from his clammy face with his sleeve. He wandered a few steps and sat abruptly on the edge of a nearby chair, nearly missing it all together.

Magda, bearing a stern expression of neutrality, put an herbal pack on my foot. It was an alcohol-based decoction, so it felt warm and then icy cold to my foot.

I fell asleep.

Endurance

I felt someone holding my foot. I opened my eyes and found Galynda kneeling beside the bed. She was looking into my foot with her hands. Her gaze was far away.

"Lynd." I said sleepily. "What do you see?"

Startled, Galynda changed her focus back on to the room. "Oh, Willow, I did not know you were awake."

"I am now." I smiled weakly. "What have you found?" I asked sleepily.

"I think you should talk to Magda. She knows all the words." Galynda spoke to the floor.

"Galynda, I do not always have to hear bad news to recognize it. Everyone has been so solemn. They dart in and out, but no one stays long. No one is making eye contact with me. If someone does not speak to me soon, I shall be forced to do something drastic.

I asked you to tell me what you see because you can see everything. You can tell me what you see and I shall decide for myself how to interpret it. I just need you to be honest with me. All this polite pity is going to be the end of me!"

Galynda bit her lower lip and tried to find words to describe what she had seen. "You remember that your foot had been broken in two places." She began slowly.

"Aye" I nodded, grateful to have my mind and my voice back, but eager to learn my prognosis.

"The place where the bones were broken, Magda had tried to align them. The bones were beginning to mend. They were a bit crooked, but they were mending. When Edward struck your foot with his staff, he disturbed the first injury and broke two more bones.

Magda found that the old injury was displaced again and one of the bones of the new injury was too.

Magda is fearful that if she could not put things right in your foot that you would not be able to walk again.

She gave you a draught of pain relieving and sleeping herbs to help you rest without pain. She kept you asleep for two full days while she waited for the antidote herb from the feast night to diminish in your body.

When she felt she had waited long enough, she gave you a combination of sleeping herbs and paralyzing herbs to deeply relax all of the muscles of your body. That is when she and Ahmad came to set your foot."

"I heard it pop. Did it go back?" I asked, beginning to see why everyone else had been so worried.

"Willow, you must listen to Magda! You must not scheme with Ahmad. Magda has already scolded Ahmad and told him she would not let him see you if she even thought you and he would create a new walking brace.

The newest break shall not heal if you put any pressure on your foot. You shall destroy your chances of walking if you try to walk while the break is fresh.

Magda has it set and has bound it to keep the bones immobile. She has threatened to keep you intoxicated until your foot heals! Her voice was stern when she said it. She is very concerned about you and I truly believe she might carry out this threat if you offer any resistance."

I was silent. My spirit was running about wildly in my chest and I felt as if I would vomit. I wanted to be alone. I wanted to cry. I was weary from the herbs and I wanted to sleep.

"How long?" I heard my voice meekly asking.

"Three moons," was her response.

A lifetime, my spirit lamented. It would be spring before I would be allowed to even attempt to walk again.

I could not speak for the lump in my throat. I turned my face away from Galynda and the tears began to flow.

"Willow," she soothed, "you cannot hide your tears from me. I can feel them in my heart." She stood and felt her way along the bed. When she found the head of the bed, she lay on her side facing me. She lovingly cradled me in her arms until I had cried myself out and drifted off into a tear and herb induced sleep.

When next I opened my eyes, the room was dark and silent. Madeline was lying in the bed next to me. She was breathing deeply and rhythmically so that I knew she was asleep.

As I lay awake, my eyes began to adjust to the limited lighting in the room. Moonlight was shining brightly outside the large leaded glass window and cast enough light into the room to help me orient myself.

Judging by the ornate leading of the window, I began to realize, we were no longer in the cottage. I could see a large fireplace at the foot of a much larger four poster bed, which was draped in rose and sage, the colors of the Princess. The fire was burning down to embers; I supposed it must be early morning and that we were back in the palace.

I lay and pondered my situation. I would no longer be able to tend to the Queen with my foot injured as it was. Nor would I be able to tend to Madame Rosmerta. I would not be able to participate in most of my typical duties for three moons. All of winter would pass before I would be able to walk and work again.

When I ruminated about such things, I felt the overwhelming urge to cry. I felt hopeless and helpless. I became angry with myself for feeling so very sorry for myself. I could see that I could very easily allow myself to steep and fester in my own pity and that such an attitude would permeate my spirits and hamper my healing process.

As I lay thinking, I realized that my mind was far more lucid. I no longer felt drunk and disjointed. I felt little pain in my foot. I supposed that Magda had stopped the mind-numbing paralysis decoction and was giving me draughts of herbs to speed the healing process while keeping pain to a minimum.

I had no idea how many days had passed since my foot had been re-injured. I knew it had to be more than two or three, for that is the number of days Magda had waited to put my foot right. I wondered how long ago it had been since she had set my foot.

However long it had been, I decided that at least some time had passed, and I now had less than three moons to endure my healing process. This helped to cheer my spirits and I vowed to find creative ways to do my chores and ways to help the others with theirs.

In Stitches

The following morning, I was stretching myself and thinking about how I might rise and make myself useful when there was an unfamiliar furtive knock at the door.

"Come in." I invited, wondering who it could be.

The door opened slowly and the Queen entered the room guiding Madame Rosmerta. I lay in my bed with my foot propped on pillows and watched the two of them moving slowly, cautiously, each in her own state of convalescence.

"I have been wondering how the two of you have been doing!" I started.

"And we have been wondering about you." The Queen said, glancing at Rosmerta with a conspiratorial smile.

I looked from one to the other and furrowed my brow. "What are you two smiling about?"

"We've been lying around long enough. We wanted to come for a bit of company." Rosmerta explained.

"There is more to this, I can see it in your expressions." I said skeptically. "What mischief are we going to get ourselves into today?" I could feel my eyebrow rise in accusation.

"We thought it might be fun to join you in here and do a bit of sewing. Magda has been telling us about the beautiful marriage quilts your clanswomen make for the bride to be. We were hoping, if it would be acceptable to you, that you might teach us more about this tradition. We wanted to be a part of Galynda's marriage quilt." Rosmerta explained.

"Oh, that is a wonderful idea!" I exclaimed. "I shall be honored to teach you about marriage quilts and to work with you on Lynd's quilt." I could feel my spirits lifting measurably.

The Queen guided Rosmerta, who was carrying and a large cloth-wrapped parcel, toward the bed and seated herself on an upholstered chair beside it.

"Rosmerta, I should like to have a look at your injuries. How do they feel?" I said, feeling more useful by the minute.

"I have not been able to smile very well, and the wound under my arm is a bit stiff." She answered honestly. "I believe the stitches draw the skin tightly and limit my movement a bit."

"How long has it been since we stitched you up?" I asked. "I seem to be in a bit of a fog about the passage of time."

"It has been a full seven day's time." answered the Queen. "And the needlework looks clean and dry."

I smiled. "Your Majesty, 'tis truly unfortunate that you are such a talented Queen."

She looked at me with an expression of utter confusion. "Why do you say that, Willow?"

"Because, Majesty, you are such a splendid healer." I replied with a smile.

"I only wish to help heal the ones I love." she said, looking deeply into Madame Rosmerta's hazy eyes and tenderly stroking her cheek.

Drawing my attention away from the couple to allow them a moment, I hastily commented, "We shall need sewing supplies and bits of colorful cloth to make the quilt."

"Alyss has everything we shall need in that magic sewing bag of hers." Madame Rosmerta indicated, pointing to the large cloth bag the Queen had draped over her shoulder.

"Excellent." I said. "First, I should like to look at your wounds Rosmerta. Perhaps we can have the stitches out so that you might be better able to smile and move."

"I like the sound of that." The Queen said with a smile. "I have some very small scissors in my bag that I am certain you will find suited to the job." She slid the bag from her shoulder onto her lap and began rummaging through her sewing supplies in search of the tool I would need.

Rosmerta unlaced her bodice and loosened the neckline of her chemise, exposing her chest and the cleavage of her ample bosom.

I quickly changed my focus from breasts to sutures. The area that Galynda had stitched had healed with no redness or weeping. I was pleased to see such neat work of what had been a terrifying and gruesome invasion of her flesh.

"Do you wish to see the one under my arm as well?" Rosmerta asked.

"Aye, I shall. Let us remove the stitches on your lip first and then we shall get to those on your chest and under your arm."

"Here are the scissors." The Queen offered, extending them to me handles first.

"Thank you." I said. "Have you a small tatting hook in there as well?"

"Why yes, I believe so." She began rummaging through her bag again. "Yes, here it is." She offered.

"Do you wish to help?" I asked, suspecting I already knew her answer.

"Very much, if there is something I might do." She nodded.

"I should very much appreciate the help." I nodded. "If

you will gently slide the tip of the tatting hook under the stitch, lay it sideways so it slides readily under the thread and raise it gently like so," I demonstrated on a stitch in Rosmerta's lip as I spoke. "I can then snip the thread thusly, and we then we can withdraw the stitch." I demonstrated one more time for good measure.

"I am learning so much from you." The Queen said with a smile.

"Aye, I replied. Not many Queens would be willing or able to do needle work of this sort." I agreed with a smile.

"Well, I am afraid my needle work is of the ornate and utterly useless variety. I do not suppose a floral pattern would have been sufficient in this instance." The Queen stated modestly.

"It may have suited me, Alyss." Rosmerta smiled. "I do love your embroidery." We all laughed.

Queen Alyssandra and I worked well together. She hooked and lifted each stitch gingerly and I clipped and pulled the stitch free.

"Now, Rosmerta, I shall see about the stitches under your arm." I said moving my focus from freshly healed flesh to warm hazel eyes.

Rosmerta slid her arm out of the sleeve of her chemise and carefully raised her arm as far as she could. "It pulls a bit if I try to move it more than this." She said with a grimace.

"It may take a bit of work and stretching to get it back to the way you are accustomed to moving it." I explained. "The newly healed tissue is thicker and tauter than the uninjured tissues surrounding it.

"I truly hate to hear these words from my own lips, but I do believe that it could, very well, have been your corset that deflected the knife from its intended target, saving your life!" I observed.

"I never thought I would see the day when you spoke the praises of the corset!" Rosmerta remarked with a sparkle in her eye.

To the Queen, I said, "This is a tighter area to work in, Majesty. If you will reach across her body, I will work from this side." I suggested.

The two of them exchanged a surreptitious smile as the Queen reached across Rosmerta's bosom to assist me with the stitches.

Inwardly, I allowed my soul to smile too. For the first time in my life I understood the secret smile between lovers. This time, as I helped with the marriage quilt, I would have a real understanding of what love was about and the kind of loving this quilt would envelop.

"Your wounds have healed beautifully." The Queen said, as she ran her fingers lovingly over Rosmerta's scars.

"Aye, 'tis true." I agreed. "I have some arnica and calendula ointment that you may massage into the scars and they shall heal with little or no mark. I do believe Galynda has made a beautiful marriage quilt for you two upon Rosmerta's breast." I said.

Rosmerta looked askance at me. "What ever do you mean?"

"Every stitch was made with a prayer for healing and 'tis infused with love. Just as the quilt we make shall be. I suspect that Lynd gave your stitching extra love, for the greatest portion of the injury was directly over your heart." I explained.

"That is lovely." Rosmerta said, looking down at her chest and stroking the scar with her fingertips.

"When our clan makes a marriage quilt, the women sit together and visit. We share remedies and recipes and tell tales of love and loved ones and share happy family stories over the quilt as we make it."

"The quilt we shall make together," I gestured a small circle in the air which included the Queen, Rosmerta and me. "Shall become the cloak that shrouds the love of the future

King and Queen and all the little princes and princesses they shall lovingly make together beneath it." I looked from one woman to the other to confirm their understanding of the tremendous importance of the quilt.

"When we have all the supplies we need, I would, very much like to work on a bit of blue cloth." I said. "I always thought that if I could make a marriage quilt for Lynd it should be in different hues of blue to match the many moods of blue I have seen in her eyes."

"We are in luck!" Her Majesty said with a smile. "That is exactly what Magda thought you would suggest. I have had Emily fetch us several lovely shades and textures in blue. I hoped you would approve."

Madame Rosmerta slid the large cloth-wrapped parcel on to the foot of the bed and untied the twine and unwrapped it. There, at my feet was a beautiful pile of pre-cut quilt patches of exotic textures and delightful hues of blue.

I immediately found a swatch I liked for Galynda I held in my hands and lovingly stroked the square of cloth. In my heart I sent up a prayer of thanksgiving.

"I love the concept of the marriage quilt," said The Queen with a tear. "It is so beautiful and so symbolic. I hereby proclaim that the Kingdom of the High Plains is officially adopting this lovely tradition!" She declared this with her tatting hook held on high. The hook pointed to the ceiling, reflecting the Queen's lofty proclamation.

"You may wish to dab your loving tears onto a bit of the cloth. That shall be the piece you begin your work on. Make that piece to reflect your tears of love." I explained.

The Queen's eyes were bright with tears. "How do I do that?" She asked.

"With love. You may shape it like a paisley tear or embroider a tear on it or you may find some other way to embellish it with your love. On the day we present Galynda with this quilt, we shall reminisce about each story and the emotions we were feeling when we made the quilt. It is an amazing archive which stores and recounts the lives and loves of the many generations it takes to create a family. It is a history and a promise of renewal with each new generation, made in love, beneath it. It is very powerful medicine when you see all of the pieces united in the quilt."

"I am going to love making this quilt!" Rosmerta choked, dabbing her eyes and then clutching her quilt patch to her tender healing breast.

I smiled inwardly. I was so pleased that these refined women understood and accepted the significance of the marriage quilt.

"Aye," I nodded. "The women of our clan cherish the precious time they have together stitching love into every patch."

As I shared this, I began to remember the wonderful women whose hands and hearts were now missing from our circle. I sent a silent prayer of remembrance for them.

"Are you all right?" Rosmerta broke the silence. "You looked sad for a moment." She frowned.

I nodded to acknowledge that she was correct. "I was just remembering." I stated softly. "Our circle was so much larger when I was a child. There are so many women whose stories and laughter are missing from our circle now."

"This is a tremendous way to celebrate them too, is it not?" the Queen asked. "We might as well stitch in a bit of the wisdom of the ancestors while we are at it."

"Aye. 'Tis true. We must honor those who are no longer in the circle." I stopped in mid-thought. "We should have Magda, Ahnja, Emily, Enid and Madeline in here too." I said.

"We shall," The Queen replied. "But not today, there is much work to be done to clean up the treachery left behind in the palace. Maddy and Phillip are awaiting the news of the craftsmen who are to assess the damage to the castle. Ahnja,

Magda, Emily and Enid are helping to organize the cleanup of the main kitchen and the great dining hall after the feast.

"Was there much damage?" I asked.

"A fair amount," Queen Alyssandra replied. "But the damage was done to things that are of little consequence to me and the children." She said with a dismissive flick of her wrist. "We three," she gestured a small circle to encompass herself, Madame Rosmerta and me. "We were the only casualties of this skirmish and I find it quite fitting that we commence this quilt alone together." She said this with finality and conviction.

"Indeed!" Rosmerta agreed.

"Well, Lynd," I thought, "You have a home and you shall soon have a husband and perhaps, babies some day soon. It is all so unexpected and so wonderful! I am so happy for you!" I felt tremendous joy in my heart. I was surprised to find I also felt relief and peace. Galynda would no longer have to wander or be lost or want for anything.

I cast a furtive glance from Rosmerta to the Queen. Each was busy with her own cloth. Stealthily, I raised the cloth to my own cheek and secretly brushed away a tear. I had waited my whole life for this opportunity. I had so many ideas for the work I would put into my very first patch for Lynd's marriage quilt. Now that the moment was upon me, I did not know how to begin.

Busy Hands

I looked forward to the daily routine of sitting in the mornings with Rosmerta and the Queen as we stitched and laughed and cried together.

In the evenings, I sat by fire and lantern light with Magda, Ahnja, Enid, Emily and Princess Madeline.

It wasn't over long before we moved our daily sewing circles from the bed chamber to the drawing room where two rose and sage upholstered settees and several matching chairs had been placed in a congenial circle in front of the fireplace.

Time passed swiftly by in the company of such wonderful women. Days gave way to weeks and weeks turned to moons.

Every woman had a unique stitching pattern. It was not long before I could identify the creator of a specific patch by her own style of stitching.

Ahnja, Galynda's mother, made precise, even stitches. Magda made methodical and functional stitches that would not come apart easily. Madame Rosmerta's stitches were much like the woman who made them. They were full-bodied and beautiful. Queen Alyssandra's stitches were delicate and ornate, as were those of the Princess Madeline. Enid had a steady hand with the needle but as her eyes had grown weaker with age her stitches had grown a bit larger to be more easily seen. Emily made a pattern of stitches that seemed, somehow, like the bird tracks a baker leaves on the top crust of a pie to vent out steam.

Our quilt grew more beautiful with each passing day. One evening, as I paused to survey our work, it struck me that something was missing. It had never occurred to me that a quilt made for Galynda would not have a single tidy stitch made by Galynda's own hand. In my entire life, I had never seen a clan quilt without her skillful handiwork included. While I was exhilarated at the thought of making the quilt for her, the absence of her voice and hands and heart as we stitched caused me deep sadness.

Magda noticed my quiet mood. "Willow, you are awfully quiet. What is it that weighs so heavily on your heart?"

I stroked the patch I was working on and smoothed it upon my lap as I searched for the words. "I was just noticing how beautiful our quilt is becoming." I began.

Every woman in the room looked from patch to patch and agreed.

"And then," I continued. "I found myself identifying each of the women by her unique stitches."

Again, the women in the group smiled and nodded their agreement and support.

"It occurred to me that I was looking for Galynda's fine stitches. Until now, I have never encountered a marriage quilt without her handiwork. I was just saddened to think such a fine quilt shan't bear a single stitch from Lynd." I explained.

"That is only a part of the lesson of the marriage quilt."

Magda explained. "We bind our woman clan together with the stitches. Everyone does her part. But the woman who is being honored leaves the clan to join another.

We must all share in the bride's joy and anticipation. But we must also be mindful of her absence. That is why you are sad Willow. You can see that you are one with the clan and that Galynda, who has always been present in your life, is now absent."

I was shocked at the deep wisdom of the quilt. It was the key to bringing our women together and it allowed us time to reflect and to grieve our loss before the honored woman left the fold.

"I always knew the quilt was important for our people. I just never understood it so deeply before today." I said. I was overwhelmed by emotions of sadness and happiness and love and joy.

"The quilt is a way to find your way through the tangles of emotions that you are feeling as you make it. It is both a powerful teacher and a comforting medicine.

I suspect you never understood all of this because you had never opened yourself up to the possibility of loving another and allowing that one person to love you, before now. Until now, you were looking at the quilt from the eyes of a child. You could enjoy the stories and laughter and you may have even shed some tears. But now, Willow, you understand that this quilt is both a gift and a sacrifice. We give away much when we surrender a member of our family. We feel it more profoundly when our heart is so deeply invested."

For a moment, we all sat in silence, needles poised in mid-stitch. We had all learned a valuable lesson from the wise wedding quilt.

A New Frame of Mind

I had become so involved with the work we were doing on the quilt, time moved more quickly than I had anticipated. Two moons had passed before I realized it.

Mornings were still somewhat problematic for Madeline as she still had bouts with morning sickness. I taught her how to make tea to soothe her stomach and tea to calm her irritability.

Madame Rosmerta taught me how to gently massage Madeline's abdomen and lower back to keep her comfortable.

By the end of her fourth moon, the morning sickness went away altogether.

I had taken to calling my Madeline "Pearl" when we were alone together.

As we dressed one morning, Madeline asked irritably, "Why do you call me Pearl? Is it because I am growing round?" She was hurt, I could tell by the timbre of her voice.

I seated myself on the edge of the bed and patted the spot beside me, indicating she should sit.

"Nay, I call you 'Pearl' because that is what you mean to me. You are precious and you glow warmly from within as pearls do. Your skin is warm and creamy smooth and very pleasing to the touch.

Maddy, you have a warm wisdom that comes from deep inside you in a place so sacred, even I cannot go there.

Pearls are the same way. They are beautiful as they are. Most gemstones need to be dressed or faceted or polished to bring out their beauty. Pearls do not require improving.

The shell of the oyster is called 'mother of pearl' for a reason. I see you housing a great and wonderful treasure there." I said placing my hand upon her slightly swollen belly.

She covered my hands with her own and I continued, "Baby pearls, as they are growing, are attached to the mother of pearl by a tiny umbilicus, just as you are united with your baby pearl.

Perhaps, I should be calling you Mother of Pearl. Have I told you that the baby is a girl?" I asked.

"No, you did not tell me this. How do you know?" She asked, genuinely interested.

You carry her in a basket. Your belly looks like a basket, smaller at the top and fuller on the bottom." I formed my hands around my own belly showing her how it would look. "If you were carrying a boy, your belly would be high and round in the middle more like a basket turned upside down. Like this." Again, I demonstrated the approximate size and shape of a belly bearing a boy.

You tend to desire bland food which also indicates you carry a girl. Women crave sour foods with boys. There are so many signs that show me you have a girl. Even your pulses tell me our baby is a girl." I ticked off each item on my fingers.

"Rosmerta tells me that the baby is a girl too. She determined this by dangling a needle suspended on a bit of thread in front of my belly! She said some women do the same with their wedding rings instead of a needle!

Rosmerta and I have come to the same conclusion; you are carrying a girl, although Rosmerta's methods are not entirely logical!" I threw my hands up into the air in mock discontent for her diagnostic techniques.

The Princess sat silently beside me, processing what it was I had just said. "Willow," she began, "I adore you. The way you speak to me and the words you use to describe things are so clear. I can see the images as you speak. I know that you love me by the way you look at me and touch me. I can feel it to my very center. You tell me in so many ways every day. You show me by your actions in everything you do for me and with me and on my behalf. Your love motivates me to learn more and to do more to show you how very much I love you too.

The following morning came with a cheerful clattering of breakfast dishes, then a loud crashing, followed by a few choice vexations I had no idea a Princess should utter.

"Good morning, Your Grace." I said with a smile. "Do you kiss your mother, the sovereign Queen Regnant of the High Plains, with that foul mouth?"

"Oh, you find yourself very amusing, I suppose!" Madeline sniffed.

"And irresistible, you forgot to mention how very irresistible I think I am." I said with a growing smile.

"Stop being so charming! I am working very hard at feeling sorry for myself!" she said, stooping to pick up the ruins of our breakfast. "I am so incompetent!" She chastised, hastily tucking a loose tendril of hair behind her right ear.

"You feel incompetent because you can not handle a tray of food?" I asked calmly. "Very well, Your Royal Highness, if being a Monarch does not work out for you, may I suggest that you not attempt a job as a kitchen maid or pub wench?" I gave her a crooked half smile as I sat up on one elbow.

She cast me a cool look. "If I did not love you so much, I think I would have to despise you for that." She gathered the contents of the spilled tray and placed the disheveled, and now unappetizing, contents onto the small table that stood on one wall in the antechamber of our quarters

"Peace!" I said. "Since I can not come to you, would you please come here and sit with me?" I invited, patting the seat next to me. I was sitting, with my foot propped upon a small hassock, in one of the settees before a warm fire.

"Oh, very well!" Maddy gave one last exasperated groan as she stepped gingerly around the wreckage that had been our breakfast and came to sit with me upon the settee.

"I can see how much you love me and how very hard you try to help. You just have to give yourself the chance to learn without chastising yourself. I can see that we both have a lot of work to do." I said.

"Whatever do you mean?" She looked puzzled.

"In a few short moons, we shall both be on even ground as new and inexperienced parents. Neither of us has been down that road. We have got to learn to allow ourselves the opportunity to learn without such harsh self-judgement. We do not hold others to such unyielding expectations, neither should we hold ourselves to that level of expectation.

We are learning new lessons every day that will teach us what we need to know to be better for each other and for the baby, Pearl. We must allow ourselves to be beginners. Babies are the greatest lesson in beginning. When they are born, we do not burden them with unreasonable expectations, we love them and guide them without judgement. Most of all, we allow them the time to be beginners. We shall celebrate Pearl's efforts, even when she cannot yet complete a task.

"It would not do to castigate a small child, whose only wish is to help, for spilling a tray of food. Shouting at a child may diminish her desire to help or to learn new tasks." I explained.

"You are the clever one!" my companion said with a smile. "I can see that my lesson in this is to allow myself, as a beginner, the courtesy of patience and kindness."

"Aye, 'tis far easier to understand the lesson than to put it into practice!" I held an index finger aloft and winked at her with a smile.

"Let us review our current life lessons." I suggested.

Do you not find it ironic that I must lie around all day and have others serving me, while you are learning to get your hands dirty helping with the chores?"

"Yes, I can see the paradox." She said nodding. "I hate it." She pouted.

"Hate is a very strong word." I could hear Magda's patient teaching about the tremendous power of words.

"Well, I certainly do not like it!" She responded tartly crossing her arms across her chest. "At all!"

"You do not have to like it. Our job now, is to learn from this situation. Every difficult task has a reward. Sometimes the rewards are small or difficult to recognize but everything happens for a reason. If you think about it, everything happens as it is supposed to and it happens, perfectly, in its own time.

I do not like what has happened either. I feel frustrated by my limitations too. I have a chance to see life through the eyes of all the patients I have ever limited to bed rest. As a healer, I can treat a disorder best if I understand it. As a caregiver, I must learn how to accept care. I am a commoner who has the opportunity to understand a little of what life as a princess is like.

Do you remember when I first met you, Maddy? I tried to invite you to share a meal with my friends in the guest kitchen. That meal was uncomfortable because as a princess, you are intimidating and you demand respect from common folk. Whether you intend to or not, you command a lot of power."

She nodded, indicating she was listening and for me to continue.

"Since we fled the castle together, you have changed irrevocably, in so many ways. That single experience alone has changed you forever." I held up my index finger, representing the singular event.

"How do you mean it has changed me?" She asked.

"Since that time, you have eaten at the same table as common people without feeling awkward. You have laughed and cried with us. You have accepted the suggestions of servants and staff. You have learned to wash dishes and how to brew tea without help and how to see to the needs of others.

Maddy, not the least of these, you accepted me into your life and convinced your mother, the Matriarch of a nation, to consider this relationship for marriage! You want to raise a regal child with what might seem, to some people, to be an ignoble gypsy!" I exclaimed.

"When you hold it in the light for me, I can see it more clearly." She said, nodding thoughtfully. "Sometimes when I am with you I feel very ignorant."

"Why would you feel that way?" I asked.

"Because I cannot see something, and you have a way of pointing it out and making it glaringly obvious." She replied.

"Again, Maddy, 'tis not that I am so much wiser, 'tis that I have had more practice observing and studying life."

"But you are so much younger than I!" She exclaimed, her frustration beginning to show.

"Only four years. And age has nothing to do with experience. As I see it, I have been a shaman for most of my life. I have been out in the world meeting people and learning from them.

You have been a Princess all your life. You have been sheltered from many of the unpleasant conditions that most humans face every day."

"What have I missed?" She asked, genuinely curious. She rested her back against the arm of the settee and draped her legs comfortably over my lap and covered us both with a woolen throw.

"I have treated sinewy, dark-skinned laborers and fleshy, soft, pallid wealthy folks. I have learned that no matter who your family is or how much gold you amass, you have the same basic needs as everyone else. All people need to eat and drink and to feel that they are valued. We all need shelter from the elements. No living creature enjoys being ill, weak or dependent on others.

This is why I feel 'tis important for you to learn to cook and clean. Could you have survived in hiding without your staff? They can most definitely survive without you, but can you survive without them?"

"When I think about trying to survive by myself, it frightens me. I feel very vulnerable." The Princess stated sincerely.

"You proved yourself to be a wise leader by listening to everyone's ideas for the plan to take back the palace. You would not have had the victory without all of their skillful help."

"That is so true!" Her voice trailed off. "There is a lot to think about." She said, almost to herself.

"Aye, Madeline, there is." I replied. After a moment of silence, I spoke again. "I believe it would be a tremendous learning experience for both of us if we were to learn to depend upon each other."

Madeline cocked her head and looked askance at me. "Whatever are you proposing?"

"I have learned to live my life independent of others. I grew up very self-reliant, not anticipating sharing my life with anyone. Perhaps, I have grown entirely too independent. And you, my little Princess, have lived your life being served by others. You never anticipated having to care for yourself, let alone others.

As you can see, we have grown up to suit our roles. You are a perfect princess, strong and forthright when you make decisions for your people. As an individual however, you are unable to tend to your own needs. You have a baby on the way and unless you learn how to tend to the baby yourself, someone else will rear your child for you.

I have grown so accustomed to doing everything for myself. It is difficult for me to accept help from others even when there is no doubt that I cannot do some things alone." I gestured at my foot with both hands.

"Perhaps," I began hesitantly. I focused inward upon the swirling thoughts inside my head, which had begun to settle and become clearer. "Perhaps," I began again. "We ought to begin our lives together on a journey!" I exclaimed.

"A clan that travels together depends upon all of its members, even the children. Every person has work to do. No one eats before the others and no one is left behind." I explained.

Another thought came to me then. "I have a wagon, part of one anyway. I am certain, now that Galynda is to be Princess of the High Plains, she would not mind my sharing our wagon with you."

"I am both excited and terrified by the idea of traveling alone with you." The Princess admitted. "Excited," she began counting on her fingers, because I would have you all to myself. And terrified, because I am quite afraid I would be a great burden to you, and I feel quite exposed just thinking about it." She ended rubbing her upper arms as if she felt a sudden chill.

"I can understand your fears. You have been protected by others all your life."

She nodded her head. Yes, I have led a very sheltered life. I admire you for your strength, Willow. I see the journey as a tremendous opportunity for me to learn and grow and become much stronger.

Phillip has had much more freedom to travel because he is a man. Mother sent him away to different kingdoms to learn the ways of other people so he would understand them and become a better ruler when he becomes King."

"That was wise of your mother to do that for him. I would like the opportunity to offer that same kind of education to you. You have already experienced life as Queen during your mother's illness."

Madeline looked down at her hands.

"What is it, Love?" I asked her. "Did I say something to hurt you?"

"No, you have done nothing wrong. I am just struggling with myself." She said, fiddling with a bit of fringe on the throw.

"Struggling? With what?" I asked.

"I have not shared this with anyone." She began. "Who has there been to tell?" She chastised herself rolling her eyes. Her cheeks flushed at her self-disgust.

"You must promise me that you shall not breathe a word of this to anyone." She said, twisting a lock of loose hair on her finger.

"Maddy, what ever can it be? Tell me!" I could feel my heart pounding in my chest. The inner workings of my mind began to weave tapestries of what if. What if she does not truly love you? What if she wants you out of the castle? What if...

She tucked the loose tendril behind her ear drew in a deep breath and straightened her posture. "Willow, I do not wish to continue my duties as monarch." Having said this, her back relaxed and bowed into a slump, giving her the appearance of melting from her former regal self into a smaller, stooped commoner.

I sat silently, allowing my mind to sort through what she had just revealed to me.

Nervously, Madeline broke into my silence. "Do you think me a bad person for not wanting to do what I was born to do?" She sat small on the settee beside me picking at a bit of nothing on the woolen throw. "I would be devastated if you thought of me as a bad person." She said in a wee, small voice.

"Maddy, please look at me." I requested softly, lifting her chin to meet her eyes with mine. I need you to understand that I love you. That will not change if you renounce your crown."

She leaned into me and wept. I could feel her body shaking as she pressed it against mine.

"What a lot of pressure there must be in the business of making decisions not only for yourself, but for an entire Kingdom." I commented. I bent and lightly kissed her hair.

She looked up into my eyes. Her cheeks were flushed and tear-stained. "I take comfort in knowing that you would love me no matter what. I want you to know that I do not wish to renounce my crown. I only wish to defer to Phillip and Galynda.

I do not care for the endless demands of being Queen. The decisions I must make are often unpopular. I feel that I can not satisfy the needs of everyone and it is truly sad when I must make life and death decisions without any time to gather my wits. I feel one war is enough for me. I am done. I shall fill in for Phillip if he should ever require it, but I shall not be sovereign Queen. The pressure and solitude are not to my liking."

"I shall love you regardless of the choice you make. You are the Princess of the people of the High Plains no matter what you choose."

"As the eldest, it is expected that I shall, some day, become the Sovereign Queen Regnant. I do not wish to bear that burden as I did when Mother was ill. I do not wish that upon Phillip and your dear Galynda either! Even though they shall have each other for support, it is a tremendous responsibility.

I would be content to remain Princess Madeline. I could never consider renouncing my crown because I carry the royal bloodlines and am growing heavy with the first Royal Grandchild." With that, she looked down and rubbed her swelling belly.

I marveled at the pressures Madeline endured because of her title. I was grateful that I could depend on the wisdom of the elders, who made all of the difficult decisions for our clan. I sent up a little prayer of thanksgiving that I did not have such responsibilities of my own.

"I have always shared my concerns with Magda. An example would be our proposed journey together. I shall discuss our journey with her and she shall take it to the Elders. They shall meet and discuss the idea before a decision is made."

"I like having Elders. It is a very wise way to take care of your people. Perhaps this is the solution I have been seeking! I shall offer this idea to Mother as a way to share the burden of administration." Madeline stated with more confidence than I had seen all morning.

"Do you not have advisors?" I was incredulous.

"Oh, yes. But their position is advisory only. I wish to have more guidance from those who have lived and know and understand the consequences of major decisions." Madeline stated decisively.

A Gift from the Elders

"It is a splendid idea to encourage Willow and Madeline to explore and learn new things from each other. Every new couple needs time to do this." The Queen began. "I like this idea, but I am uncomfortable with them going unaccompanied by the guard."

"Begging Your Majesty's pardon, but being accompanied by the Royal Guard rather defeats the anonymity experience." I said bowing my head in deference.

"I know, Willow, Dear, it is just that I worry so." She replied.

"Willow," Magda turned to address me "You are as strong a woman as any I know. But you are just that, a woman. By being out on your own, you would be putting Her Highness, the baby and yourself at risk. I would not want anything to happen to any of you and unfortunately, two women alone are far more vulnerable than a man and a woman."

"I quite agree." Ahmad said, nodding his head and

brushing his bushy mustache with his hand. "I am thinking that two women alone is a big risk."

"'Tis imperative that I gather springtime herbs to replenish our supplies." I countered. I knew in my heart that I could do little to change their current frame of mind.

The meeting with the Elders was not as unsympathetic as I thought it would be, but the outcome was disappointing, nonetheless.

We returned to Madeline's bedchambers and discussed the meeting. It was disappointing. Neither of us wanted to hear the answer we had received, but the Elders had passed their decision down to us and there was not much we could do about it.

"Maddy," I said thoughtfully. "I have something I need to do. I shall meet you here, in your bedchambers, before the evening meal."

Madeline searched my eyes for a hint of what I was thinking.

"Very well." She said with a hesitant nod of her head. Her expression asked for explanation but when none was forthcoming she simply bowed gently, granting me my leave.

I hobbled from the bedchambers, headed directly for the harem.

Outside of Rosmerta's door I knocked and awaited an answer.

"Why Willow! You are up and about! How nice!" She began excitedly. Then in mid-thought she added hesitantly, "Does Magda know?" Unconsciously she looked over my shoulder to see if I had been followed.

"Aye, she does indeed." I acknowledged. "Ahmad has been making me a walking stick and I have been given my brace on the condition that I take care not to walk on it over much. I do believe the pain will be an apt monitor of my activities." I said.

"Oh, do come in!" Rosmerta exclaimed, stepping aside to

allow me passage.

It was comforting to be back in Rosmerta's private quarters. I had missed our visits and heart to heart discussions.

"I need your counsel on something." I began.

"How can I help?" Rosmerta wanted to know. She directed me toward her sitting room.

"I know in your specialized training, that you have to know a lot about men and their likes and dislikes." I was having difficulty finding the words to say what I wanted to say.

"Where are we going with this?" Rosmerta asked with her eyes squinting and her brow furrowed in utter confusion.

"Well, I have brought a proposal to the Elders that Maddy and I should spend some time away from the castle. We need private time together so that we might become better acquainted with each other before the baby is born. I need to learn how to accept help from Madeline and she needs to learn more about how to take care of herself and others before she becomes a mother."

"You do realize that a Princess does not raise her children. That is done by the nurse maids and wet nurses." Rosmerta began hesitantly, still puzzled. She moved a woolly throw from the settee and seated herself upon one ankle in a tailor sit position, with the remaining foot dangling.

I sat across from her in a matching wingback chair.

"All of which has important ties to what I have come here for, but just off the point at the moment." I replied.

"Very well, how may I help? Where do I fit into the scheme of things?" She asked with her hands upon her ample hips.

"I realize that others tend to royal babies, but Madeline and I have discussed it and we both have decided to raise the baby ourselves so that we can grow in each others' hearts from the very beginning."

"That's very admirable of you both. Babies can be a lot of work." Rosmerta stated.

"Aye, as can anything worth having." I agreed. "A baby has been given to us that we may care for it and love it. We cannot fully love someone we do not know. We want to love this baby with our whole hearts."

"You are such a sage." Rosmerta said with admiration. "Sometimes I regret the choice I made not to have children of my own, although, the Prince and Princess are very much like my own."

"The Elders have rejected the idea of our travels because they are troubled about our safety."

"They would feel better if you were accompanied by a man?" Rosmerta concluded.

"That is a fair assessment." I nodded.

"And you need to know what the best characteristics of a gentleman are so you know who to hire to drive you two?" She asked.

"You are partially correct, but my intention is not to hire an escort or a chaperone. I want to know about the behaviors of men so that I might be able to behave as such myself."

Rosmerta sat for a moment with her mouth agape looking rather like a fish out of water. When finally she was able to recover her composure, Rosmerta gasped, "You mean you want to disguise yourself as a man?"

"Aye, that is exactly what I am proposing. Will you help me?" I replied.

"How can I help?" she sounded bewildered.

"I wish to look and behave as a man does. I had hoped you would tutor me in the fine art of walking, talking and behaving as a man does."

"But Willow you are such a beautiful woman!" she exclaimed.

"Aye. That may be, my dear friend. Unfortunately, as a woman, I am bound to this castle. Will you not help set me free?" I requested.

"Oh, yes! Bunny, I will. How liberating!" She exclaimed. Rosmerta clapped her hands together silently in her enthusiasm and then scurried to her dressing table. She returned with her scissors and hairbrush in hand. "Your hair is definitely a very feminine feature which shall be easy to remedy."

Come into the bedchamber, where the lighting is better, and there are no carpets.

I followed her obediently into the next room and seated myself on the small bench that she used at her dressing table.

She removed my hat and began to uncoil the braids from my head.

As I felt my plaited hair lighten on my head, I wondered if I had made the best choice. As the first braid was cut from my head, I decided there was no turning back and no room for self-doubt.

Rosmerta fussed over my hair for what seemed an eternity and then, when she was satisfied, she stepped away from me to fetch the hand mirror which was on her dressing table.

I was taken aback when I saw my own image in the looking glass. I nearly did not recognize myself looking back. It was difficult to see myself in the man-boy with short, curly hair who stared back at me in shock. The transition was almost complete. The change in wardrobe, I was certain, would only confirm that I was, indeed, a man.

"Rosmerta," I began breathlessly. "Rosmerta, I can not believe that is me in the reflection. The change is so absolute!" I said stroking what was left of my hair over and over again. "My head feels so much lighter! I am certain that Magda would have done this for me when I was small if she felt the Elders would have accepted it. My hair was always so unruly, and I am so active that 'twas often quite a mess!"

"That I can well imagine!" she said with a smile.

"Do you like it Willow?" She asked, indicating with the hairbrush that she meant the haircut.

"It serves my purpose. That pleases me. 'It shall be far easier to care for and that also pleases me. I am not accustomed to my reflection yet and that shall require time. I pray that Madeline does not take offense."

"You mean to tell me you did not tell Her Highness?" A disconcerted Rosmerta asked clapping one hand over her gaping mouth. "Why do I allow you to talk me into such trouble?" Her suddenly weak knees gave out and she sat upon the bed with a plop.

"I have not told her just yet." I replied shaking my head. "You were the one person I thought of who would be willing to listen and mightn't think me crazy."

"Oh my, I am going to have to ask more questions before I leap in with both feet next time." Rosmerta said rising to her feet. She placed her scissors and brush in their respective places on the dressing table.

"I did not allow even myself the time to think." I stated. "Have we any clothing that I might wear that shall complete this look?" I asked, tugging at my shortened hair.

Rosmerta began to pace the floor. All the while she tapped her chin with her index finger. I was quite taken aback when she suddenly whirled about and asked me "Do you wish to appear as a peasant or a nobleman?"

"Perhaps," I began, "I should appear as a nobleman since Madeline will already have to struggle to learn independence. I can not imagine how it would be for her to have to live as a peasant as well."

"Or, perhaps that is just the guise you will need to make your transformation complete." Rosmerta replied, deep in thought.

"Poor Maddy." I said shaking my head. "Whatever will she do?"

"Whatever she does, she will do it all by herself, with

your guidance of course." Rosmerta commented. "I can get you some trousers and a tunic from our trunk of left behind items. If you will excuse me, I shall make haste." She curtsied to me and backed from the room.

While Rosmerta was out of the room, I walked to the dressing table and took up the looking glass and peered at my image once more. There, in the mirror was that curious man-child gaping wide-eyed at me.

I ran my fingers through my shorn hair. There was little left of it. 'Twas truly exhilarating and liberating all in the same instant, once I realized I would be free of endlessly having to brush and braid it. There would be no more endless plucking of grasses and seeds out of my hair after gathering medicinal plants and no more frustrating tangles.

Rosmerta was back quickly with trousers, tunic, and a short chemise. "Here Bunny, let's have you try these for size. No one will miss these; they have been here for ages. We had them laundered and pressed, but their owners have never called on us to claim them." She stated with outstretched arms offering me several articles of clothing.

The tunic, far less confining than a corset, was a welcome and easy adjustment. Wearing the trousers however, seemed somehow indecent. It felt very much as though I were wearing my pantalets on the outside of my clothes.

Madame Rosmerta placed the tips of both hands to her lips. "Oh Bunny, I would not recognize you if I did not know it was you. You look very much like a man-boy!"

"Rosmerta," I faltered, "do you think it will matter that my hands are so small?" I said, holding them up to inspect them.

"No, I should not think so." She answered honestly. "I have met many fine-boned gentlemen in my time." Her speech slowed and then she turned to face me. "You know, it is a good thing that you have a bit of a limp, otherwise we would have to work to make your walk less feminine."

"My walk is feminine?" I asked genuinely intrigued.

"Oh yes," Rosmerta replied, tucking her hair behind an ear. "A woman walks in smooth, fluid movements almost as if to keep from disturbing her skirt ruffles." She demonstrated an exaggerated version of a feminine gait.

"A man, on the other hand, walks in long abrupt steps as though every step has a purpose and he has somewhere important to be." She lifted her skirts, exposing her bloomered legs and demonstrated a masculine stride.

The effect was comical, and I had to laugh to see such a spectacle. "Oh Rosmerta, I can see that fine ladies oughtn't to walk as you just did! I would never be able to get through my day for all the laughing!"

Rosmerta smiled at me. "So, you agree, men and women do, indeed have different manners of walking."

"Aye, they do." I agreed still smiling. "I shall be aware of my stride from this point on." I promised.

"I shall bring these new changes to the Elders tomorrow. Would it be possible for you to arrange a private meeting with Madeline in the conservatory? I should like to break this to her before I present myself to the Elders. I promised to meet her in her bedchambers before dinner. I can not do that now." I said.

"I should say not! Bunny, I would not want to be you attempting to enter Her Royal Highness' bedchambers without a formal introduction. You could end up in shackles!" She told me this warmly, but there was a sense of genuine concern in her voice.

"That is why I have come to you, Rosmerta, because I trust that you would know what to do, even in some of the most unusual of circumstances." I replied.

"More unusual than you know, Honey." She replied. "Now, we should see to it that you and the Princess have a chance to have a late supper and get acquainted. I think that would be a wise approach." Rosmerta agreed nodding her head in thought. "I shall tend to the details, but we must make haste. Darkness is already upon us," she said, making shooing motions with her hands.

"Might I find a path to the conservatory from here, to avoid being seen?" I asked.

"Of course," Rosmerta said, hastily tucking a loose tendril of hair behind her ear. "I shall tend to your dinner request and then guide you there. Why don't you practice your walking, and I shall return for you in a moment." Rosmerta grasped the front of her skirt, and curtsied as she backed toward the door.

Moments later we were making our way through the walls of the castle as hastily as my injured foot would allow.

Dinner for Two

Rosmerta seated me in the conservatory; at the very same table she had seated Galynda when she had surprised me with her arrival.

I wondered how many meetings and trysts she had arranged in her time at the castle. My mind began to wander into uncharted territory, and I had to close my eyes and shake my head to rid it of unsavory images.

As I waited, in the dimly lit conservatory, I sat and listened to the myriad of exotic, colorful songbirds as they settled for the night. I knew they were there, even if I could not see them now. I had seen them by day, as they flew through the canopy of trees and plants.

These rare and wonderful birds were safe from predators in this room of glass and black and white tile. There was water for them in the ornate fountains and the waterfalls and streams. There were seeds and fruits and suet for them hidden throughout the room.

They were safe, but, I wondered, were they as happy as

they would be if they were free? I realized that Maddy was the same as these birds. She had all of her needs tended to for her. Everything she could wish for was brought to her, but she lacked the one thing that could truly make her flourish, her freedom. She was not at liberty to pluck the fruits of her desires for herself.

As a small child I had imagined life in a castle would be very liberating. The royalty who lived in castles surely would have no chores and I was certain that they could do as they pleased.

It occurred to me now, as I sat pondering her life, that Princess Madeline was quite possibly the most confined human being I had ever met. Everything she did or said was under great scrutiny by the Royal Family and all of the people of the Kingdom. 'Twas at that moment that I realized I felt pity for her.

I had never imagined how it would be not to be able to run, unshod, in the dew-dampened grass. I could not imagine how miserable I would be, were I to live my life as these birds and Madeline did.

My thoughts were interrupted by approaching footsteps. I felt the color drain from my face. I felt cold and suddenly, I felt afraid. What would I do if Madeline and the elders hated what I had done to my hair? What if they felt I had been insubordinate?

I could hear hushed voices as Madame Rosmerta ushered the Princess into the conservatory and took her leave hastily.

"I am so sorry to keep you Sir," Princess Madeline said crisply. "I was unaware we had a guest." she said with a regal curtsy in my direction. It took me a moment to realize that it was me she was addressing.

In that moment of hesitation, I gathered my best gentleman's manners and rose from my seat and gave her a gentle bow, careful not to forget I was a man and curtsy by mistake.

"Please," the Princess began, "won't you have a seat?" She gestured toward the chair I had just vacated. "Madame Rosmerta tells me you have business with me." Her eyes studied my face, taking in every detail.

So intense was her gaze, I felt myself shrink under her scrutiny. She appeared certain she should know me, but she could not quite place me.

"It must be the late hour. I really must apologize for staring. You seem so familiar, and yet, I can not recall a name. Have we met?" She asked sweeping my face with her gaze again.

I nodded my head slowly.

She looked relieved.

Breaking all castle protocol, I leaned in toward her, across the table.

"Sir, I beg your pardon!" she stiffened and pulled back from me.

"Maddy," I said softly, "'Tis me, Willow."

Her breath caught in her throat and she did not speak for what seemed an eternity. Her face flushed and her eyes filled with tears.

My heart sank. I felt certain that I had frightened her, that she felt threatened by me. Perhaps, she despised me for what I had done. To make matters worse, I had not consulted with her and then I had sprung this on her with no warning.

I felt a knot in my throat. I tried to swallow but my mouth had gone completely dry. I could not speak, for the lump. I could taste the tears in my mouth before they welled in my eyes.

"Willow," Madeline began, "oh my." she spoke in starts and stops as if she could not find the words to say. She placed her palm against her chest. With her free hand, she grasped one of the napkins from the table and lightly whisked the tears from the corner of her eye.

I managed to find my voice and spoke again. "Maddy, I..."

and then my voice wavered with emotion and faded.

"It is such a curious thing to have a young man seated before me who has the voice of the woman I love." The Princess spoke meekly.

"I am sorry, should I not speak? Would you rather I went away? Do you hate it?" I rambled on stupidly once I found my voice again.

Madeline brushed away another tear with her fingertips and patted her chest with the hand that clutched the table linen. "You gave me quite a start!"

My own heart was pounding so hard I had to strain to hear her speak. "Is it awful? Would you rather not see me?" I queried.

Madeline, still flush-faced smiled through her tears. "No, that is not what I need, nor what I meant to imply." She waved the linen-filled hand back and forth as if to rub out the idea as it hung in the air between us.

"You really gave me a start!" She gasped. "I could not explain it, but when I saw you sitting here I felt... I felt..." She hesitated, searching for words that seemed to elude her. Finally, she burst out, "I felt amorous toward you!" She gestured toward me with a sweep of an upturned palm.

"'Tis a good thing to feel is it not?" I asked.

"No, it is not." She defended. "Not when I am promised to someone else!" her voice was rising. "I did not recognize you as Willow!" she said more quietly. "I thought you were some unknown young man from a neighboring village!" she waved her hand in a dismissive manner. "I was beginning to wonder what was wrong with me!" she said stabbing herself in the chest with an accusatory finger. She leaned across the table toward me and spoke in a conspiratorial tone, "Aside from you, I have never felt that amorous feeling for anyone, until now." She paused, rolling her eyes. "I felt as if I were being unfaithful to you!" She began to cry in earnest.

That was not the answer I had anticipated. It never

occurred to me that she would not recognize me. I had also never considered the possibility that, as a man, I might be more attractive to her. Suddenly I was frightened.

"Do...do you like me better as a man, Maddy?" I asked in a small voice, frightened to hear the answer but compelled to ask anyway.

"No, Willow. That is not what I meant to infer either!" She shook her head in frustration. "I was not anticipating meeting the one person on this earth that means everything to me. I was thinking that I was just tending to castle business when suddenly, there you are in an unexpected form!" She gestured toward me with both hands. "Princess Madeline may not have recognized you, but something deep inside me sure did!" She said in frustration.

"Are you angry with me?" I asked.

"Oh, Willow! You are so impetuous sometimes, you exasperate me!" she leaned back in the chair heavily.

"I knew if I spoke with you about it, you would tell me 'no,' so I decided to enlist the help of the one woman who knows more about the behaviors of men than anyone I know."

"Oh, that Rosmerta!" Madeline made a cross face and balled up the napkin-filled hand into a fist that she shook in mock threat. "There can be nothing but trouble when the two of you put your heads together!"

"Then you are not angry with me?" I asked again.

"No, Willow, my Dearest One. I am not angry with you." She said as she sat forward again and lightly cupped my chin in her hand. "I was taken aback. I was angry with myself for having inappropriate feelings for someone other than you!"

Her touch brought a light, tingly feeling up from my loins into my middle. I found it very difficult to concentrate when she touched me.

"I plan to go before the Elders tomorrow and see if the transformation I have made will change their minds." I said.

I was deeply relieved that she still loved the person who was Willow.

I bravely continued. "As I see it, if I could successfully deceive you, then I know that we can deceive everyone on the outside without any problem."

"You have made your point." She said. "It is just so amazing, the difference a little less hair and a change of clothing makes." She said, shaking her head as she scrutinized my face and body.

"I ordered a late dinner for us." I said.

"That's a good thing, young lady," Madeline said. "You are going to need your strength, because I intend to take you into my private chambers this evening and do a thorough investigation into these changes to see just how extensive they are!"

A Second Meeting before the Elders

When we returned to the private chambers of the Princess, she held me out at arm's length and inspected me by the firelight. She lighted another lantern and turned me slowly to inspect me from all angles.

"My, oh my, you do indeed look like a young man!" the Princess gasped. "I cannot get over it!"

Madeline helped me remove my tunic, leaving me in my short chemise and trousers. I felt a small shiver of anticipation run up my spine.

"Come closer to the fire." She invited, beckoning me with a hand gesture.

I obliged, stepping into the light.

Maddy had me turn this way and that. Raising and extending my arms.

"Whatever are you doing?" I queried.

"Now, come closer and bend, at the waist before me as though you were serving me." She replied without answering my question.

I did as she requested, now more curious than ever.

"Willow, you do look a lot like a young man. You do, however, possess a pair of very beautiful, feminine breasts, which upon close examination, I can detect from several different angles."

"I can bind them." I volunteered, hating the idea already.

"I think that would be a wise choice, I do not care to share them with anyone else. Besides we don't wish to reveal our secret to anyone else now do we?"

"Aye," I replied, nodding. "I have treated patients with injuries to their ribs. I have made support wraps that fit rather like a tight vest that can be worn under a chemise."

"That is a very a good idea, but we shall have to resort to strips of cloth for our meeting tomorrow," she replied matter-of-factly. "Let's bind you now so that we are certain that your new persona is flawless by morning.

When we had conceived of all the possible ways that I might reveal my identity accidentally, we fell into bed, exhausted, just as the sun was breaking over the edge of the mountains.

With only a few hours' sleep we were awakened by a knock at the chamber door.

Madeline rose to a sitting position and placed a finger upon her lips. "I shall take care of this. You stay here."

I suddenly remembered my decision to cut my hair and ran my fingers through it. It was still close-cropped and very curly.

I lay in bed smiling to myself. Madeline had loved the texture of my hair and could not keep herself from running her fingers through the thickness and depth of my curls, which she stated were remarkably similar to curls I had on other regions of my body.

Madeline had said, "Now every time I look upon you, I shall be able to imagine clearly how you look with no clothing at all. I can run my fingers through your hair and I

shall be making love to you and no one will know but us."
She said this and then ruffled my hair. I could feel the tingles
start between my legs and rise to my chest, where my heart
skipped a beat.

"That was Madame Rosmerta," Maddy said, interrupting
my reverie. "These boots are for you." She set them beside
the bed.

"Rosmerta says the elders have agreed to meet with me
in the throne room before breakfast is served." She appeared
concerned.

"Are you well, my Love?" I asked. "You look pale."

"I think I am going to be sick," she replied as she sat
beside me on the bed, clutching her chemise shut at the
neckline. "It does not bode well for us that they wish to have
a meeting so early in the day. They have had little time to
deliberate. I suspect that they have already made their
decision."

"How do you feel about all of this?" I asked. "I want to be
sure this is what you want."

"Willow, we have gone through all this before, I am
frightened. I have no practical skills. I do not wish to be a
burden on you, especially now."

"What do you mean 'especially now'?" I asked.

"I mean, now that your foot has been re-injured, thanks
to Father. And with the baby on the way, you shall have two
children to be responsible for."

"Nay, Madeline, I shan't have. We have discussed this at
length. We shall have at least three moons before our baby
pearl is to be born. We shall have plenty of time to prepare
for the baby and you shall know a great many things about
the world around you by then."

"I am still frightened." She said with a pout.

"Perhaps, your fears will resolve as a consequence of
learning to be independent." I tried to reassure her.

"I do wish to learn. You have already taught me so much.

I believe the two of us together can do almost anything!" she said, perking up and forgetting to pout.

"Now," she said, resuming her confident regal persona, "We had better wash up and prepare for our meeting with the Elders. We do not want to keep them waiting!"

As she prepared the water for washing and assembled our clothing and toilet things, I stoked up the fire and made our bed.

We hastily washed before the fireplace. Suddenly I burst into laughter.

"What do you find so humorous, Willow?" Madeline asked.

"Madeline, darling, do you really expect me to fool anyone wearing the lovely dress you laid out for me?" I asked.

"Oh, my!" she laughed. "That could make the deception a bit less effective!"

I quickly climbed into the borrowed trousers and began to bind my breasts with the strips of old chemise. When the ends of binding were neatly tucked away in the wrapping, I donned the short chemise and tunic.

"Come, Willow, and let me wet your hair."

I teased her with a flirtatious smile.

"Stop that! We have serious business to tend to!" She scolded. "We can tend to more pleasurable tasks later." She soothed

"Now that it is short, your hair is free to run and play in every which direction it pleases!"

A quick glance in the looking glass in the light of day was all the fuel I needed for my wavering confidence.

"Are you ready then?" Madeline asked. "Holding me out at arm's length for a final inspection

"I am as ready as I shall ever be." I replied.

As we left the bedchamber and turned in the direction of the throne room, I nearly ran head-long into Madame

Rosmerta.

"I requested that Rosmerta escort you into the throne room." Madeline said. "I shall walk on ahead and meet the two of you there."

My expression must have been one of confusion, because before I could form the words, Rosmerta was answering my questions.

"Madeline has devised a great plan to gain the favor of the Elders. We are going to go along with her plan, and I am certain all will be well."

My mind was reeling with what if's as I hobbled down the long corridor to the throne room in my overlarge, cumbersome boots.

When we arrived, the door was left slightly ajar. An action I knew must have been intentional on the part of the Princess. Meetings important enough to be held in the royal throne room demanded the highest level of secrecy and confidentiality.

Rosmerta and I leaned in close to hear what Madeline would propose to the Elders.

"Good morning Princess Madeline. You look weary. Are you well?" It was Magda, always the healer.

"Yes Magda, I am quite well, thank you. I simply did not sleep much." I could hear a rustle of skirts and knew Madeline was curtsying out of respect for the venerable healer.

"I am thinking you make too much worrying in your mind young Princess." I could imagine Ahmad tapping his temple with his index finger.

"What is it, Dear, why have you assembled us here?" I could hear concern in the Queen's voice.

"I wish for you to reconsider your decision about allowing Willow and I to travel together." I could hear a slight waver in her voice as she spoke.

"Maddy, you know that decision was for your safety." I

was surprised to hear Prince Phillip's voice.

"Yes, I know." She replied. "How would you feel if I told you I had engaged a young man as an escort?"

"No disrespect, Your Highness, but you were given that option yesterday and you declined." Now it was Galynda's voice I heard.

I had never imagined that Galynda would ever serve as my Elder. She had always been my friend, my sister, my companion, my equal, but never my Elder.

"Yes, this is true, Highness, however, the young man would have been of your choosing, not mine and not Willow's."

"I see." Galynda responded. "And you have found such a young man? I can not believe our independent Willow would stand for an escort of any kind, male or female."

I cringed inwardly. No one knew me as well as Galynda. She knew how independent and strong-willed I could be. I could envision this working against me, now when I needed her support the most.

"It was Willow who selected our escort. With your permission, I would like to introduce you all." She spoke in a level and calm tone.

"Okay, Bunny." Rosmerta whispered as she squeezed my hand. "That's you! Do your best."

The Princess directed the doorman to show me in.

I remembered to keep my pace as confident as my tender foot would allow. The heavy boots helped to modify my gait. I hoped it was enough to disguise my limp long enough to get me before the Elders.

"Come in young man. Come closer to the dais." The Queen indicated with a beckoning hand.

Perhaps, I thought, she felt that my slow pace was due to timidity. That was acceptable to me. As I strode forward, I noticed Ahnja was also seated on the dais with the rest of the Elders.

When, at last, I reached the foot of the platform, I bowed deeply to show my respect for the great minds seated before me.

Beside me, Princess Madeline addressed the Elders again. "This is the only companion I wish to have escort us on our journey together. I have reviewed both background and education and find that all qualifications surpass your prescribed requirements for hunting, gathering and defensive skills.

Pieter has provided me with a very strong recommend-dation, stating that he has gained much knowledge and many new skills from their time together and would not hesitate to travel far and wide with present company." She indicated me with a formal sweep of her hand.

Everything Maddy was saying was true and supportable. Naming references only lent strength to her argument.

"Well, young man. You must be quite the marksman." The Queen seemed impressed.

I bowed a silent thank you to the Queen.

"If Pieter has spoken on your behalf, then you must possess superb defensive skills as well." Prince Phillip added.

I gave him a small nod and bowed respectfully.

I could see Ahmad pinching the side of his mustache thoughtfully. His eyes traced my frame and came to a rest on my feet. I was grateful to Rosmerta for presenting me with a well-worn pair of boots on our way to this meeting.

"Your boots," Ahmad indicated with his chin, "they are old. Not road worthy." He said shaking his head slowly. "I am thinking, that if the others agree to this. I must, for you, make new boots."

My head was reeling. Even my beloved Ahmad did not seem to recognize me. I respectfully bowed in gratitude for his generous offering.

"The Royal family has known and trusted Pieter and his family for generations. His recommendation does not come without great consideration." The Queen addressed the others.

"If there are no other questions of this young man, I believe we shall dismiss Madeline and her guest so that we may discuss this matter in more detail." Queen Alyssandra stated with authority.

No one made a move to produce further questions.

"Very well," the Queen nodded. "Madeline, please escort your companion into the outer chamber where you will await our decision."

Madeline, careful to find my left elbow, acted as support for my injured foot while maintaining my cover of being a gentleman.

The door was again left the slightest bit ajar in the hope that we might hear some of the deliberation.

Rosmerta waited eagerly at the door. She silently shook with excitement. "It appears to be going well." She whispered.

"I think so too." Maddy breathed.

"Aye and nay," I said in a hushed tone.

"Whatever do you mean?" they asked in unison.

"The Royal family is only one portion of the Royal Elders. We must also consider what the Family Tsigani has to say and they are tough to convince on someone's word alone."

Just then we could hear voices in the throne room. They too were speaking in hushed tones and I could only hear bits of what they were saying.

"...did not speak for himself." I heard Ahmad say.

"Nay, that is true he did not." Came Ahnja's familiar voice. "... rather small, hardly any bigger than the Princess."

"... have the youth return to the room," Galynda suggested. "...conduct my own interview..."

I felt myself cringe.

"What is it?" Madeline asked.

"Oh, I think I know," Rosmerta offered. She too was

flinching outwardly.

"What?" The Princess repeated more urgently.

"Galynda..." was all I had time to say.

The great door to the throne room opened and we were beckoned inside by the kindly doorman.

Rosmerta hugged us both and we returned to the throne room to face the Royal Elders.

"Come here to me." Galynda summoned me.

Reluctantly I made my way to the dais and stood before her.

"I have not heard you speak. 'tis important that your voice be heard. Do you not agree?" Before I could respond she spoke again. "Come in closer to me and give me your hands."

I knew without question that Galynda knew 'twas me. Touching me was only going to bring that more clearly into focus.

The room held its collective breath as Galynda silently held my hands.

"What do you see, Dear?" The Queen asked.

Galynda lovingly squeezed my hands with hers. "There is no other person who shall provide for your Princess or protect her as valiantly as the person before me. All that Princess Madeline has stated is true. You have in this one a gifted hunter, gatherer and healer. Were I in the place of the Princess, I would want or need no one else to tend to my needs and wishes."

"And what of Willow's needs?" Magda asked in my defense.

"I shall see to them." Madeline answered. "I have much to learn but I shall work hard to do my fair share." She curtsied respectfully to Magda.

Magda seemed to be placated by this answer. She gave Madeline a small nod of approval.

"If I might suggest something," Galynda began.

"Yes, Princess Ra Ahnan, go ahead." The Queen gestured her consent.

"I feel it is best if we allow Willow to share her feelings with all of us." She squeezed my hands in hers again showing me her support and then she released her grip.

I took several steps back from the dais and curtsied to the Queen.

"My Dear Queen Alyssandra," I began.

Upon hearing my voice, she clapped a hand over her mouth and gasped in response.

"I apologize for deceiving you. 'Twas only my wish to demonstrate that I could be a convincing enough man to travel alone with Princess Madeline."

Lowering her hand from her mouth to the dimple at her throat, the Queen replied. "You certainly had me convinced!" She breathed.

"Aye," I continued. "But I knew that Lynd knew the truth. She can see me clearly no matter how I try to hide my feelings or my identity."

"I am also thinking that Ahmad had me figured out." I jested as I imitated his word choices and stroked my invisible mustache. "This man has made shoes for so many people and horses, he can recognize anyone by their footsteps, foot-prints, or the wear patterns on their shoes." I nodded in Ahmad's direction and he returned the gesture.

"Even if she were not my mother, Magda is such an amazing diagnostician; I am certain she had spotted my uneven gait, knew the level of my pain and had uncovered my upset, nervous stomach before I came through the door. I can no sooner fool her than I could Galynda!" I said

"I knew the plan would work when I was able to convince the Princess herself that I was a stranger."

"Yes, that she did!" Madeline joined my defense.

"Considering the change in circumstances, I believe we ought to dismiss Willow and Madeline so that we can discuss these matters in more detail. Does anyone have something they wish to add?" The Queen addressed the Royal Elders.

No one offered any further ideas or arguments, so Madeline and I curtsied and we took our leave.

This time, the door closed behind us with a soft click.

"Oh, blessed gods in the heavens!" Rosmerta was beside herself with nervous anticipation. "I think I could just die right here! I can not bear the agony of waiting a moment longer!"

"Rosmerta!" I said, comforting her with an embrace. "All shall be right. No matter what they decide, we shall all still have each other. Decisions made by the Elders are made together for the welfare of everyone. This is why we choose the wisest members of the tribe and now, the Royal Family, to serve as our decision makers."

"Oh, I know, Bunny. It's just that you worked so hard to show them that you can be the man they wanted you to bring with you." She said, wringing her hands.

I looked over at Maddy who appeared to be equally as shaken.

The door opened and the doorman summoned us inside. As we made our way up the aisle, I heard the latch of the door click behind us.

"Poor Rosmerta." I thought.

"Madeline, Willow," the Queen looked from her daughter to me and back again. "We have decided to grant you your wish. You shall be allowed to travel alone together for the period preceding the birth of my grandchild, at which time, you shall return to the castle to share what you have learned."

My heart was bouncing off the insides of my ribs. I hardly knew how to contain myself.

"I am thinking you shall be needing those new boots, but I am also thinking you shall be needing a wagon that is not a heavy vardo." Ahmad offered. "I shall be working this out with the craftsman in the carriage house."

"Ahnja and I shall create a very useful space inside the wagon with a place for everything you shall need for the two of you, and, eventually, your baby." Magda stated.

Magda and Ahnja were the best women here for that job. Aside from Galynda and me, no other woman present had lived in a vardo. Magda, I knew would create spaces for medicinal supplies and Ahnja would make cozy nests for us and useful spaces for all the necessities.

"And Willow, I shall see to your wardrobe personally." Ahnja stated.

Until this moment, I had not realized how very much I missed my home under the great big sky.

"We have some fine breeding stock in our paddocks as well," added Phillip. "We shall choose the strongest of these to pull your wagon. Your ponies are so well suited to the life. I only hope our finer boned horses are up to the task."

Home! I was going home and I was taking someone I deeply loved with me. I could not have asked for a greater gift.

"When shall we expect to leave?" Princess Madeline asked.

"The Royal Wedding is less than a moon away. I believe our craftsmen are capable of creating a wagon by that time. I do not see any reason why you two can not leave soon thereafter," was the Queen's reply.

"Thank you all," I said with a deep, heartfelt curtsy. "I know that we shall be successful. All your love and support shall guide us safely along our journey. You have given us so many gifts that shall serve us well in our lives together. Thank you."

I am certain I broke most of the Royal Rules of Protocol as I stepped onto the dais and hugged all of the Royal Elders and thanked each one personally for his or her part in the decision-making process.

Preparing for the Future

The days flew by as we hastily met in secret to put the finishing touches on the beautiful marriage quilt for Galynda.

"That was an amazing thing that Galynda did at the meeting with the Royal Elders." Queen Alyssandra marveled.

"Tell me what she did!" Rosmerta's eyes sparkled with anticipation. She was eager to hear all the news from every perspective possible.

Alyssandra stopped mid-stitch. "She took Willow's hands in her own, and she knew right away that it was Willow, even though Willow had not uttered a single word to that point.

"That just amazes me!" Rosmerta said shaking her head.

"Nothing Lynd does amazes me anymore." I said shaking my head in turn. "When I am with her, I am totally naked. I can not hide a single thing from her I gestured with a sweeping motion, pulling my latest stitch taut. She knows where I've been and who I have spoken with and if I've treated someone. She knows how serious the illness or injury is because of the herbs I've treated them with. 'Tis a very good thing I am an honest person.

"Thank the gods that Phillip is a one-woman man!" The Queen said with a smile.

"That is almost not funny." I said shaking my head.

"'Tis funny now," I said resting my hands in my lap. "But when we first arrived here, it wasn't. Do you remember how jealous of you Galynda was, Rosmerta? Every time I came from your chambers, she could smell the perfume and incense. She was afraid you had led me astray and that I was calling on you for your professional services!"

"Oh, my." Rosmerta replied. "I do remember that." She thoughtfully threaded her needle and began to stitch again. "I never intended to threaten anyone. I was only trying to help you become acclimated and to make you feel more at ease here."

"I know, and she does too, now." I agreed. "I was very nervous to be here at first. Your ways were so foreign to me. I was not certain of anything. Your kindness, wisdom and guidance made all the difference. Thank you."

"Oh, you're welcome, Bunny." She said waving a hand to dismiss the serious note I had struck.

Maddy caught my eye and furrowed her brow at me. She mouthed "Bunny" and looked at me askance. Then she winked at me and resumed her sewing.

"Galynda knew too, that you might be leaving her soon because of the visions she had been having. She had learned that you would be of the third sex and she was frightened that you would find someone and abandon her for your new love. She did not wish to be alone and dependent upon her mother all of her life." Magda added.

I nodded my head in agreement. "Aye, I think 'tis wonderful the way things have worked out." I remarked. "Galynda has a home where she can find everything she needs. She has so many wonderful people here who want the honor of escorting her to the throne room or to fetch things for her. They want to do these things for her because it is an honor to do so, not because they pity her or because of her blindness."

"Aye, truer words were never spoken. Most who serve her do not even know that she is blind." Magda commented.

"I pity the fool who tries to hoodwink that one." Ahnja said with a smile. "I am sure Willow can tell you, my Galynda can have a fiery temper when things are not going the way she wants them to."

"Aye," I said, nodding my head in agreement. "But a lot of the times she lost her temper with me, I believe she had good reason."

"Are you a bit of mischief?" Maddy asked with a smile that showed the beautiful dimples in her cheeks.

I watched her as she tucked a loose hair behind her ear. My, but she was beautiful.

"Aye, I suppose Magda might attest to my mischief making days." I said shyly.

"Nay, nay" Magda said warmly. "Willow was almost always too serious. She started the work of an adult too early on in her young life. That would be my fault."

"Nay, Magda, I find no fault with you. I followed you about, asking questions strung together like beads. I wanted to be involved in everything you did."

"Aye, that is a fact." Magda replied, nodding.

"But I do remember coming back to camp with all manner of slippery, slithery, jumpy creatures in the pockets of my pinafore." I said laughing. "I think poor Lynd had to learn what they smelled like just to avoid a fright when something popped out of my pocket and landed on her head or in her lap."

"That was when she would really blast me with her temper." I said smiling. "As I said before, the times she lost her temper with me, I undoubtedly deserved it."

Everyone laughed then.

Still laughing Ahnja said, "Poor thing, I'm afraid she still hates to get dirty and she has never liked snakes or frogs."

"I can't imagine how she and Willow became such good friends." Magda smiled. "I spent so many, many hours picking grass and twigs from Willow's hair and always there was mud and tears along the edges of her skirts."

Madeline's gaze caught mine and held it. I saw an amused twinkle in her eye before she looked down and resumed her sewing.

"Oh my goodness, yes," Alyssandra said. Her gaze was far-away, focused on a different time. "Phillip and Maddy were almost completely opposite too. When they were little Maddy, my little adventurer, would disappear behind tapestries or inside cabinets. She found more hidden passages than we knew existed!"

I looked up and caught Maddy's eye. We shared a sense of adventure. I was looking forward to our travels more than ever.

"That's a fact. That child frightened away some of the more superstitious kitchen maids!" Emily agreed.

"I was always having poor Emily pack some sort of lunch or snack for Maddy." Alyss said. To Emily she asked, "Do you remember that, Dear?"

"Oh my, yes!" Emily said with a smile.

"That child would be gone for hours at a time." The Queen said. She found Maddy's gaze and held her daughter's eyes lovingly in her own. "And now you will soon be off on another great adventure, won't you?"

Maddy smiled a sly smile at her mother. "Yes, I shall!" she said smiling and greedily rubbing her hands together."

"Phillip," Alyss continued, "was quite a different story. He was not one for the dark or musty places and preferred to play in the bright conservatory or to sit quietly reading in the library."

That shall suit Lynd just fine!" I said with finality. "I have just finished my last patch."

I raised my corner of the quilt and said, "Here's to their clean and tidy life together, a life free of bugs and frogs and musty places."

"Until they have children like you and me!" Maddy said, looking at me with a knowing smile.

We all sat back and admired the quilt we had just completed together. Every stitch made the quilt stronger. Every story bound us together more securely as a family. Stitch by stitch, we sewed our way through lifetimes of love and relationships. Each stitch held the promise of new generations of loving people who had not yet populated this Earth.

The Wedding Day

The day of the wedding had finally arrived. Activity in the castle had increased tenfold. The only place I could recall being nearly as busy was the inside of a beehive that had been cracked open for its golden honey. My best defense with the beehive was to stay away from it and let the worker bees do what was necessary to put their home back to rights.

My best defense in the castle was the same. I avoided the activities I was not directly involved in, and I left the fussing and bustling to those who were more qualified to fuss and more directly involved with the bustling.

I slipped away from the castle to see how the wagon was coming along, Ahmad had told me it was nearly completed.

A short walk down the grey gravel road brought me to a beautiful stone barn and carriage house. The half doors were open offering fresh air and sunshine to the livestock that occupied the stalls inside. I could smell the earthy aroma of cow and horse manure and the pungent scent of horse sweat intermingled with the sweet smell of hay. I closed my eyes, breathed deeply and was comforted to hear the contented snort of one horse answered by the low nicker of another. My reverie was interrupted by a man dressed in tattered clothing who was seated outside on a low wall, whittling a stick aimlessly.

"I'm sorry sir; I can't allow you in." He said, standing to bar my path to the door.

I resisted the impulse to look over my shoulder for the 'sir' he was addressing. "Why ever not?" I asked.

"Dunno," he said, shrugging his shoulders loosely. "Something 'bout a weddin' and not to let no one from the castle or the village in. I dunno anymore 'an 'at." He said and he sat down to resume his whittling.

It was clear to me that his mind was not as sharp and strong as most. I surmised that he had probably asked to help, and this was the only job the other men felt he would not make a botch of.

"Well thank you just the same." I said. "You did your job just fine. No one shall find fault with your work today." I said with a reassuring smile.

He drew himself a little taller as he swelled with pride. "Thank ye!" he said with a toothless smile. "Thank ye a lot." He repeated, waving his hand with the whittled stick in it.

Suddenly I had the overwhelming compulsion to see Galynda. Unlike my visit to the stables, I would not take no for an answer. Something felt very wrong and I had to see her for myself.

Moments later, I was knocking on her chamber door. A small chamber maid answered my knock. I recognized her as the young maiden, Rose, who had been chosen by Galynda to see to any little detail her beautiful young mistress might need.

"I am here to see Galynda." I said to Rose.

"Yes, she is expecting your visit. If I may be so bold," Rose said with a curtsy. "Her Highness is not faring well today, and I am grateful that you have come to her."

"Show me to her?" I asked.

"Yes, follow me." She invited me to follow with a gesture of her hand. She gathered her skirts and turned. I followed closely on her heels.

Galynda's private chambers were decorated in the royal colors of purple and green with accents of silver. Her sitting room was bright with sunlight. She had a settee and several wingback chairs arranged before a large marble fireplace.

Her bed was draped in green and silver bunting, with purple and gold bolsters and pillows.

I found Galynda seated before a gilded dressing table in a tangle of women each involved in her own detailed activity. Each activity involved a part of Galynda's body.

One woman was busy with Galynda's hair, one was at her feet buffing her toenails. Two others were fussing about her hands filing and buffing her nails. Another was laying out the Royal wedding gown.

"Oh, Willow!" Galynda wailed. "I am so thankful you are here!"

"Excuse us please?" I said.

Each woman stopped what she was doing and took her leave with a polite curtsy.

Rose stood silently in a corner awaiting orders from her mistress.

"Rose," Galynda spoke. "'Tis all right now, Willow is here, you may go as well."

Rose, too, politely took her leave and we were alone in the room.

"Lynd, you look as if you have been crying for hours."

"I have been. I was crying out to you with my heart. I was afraid you would not hear me!"

"What is it? What can I do?" I asked, feeling helpless.

"Willow, how can I leave you?" She cried.

"Leave me?" I repeated.

"Yes," she sobbed. "I always thought we would spend our lives together." She stopped to catch her breath. "I...I always thought you would be here for me. And...and...and then, I thought you would find somebody and leave me!"

"And now?" I asked.

"And now, I shall be wed today and we shan't share our wagon and you shall have to share it with Madeline and Phillip tells me there is another castle and when I look into my future, I am not here...and..." she was sobbing so hard she could no longer speak.

"Does it bother you that I have found someone and that I will share a wagon with her?" I asked, secretly dreading the answer.

"Nay, I am happy for you." She replied through a stuffy nose. Her face was red and tear stained. Her eyes were puffy and her nose was red and running. She was not the composed and wise *drabardi* I knew.

"Lynd, what is really bothering you? You are not leaving me, no one has spoken of the other palace and I am not leaving you. We have both found wonderful, loving people to share our lives with! Our lives shall be different than what we ever dreamed they would be, but I believe we shall be happy here. Since you are marrying the Prince, and I shall be with the Princess, we shall finally be sisters after all!" I said hugging her with one arm.

Galynda leaned into me for security and support. I found the abandoned hairbrush and gently began to brush my best friend's hair. I began to hum and old Rom folk song.

"Does it hurt?" Galynda asked suddenly.

"Hmmm?" I asked, half in thought. "Does what hurt?" I asked.

"You know," she said, "the intimate part. Does it hurt?"

I stood blinking numbly for a moment uncertain how to answer such an earnest question.

"I can not deny that I have lain with Madeline, you know

that I have. That is not the issue." I said. "I am having difficulty finding the right words to paint the picture with."

"I am listening." Galynda replied, calming down visibly.

"So, what I am hearing is, your biggest concern right now is not really me or the clan, but the wedding night. Is that accurate?" I asked, brushing her hair in long, even strokes.

"Well," she began. Her face was a contorted blend of pain and relief. "Aye." She admitted. Her face flushed.

"Do you and Phillip... show affection at all?" I asked. "I mean, do you embrace or hold hands?"

"Aye." Galynda nodded.

"Have you kissed?" I asked.

Galynda's face flushed again. "Aye." She said shyly.

"I would say, by that expression, that your kisses have been deep and intimate."

She gave a little nod. "Aye, many have been."

"And did that kind of kiss give you any feeling in particular?"

"Feeling?" she feigned confusion. "What ever do you mean, 'feeling'?"

"Was the experience good for you? Or was it scary? Did you want more, or did you want to stop?" I asked. I set the brush on the vanity table and sat down on the small foot stool at her feet.

"Is it possible to choose all of those options?" she asked, bewildered.

"Tell me about that. It sounds like an awful lot to experience all at once." I replied.

"Phillip is a kind and gentle man. He has a very good heart. When he touches me or kisses me the feelings I have are almost overwhelming."

"Overwhelming in a good way or in a scary way?" I encouraged.

"Again, it feels as if 'tis both things at the same time. I

like it and it feels very good but then I feel foolish and I want him to stop." I could see her frustration as she beat both fists into her lap.

"Why? Why do you feel foolish, Lynd?"

"Because," she said "because I want him to do more but I don't know what 'more' is! I am not certain I shall like it. I am afraid I shan't like it and that I shall be awkward at it. What ever 'it' is!"

"The feelings you have before you become frightened. Do you enjoy them?" I asked.

"Very much." She nodded with a small private smile.

"Phillip is a kind and patient man. I can not see him forcing his intentions on you. He is not like his father. He is more like his gentle-natured mother. I am certain he will wait for you, until you are ready to take the next step with him."

"But will it hurt?" Galynda persisted.

Again, I sat blinking and uncertain how to proceed. "Lynd, I do not know if it hurts to be with a man. When I am with Maddy, I feel as if I can not get close enough. I want to breathe every breath she exhales because it was inside of her."

"The first time we were intimate, I must admit, Maddy did not leave me time to sit and worry about my technique." I recalled with a crooked, private smile.

"Did she force you?" Galynda was alarmed.

"Nay. 'Twas more like she took me by surprise." You remember I told you how we accidently ended up in the same bedchamber at the cottage. Apparently, out of habit she had gone to bed in that room." Telling the story aloud, made the events of that night come into clearer focus for me. "'Twas the night you were up so late getting acquainted with Phillip. 'Tis the reason you were not in the bed with me." I slowly realized.

"So, then what happened?" Galynda asked eagerly.

"Once she knew 'twas me, she taught me what a kiss was!"

"Really! Did you want her to kiss you?" Galynda asked.

"I did not know that I did, but once she kissed me, I knew I had been starving for her all of my life." I spoke slowly, realizing how true my words were.

"Did you feel awkward?" my best friend asked, hanging on my every word.

"I knew nothing about showing affection. I never expected that I would ever need that set of skills." I replied honestly.

"That is how I feel! Here 'tis my wedding day and I know nothing about how to please my husband!" her bewilderment was growing and she had begun to tear up again.

"Wait a moment! This *is* your wedding day, the things you need to concern yourself with are: do you love him enough to give your life to him, and does he feel the same way about you."

"Aye. We do" she confirmed with a nod and a sniffle.

"Then, I think any physical expression of your love for each other will be deeply meaningful for both of you."

"But, did you like Maddy before...before?" She lost momentum, unable to bring herself to utter the words aloud.

"I was very attracted to her. I asked Rosmerta many questions." I admitted.

"Which is why you spent so much time with her?" she asked.

"Partly, you were not here to talk to. I was here in a strange land, I knew no one, and I was experiencing so many new feelings and physical symptoms. I thought I might be ill!"

"You did?" she asked with a smile.

"Aye! My body was not behaving in the calm and sedate manner that I was accustomed to, so I saw each new physical reaction as a symptom. Did your mother ever teach you anything about physical attraction or physical reactions?"

"Nay. 'Twas assumed I would never marry so I would never need to know." She plucked at the corner of the kerchief she held in her lap

"And 'twas the same for me." I said nodding my head. "I am only glad that I found someone who will love me for who I am and who is just as new to love as I am."

"I am happy for you. I know I could not bring myself to tell you all this before because I was blinded by jealousy and worry." Galynda sniffed.

"I am happy for you too." I smiled. "Now you shall have your home and all the guides and fetchers you could possibly wish for." I said with a smile.

She sat with a frown upon her face.

"What is it that bothers you so, Lynd?" I asked.

"I still wonder if it shall hurt." She said with a small voice.

"Perhaps," I said matter-of-factly. "I have heard that the first time can be painful, but my experience with Maddy was so flooded with excitement and desire, I can not imagine any pain that would have stopped me from sharing such a wonderful moment with the one person I love more than my own life! Just trust your feelings, trust Phillip and let your body be your guide."

That seemed to be the answer Galynda was looking for. "Then I shall be just fine! She said. "I have plenty of desire and when I am with Phillip, I feel such overwhelming exhilaration I almost forget to breathe!"

"No more tears then?" I asked.

"Nay. I think I am done for now. Thank you for understanding and helping me through this!"

"I hate to be an old nag, but do you not have a wedding to prepare for?" I asked with a smile.

"Oh! I do! Oh, Willow, what shall I do?" she became frantic again.

"You trust the worker bees to get you all in order and then you walk down the aisle where the minister and Magda wait to bind you to your betrothed." I responded. "Shall I send Rose to assemble the ladies?" I asked.

"Please." She breathed.

"I shall take my leave for now, but know that I shall be cheering for you from my seat." I kissed her gently on the cheek as I hobbled toward the door.

"Willow," Galynda called to me.

"Aye?"

"I expect to take a closer look at that foot before I consent to your leaving this castle." She asserted, waving a sodden kerchief in my direction.

"Welcome back, Lynd. I have missed you!" I said over my shoulder. "Are you ready for this?"

She closed her eyes and drew in a deep breath. "I cannot think of any way to prepare myself more for this moment." She replied.

I remembered hearing those exact words, the day we returned to camp after the attack in the cave. I wondered if this meant that she was trusting in providence or resigning herself to the fates.

I found Rose and all the ladies awaiting the next order in the ante room of Galynda's chambers.

I summoned them in and went in search of Maddy.

Before I could reach Maddy's bedchamber Madame Rosmerta came scurrying out of the wings with her skirts in both hands. "There you are! I have been scouring the castle in search of you!"

She looked spectacular. Her dress was made of fine silk brocade of gold and wine. The décolleté bodice was drawn up tight and the low neckline allowed for a tantalizing glimpse of her ample bosom.

Her hair was swept up into a tight, shiny bun at the top

of her head and was decorated with a delicate diamond tiara that rested at the base of it.

Her ears were adorned with large tear drop shaped garnet earrings which matched the short necklace that she wore. The scarring beneath her collarbone was not visible and I sent a loving prayer of thanksgiving to Lynd for concealing such an angry wound so artfully.

"Was I supposed to be somewhere in particular?" I asked, genuinely confused.

"We have a wedding to prepare for." Rosmerta nodded, as she grasped me by the left elbow to guide me down the corridor toward her quarters.

"Aye," I agreed. "But I was just in talking to Galynda, she was not faring so very well."

"I am sorry to hear that. How is she now?" Rosmerta asked, concerned.

"She is quite frightened. I could have used your expertise."

"Oh, poor thing!" Rosmerta clucked. "It does not have to be that way!" she said as she shook her head.

"Our clan taught her nothing of the marriage bed because as a Chosen One, she was not expected to ever marry." I explained.

"Tsk! But still!" Rosmerta persisted. "Why is it that the women are always left in fear, but the men are encouraged to go out and bed as many women as they can?"

"Perhaps, women live in fear because so many men live by that philosophy." I offered.

"That, my dear, is entirely possible." She retrieved the key to her chambers from between her ample breasts and slid it into the keyhole on her door. A soft click and we were inside.

"The wedding is very soon. We haven't time to bathe you and..." She became almost frantic, wildly tucking a loose tendril of hair behind her ear.

"Rosmerta, I bathed this morning. I have only had a meal, a walk and two conversations since then! How dirty can I be?"

"Oh, oh, that's good! That saves us some time! Come on then, let's get you dressed, shall we?" She said gesturing me toward her the way a mother urges a toddler to take a furtive step.

"I'll be right back." She said, disappearing into the closet.

I could imagine the beautiful dress of blue that had been laid out for Galynda. I allowed my mind the opportunity to wonder about the beautiful dress the Royal Tailors might have designed for me to wear.

I removed my tunic and sat upon the bed to unlace my brace and boot.

"Here we are!" Rosmerta reappeared with an armload of green velveteen and satin. "Stand up and put your arms over your head." She instructed.

I obeyed. Arms in the air I asked. "Since green is the color of the High Plains Crest and blue the color of my people, if I am wearing green am I to be seated on the groom's side?"

Rosmerta stopped pulling my chemise over my head mid-task. "You know, that is a truly fine question." She said thoughtfully as she continued to remove my undergarment.

She rummaged for a moment in the pile of fabric she had laid on the bed. "Here, she said put this on."

I pulled a new chemise over my head. It was a fine soft fabric of the purist white with beautiful white embroidery over the yolk and mandarin collar.

"Here, now this," she said producing a green silk waistcoat.

I had only just gotten my arms through the vest and she was holding out another garment for me to put on.

"That does not look full enough to be a skirt." I said buttoning the waistcoat. "What has happened to it?" I queried as I stepped out of my trousers.

Wordlessly, Rosmerta held the garment up for my inspection. It was the finest pair of velveteen breeches I had ever seen. The drop front was fastened with four brass buttons and the sides of the legs were edged with gold braiding

"Trousers, my lady?" I puzzled.

"Yes, we thought it best, since you have taken on the persona of a man, we can not introduce you formally in a dress! We would really confuse the people of the Kingdom!"

"Aye, that makes sense." I agreed. "There is more to this whole wedding ceremony than I know, isn't there." I observed.

"Oh, yes. More than you can imagine!" Rosmerta nodded vigorously with a smile.

"I have never worn such finery." I breathed. "Even as a woman!"

While I stood admiring the gold embroidery of the waistcoat, Rosmerta guided my arms into a sage green, layered tapestry, dress coat which was accented with gold braiding at the mandarin collar and cuffs. It had two rows of brass buttons down the front.

"Your father, Ahmad sent these for you." She said disappearing behind her wardrobe curtain and reappearing with a cloth-wrapped bundle in her arms.

I could smell the fine leather before I could unwrap it. I had never seen the likes of these beautiful, brown, riding boots.

As I pulled them on, I realized the front portion of the ankle was open, making getting into them easier. Across the front of the ankle was a half spat that buckled up the side adjusting the amount of support the boots offered.

I felt taller in these beautiful boots and I adored the fact that they squeaked a little, like horse tackle, when I moved about in them. I loved them and sent a prayer of thanksgiving to my father, Ahmad, and to all the hands that made this day possible.

"Oh, Bunny!" Rosmerta breathed. "Ahmad has truly outdone himself. Those are beautiful!"

"Oh, Aye!" I agreed. "I have never owned a pair of knee-high boots before!" I exclaimed, trying to see all of myself from varied angles.

How does the fit feel? It does not bind or pinch? How does your foot feel?" My companion enquired.

"'Tis a perfect fit. No discomfort at all." I noted honestly.

She wetted her hairbrush and brushed my unruly hair into submission. "The tailors thought it fitting to make a special hat for the occasion." She said producing a fine, green velveteen pill hat that was fringed with white fur.

"Done!" she announced after she had placed it upon my head. "Come along! We must make haste to the Royal Chapel."

"Is it here in the castle?" I asked.

"Yes. But we really must make haste." Rosmerta urged, grasping my elbow lightly to both direct and support me.

"Is that music I hear? Or am I just delirious from the great speed at which we are doing things today? I dare say, any faster and my head will spin!"

We opened a door which looked into a heavy drapery. I had grown accustomed to Rosmerta's secret passageways and was not surprised to hear the music of a powerful pipe organ with much more clarity.

"Now, Bunny, go and guide Galynda over to the foot of the dais and wait there with her." She directed. "I am going to take my seat."

Upon her head, Galynda had drawn her hair into a bun, save for tiny ringlets, which hung in front of her ears. She donned her silver circlet and was dressed in the beautiful royal blue dress I had glimpsed on her bed. She wore a beautiful necklace of sapphire and diamonds that I had never seen before.

Galynda's form-fitted bodice of silk brocade was laced at the front and outlined with silver twist at the waist. The long, slender sleeves of the chemise were of silver blue and fitted close to her arms. At her waist, the overskirt was divided in front, to reveal the shimmery silver blue silk of the chemise, and formed an elongated, ruffled peplum which served as a train.

She was stunning. For a moment, I hesitated to reach out and touch her, for fear I might spoil her.

"Hi Lynd, It's me." I whispered in her ear. "You look gorgeous!"

"Oh, Willow!" She breathed. "I am so happy that you are here with me!" She said as she found her spot at my elbow.

"All will be well, my sister." I quoted her. "Shall we go for a little walk?" I asked, as if it was something we had done every day of our lives.

She smiled then. "Yes! Let's!" She squeezed my arm.

The music changed then, to a more formal tone, and everyone rose and looked to the back of the chapel where we stood behind closed doors.

The great, heavy wooden doors to the rear of the church opened slowly, allowing in light.

The chapel was decorated with green, purple and blue bunting. Great floral arrangements flanked the substantial marble altar. The air was stifling with the pungent aroma of frankincense, cedar and sage.

Everyone in the chapel was dressed in finery, the likes of which I had never imagined. I felt a growing lump in my throat as I spotted my clan standing together at the front of the church.

I proudly led Galynda up the aisle. She lovingly squeezed the inside of my elbow as she had done so often. I squeezed her back by flexing my elbow and positioned her before the altar.

It was truly an honor to be there with her on such a

momentous occasion. I felt excited for her and sad for myself, as I knew she would no longer need me to guide her as I had done for so many years.

Behind us, Princess Madeline entered the church with her brother, Prince Phillip at her elbow. Watching them approach, I was made dizzy by all the emotions that surged through my heart all at once.

Oh, how I would miss being Lynd's eyes. She and I had always worked so well together. I was happy for her too. Now she would have a home and all the helping hands she would ever need.

As I stepped away from my sister, I allowed myself to look at her one last time before turning to look upon the Prince and Princess. Galynda's dress was even more magnificent on her than it had been when it was laid out upon her bed!

When at last I turned my eyes to Madeline, she was looking right at me. She was smiling shyly and I could see her endearing dimples. She quite took my breath away.

She was shrouded in silk and velvet and fur. There were so many lovely textures that I ached to run my fingers over her and experience all of them.

A silken corset of sage green silk brocade embraced her breast and was elaborately laced with gold silk ribbons at the back. It was outlined by gold twist and embroidered with fine gold thread in a filigree vine pattern. A scattering of pearls of varying sizes, were strategically sewn in place to look like berries on a vine.

I pulled my eyes away from her, for fear that if I did not, I would stare unabashedly. I bowed my head and caught sight of my own waistcoat. 'Twas made just the same as her corset! I, too, had baby pearls embroidered upon my bodice. My stomach shuddered just then with tears of joy that I could not shed.

I lifted my eyes to drink in the vision of the woman I

loved. Indeed, I was beginning to feel intoxicated. I was no longer certain that I could trust my legs to support me as I stood there.

The golden silk chemise she wore had a broad, sweeping neckline with dropped shoulders, leaving her beautiful smooth shoulders bare. The flowing chemise billowed slightly at the top of the tight bodice and reappeared at the waist as the underskirt. The sleeves of the chemise were fitted at the upper arms with sage green silk cuffs to match the bodice. The golden silk sleeves of the chemise flowed freely at the elbow. The layered sage green velvet tapestry overskirt divided at the front of the waist and formed a flowing train that was edged with white fur trim.

Again, I had to pull my eyes away so that I would keep my mind from wandering beyond the boundaries of her lovely dress. In that moment, I recognized that my trousers were of the very same sage green velvet and my hat was also edged with white fur.

The Princess wore a necklace of diamonds and emeralds. The light from the windows struck it from different angles as she moved up the aisle, causing it to flash and sparkle brightly.

Prince Phillip was so majestic in his regalia. His double arched crown was topped with a golden orb, lined with royal purple velvet and edged in ermine. It was heavily decorated with gemstones which caught the light as he solemnly strode toward Galynda, who awaited him, at the altar.

His black dress coat was made of layered velvet tapestry and edged with silver braiding about the cuffs and mandarin collar.

His shoulders were squared and fortified with the royal blue velvet sash draped gracefully over his left shoulder and pinned on the right at his waist with a gem crusted brooch; like the very one Madeline had pinned upon my chest so long ago. Over his right shoulder, he wore a royal blue velvet cape edged with ermine.

His silver waist coat, like mine, was silk brocade. His black velvet breeches were tucked, at the knees into shiny, black riding boots which were embellished with silver spurs.

For a moment, I stood stunned, giddy and breathless. This would be a moment in history, for so many reasons. I was here to witness it all. I must straighten up and pay close attention, for I would have great stories to share with all of Lynd's children for generations to come.

In a rustling of skirts, Galynda and Madeline knelt at the foot of the altar.

I realized the event had begun without me and I turned to face the altar. For the first time, I recognized my mother, Magda, who was standing beside a minister. Each was dressed in full, religious regalia.

The minister wore a gold cape and stole over his snow-white chasuble, his gold, pointed headdress stood tall and stately upon his head.

Magda was magnificent in her snowy white cotton robe. It was embroidered with forest creatures in white cotton thread. The waist was drawn in with a wide, raw-edged, leather belt, which had several pouches for personal and ceremonial items.

Over her robe, she donned her magnificent olive green hooded woolen cloak. She wore the hood down, over her shoulders, and draped the cloak over her left shoulder, where she fastened it with three leather thongs and deer antler toggle buttons. Her hair was braided and wrapped around her head as it always was, but today, she wore a crown of peacock eyes and pheasant feathers. The time-worn badger's head medicine bag hung at her side.

The music stopped and the room was so still I could hear my heart pounding in my ears.

My eyes scanned the crowd and I found her Majesty, the Queen, seated proudly, on the right side of the church beside her Rosmerta. She was resplendent in her golden dress. Her hair was swept high in a tight bun. A dazzling diamond crusted crown sat nestled in her hair. She wore a beautiful diamond, garnet and yellow topaz necklace and earrings. I was grateful that she had recovered so fully and was able to be here to celebrate her children in such a grand manner.

Magda raised her hands, offering a blessing upon the people of the Kingdom and its new rulers. The minister did the same.

Magda introduced me to the people. "I present to you, Rajani, drabarni, healer to the Tsigani people, healer of your Queen, and the child of my own heart."

I dumbly turned and made a slight bow to the people. Everyone cheered.

"Willow, do you profess your love and devotion to Princess Madeline?" Magda asked.

I stood in silence, blinking, unable to process the question.

Magda leaned in toward me and warmly repeated the question that was swirling in my head.

Stunned, I turned to her and replied. "Aye."

"Will you look at her, hold fast her hand and tell her so?" Magda requested with a smile that sparkled in her eyes.

Puzzled, I took Madeline's hand in mine and realized at once that she was as mystified as I was. Her palms were sweaty with the uncertainty of the moment.

"Princess Madeline." I heard my voice call to her in a formal, hollow tone. "I love you now and shall always love you." As the last of these words passed through my lips, I realized that Magda was performing a hand-fasting for Madeline and me. We were getting married!

"Princess Madeline, do you profess your love and devotion to Rajani?"

She hesitated for a long moment. My busy mind began to worry. What if? I thought, perhaps she would decline to profess anything before her people.

She curtsied deeply to Magda. "Magda, she replied. I do profess my deepest love and devotion for the child of your heart. I promise to love and provide for you and your family for as long as I draw breath.

Magda, smiling, addressed the Princess. "Then, Your Highness, perhaps you would present this proposal to Willow, directly."

Without hesitation, Madeline turned to me and stated, "Willow, Rajani, I love you with everything that I am, and I always shall. I promise to care for you and provide for you and your family for as long as I draw breath."

Magda reached inside her medicine pouch and withdrew a golden bit of rope and tied it around our hands as we held onto each other for support.

"With this golden bit of rope, we bind two lives together for all eternity."

Madeline grasped my hand tighter and I could tell she was just as surprised by all of this as I was.

Someone came from the wings bearing a pillow, upon which, were two gold circlets each embedded with a cabochon in the middle. One bore a green stone and had more ornate filigree. The second circlet bearing, an enchanting stone of the richest red garnet, was beautiful in its simplicity.

As I stood and stared at the lovely circlets, Magda unbound our hands and tucked the golden rope back into her badger skin medicine bag.

The circlets were presented to me. Magda laid her hand upon the crown with the green stone and turning to me she said, "Place this token of your unending love upon the head of your bride."

Nervously, I took the ornate crown and gingerly slid it onto Madeline's head. It was a perfect fit. The color of the stone was an amazing compliment to her beautiful grey-green eyes.

To Madeline, Magda said, "Place this token of your unending love upon Willow's head."

Madeline cupped the circlet in both of her hands and raised it to her lips, kissing the blood-red stone before gently placing the crown upon my head. "With this, I give thee my heart."

"Before these witnesses," Magda gestured to the throng, "you have bonded your love and fasted your hands. You are forever joined from this moment hence." She raised her hands in celebration.

The congregation cheered and my head reeled.

The ceremony was turned over to the minister in golden robes. He addressed the people of the Kingdom and then the regal couple before them.

There was much cheering for the Prince and his new bride. I regret that I have failed my best friend and sister. In my selfish reverie, I had let her and her new groom down most completely.

'Twas my true intention to record all the momentous occasions of Galynda's amazing life as they unfolded for her. 'Tis with shame and sorrow that I admit that I was rendered utterly incapable of paying close enough attention to such an important occasion. I was so astounded by the tremendous gift the Elders had bestowed upon me by allowing me to marry Madeline in such a formal and forthright manner that I quite forgot to remain an objective observer.

I was there, in the Royal Chapel, holding hands before the Kingdom with the woman I loved and would spend my life with.

The Reception

The ceremonies were over before I knew what was happening and Princess Madeline and I were being directed down the aisle to the awaiting crowd. Galynda and Prince Phillip were close behind.

The cheering encouraged my racing heart to beat faster. People in the crowd were throwing bits of bread at us and shouting wishes for wealth sufficient to ensure that we always had enough to eat. Others were tossing tiny pinches of salt and wishing us just enough variety in our lives to keep the flavor fresh.

Well-wishers and back-clappers surrounded us for what felt like hours. As a man, I noticed that well-wishers were heavy-handed with my person, smashing my hand in rough handshakes and clapping down hard upon my aching shoulders.

We were guided to the great hall where we were to have the reception.

The great hall had never looked as grand as it did this

day. It was shrouded in buntings of the now familiar royal green and purple as well as the royal blue, representative of Galynda. The long table was laden with brilliant candelabras and arrangements of colorful and exotic fruits and flowers and baskets of breads and platters of meats and cheeses.

Wine was being served liberally and was consumed as quickly as it was dispensed.

The great hall was filled with the din of talking and laughter and music and toasts.

"Maddy," I said. "I'd like a moment with you, please."

She took my hand and led me away from the crowd. "What is it, my dear husband?" She asked with a flirtatious smile.

For a moment, I was lost in her dimpled smile and could not recall what it was I wanted to discuss.

"You are so stunning," I said. "You shall have to allow me a moment to gather my wits!" I defended.

"Willow, did you have any part in planning this?" Madeline asked.

"Nay," I denied, shaking my head. "I brought you here to ask you that same question! It would seem that if you did not plan it and I did not, then I believe that the Royal Elders are the ones to whom we should give thanks!" I declared.

"I quite agree!" Maddy said squeezing my hand and smiling into my eyes.

"Is this an awful thing to say?" I asked. "You look more beautiful today than I have ever seen you."

"No, that is a lovely thing to say." Maddy responded with another warm squeeze of my hand.

"But you are so lovely and I can scarcely wait to have a moment alone with you when I can disrobe you and cause your hair great disarray!" I confessed feeling utterly stupid.

"I am so relieved to hear you say that!" she replied steadily. "Because that is how I feel too! I have a theory about these feelings do you want to hear it?"

"Indeed I would," I said. "Very much."

"I believe a gift when it is wrapped in bright cloth or paper makes it more interesting and therefore more desirable. The same is true for wedding dresses and wedding cakes, have you ever seen one?"

"Nay. Not one from your culture." I said.

"Come and see it!" she said leading me by the hand.

The cake was a tower of white, with intricate, ornate patterns of icing upon it and border piped around it.

"Wedding cake is very ornate. It is created for its beauty and to elicit our feelings of desire for it and for other beautiful things." Maddy explained.

"Your theory is quite logical. I like it." I said smiling.

Maddy casually swiped her finger through the icing and without hesitation extended her finger to me for a taste.

As I suckled upon her finger, my mind took its leave of the great hall. I was floating and drifting off to a downy soft bed filled with humid moments of soft mewling sighs.

Someone in the crowd had spotted us near the cake and began the murmuring. "I think they are going to cut the cake now!"

"Willow!" Maddy shout-whispered to me. "Willow, they are coming this way."

Maddy cast me a furtive look of mirth as the crowd gathered around us. Great cheers brought Prince Phillip and Princess Ra Ahnan to the table as well.

Together, we cut the cake and fed our new spouses and made toasts thus, commencing the festivities.

It was an evening of music and eating and dancing.

Madeline spotted her mother on the opposite wall and grasping my hand, waded through the crowd to her mother. She allowed her mother to finish her conversation and then kissed her on the cheek. "Oh, Mother! Thank you for making this possible!"

"'Tis my pleasure, Madeline. I hope that the two of you

shall be happy together always." The Queen said embracing her daughter and then me.

"Thank you, Majesty." I said "With all that I am."

"Willow, Dear, you are most welcome. You have brought great and wonderful healing changes to our ailing Kingdom. This feels as if it pales by comparison to all you have given to us. I know that you are intelligent, gentle and kind I could not want more for my only daughter."

"But Majesty, I am not regal, nor am I a man." I said, feeling myself unfit to wed such a fine woman.

"Willow, Dear, Madeline has endured both royalty and masculinity. Neither of these was agreeable to her. I, too, have endured both and prefer kindness and humanity."

"I..." I began. "I ...I am astounded! I never imagined this in all my life." I began.

"Yes, I know. It is the unexpected gifts that often bring the greatest rewards." She said with a smile. "That is why the Royal Elders, as you call us, made the collective decision to allow this marriage to happen." She lovingly stroked Madeline's face and then mine.

"Come, let's go for a little walk." The Queen invited.

On our way out of the great hall, we were joined by Phillip and Galynda, Magda and Ahmad, Ahnja and Emily, Enid and Gus, Madame Rosmerta and Pieter. Those few who had stood together with us and plotted to save the kingdom from Edward.

We had assembled in a neighboring room which housed stray dining room chairs and the rolled-up carpeting from the great hall.

"We thought you may need a respite from the crowd." Rosmerta said. "That, and we were dying to give you your wedding gifts! Sit, sit!" she gestured with widespread fingers to a small grouping of chairs set in a semi-circle. "I'll be right back!"

Rosmerta scurried away and returned with the marriage

quilt that we had made together. She handed the quilt to me. I in turn, carried it to Ahnja and placed it lovingly in her lap.

"'Tis for Ahnja to give." I said.

Ahnja walked to Phillip and Galynda embracing the quilt, tears streaming down her face. "For the new couple, on their wedding day" she said, smiling through tears.

Magda rose from her seat to put her arm around her sister's shoulders to console her.

"Oh, Phillip!" Galynda announced. "'Tis a marriage quilt!"

"Galynda has told me wonderful stories about the rich and exquisite quilts your tribal family makes!" Prince Phillip addressed the tan, Tsigani faces in the crowd. "I am so grateful that you chose to honor her in such a beautiful way! Thank you!" Phillip said with a polite bow.

"We honor you both as important members of our family." Ahmad declared.

"Aye, aye, tis true." The others agreed.

"'Tis amazing! Galynda marveled as she unfolded the quilt and ran her sensitive fingers over the loving stitches that held it together. This one was made by Aunt Magda! And this one by my Mama! Who made this one?" She asked pointing to a particularly ornate patch.

"That one is mine, Galynda, Dear." The Queen flushed with pride.

"Oh, the stitches are so beautiful!" Galynda breathed, hugging the patch to her bosom.

"Oh, these stitches are lovely too," Galynda cooed. "Who made these? There is so much attention to detail." She observed out loud.

"That would be mine," said Rosmerta, raising her hand.

"Oh, Rosmerta!" She nodded recognition "Of course." Galynda began. She stopped herself before her thought became vocal, but I suspect she was thinking about our little discussion about Rosmerta and her skills in observation and attention to detail.

"Willow, I would know your chicken scratch anywhere!" Galynda exclaimed, laughing through tears. "'tis a comfort to know your hand will always be near my heart." She held up the patch that I had made and pressed it against her bosom.

"Oh, my, these stitches are so extraordinary." The new bride exclaimed as she ran her fingers over and over the stitches. "Your Highness, your needlework is exquisite! Thank you ever so much for sharing your brother with me!"

Princess Madeline sat back with her mouth agape. When her wits returned, she gasped; "How ever did you know that was my patch?" she puzzled.

"'Tis quite obvious, really. I found your mother's needlework to be lovely and ornate. Your stitches are very similar to hers. You both have a unique feel to your stitches. The length and tautness differ from ours. Each person has her own signature stitch. 'Tis like a voice, it has its own unique accent. Yours and your mother's stitches do not come from any place I have ever been before."

When her fingers reached the center of the quilt, tears welled in Galynda's eyes.

Everyone searched each other's faces for an answer to her sudden change in mood.

"I never thought I would ever be a bride." She finally said. "I never thought I would ever have a marriage quilt of my own." She sobbed. "I never thought...oh, Mama! I never expected to find myself holding a quilt with your love stitched into the very heart of it!" she sobbed so hard then that she could no longer speak.

Ahnja rose from her seat and went to her daughter. "Oh, my Galynda," she said, hugging her daughter. 'Twas a bittersweet thing, making this quilt for you, my only child." She slid into the chair next to her daughter, which Pieter had vacated for her. She nodded thanks to Pieter and slid one arm around Galynda and rocked her gently. The mother kissed her sobbing child's hair. "I wept many tears for you. These women," She said looking into the faces of all who were present. "These women, your tribe, have heard stories and have wept and laughed and wept again. This quilt is only a small token of all the love that makes this tribe your home."

Tucking a small stray tendril of Galynda's tear-soaked hair behind her ear, Ahnja lovingly continued. "I am not abandoning you. You are not leaving me. We are binding together two families." She laced her fingers together with Galynda's for emphasis.

Everyone nodded his or her agreement. Each of us had tears in our eyes.

"Come on now Galynda, let's finish admiring your beautiful quilt." Ahnja said.

Galynda inspected the entire quilt and thanked each woman in turn.

Rosmerta left the circle with tears in her eyes. "This is more emotional than I could have ever imagined."

I had formed the words in my mind. I wanted to ask Rosmerta if she was all right. My head was swimming with the activities of the day. Everything seemed to be moving very slowly in my mind. I made a move to speak, suddenly, Madeline squeezed my hand tightly. I turned to face her, to ask her what was wrong. The next thing I knew, I felt something heavy upon my lap.

I turned my head to see what was happening. My mind was moving so slowly, I couldn't understand what was happening.

Beside me, Madeline began to cry in earnest. Before me, Magda stood with tears in her eyes too. Madeline squeezed my hand more tightly and then placed my hand upon the bundle that had been placed upon my lap.

I turned my eyes from Magda to Madeline and then to my lap. There, before me, was a mass of brown and green cloth.

Slowly, it came into focus, it was a marriage quilt!

My voice was gone. I could not speak. I bowed my head and wept openly. Madeline wrapped her arm around me, and Magda knelt before me. Both women held me and allowed me to cry myself out.

"I never imagined..." was the only intelligible thing I could manage to say.

I had never imagined. I always knew. I knew I would never have a love, never take a spouse, never have a marriage quilt and yet, I had found all of these things. I had found someone to love and somehow, she had become my spouse! And now, we had the blessings of our families bound together, piece by piece, one strong stitch at a time. We were bound to each other by a hand fasting and the marriage quilt confirmed it.

Everyone gathered to admire the quilt. It truly was beautiful.

I recognized Magda's familiar needlework in the very center on a brown patch. Next to it, was the very intricate work of the Queen on a green patch.

"Your blessings mean so much to me, Magda. How do I ever begin to thank you for all that you have given up to care for me? Thank you, for everything, but mostly, thank you for being my mother. Thank you." Tears streaked down my face. Magda, still kneeling before me, cupped the back of my head in her hand. She drew my forehead to hers.

"Willow, my child, I have cared for you because I love you. I have loved you since the moment I knew your mother was with child. You will always be in my heart." She smiled through tears of her own.

Examining the quilt further, I found Galynda's patch. It was more beautiful than any I had seen she her make.

"Oh, Lynd, this is truly your finest work. I shall treasure this." I hugged the quilt to my chest. "Wagon or no, you shall be with me always!" Tears began to flow from my eyes again.

Just as I began to wonder if there was an end to my tears, the Queen rose to her feet and said "I believe our poor children have endured all the powerful emotions that they can manage for one day. Perhaps we ought to leave them to recover and rejoin the festivities." She made a sweeping motion with her elegant arm toward the great hall and made a move to lead the others in congratulations.

"My Madeline is in good hands; I know this with all my heart. I love you as though you were my own, Willow dear, and I always shall." The queen embraced me warmly and kissed my cheek. I was overwhelmed and felt the urge to cry again.

"Thank you, Majesty, I love you and your family. I am honored to be a part of it."

Each member of our party wished us well in turn, until it had dwindled to the two new couples.

"I am weary from all that has happened today." Madeline stated with a bow to Galynda and Prince Phillip. "Come Willow, we should retire to our rooms."

My mind was reeling. "Our rooms" I was a permanent part of this family. I was no longer a visitor in the guest wing. I was bound for life, married; hand fasted with the most beautiful creature I had ever known.

My stomach felt fluttery inside. I could hear, nay, feel my heart beating in several places at once.

The Wedding Night

I felt myself being led by the hand to Madeline's quarters. I hobbled on behind her, having difficulty keeping up. My mind was working very hard just to focus on any single thought and just then I was hoping I could keep up without stumbling and falling.

Madeline held one hand and in the other, I still embraced the beautiful quilt that bound our families together.

Once we were back in our rooms, Madeline pressed the heavy wooden door shut and leaned her back against it. She blew a stray tendril of hair out of her face and said "Oof! What a day this turned out to be! How long had you been planning this?"

"Planning? I knew nothing of this until Magda guided me through the ceremony!" I defended. "I thought, perhaps, I was the only one who was not involved with the planning. I knew nothing and suspected nothing! I am stunned just recalling the ceremony, even now that 'tis over!"

"I agree. That was quite a surprise, wasn't it?" She gave

me a warm enchanting smile. Her eyes sparkled gaily. I lost myself somewhere between her beautiful dimples and her full lips.

She led me to the inner chamber, where our marriage bed would be. I could see that someone had taken the time to fill the room with bouquets of fresh roses and wildflowers.

"'Tis much too early for roses." I observed out loud.

"We cultivate them in green houses so that we may enjoy them all year." Came the response.

"They are beautiful. I love the small native flowers too! They are so bright and cheerful."

"I am certain that is why they were included in these bouquets. I have never had flowers of this kind in my chambers before, except on the rare occasions that Phillip and I were allowed to go outdoors. We picked some like these for Mother." She said, lovingly stroking a small, blue flower.

I spread the marriage quilt upon the bed so that I could appreciate it in its entirety.

It was beautiful. I had never seen a marriage quilt through the eyes of a recipient. Before today, I had never understood why the women would become so emotional. Today, I had crossed a threshold. I suddenly knew things today that I never would have imagined I would be privy to.

"I don't believe I have ever seen anything quite like this quilt. I can see why it is such an important tradition for your family. I don't believe I have ever received such a meaningful, heart-felt gift before.

I enjoyed making my patch for Galynda and Phillip's quilt. It meant a lot to me, being a small part of it. But this, this is so different. Having this great outpouring of love from your family is very different. I never knew a gift could make me feel this way." Maddy said as she removed her circlet and let her hair down.

"Neither did I!" I agreed. "I have seen many quilts being made and have given a bit of myself to many people, a patch at a time. This one, this one is so different. 'Tis so much more personal this time, when the love is directed toward me, than all the times when I was directing love out to others."

"That must be the difference, Willow. It is far easier for some to give until they are empty than it is for them to receive, a trait I often see in you, my husband." She said with a flirtatious flash of her dimples. She replaced the circlet upon her head.

Madeline stroked my back with one hand. Gently, she pulled me toward her and my lips brushed hers lightly. The light that had been sparkling so brightly in her eyes blurred softly out of focus.

She backed against the large post at the foot of the four-poster bed. She pulled me close to her and kissed me warmly with her full lips.

I felt the pressure of her full belly against my abdomen and something melted inside of me. I felt flushed and kissed her back with fervor.

The roses in her cheeks flushed as our kisses became more impassioned.

She was breathless as she spoke, "Willow, take me to our marriage bed and bind me to you forever."

That night, we created our new life together upon our marriage quilt. It was a quilt which had been thousands of years in the making. It was bound together by the stitches of our ancestors and Royal Elders. These sutures crossed cultures and bridged time between generations. It was an experience so sacred, that I can not even bring myself to pen the words here.

A Journey for Two

The morning following our hand-fasting, Madeline and I were awakened abruptly by a loud knocking upon our chamber door.

"You stay." I volunteered, still groggy from the deep sleep one can only achieve after a night of passion. "I shall go and see who 'tis and what they want." I stumbled from our marriage bed, wrapped myself in a dressing robe and limped toward the door.

"Aye, what is your wish?" I asked from my side of the door.

"Bunny, it's me, Rosmerta." The reply came.

I laughed in my heart. It seemed odd that she, who taught the art of love making and pleasuring to the Royal Family, would be the one to disturb my first night of hand-fasted bliss with Princess Madeline.

"Is it customary for courtesans to make house calls to newlyweds?" I blinked sleepily, opened the door slowly and admitted Rosmerta into the anteroom of our private chamber. "Good day Rosmerta. Have you been up celebrating all night? Have you not been abed yet?" I was incredulous.

"I have a wedding gift for you two. I couldn't wait to give it to you!" she said with a sparkle in her eye.

"Now?" I asked still feeling muzzy-headed. "Can it not wait until a decent hour?"

"Please!" She pleaded, tapping her spread fingertips together.

"Oh, very well," I conceded. "Bring it in." I gestured with a sweeping hand.

"You shall have to come with me." Rosmerta shut one eye and bit her lower lip as if she were anticipating a beating.

Rosmerta had captivated my whole heart almost from the moment I had met her nearly half a year earlier. It was difficult to deny her anything. 'Tis truly a blessing she never used this to my disadvantage.

"Rosmerta," I looked at her sideways. "I know you well enough to know when you are up to mischief." I crossed my arms over my chest. "You have rousted us from our wedding night and now you ask us to leave our bedchambers." I rubbed my imagined bushy mustache the way I had seen Ahmad do and looked at her down my nose, pretending to be in deep thought.

"Willow," my bride mumbled from the next room. "Who is it? And what can he possibly want at this hour?"

"'Tis Rosmerta. She has come bearing wedding gifts." I explained.

My new bride padded into the anteroom in a robe matching the one I wore. My heart smiled when I realized she had taken time enough to brush the evidence of our passion out of her previously tousled hair. Now it was brushed and swept up in a tidy bun at the back of her head.

I marveled at her stunning beauty. She was still flushed with sleep. I knew that, were I standing near enough to her, I could smell the warmth of sleep and the smell of our passion on her skin. I felt a tiny fish flip in my abdomen at the sight of her.

"Gifts?" Madeline supported her lower back with the flats of her hands and swept the room with her eyes. "I see no gifts." She crossed her arms across her breasts and feigned an exasperated look.

"She tells me we shall have to accompany her." I informed.

Madeline could see my thinly veiled mirth and played along with me.

"Of course you realize we have had insubordinate subjects put to death for lesser offenses than disturbing a Princess in her most private hours." Madeline cocked a haughty brow as she paced with her hands resting in the small of her back again.

"Oh! The two of you!" Rosmerta exclaimed as she looked from me to Madeline and back again. "Don't kill the messenger!"

"Ah ha! I knew it! There are others involved in this plot!" Maddy turned on her heel, shaking an accusatory index finger in Rosmerta's direction.

Rosmerta stood blinking innocently with a palm pressed to her chest.

"Aye, I agree. I have an idea we might find a fair number of co-conspirators involved in this escapade."

"So, are you two going to come along willingly or am I going to have to resort to force?" with this Rosmerta began to push up her sleeves.

I began to laugh. The others joined me.

'Twas a great feeling to know I was loved and that I no longer had to live in fear for my life or the lives of my loved ones. I reflected on the life I had lived, leading up to this moment. I had grown up a Rom nomad. My caravan had lived under constant scrutiny of villagers that had fallen victim to horse thieves and scoundrels who ruined trading for honest families such as mine. Until this moment, I had never realized what a tremendous relief it truly would be, to have a permanent residence, where I was free to live in warmth and safety in the company of good friends.

I draped one arm around my dear friend's shoulder and the other around the shoulder of my new bride. I looked from one to the other. "Very well, then. How should we dress for the occasion? I hardly think Her Highness should greet her people in her dressing robes."

"I should think not." Rosmerta agreed. "Perhaps you would dress as you would for a Royal meal. Emily and her kitchen staff have prepared a delicious breakfast for the royal couples. By your leave, I shall wait here." She seated herself in a small armchair. "I was given strict instructions to escort the two of you to the great hall for our meal. Make haste now." She said clapping her hands. "There are a great many details to attend to."

I smiled inwardly knowing that in other kingdoms, subjects were often treated more like objects. Here, everyone was treated with warmth and dignity. Rosmerta had been a dear friend to Queen Alyssandra long before she was wed to Edward, the man she made King consort by her birthright. Rosmerta was part of the warp and the weave that held the fabric of this Kingdom together. She was subordinate to no one, save her beloved Queen.

Madeline took me by the hand and guided me back to the inner chamber of our rooms, closing the large heavy wooden door between us and the anxious Madame Rosmerta.

"Willow, my new husband, my wife, what ever shall I call you?" She looked at me deeply with eyes that blurred out of focus. "What have I been doing all my life without you?" She began to kiss me then.

"I am sorry, Maddy." I began. "I can not do this right now. I do not wish to disappoint you, but you must know. I am inhibited with Rosmerta in the anteroom. She is so learned in the ways of passion and pleasure. I feel odd knowing she is outside that door. I might make a noise or something!" I whispered in a hoarse voice.

Maddy's countenance softened into a warm smile. "Oh, Willow." She shook her head. "It is impossible for me to be angry with you." With that, she cupped my breasts together, as one cups water to wash one's face, she bent and kissed them both and then wrapped her arms around me in an embrace.

"I think I should tell you; no one understands how we feel better than Rosmerta. She has remained with us for so long because discretion is her business. That, and she and Mother are intimately involved." She said with a conspiratorial smile.

"How do you know this?" I asked.

"Can you not see it in the way they look at each other?" She cast me a look over her shoulder as she prepared washing water behind the dressing screen.

"You implied that you know more than that." I urged.

"Oh, I do!" She smiled. With that, she bent over the washing basin and cupped water, as she had done with my breasts, and brought the water to her face. She looked up from her washing, water dripping from her face. "You have no idea how long I have wished for someone to share all of my most delicious secrets with! And now, here you are!" She said with a flourish of her dripping hands.

"I have seen Mother and Madame Rosmerta together. At first, I was so young; I was confused by what I was seeing. All the thrashing about and screaming, I thought surly someone was being hurt. I was ready to spring from my vantage point and rescue Mother, until I heard Mother moan 'Rosmerta, Darling, you feel so good, don't stop.' That is when I figured out what I was witnessing. It surprised me how comforting it was, seeing my own mother in love.

I believe that seeing Mother and Rosmerta together in the

act of passion helped me to recognize that part of myself that could only be satisfied by the love of another woman." She concluded her ablutions and stepped into the wardrobe in search of an appropriate dress.

I refreshed the bathing waters and took my place at the basin. "They have no idea that you have seen them being intimate? That you know they are lovers?"

"They try to be discrete," Maddy replied from her side of the dressing screen, "but since I have seen them together, I look for little signs." She gestured a small measure between thumb and index finger.

"How long, when, how old were you..." I could not find the words to ask the right questions and bathe at the same time. There was so much to learn, to know, to experience.

"I was quite young; it was just before my first moon cycle. I was growing and changing and just beginning to experience curiosity about such things."

"So you have known for nigh-on 15 years?" I froze in mid- scrub. I was astounded.

"Yes, I suppose so. Come along Love, make haste." She said.

I could only muster a turtle's pace. She was stunning. Surly she had to know the power she possessed over me.

"Here my Love, put this on, our breakfast is waiting." She handed me some trousers and a tunic to don.

I dressed myself hastily. "Maddy, how is it to have such a secret for so long?" I queried while tugging on my trousers. I pulled the green tunic over my head and adjusted it over my hips.

"Now, come along," she summoned me. "Let me put this on you." She raised the circlet to her lips and kissed the garnet and placed it upon my head and guided me to the anteroom door.

Rosmerta sprang to her feet and set the pace for our procession to the great hall.

My injured left foot was healing nicely, I noticed, as I was able to keep pace with my companions as we scurried down the corridor.

The great hall was bright. Sunlight streamed in through the floor-to-ceiling leaded windows. The buntings and the floral décor from the wedding celebration had been freshened and the great wooden table was laden with platters of fruits, breads and smoked breakfast meats.

The Queen was already seated at the head of the table. Princess Madeline took her seat to her Majesty's left and I, Maddy's consort, was seated beside her. This was how it would be from now, forward.

Today, Prince Phillip, would be seated to Her Majesty's right, and his new bride, Galynda, would be seated across from me to Phillip's right. I smiled as I noted that Phillip and Galynda, were still absent from the table. I prayed that this was a good sign.

My thoughts were interrupted as the crowd at the table turned their heads collectively toward the entrance. Prince Phillip and his new bride, Princess Ra Ahnan, had arrived. They nodded apologetic greetings and found their seats.

I studied my sister for signs of her mental state. Her cheeks were flushed and her eyes were bright and sparkling. Her gaze was softened and out of focus. The worry I had seen creasing her face had smoothed out and she appeared more serene. Her circlet was in place, but ever so slightly askew. Her lips seemed redder and fuller than I was accustomed to seeing them.

"Good morning, Lynd." I whispered across the table.

"Oh, Willow, good morning!" Galynda replied, out of breath. "How are you?" she asked with a smile. She reached out across the table for my hand.

"I was going to ask you the same question! Are you well?" I grasped her seeking hand warmly.

"Oh Yes, I'm feeling much better. Thank you." She

nodded with a smile. Her hand squeezed mine reassuringly. She would be just fine.

A merry meal was enjoyed by all. When we had finished, the Elders lead the two new couples toward the main entrance to the castle.

I had not seen this door in the five or six moons since I had arrived here. I wondered how long it had been for Madeline, since her father forbade the children to go outdoors. Perhaps, I thought, it had been since that terrible day when she had been shuttled away to be wed to Alexander.

The doors were opened and fresh, spring air rushed inside. The sunlight streaming in was so bright I could scarcely see.

We were guided outside to the covered portico. There, before us was the most magnificent wagon I had ever seen. 'twas painted crisp white with dark green pinstripes and thistle leaf accents. I did not recognize the handiwork as Rom. Perhaps a craftsman from the castle had lent his or her hand to the wagon.

The roof was the most stunning feature of all for it was made of copper. The sunlight glistened and reflected off the roof, making the bright sunlight seem brighter still. The wheels seemed taller and were definitely more spindly than the wheels of our heavy vardo. The whole wagon appeared sleek and more fine-boned than any caravan I had ever seen.

The matching pair of dun horses was also more fine-boned than the fells ponies I was accustomed to. The combination of horses and wagon was simple, yet elegant. I would never expect to see a Rom nomad in a wagon so spindly and beautifully understated, which was exactly why it had been so finely crafted.

"'Tis beautiful!" I exclaimed.

I knew right away, Pieter, the groomsman, who stood proudly at the head of the horses, had personally selected the team that would pull our wagon and the tack that would tether them to the wagon. I also knew that my surrogate father, Ahmad had carefully made the shoes for our horses to guarantee surefooted travel.

"You must look inside!" Ahnja invited as Magda opened the door in the back of the wagon and stood back for our inspection.

I knew Ahnja and Magda had helped to create a very functional living space inside. No doubt, Her Majesty, the Queen and Rosmerta had something to do with the more ornate and comfortable features I was certain I would find inside.

I was so excited I could scarcely contain my enthusiasm.

"After you Maddy." I helped the Princess maneuver the small steps which gained passage to our living space within the wagon. I followed her inside.

I had never been inside a new wagon before. It smelled spicy of new wood and oily of fresh paint.

The Dutch door, which could open at the top only for air ventilation, was painted dark green to match the pin striping and scrollwork. The windows in the door and walls, while in the very places that we had them in our vardo, were made of ornate leaded glass with beautiful colored gems.

The sitting area was well appointed with an upholstered settee in rose, sage and garnet. A small occasion table flanked either side. A sconce hung upon the wall above each table. Framed needlework that I recognized as Her Majesty's handiwork, hung upon the wall. 'Twould be a loving and cozy place to sit and visit in the evenings or on rainy days when travel would be difficult.

The kitchen was across from the sitting area, making access to the stove easy for both spaces. The wash tub was of hammered copper, an accent I was certain Ahmad had crafted. The work top was well-oiled and ready to be put to service cutting and chopping with knives I knew would have been lovingly made by Ahmad. Cast iron pans were nested in a drawer, just as they had been in Magda's wagon.

I felt a tangle of pride in my new love and our new wagon and deep, stab of grief, recognizing that my days of journeying with my loving clan had come to an end.

Everything had been prepared and was well-stocked and set for a journey. Herbs hung drying from the ceiling and would be accessible for cooking and healing needs. I turned then, to look back for a hook beside the door, knowing that I would find it there. There it was, in pride of place, a well-travelled otter skin medicine bag, prepared and at the ready for another adventure.

"Oh, look!" Maddy exclaimed from the front of the wagon. "Our Marriage Quilt!" She lovingly stroked it with her fingertips.

"Aye," I nodded, too emotional to say more.

Seeing the quilt there upon our bed, in a new wagon that had so lovingly been crafted just for us, turned this amazing fantasy I had been living into a tangible reality for me.

This journey is about you and me and the life we shall make with each other. Are you ready for that?" I said, fighting the emotions that had lodged in my throat.

"Of course, I would follow you to the end of the earth." She said with a wink.

A Change of Direction

We stepped outside the wagon into the brilliant sunlit day. The breeze played softly in my hair and I was aware of a chill on the back of my neck. I rubbed my neck to warm it, thinking 'twas only the absence of my plaits.

Galynda was beside me, her hand in the crook of my arm as it had always been.

"You feel it too, do you not?" She whispered softly for my ears only. "You have gooseflesh."

"I do feel something in the wind." I nodded rubbing my arm and her warm hand, acknowledging that the chill was not about the weather at all.

"Do you remember the dream about the wagon wheel, the one that has been eluding me?" She began.

"Aye." I replied. "Of course, 'tis been a truly vexing mystery."

"The mystery is unfolding its wings." She stated matter-of-factly. "The wagon wheel shows me that the changes are in motion." She spoke slowly with a furrowed brow as she worked through her thoughts. She pursed her lips around each word to prevent them from coming out of turn.

All around us, spring was bursting forth in the brilliant spring sunshine. Family and servants packed and prepared the wagon for our journey, all unnoticed by us. We slowly began to walk together as we talked. Walking always seemed to help keep the messages flowing smoothly.

I marveled at how seamlessly we worked together and I hoped that, someday, Maddy and I would share such a symbiosis.

"Willow, the wheel is not a wagon wheel at all, but it offers direction to us as we travel." She hesitated, searching for vocabulary.

"Lynd," I hesitantly interrupted her process. "Is it a compass rose? Does it tell you North, South, East and West?"

She squeezed my arm tightly. "Aye! Aye, it does!" She agreed.

I solemnly pursed my own lips and nodded in determination. "I have something to show you." I said.

We found ourselves in the throne room. It was the very room in which I had very first laid eyes upon the Princess. That moment seemed so long ago. How very much our lives had changed because of and since that moment in time.

"Willow." My thoughts were interrupted by my companion.

"Aye?" I returned to the present.

"What is this place?" Galynda asked. Her face had become ashen.

"'Tis the throne room." I replied.

"Aye," Galynda acknowledge. "I have been here before." She nodded. "Each time I am here I feel dizzy and nauseated."

"Do you feel that now?" I queried, concerned for her health.

"Aye," she answered. Her gaze was distant as she

searched the ethers for answers.

"Shall we take our leave?" I asked, turning to guide her out the door.

"Nay. Nay. You have found the answer to our mystery!" she replied holding me fast to the spot. "The wheel has been here all along." She indicated, pointing to the floor.

I looked down at the marble floor with the intricate inlaid compass rose and the tendrils of vines and thistle leaves that I had been too terrified to really notice on that fateful day. Observing it now, it was beautiful, nay, breathtaking and perfect.

"It is perfect." Galynda stole her way into my private thoughts, as she so often did. I smiled, loving her for it. "Rather, it is nearly perfect, save for a growing fissure that runs through it."

I looked again at the craftsmanship there directly between my feet, was, indeed a clearly defined split. I felt an icy finger slide up my spine.

Her warm hand gripped my arm. "Aye, Willow, the fracture is running from the East toward the West. It guides us to seek shelter to the West."

My mind reeled. Leave here? I had been so certain that we had found our forever home. I could feel tears burning in the backs of my eyes. A large lump knotted in my throat and I could scarcely breathe.

"Willow," my sister began. "All will be well if we heed this message, but we must make haste. All of us."

I stood stock-still, frozen by the overwhelming emotions of fear and hurt and confusion and devastation and so many other things that filled me at once with panic and dread.

"Willow," Galynda began again, "'tis a message for us all to leave this place of hurt and pain and suffering. We are to move forward to a place of new beginnings, healing and hope." She stroked my arm lovingly with her free hand.

"All will be well?" I shakily asked for reassurance.

"Aye," she said with genuine confidence and warmth.

"Do the others know anything of this?" I asked.

"There has been growing concern as the fissure has been growing and widening with each passing day." Galynda stated. "I simply did not know that it was related to my vision until now.

"Now that we know, we should make haste to warn the others!" I declared, tugging to move my precious friend from the face of danger.

She held me there. "Willow, the wheels are in motion! The journey has begun." She said with a free smile.

I was dumb with confusion. I wanted to run from the room with Galynda in tow. I wanted to yell or to melt into a sodden puddle of my own tears.

Galynda, sensing my despair, cupped my face in her hands and kissed me on the forehead. Willow, you are leading the caravan to safety. You are our true leader."

"Nay, that is not correct." I puzzled. "The Queen..." I began.

Galynda covered my gabbling mouth gently with the palm of her hand. "Willow, trust me. All is as it should be, and all will be well. Listen to me please." She soothed.

I silently nodded my head that I would and she slid her hand from my mouth.

"I have been very involved in the meetings with the Royal Elders. The Queen is quite concerned about the fissure and has conferred with several master craftsman who all share deep concern about the integrity of the palace, as the fissure runs through the very heart of it. The Queen has another castle, the one that Phillip was living in until his return. It is west of here by the sea. I have visited it in my dreams. It is more beautiful than you can imagine. It is to be our beautiful forever home.

Since you and Madeline are prepared for your journey, you shall lead the way to the castle by the sea! Phillip has asked the craftsman who built and prepared your wagon to prepare all of the others in the fleet. I shall speak to the others as we must all make haste; time is of the essence!"

I could sense the resolve building in her as the mystery unraveled. Her eyes sparkled with hope as she spoke.

I heaved a great sigh and felt my muscles unwind as I began to relax.

"Come Willow," my sister tugged at my arm as she turned to lead me toward the others. "You have a journey ahead, and we shall all be right behind you!"

I felt the joy return to my heart as we stepped out into the brilliant morning sunlight. The sun had risen higher in the sky. Daylight was slipping away from me. I would need to leave soon if we were to put any road behind us this day.

"I shall inform the others of all that has happened." She slid her hand from my elbow and grasped my hand warmly. "Now go, Willow." She smiled through tears. "Lead us all home."

The cold water of the Pacific didn't bother him, but Tristan was pale, shivering as he wrapped his arms around his chest. "C-c-cold…"

"I know." Aran managed a brief smile and helped the younger, smaller boy towards the rocky shoreline. He could have survived the pull of the undertow and the drowning, but their parents never would have forgiven him for losing their younger son. Not for the sake of a swimming lesson.

The towels were new, thick and white fluffy things he'd bought the other day and stuffed into a knapsack just for this lesson. None of the threadbare towels at home would have served the purpose intended for the morning swim.

Even with two of them draped over Tristan's shoulders, the five-year-old still looked cold,

wrapping both layers of terrycloth tight around his body. Teeth biting into his lower lip as he tried to hide the shivering as he warmed himself beneath them.

Aran ruffled Tristan's hair before looking at the Pacific beyond the rocky crescent of beach. They were three hours from Seattle, and it was just early enough in the morning that they weren't going to be disturbed by anyone human. He'd chosen seventeen, not for the question of why there was a twelve-year gap between them but because he wasn't comfortable taking a form closer in age to his little brother's.

Tristan wasn't shivering now. Aran pulled the towels from his brother's shoulders and stuffed them into his knapsack, offering a light-yellow t-shirt with a dinosaur printed on the front. His brother's ratty

swim t-shirt was salt stained and laundromat abused, looking more pink in places than the red it had been when new. "Get dressed. You need this more than I do."

A little September chill was nothing to him when he'd dared to swim the Antarctic Ocean before.

Tristan's look at him was meant to be scathing but only managed to appear cute as he pulled the t-shirt over his head, fumbling with the sleeves and neck hole. "Don't see you cold."

"I'm older than you and stronger." Aran smirked briefly, pulling the five-year-old down against a driftwood log. "Want to see a trick?"

They were sheltered enough by the stand of trees between the little beach and the parking lot. It was unlikely anyone would see them at this hour

unless they were an unlucky hiker or dog walker seeking to take in nature for a few minutes.

All he had on was a pair of swim shorts for modesty's sake, shoes and shirt hadn't occurred to him when he had packed the backpack this morning for their little swim lesson. Aran took a couple steps away from the improvised park bench and stood, letting the soft light of the change surround him. It faded a few minutes later, leaving him dressed in a plain knee length tunic and leather sandals.

Tristan's eyes were wide with amazement. "Think I can do that?"

Aran chuckled and sat down on the log, stretching one leg out to study the sandal on his foot. "Probably not, sorry to say. You're stuck having to

scavenge clothing or cache it after you make yourself human again. I'm not like you or our parents. I'm…"

He trailed off, pulling the younger boy closer to his body. "I'm more like Coyote than you are. He's able to do that clothing trick as well."

"Oh." Tristan quieted, snuggling between Aran's arm and side with a happy little sigh, his interest in the clothing matter fading as quickly as it had come. "Mmm."

Aran winced as his brother jostled his arm, turning the wrist toward the morning light to see the dry, peeling skin at the base of his hand. Tristan hadn't meant to hurt him, but the slight burn itched, prickling against the undamaged skin on his forearm. A couple hours swim hadn't been long enough to do

him good, but the five-year-old shapeshifter didn't have the strength yet to make their lessons longer.

"Ari?" Tristan's voice was small as he noticed and poked at the burn on Aran's wrist.

He snarled softly, warning the little shapeshifter to back off as he covered the dry skin with his hand and dropped the injured wrist back to his side. His brother hadn't meant to hurt him, but the pup was mortal. Tristan would never know what it was like to have such a close tie to the ocean, that being on land for a week or two – or longer was a trial. "Don't."

Tristan drew back with a small, frightened whimper, wetness streaking his cheeks that had nothing to do with the finished swimming lesson. "Sorry."

Aran sighed, towel drying his hair with his brother's ruined t-shirt before balling it up in his hands. "I should be sorry, not you. It was a moment where I lost myself and it shouldn't have happened. Won't happen again, promise."

"'kay." Tristan swallowed, scrubbing the tear tracks away from his face. "How come you burn like this? I'm fine – I don't need to go swimming like you."

So his brother had noticed that. Tristan could get a point or two for being observant even if he didn't know what he was looking at. Aran laughed though it was hollow. "Kit, you're mortal. I'm not. Remember what I told you a few minutes ago about Coyote and his clothing trick? About his- our kind? I've got all of that man's power with some of his

weakness. He can't travel more than half a day from the coast. I can't be on land for longer than a few weeks."

He folded his brother's hand in his own, teasing a fingertip between the five-year-old boy's fingers before releasing it. "Not without coming to the point where it's a struggle to breathe and my body starts to fail on me."

Tristan crawled into his lap, nestling against the cotton tunic and clinging tight to it. "Yucky."

"Yeah, yucky." Aran wrapped his arms around the smaller boy's body. "All that nasty stuff that goes on inside your body. Poop included."

Tristan's nose wrinkled for a moment but he subsided, snuggling close once more. "Mama says it's

your story to tell, not hers. Can you? You're older than she is."

Maybe he could but not while his brother was on his lap. Aran coughed, setting the younger boy next to him. Tristan was like a little radiator when he wanted to be. Too warm and too close for comfort at times. "Which one? My former lover's? Or something else?"

He touched the silver and diamond pendant at his throat and sighed. It was too delicate a thing for a man to wear but it had been a gift a century ago. His lover would have expected him to keep it. "She died eighty years ago. Titania isn't worth mentioning now."

Guilt flickered across Tristan's face and he wiped a grubby hand across the bridge of his nose,

leaving a streak of dirt behind. "The one you never say about. Mama says you've had girls in your bed, but they don't stay."

Leave it to a five-year-old to ask about his sex life with human women. As for the rest, he was going to have to talk to his adoptive mother about mentioning *his* private life to Tristan. There weren't many boundaries in their family, but this was one of the ones he would have preferred her not to mention. Aran glanced towards the sky, shaking his head. "Danu have mercy on me. You should have been a fox or cat, not an otter, kit. Something to match that endless curiosity of yours."

The goddess he'd named wasn't inclined to answer him, so far from her homeland but even calling her by name was a small comfort to him.

"Fine, I'll tell it, but this isn't a pretty story. And Titania is only a small part of the tale."

More than that, there had been a small part of him that wanted to tell the story. Tristan deserved to know the truth. At least as much as he was willing to give the little shapeshifter. There would always be parts kept from his brother, but Tristan had earned most of what he was willing to share.

Chapter Two

Early Helladic Period III – Approximately 2100 BC

Lightning cracked overhead, splitting the dark sky with fire as the horse shied, small ears flat against its skull. The storm doing more than the smells of blood and shouting warriors could to frighten it. War

trained and bred for the task. And far more intelligent than any mundane horse could be.

He felt it when the weight vanished from the chariot he was pulling, its owner up to his knees in salt- now brackish water and mud with sword in hand and spinning to counter a blow from a misshapen stone like beast.

Fire traced its way across his flank, and he slowed, stumbling on a tuft of hidden grass in the muddy battlefield. Only his mate and kits kept him from losing pace entirely. His family and the chariot he was pulling in an arc back to where Poseidon had turned from fighting the stone beast to fighting something much more shadowy in nature. Whatever it was, smelled of burning things and fire, and the bitter, acrid scent of Hephestus's forge.

Mortals painted romantic battles between the gods and the titans, this as far from rosy as the tales they told around their firepits could be. It wasn't god against titan, it was brother against brother and neither were well disposed to each other. Only Agesander could bring an end to the fighting between the lord of the heavens and the ruler over the seas.

A massive wolf howled somewhere in the distance, briefly visible as an outline as lightning ripped across the sky again. Baying answered the wolf's call as Artemis's hounds scented their prey.

The howl turned from triumphant to the worried song of a hunted animal, the goddess's hounds hard in pursuit. They had the wolf's scent now; nothing would shake them from their chase save for the creature's death. They just had to catch it first.

If his master shouted for him, the words were lost amid the thunder overhead but not the tone – the call echoed to his core, forcing him to obey even if he wanted to refuse. It was an honor to fight for Poseidon, to serve him a blessing.

He shifted to human shape without thought, reflex and years of habit in obeying the Earthshaker making him join the god's side. One man's blood streaked, and lost sword retrieved from the fallen mortal warrior's slack grip. The chariot was more a hindrance than a help now.

Fire blossomed in the distance, and he flinched, drawing back as the god's hand tightened in warning around the wrist not clutching the weapon by the muddy hilt. A circling eagle screamed and dove, talons outstretched towards Poseidon. Only to fall

short onto the filthy ground, a pool of salty water bubbling up around it as it fought to free itself. And failed in its struggles as the water swallowed it whole.

A nearby pair of warriors in mud-streaked tunics fought each other in grim silence, except for the sparks thrown by bronze swords, heedless of the other battle going on between gods. Or nearly so as one of the men dared a look over his shoulder, spun away to duck a slash from his opponent and freeze, eyes widening in disbelief at the sight of Poseidon there.

To his cost as an arrow pierced linen armor from behind and sent the warrior to his knees before falling almost gently into the muck of the field.

They were seen now, not just nameless warriors on a soon to be forgotten war. The survivor

grinned and lifted his sword high, giving just the hint of an acknowledging nod. Not triumph at the god's favor but an invitation to join him in battle.

Only one would walk away from this tonight. It wasn't going to be the mortal warrior. He met the warrior's attempted blow with his borrowed weapon before ducking beneath an ill-timed outstretched arm. His sword found the man's throat and cut through it, just shy of the bone.

"Enough!" The voice shouldn't have been heard over the thunder or the cries of the nearby warriors but somehow it slowed the tide of the battle – a few of the men lowering their weapons in uncertainty as they swept their gazes around for the source and owner of the voice.

He looked back over his shoulder, daring to glance at Poseidon's remote expression painted on a heavily and graying bearded face, yet finding no clue to guide him by. There was no order to obey as he went to his knees in front of the sandy haired newcomer in a sober, undyed tunic. Or the man's red-gold haired daughter, lingering a step or two behind her father with a burning bird of prey perched on one outstretched wrist. Falcon or hawk, it mattered not.

He kept his gaze on the ground, not daring to look above or beyond the churned-up patch of mud he was focused on, though it was impossible not to overhear the words, either.

Poseidon's voice deeper than his brothers' grumbling his answers, Zeus arguing hotly with a rough shake of a hand towards the lord of the sea.

Agesander far more measured between the two, though tight as he stepped between them and forced them apart with both hands slightly outstretched.

A woman's touch, far gentler than expected as her hand cupped the side of his face and lifted it to meet her gaze. He pulled away, not daring to look longer than permitted. Hecate was a goddess; he was only a soldier – not worthy of looking at her. "Mistress."

Her laugh was soft, somehow still sad. "Hecate. I'm no mistress of yours anymore than you should belong to Poseidon. This battle was unneeded and only my father could have intervened between my…"

Her mouth tightened, eyes flickering a falcon's gold for a moment. "My dearly beloved uncles."

What could he say to that? He owed his life and creation to Poseidon – to turn away from the god, despite Hecate's claim of his freedom was unthinkable. His wife's hand slipped over his shoulder, soft – encouraging him to stand and rejoin her. Somewhere unseen, unnoticed she had claimed human form though the style of her hair more resembled the dark mare's mane from before, cut along the sides, long and loose behind her back. "I owe Poseidon too much to leave him. He gave me my life."

He stood at last, reluctantly turning away from the witch and shapeshifter to shift back to his natural

form. The battle may have ended but the war wasn't over yet.

Chapter Three

"But I thought the titan thingy was a long time ago and it wasn't Posy against Suzie." Tristan's voice intruded on the story mid telling.

Aran snorted, glancing out toward the water hitting nearby rocks at the edge of the beach before the tide pulled it out again. With a slight gesture the little wavelet took the shape of a white horse running across the stones before it collapsed into seafoam and water, once more reclaimed by the sea again. "The titanomachy was a long time ago, before I was born and it was the last time Poseidon, Hades and Zeus cooperated with each other, when they succeeded in imprisoning their father."

Tristan scrambled from his perch on the driftwood log, splashing through the water in an attempt at catching one of the horses before he came back, dripping but not soaked through like he had been. "Awh."

His disappointment didn't last long before his expression brightened with childlike hope. "Are you going to let me ride you one day?"

Aran went still, hand going tight around a sharp-edged bit of rock Tristan had gifted him after playing on the beach. The five-year-old would be good with weapons one day if the roughly knapped bit of stone was anything to go by. He closed his eyes, using the pain as much as the warmth of blood trickling across his palm to focus. "I'm coming to that

answer, kit. But no, that's one thing you can't ask of me. It's dangerous, especially for you."

He took a breath, raking his free hand through the drying strands of fair hair. "Are you going to let me finish or do I have to tell your mother to threaten you with a human elementary school to keep you quiet? Dad won't hear of it but there's more education out there than a mechanic's shop and passing him his tools."

Tristan opened his mouth and quieted, though it was only the kind of quiet brought on by a chocolate chip and peanut butter cookie sandwich. "Mhm…"

"Thanks." Aran let the crude spearhead fall to rejoin the other rocks at their feet. The blood drawn was only a minor wound, one that would heal in a day

or two, in contrast to the tight, itchy feel of his skin. "Poseidon was my master, but I didn't know how little he regarded me or what I was to him. I…"

"What I was to him. I…" He took a breath, steeling himself against some unpleasant memories as he closed his eyes. "I thought loyal soldier, he thought slave."

Tristan cast him a hurt look, slipping a chocolate streaked and sticky hand over his arm in sympathy, despite the mouthful of sandwich he'd stuffed into his mouth. Somehow managing to talk around the bite he'd taken. "s'notfairy- ee's mean."

The logic of a five-year-old shapeshifter. Aran shook his head, teasing a bit of Tristan's dark hair into a damp rat's nest. "Swallow first and then talk, please. No one needs to see the crumbs on your shirt.

Or what's in your mouth. I like the scent of chocolate as much as the next male but don't turn two cookies into your peanut butter sandwich. I'll ask again, can you keep quiet for ten minutes?"

"S'rry." Tristan stuffed more cookie sandwich into his mouth though he did manage to keep the crumbs from escaping this time.

Finally. Goddess blessed silence from his little brother. Aran sighed, relieved by Tristan's difficulty in speaking. He could get through the next few minutes or however long it took for the little shapeshifter to polish off a half-eaten sandwich made from two chocolate chip cookies and peanut butter.

Chapter Four

Early Helladic Period III – Approximately 2100 BC

Soft, pale blue light glittered through the stable's open windows. The color of the sea in the mortal realm and a near match for the blue of his wife's eyes. He kissed Theia, not caring that they were tangled together on a pallet in the barn's loft rather than in the hall with the sailors taken into Poseidon's care after a death at sea.

A fish swam by, odd to anyone not used to the sight, barely worth mentioning to either of them despite the apparent lack of water in the stable, or for the horses resting within their stalls. Theia smiled, following its meandering path before it vanished through one of the stable walls, returning to its true element.

Poseidon's realm with both within the water and outside of it, little difference made by the sea life that interrupted their trysts on occasion.

Theia flinched under his touch, and he pulled back, moving his hand to see the flushed and peeling skin across her shoulder and upper arm. "What's this?"

He knew full well what it was and the reasons behind it, but the question needed to be asked regardless.

"It'll pass." Theia's voice was quiet. "Just too long on mortal land. It was worse before."

If she was unwilling to talk about it, who was he to press the matter? He sighed, interlacing his fingers with hers. Unlike him, her hands were free of

the webbing that joined his fingers halfway to the first knuckle. "Fair, I suppose."

She braced herself on one arm, pressing her mouth against his and pushed him onto his side, rolling him so that she was sprawled full out across the length of his body, chin resting on her forearm as she looked into his face. "Not fair, but you always were too serious. The burn will pass."

Too serious? He rolled his eyes, tangling a hand through Theia's black mane and teasing the dark strands through his fingers. She smelled like sunshine and sand. All the things they struggled to see without Poseidon's protection. "I thought that was Athira, of the four of us. Danae was always pulling little tricks on the other mares or Poseidon's kin."

Theia's mouth quirked as she slipped a hand over the curve of his shoulder and upper arm. "I remember that one. She stole honey from Aphrodite and mixed it with sweetened sunflower oil. It wasn't the most difficult trick she could have planned. Wasn't that one you taught her?"

"I'll never say." He pulled her close, breathing in her scent once more before draping the blanket across their bodies. "And honey was safer than giving fire to the mortal kind. I pity Prometheus, bound in some northern wasteland for his crime."

"I suppose." Theia's voice was unconvinced, but her eyes were dancing with amusement at the memory of Danae's little trick. "Do you ever think we'll see more than our homeland or Poseidon's realm?"

Those were dangerous words for his wife to consider but a good question regardless. He cupped the back of her neck with one hand and nipped gently at her collarbone, barely drawing blood with the small bite. "If we serve well enough, perhaps. Not before."

She lay back against the pallet, pensive and one hand resting across her stomach. "Do you ever think about it? Freedom? A chance to do what we will instead of obedience to Poseidon?"

He hadn't thought of that, truth be told, and he sagged back against the pallet they lay on. "How much freedom can there be when he can force us to obedience?"

"This is something you've thought about?" The question came unbidden before he could stop himself or silence it before it could be spoken.

Theia sat up, moving to his side before she sat, legs drawn up underneath her body. "In a word, no. But I've… noticed how Poseidon watches me. He loves his servants but I'm not certain his is the kind of love I want to return."

Her hand slipped over his and she pressed a chaste kiss to his mouth, wrapping an arm around his waist. "Yours is the only love I want. Yours and our daughters."

He hesitated and welcomed her unspoken invitation, spreading Theia's legs with one knee before slipping inside her.

His breath caught and he went still, freezing mid act as Poseidon's silent call echoed in the back of his mind. Theia's expression was no less stricken as

she put a hand to her temple, hearing the same call in her thoughts he did. "Ah…"

Words alone wouldn't have been enough to enforce the summons for them but Poseidon's silent call and the power behind it could. And often did, nearly stripping choice from them. They wouldn't be able to resist his command today. "So be it."

Like it or not they were Poseidon's soldiers and bound to obey the god.

It wasn't his place to question what the god's mood was like – only to serve and obey Poseidon's will without questioning it. There was some safety in speaking to Theia in the stables, much less so in the open where their master might overhear their hushed words.

All he knew of the nameless little village was that its residents had failed to respect the Earthshaker and for that, had earned the god's fury. Poseidon and his kin were fickle creatures, as willing to bless mortals as take their favor away.

Theia's hand slipped into his and he squeezed it for a moment, feeling the warm, combat worn skin across her palm. She could have healed the damage done by years of training with sword if she had wanted it. His wife hadn't for his sake- she knew what he liked.

She pulled him close, wrapping one arm around his waist as she rested her head against his shoulder, dark hair a stark contrast to the fairer coloring of his hair. They could have been any young

couple sneaking away from the village for a moment alone on the pale sand of the nearby beach.

He'd chosen his shape to mimic a young man in his eighteenth summer. Theia had favored something a little younger than that. Fourteen to his eighteen.

They stood in that space between land and sea, the saltwater lapping at bare feet. Either one of this could have done this on their own but Poseidon had made them both go, leaving their daughters in the god's care.

It went unsaid but he couldn't help tasting something bitter at that. This wasn't a question he could ask his master, but it felt as though Poseidon was holding the young female shapeshifters as

collateral against their good behavior, obeying his order for the sake of protecting Danae and Athira.

The water pulled away from the shore, leaving small boats and fishing vessels listing on the wet sand as their owners looked on in confusion. It wasn't fear, not yet but they would learn that Poseidon wasn't a god easily crossed. A few human children paused in their play to watch the retreating water, wide eyed. The youngest couldn't have been more than three summers old, clinging to his half-grown brother's hand.

One red-haired woman's eyes widened, fixed on them in fear before they narrowed, and she scooped up a young girl into her arms and hurried from the shoreline. Not quite a full out run but not a calm walk away from the coming fury.

A horse grazing at the edge of the beach where the shore turned from sand to scrubby grass, lifted its head at the woman's approach as she scrambled onto the gelding's back. The child held securely in a one-armed hold as she nudged the beast into a trot and then canter. And then a full out run in her haste to escape what was about to come.

He couldn't focus on the woman or the way her hair drifted behind her in striking contrast to the silver mare's body, like copper against seafoam. Theia clung to him as the water rose up behind them, looking more like a solid wall than the gentle waves it had been a day ago.

Theia's arms wrapped around his waist, holding as tight as she could with wetness clinging to her eyelashes. Saltwater or her own tears as the wall

broke, rushing forward to sweep away the boats and nearest wooden homes.

There was little time for anyone to run or cry out as Poseidon's fury swept the village away. The water was before, behind and around them, holding them suspended for a moment. Black spots danced in front his vision as he inhaled water, choking on the taste as he fought his way to the surface. Oiled canvas and broken wood tangled around him. Theia's hand was limp in his own as he brushed a strand of her dark hair out of her eyes. Death wasn't the end for them, and he could see the change as it started at her fingertips. Flesh and dark blood giving way to seafoam and a soft light before Theia's natural shape stirred, once more horse formed.

She twisted, turning to look back at him and whickered. He smiled briefly, swinging a leg over Theia's back as he tangled both hands in her black mane. Death was a minor thing for them, not something they needed to concern themselves with as he sagged against her neck. It was a relief to finally go home. The sea was as much a part of them as they were a part of it.

Chapter Five

September 18th, 1993, 1:45 AM. Seattle, Washington

Most nights he slept in his own apartment, but Tristan had all but begged Aran to stay the night over in the house. September was in the wrong season for a thunderstorm, but the old house was poorly insulated. The wind rattled at the windows, slipping

inside the ill-fitting frames where it could, rain pounding against the roof when it couldn't.

The front door screeched on rust stiffened hinges as he opened it. Aran winced, stepping through before he shut the door behind him. "Tristan?"

A softer creak came from the uncarpeted stairs up to the second floor. Aran went still for a second, one hand on the light switch. He didn't need the light – their kind could see in the dark as easily as it was day when they wanted to but flicking it on would give Tristan a little forewarning that he was in the house.

Aran sniffed, catching a whiff of his brother's scent. "Your parents left you again?"

"Yeah." Tristan crept out of the bedroom at the end of the hall, wiping his nose on one sleeve of a

second-hand set of dinosaur pajamas. "'s why I called."

Aran sighed, sitting with his back next to the wall as he pulled his brother close, absently teasing a hand through the rat's nest that was Tristan's chin length dark hair. He couldn't fault the five-year-old for being terrified of the storm or calling him over but one or both of their parents should have stayed behind to make sure the kit was safe and happy, not abandoning him for duty. "Mom's a kitsune and a guardian for Chinatown. Dad probably went with her just to add a little protection. You know what she went through during the war, right?"

Tristan's nose scrunched as he looked up at him. "Uhm… Mama was put into a cage because she looked different from people?"

It was a bit more complicated than that but for a five-year-old, Tristan's answer was more aware than most human kits. "Yeah, something like that. Northern California... wasn't fun."

Tristan blinked, eyes catching a little of the light overhead and reflecting it back as he looked up at the photograph hanging on the wall between the bedroom and the bathroom. "You went too?"

"In as much as I looked Japanese then, yeah." Aran shook his head, pushing the memory aside. "Illness and death was a blessing that time. Left a few questions for the interment camp guards but made my escape easier. As long as her people keep being caged for how they look, she made a promise to stop that. No more camps or prisons based on appearance or culture."

He stood, offering his hand to his brother. "C'mon, I know you hate going into the attic but there's something I need to show you. Someday if you want it, it'll be yours."

Mariko intended the gift for him, he was planning on refusing it. He wasn't Japanese by birth or blood. He had no right to the sword that had once belonged to Tristan's grandfather. "C'mon, I know you hate going into the attic but there's something I need to show you. If you want it, it'll be yours someday."

Tristan's mouth opened and closed, eyes going round. "Ari?"

Aran chuckled, shifting the ladder under the attic entrance, and shoved at the small wooden 'door' covering. "C'mon, little one."

There wasn't much in the attic except for dust and one old steamer trunk tucked behind a canvas sheet. He flipped it off, sneezing in the puff of dust that rose up. "*Ifreann.*"

Tristan smacked his shoulder. "Mom says hell is rude."

"It was a very dusty box," Aran said dryly. "And the only hell I believe in is Tartarus, Tír na nÓg doesn't have a hell in the same way my homeland does."

He touched the lock for a second before pulling the key from his jeans pocket. It only took a moment and the right amount of force to open the trunk before he lifted the lid up. The black and white photograph album was less important than the sheathed weapon resting on a fluffy furniture blanket.

Aran lifted the curved sword out in both hands and set it in Tristan's lap. "This was your grandfather's; it could be yours when you're old enough."

Tristan looked down uncertainly at the katana. "Shouldn't it be yours, Ari? You're older than me an' the fighter. I've saw you down in the backyard practicing with that Greek thingy. The pretty sounding one."

Tristan's "pretty sounding sword" had a name. Aran tried to smile. "They called it a makhaira, little brother. Anyway, I'm not Japanese. I don't have any right to your grandfather's weapon."

Tristan looked like he was about to cry, touching the hilt of the sword with a trembling hand. "It's yours. Don't care what Mom thinks."

He curled up in Aran's lap, forcing him to close the steamer trunk on the fifty year old memories. "Never finished your story after the swim lesson."

"Ah." So, there was more to the phone call from a shaky landline than just fear of a storm. Aran arranged his arms so that he was cradling the young shapeshifter in his lap rather than being trapped by him. "I ended it after being ordered to drown people in a tsu- a really big wave. There's no justification for that, even if I didn't have a choice in refusing Poseidon's demands."

Tristan sniffled, quieting before speaking barely above a whisper. "You didn't do it 'cause you wanted to. Your boss guy made you do it. Better than

what Mama did to the Mogli people when she tells about when they came to her home."

"Mongolians." Aran corrected. "I guess. But I still could have gone into that little village and made an attempt at warning them to run. Poseidon would have been content with the destruction of the village and their livelihoods. Their lives were only collateral in the flood. They weren't warriors or soldiers able to defend themselves. Not like the sailors who invaded Japan."

It was easier to find his place in the story than it had been in earlier breaks between telling. The tsunami and its destruction were burned into his memory in a way other events had faded, lost to time and distance. Tiryn's red hair as it caught the wind behind her, flying like a flag while she rode her mare

hard, trying to escape with a child in her arms. He hadn't known her name then. He'd learned it since, much to his regret for that long ago flood.

Chapter Six

He was the first to wake, sprawled out on the tiled floor of Poseidon's hall and watery blue light streaming in from the crystalline roof. A school of fish nosed at him before he brushed them off with an irritated hand. They scattered, frightened before returning to their place in the physical world.

Theia stirred next to him and coughed, rolling onto hands and knees before she spat a mouthful of water out onto the floor. Her hair was already drying, untouched by the destruction, she – they had caused.

He drew her close to his body, seeing her not as the fourteen-year-old woman she had chosen to be

several hours earlier but a woman closer to him in age. Nineteen or twenty or so. Her cheeks were still wet with tears as she rested her head against his chest. Theia held him tight until the last of her tears fell and she glanced at him, looking older – more tired despite the young female shape she wore. "We'll figure out what to do. I promise."

They were feeble words at best, barely worth the oath he'd made to his wife but she accepted them regardless, standing and shifting back to her black mare form. Emotions were easier, simpler in a form that matched their spirits. He would join her but there was still business he had to attend to.

He knelt on one knee, barely daring to lift his gaze to look up at the god. "It's done. The mortals

will remember the destruction of the village for as long as they keep telling the story."

Poseidon gave him a long, lingering look and stirred from his throne, teasing a hand through his fair hair. Lysander kept his head bowed, trying to keep his expression blank, expressionless. Whatever his feelings on the village's death, he was still Poseidon's soldier. Confronting the god who had created him was not a wise course of action. Not if he wanted to live longer than he had. Any... indignity was worth keeping his life. "There were no survivors."

Save one, but it was doubtful she had been a resident of that village.

Poseidon pulled away, a shadow of satisfaction crossing his face before he sat back down

again, acknowledging his wife in the equally matched golden throne next to his. "Go then."

He left, ducking his head in respect before turning away, expecting the sting of a lash across his shoulders and back. It wasn't the first time; it wouldn't be the last time for some minor slight or slip of memory.

His path led him not to the stables as intended but to the meadow where Theia was cropping listlessly at a tuft of grass. He brushed a hand through Theia's mane, tangling the coarse hair through his fingers before he swung a leg over her back. Neither of them had been trained to saddle or bit in their horse forms so he rode without, guiding her with touch and his knees.

She went where she wanted as often as he asked her to go where he wished. If he had been in her place, he would have done the same as the soft, sea blue light surrounded them. It faded, leaving him dizzy for a second, clinging to Theia's neck until the spinning faded. The twisted knot in the pit of his stomach took a moment longer to ease and he steadied himself against the comforting body of the mare by his side.

The sun was too hot against the back of his neck, his skin too tight, itchy and he closed his eyes against the prickling sensation in them. Not tears of his own for what he had done, just a reminder of how vulnerable he was on land.

All he could say of Thera was that his current place was small and uninhabited with a good view of

the sea. Gulls circled overhead, crying out and the wind teased through his hair, making her presence known before she subsided, tiring of her game.

He sighed, picking up a rounded stone from the beach and tossed it into the water, watching it as it leapt a few turns before sinking out of sight beneath the waves. The stone would be an easy find again if he wanted to, but he was in no mood for the human pup's game.

"You think too much, warrior." The woman's voice was dry, as cool as the little cave she shared with her sisters.

He glanced at her, trying not to show disquiet at the sight of dark-haired Atropos standing not a few feet from him, dressed in a gray dyed tunic and lightly veiled. The delicate cloth didn't hide her face

completely, but it obscured her features from him. Atropos had come up on him so silently it was as if she had materialized there instead of making her way down to his side. He would have preferred her younger sisters. They weren't responsible for cutting the life thread of a mortal when the time came for them to descend into Hades' realm. "I like it here, it's… peaceful."

Atropos laughed, placing a gentle hand on his shoulder before she pulled him down to sitting next to her. "Peace? From my kinsman's best soldier? I see much, but I never expected that from you, little one."

"What purpose did Poseidon have in using me to send a wave to flood a village?" He forced the question out, tasting the sourness of it. "I know who I am but this, I-"

He cut himself off short, shaking a head. "I'm changing and I don't know if I should be."

Her smile was hidden behind the veil, but it was in her voice as she placed a hand on his wrist. "You're a shapeshifter, it's in your nature to change."

"Not like this." He cast a longing look towards the water, chewing on his lower lip. "Not so… mortal."

"You would prefer a life as Poseidon's slave?" Atropos's voice sharpened though there was no anger in the question. "I can read the history of his treatment on your back without asking you to remove your tunic. My sisters told me what was to come, and how the scarring would fall across your shoulders. Your only value to him is in obedience and as a soldier. That isn't life, that is a cage you made

yourself. He cares little for you beyond your skills as a warrior."

He wanted to deny the words she spoke and couldn't find a rebuke to them. Life as Poseidon's pet, now that he was aware of it, wasn't for him. "What do I do now?"

Atropos couldn't be proposing rebellion against a god, could she? Acknowledging the truth was one thing, confronting Poseidon was another. As powerful as he was, the god had made him – there was every chance Poseidon could end him if he was driven to it.

"Then run." The oldest of the moirai gave a shrug, looking past him to the ocean lapping at the shoreline. "I will not tell your future, there's a mercy in not knowing what may happen but I see you on

some emerald island, a rider on your back. I cannot say more than that."

"I understand." He picked up an attractive rock and turned it over in his hands before tossing it into the water. As pretty as the stone was, it was still just a stone. "I'll return soon enough; I just need a word with Theia."

"Of course." Atropos inclined her head and took a step away from him, climbing the narrow path she had used to find her way to him.

Theia shifted back to human shape, the black mare giving way to the woman as she rested her head on his shoulder. "I heard what was said. Is she telling us to leave Poseidon's service?"

"She may be." He didn't want to make a guess on so little information mentioned. The Moirai were

difficult to interpret one way or the other and it was wiser to see how things unfolded rather than fighting against the river's current. "They rarely tell everything to the one asking. There's… wisdom in that, I think."

How much, he couldn't say but it wasn't for him to judge what the fates told him. They always had a reason even if the motivations were unclear until after the action had unfolded. "Stay with me or return home?"

"Return home." Theia wrapped an arm around his waist, scuffing her bare foot through the sand bordering the shore. "I know when you need your space and when you want my touch. I'll speak with you when you feel ready to."

She released him and waded out into deeper water before diving below the surface with barely a ripple left behind to betray her ever having been there.

The sun drifted across the sky for the space of an hour or two before he followed his wife back home, back to where they belonged. The seed of a plan was beginning to take shape but that was all it was in a secret corner of his mind. A seed of an idea, nothing more.

Chapter Seven

September 18th, 1993, 4:00 AM. Seattle, Washington

Breakfast at four AM wasn't a habit for his little brother but Tristan deserved something sweet and sugary after the traumatizing piece he'd told this

morning. It had taken three hours to go through that part of the story and the rain was finally letting up, no longer as strongly scented as it had been when the five-year-old had figured out the right number to call to get ahold of him.

Aran glanced toward the upended bowl of milk spreading across the ancient kitchen table and let it linger there. Napkins would clean that mess up easily enough but there were none in the kitchen drawer. Tristan had spilled it several minutes ago when a crack of lightning had split the sky and turned the kitchen briefly silver white. Unusual for a September morning but fitting for the story hour.

He sighed, holding the bowl below the level of the table's edge and passing his free hand over the creamy puddle. It flowed, collecting into the dish

before he set it well out of his brother's reach. "I did tell you it wasn't a pretty story. Do you want me to continue?"

His past was a lot to put onto a five-year-old's shoulders, whether they were human or a young shapeshifter and if Tristan wanted to end things here, he'd understand. A change of subject was in order though any plans for travel would have to wait until eight or so. "Why don't we go out instead? It'd do us both good to get out of Seattle for a while."

It was good Tristan wasn't the most observant of people around or he would have noticed the change from the t-shirt earlier to a long sleeve shirt and denim jacket Aran was wearing now. No trick this time, just a spare change of clothes taken from the backpack cached in the master bedroom while Tristan

had been occupied with his early breakfast. Fates
willing, his little brother wouldn't ask.

Tristan's expression fell as he looked from the
cream filled bowl to the shirt. "But you like t-shirts,
why're you borrowing one of Dad's shirts now?"

He slipped from his perch at the table and
grabbed for the sleeve, pushing it roughly past Aran's
elbow. "Ari?"

The mild burn and peeling skin from a day
before was raw, red and angry now, stinging as the
cotton brushed across the ugly wound. Tristan's touch
was gentle, barely skin to skin skimming across his
arm but the brief touch against the burns had Aran
flinching away from the child's touch, teeth bared and
a low hiss threatening before he could keep it from
escaping. Tristan blinked once or twice, chewing on

his lower lip before he rummaged through the clutter stored in the drawer next to the ancient refrigerator. He reemerged with paper towel, folded and damp from tap water, and tape. "This help?"

Aran accepted the paper towel, laying it against the inside of his arm. Burn cream and specially treated cloth bandages would have been better, but he couldn't fault a five-year-old for trying to help. And even as small of a gesture as lukewarm tap water and paper towel was better than nothing. "Thanks."

He tugged the shirt sleeve down over his arm, grateful that the boy had been able to identify medical tape rather than paper tape this time around. And for that, he was willing to reconsider his plans of waiting until full light to travel. "Let's go to the cabin."

Tristan brightened at that, easily distracted and grinning at the prospect. "Yay!"

He quieted a moment later, uncertainty crossing his face. "Can I keep up with you? I'm still a pup."

"Kid, Tristan, kid. Not pup, remember? And we can take our time hiking there." Aran smiled wryly. "I know it's sixty miles from Seattle to Rainier Park, but we're in no rush to get there even if it takes us a week. And your mother wants you to build up your strength."

"'kay." Tristan shifted from one foot to the other. "How…?"

"Come out back." Aran let the bowl into the sink with a note scribbled in Welsh for their mother. Mariko wouldn't worry about them if there wasn't a

note, but it was worth telling her where they were going. "We're traveling light, don't bother with a backpack."

He was first out into the weed choked excuse for a backyard before he closed his eyes. The change was like warmth, a gentle light sliding over his skin as the human mask fell away and left the wolf in his place. It wasn't a comfortable shape for him to wear but a horse in the company of a little mountain lion kit would raise a few eyebrows from hunters. If he wasn't shot by mistake by those men looking for deer.

Tristan's change was a moment later and into the squeaking mountain lion kit he'd thought would happen. Aran let out a huff, picking his brother up by the scruff of the neck, carrying the kitten out of the backyard and into the scrap of woods behind the

house. It was going to be a long four days run if this was the shape Tristan preferred. Wolves and mountain lions were as unlikely as a young cougar and a horse traveling together. The sooner they could get out of the city, the better. No one needed a strange picture of an unlikely set of animals cooperating with each other.

Their first break came twelve miles after leaving the house and backyard behind them. Aran shifted back to human shape, regretting the action despite the necessity of it. He needed hands for this, not paws.

Tristan snuffled in his sleep, curled up beneath a stolen blanket. Aran brushed a hand across the child's dark hair before returning to the task at hand. The flint and steel were stolen as well, taken from a

sporting goods store while the salesclerk's back was turned. Sparks flew, bounced, and vanished before the second attempt set the small pile of paper and twigs alight.

They weren't out of danger yet, there was every chance a homeless wanderer could find them, but the abandoned warehouse was safer than the alley next to it. He'd made a circuit of the area before stealing the minimal supplies they needed.

Tristan mumbled something and stirred at last, eyes catching the firelight and reflecting it back for a moment as he burrowed deeper into the pocket of warmth his body created underneath the layer of fleece. "Will I be able to do this someday?"

"Run twelve miles and not tire? Eventually, maybe." Aran sat down cross-legged before the fire

and pulled the too restrictive shoes off, tossing them into a dark corner of the warehouse. Some lucky scavenger could make better use of the footwear than he could. "Not now though, you're still too young for it."

"Too little for everything." Tristan said. "Can't keep up with you, can't swim or anything. When'll I be able to keep up with you?"

Aran looked at him from across the small fire between them. "Don't wish your childhood away, kit. At least you had one. I never did. Poseidon was never interested in raising a child so he... well..."

There were no words to describe the act of his creation. It couldn't be called birth since neither mother or father had been involved in the act. His earliest memories had been of choking on air as he

fought to breathe for the first time, and the first

unsteady steps on two legs, not four. "I had to teach

myself everything you take for granted and Poseidon

wasn't interested in playing 'father' to me."

The emphasis on father was bitter. Once he

would have welcomed even the slightest bit of

approval from the god for an act done well. Now he

knew better. Poseidon had only thought of him as a

useful pet to do with what he wanted. "Just sleep.

You need the rest more than I do."

He brushed a hand through Tristan's hair,

tucking a strand out of his eyes as he drew on a little

of his power, sending it his brother's way. The little

shapeshifter would sleep now, comfortably until

dawn came when they needed to travel again. Their

campfire would be enough to keep the pup warm until

dawn, until then – he needed time alone with his thoughts.

Aran tucked a fallen corner of the blanket around Tristan's shoulder, glancing towards the flames before peeling the crude bandage from his forearm. It hurt to remove and he gritted his teeth, pulling the paper towel and tape off at once rather than picking at the tape holding it against his arm bit by bit. Humans were oversensitive when it came to pain, what laid them out for weeks wouldn't have stopped him for long on any other day. Thrown against a wall, taken an arrow in the shoulder. Those were mundane dangers. There had been a grandson or daughter of Lycaon spoiling for a fight once, they had buried a claw tipped hand in his chest and given him the unwelcome 'pleasure' of seeing his heart eaten in front of him, moments before death and return to his

69

element. A little pain from pulling a used bandage off his forearm should have been insignificant, no more than a minor papercut was.

The paper towel came away with spots of dark blood and drying skin where the crude bandage stuck to the edges of the burn. Raw flesh laying beneath the stiffened layers of white paper.

Aran sighed and cast the paper towel into the fire. It caught at the edges, curling into a brown and then blackened ball as it was consumed. The orange light showed what he wanted to deny to himself; the burn damage was spreading across his arm faster than hoped for. Being on land was more risk than he cared to acknowledge. Nothing as flashy as the paper towel being consumed by fire in front of him but the effects

were the same. Spontaneous combustion was a myth, his frailty, less so.

The burn on his forearm was the least of his worry. It could be hidden, deflected from. Everything else, less so unless he kept his shirt and jeans on. . There was no telling how the rest of his body looked other than the tight, itchy feeling beneath the cotton shirt and jeans. It was lucky Tristan wasn't observant. He'd have noticed the flush across his hands and how cracked, dry the webbing between his fingers had become. "You didn't ask for the next part of the story, but I'll tell it anyway, kit."

The sooner he finished with his story, the better. It didn't matter if Tristan was too far asleep to overhear this part of the tale.

Chapter Eight

Early Helladic Period III – Approximately 2100 BC

The wreck was new enough that it hadn't there long enough to be lost beneath the shifting sand and silt, but it wasn't so recent that survivors were still struggling to make their way to shore. If they could swim at all.

The sailors not lucky enough to wash ashore for their wives and mothers to deal with were tangled amid ropes and shattered wood. Agesander could deal with the souls of the men given proper rites – the ones bound and trapped on board when it sank – they belonged to Poseidon until he was willing to let them go to their final rest.

His attention wasn't on the decaying cloth and flesh of their bodies as much as it was on what the

doomed ship had carried. Wine and fish were worthless, but it was something just as mundane that caught his eye. The gold was as bright and clean as ever – would be for as long as time and tide didn't scatter it, the silver was already turning black from the salt water.

He knelt, sorting through an overturned chest before slipping a few of the coins into the small pouch he'd scavenged from the captain's belt. The dead had no need for money, except for what he'd placed in the man's mouth as payment for the ferryman.

There would be time to return to the wreck later if it wasn't lost by then. For now, he had what he needed from the crew and its captain. They served no further use for him now.

He couldn't go directly against his master. That was a sure way to invite death even for one like him, so running and offering a prayer to whatever fate was looking out for his family was the only choice before him.

Theia was willing to sacrifice everything to accompany him, but he hadn't mentioned the seed of his plan to his daughters. Fear of them as much as fear for them. One could be trusted, the other was stubborn in her devotion to Poseidon. Whether that meant she would betray her own family to the god was unknown, but his plan needed a little more time to form before he dared mention anything to them.

"Father?" A young woman's soft voice sounded from the stable entrance before she

approached him, gaze on the small pouch of coins in his hands. "What is this?"

Lie and risk his younger child's dismay or tell her the truth and earn her fear instead? He sat on a sack of grain, resting the back of his head against the wood of the stable's half door. Danae had chosen her shape to mirror his own, fair blonde hair and a stockier build than her sister and mother's. His daughter could have been his twin in appearance if things had been different. She had even mimicked the webbing between his fingers for herself.

Truth won out as he turned the little coin pouch over in his hands and dropped it behind the sack where it lay out of sight. "I'm thinking I might…"

The words wouldn't come as much as he wanted them to. He sighed, frustrated and ran a hand through his hair. "I learned more about... free will than Poseidon may care for one of his soldiers to know about. And your mother never wanted to use her power to kill innocents. What happened to that village..."

Those deaths had left a mark on Theia's soul and his own. Fighting as a soldier against an enemy made sense, was fair but not the deaths of mortals. "Theia has... started questioning Poseidon's ways. I cannot let her go alone."

Not with the secret his wife carried in her belly. The child's father was undetermined but even if it was Poseidon's pup, he'd raise the boy as his own.

Danae's expression was pained as she took a seat next to him on a nearby crate. "You're one of our master's best. Do you think he would permit you to leave for the… sake of my little brother? And if you do flee like the Erinyes are hunting you, what makes you think he won't find us? We swore an oath to serve him, breaking it…"

It wasn't hard to hear how she included herself in the little group. He lifted his gaze to her, sweeping a strand of Danae's hair behind one ear. "This will work, it must."

The other horses drowsed or cropped contentedly at their food and for that he could envy them for such a simple life. No thoughts beyond running with the herd or for the males, guarding their mates from rivals. Mere animals for the long lives

they had before them. More than any mundane horse anyway. Of all of Poseidon's creations, they had been the only ones gifted with shapeshifting and a share in the god's power. "I don't feel we have much of a choice now, Poseidon isn't the master I thought I knew during the wars with his kin."

If the god had ever been and it had taken him this long to see the truth for what it was instead of loyalty to Poseidon. There was a cruel streak to the Earthshaker that he had been blind to, or willing to ignore until he couldn't. Poseidon was more akin to the northern wolf god who had adopted Ares as his name than an honorable warrior or a man worthy of respect.

"Where will we go?" Danae's voice was soft as she smoothed the skirt of her tunic. "He can track

us anywhere he wants to and land – you know how it is for us, Father. A month's turning and we're forced back to our- his element."

That was the flaw in the half a dozen plans he'd thought of and discarded. He sighed, briefly touching the bronze blade at his waist before dropping his hand back to his side. Poseidon claimed the oceans and the only way to avoid his eye was to make a living on land. Something none of them could do for long without sacrificing the power the god had given them. It wasn't a sacrifice he could make himself though; he wasn't going to pretend to know his daughters' minds. Danae might consider the idea, Athira never would. "Can your sister be reasoned with?"

Danae's expression fell and she turned her hand to study it in the watery blue light of the stable. Like his, her hands were webbed halfway to the first joint of her fingers. "She's devoted. Serving Poseidon, she won't see a word spoken against him. It may not be your choice, but Athira would love a chance to be welcomed into his hall and bed. All she dreams of is being a goddess like him. If that means turning her back on her own family, she may."

She sagged against his shoulder, closing her eyes. "Athira's... fury and blood, more like Ares than you. She has a taste for it."

He wanted to deny it but couldn't. His firstborn had always been... fiery, hot tempered and just as quick to lash out as she was to forgive

someone. The scarring she'd left across his upper arm was a memory of her temper.

Danae's hand slipped across his arm, comforting as best she knew how. "Neither Poseidon or Athira will hear of your plans, you have my word."

"Thank you." There was little else to say, except turning his thoughts to the uncertain future before them.

Chapter Nine

September 18th, 1993, 8:00 AM. Seattle, Washington

The swimming pool outside the century old cabin was just a spring fed pool of water Aran had made deep and wide enough to splash around in. Not enough for him to join in but it would suit a five-year-

old shapeshifter still learning how to do more than a doggie paddle in human shape.

Aran knelt at the edge of the spring, splashing water onto his face before pulling the cloth bandaging from his arms. It stuck briefly, dark blood spotting the beige strips before coming free. And tearing a layer of skin with it. He winced, grateful Tristan was such a heavy sleeper. The kit wouldn't be up for an hour or two unless something did manage to penetrate that exhaustion. He'd pushed his brother harder than he would have on any other day, needing them to leave the confines of the city for the safety of Rainier Park.

He hadn't slept, keeping half his senses on his little brother and half for other danger outside their haven. There were times he did but only when he needed to recover from his wounds. In health, apart

from the burning on his hands and arms, it was an option, not a necessity.

A prickle in the back of his mind had him going still, wary until he relaxed. It was only the spring's spirit greeting him with a bubbling kind of laugh. Tristan couldn't have sensed the creature and she wouldn't have answered the pup's halfhearted prayers anyway, not in the same way she did for him. "Help me, please."

The spirit stirred from her rest and the water bubbled, foaming briefly before settling again as a cat like creature formed from the water of her home sprang out to land next to him with a slight splat next to him. Aran chuckled, rubbing the water cat between the ears, careful not to break the tension of her body

with his touch. "The longer I spend on land the harder it is for me. See?"

She bubbled, almost mimicking a true cat's purr as she batted at one burned forearm and nudged at his wrist with her head. *You smell of salt water and sand, not these woods and the coming rain. You could heal your own wounds if you wanted to.*

There was gentleness in the words despite the chiding tone. Aran sat back on the flat-topped rock, pulling his shirt off to reveal what he'd managed to hide from Tristan so far. The burning wasn't as severe across his back and chest, more of a deep pink flush but it was only a matter of time before it did start to peel and burn on him. Before he was too ill, too weak to make the return on his own. "I could but I'd have to leave my brother for that."

Brother. She sniffed at one wrist, eyes going as flat white as winter ice on him. *Suppose I must then. The little one is sweet and had I been one of your people's naiad's I would have claimed him for my own. That fight isn't one I'm willing to engage in – not against one of the Earthshaker's pets.*

"Former pets, I'm my own now." Aran said. "Have been for a long time."

She sneezed and a little silty green liquid stained the stone between them. *Once his, always his, kelpie. He doesn't forget any easier than he forgives betrayal. Time is meaningless for a god. Still...*

Her silent voice was resigned as she released her hold on her cat form and flowed up and over the worst of the damage on his skin, healing in minutes where it would have taken him hours or a day or two

to heal on its own. Fair skin smoothing over the raw, reddened wounds. *So be it, Aran.*

The sun was rising over the treetops and making it an unusually sunny day for Washington as the cat spirit finished her work and slipped back into her water to rest. Aran sniffed, not looking over his shoulder as Tristan finally wandered out of the cabin in nothing but a wash abused t-shirt. "You're up. I was just about to cook something for breakfast."

Eggs or toast over a campfire, most likely. He'd never been much of a cook – never needing the skills for himself. "I-"

His words died, cut short as the wind shifted, bringing with it a scent of ice, snow and winter. Alone he could have ignored it as nothing, with Tristan, he wasn't going to. The little shapeshifter

was a child in appearance and experience. "Stay back."

The wind was too still now, the animals too quiet in a way that had nothing to do with him. He was an apex predator in his own right but that was only his own element. On land, he was vulnerable and wary. And he had his brother frozen in fright next to him. "Takara, go inside. Now."

He didn't have the power to enforce the order behind the words and even if he had, he wouldn't have used it. Memories of the ill-use Poseidon had put him to, still left a bad taste in his mouth, several thousand years after earning his 'freedom' from the god's service.

Tristan's spell broke at the use of his proper name. "Ari?"

"Now." Aran sniffed at the light breeze, grateful that the wind had given this much to him. There was a scent of the rival again, cold wind in and of itself, ice, and a memory of cold. Not Coyote then, the Native American shapeshifter smelled more like a storm when he was in a bad mood. Like the air after a lightning strike. This wasn't him, as small a relief as it was to know that.

He didn't need to see his reflection in the naiad's pool to know what he looked like now. His physical shape hadn't changed much, except for the telling eye color. Or the lack of it. The blue washed out so much that it was nearly white despite the perfect vision.

Tristan wasn't in sight or scent as he closed the cabin door behind him, the latch being turned a

second later, followed by a whimpering little cry from behind the door. He ignored all of that, fixed on the newcomer stepping out from behind a tree and into the cabin's clearing.

Aran dropped into a crouch, baring his teeth in a warning snarl. If the inhuman sound wasn't enough to drive the stranger away, there would be no choice but to fight it out, for his little brother's protection. Scent alone was enough to tell him who the stranger was, even in the relative warmth of a September day. "Sieh."

He'd know the male wolf anywhere and would kill him to protect Tristan. More recent to his memory was the time Sieh and Coyote had fought; Seattle had burned during that battle though with only one or two deaths connected to it.

Sieh shifted, leaping the naiad's pool of water to tackle him against the ground, teeth bared and a bare inch from his exposed throat. A line of fire traced its way across the bare skin of his side and he twisted against the wolf's weight on his body, throwing it a foot or two away before the other shapeshifter was on all four paws again, amber eyes narrowed in dislike.

Aran cursed and threw himself to the side faster than any human could have as the water in the spring bubbled, the naiad bound there responding to his fury with helpless anger of her own. She could only heal; she couldn't join him in this fight.

He let his control slip at last, and with it – the human guise as the black horse stood there. Predator and prey but only in a mortal's limited view of things.

He was Sieh's equal in power despite his natural form. This would end in one of their deaths or both – surrender wasn't an option, not for them.

Sieh snarled, ears flattening against his skull and leapt again, narrowly missing Aran's back as he fell and rolled on the other side, scrambling to his feet. Aran reared, intent on bringing the full weight of his hooves down on the wolf's side. Crushing the other shapeshifter's ribs if not killing him outright.

The sun visible overhead slipped behind a cloud as the sky darkened and raindrops pelted the ground and them, rattling against the cabin windows.

Sieh blurred, moving faster than any wolf could have and shifted back to human shape, crouched on bare feet and expression empty of any emotion before he changed again, taking a falcon

form several times the size of anything natural. Aran followed him into the sky, hawk shaped as far as he could go and lingered there, teasing the falcon before he dove again, racing the wind as much as Sieh back to the ground. Wings and talons locked together in a fight that would end with someone's death. It wasn't going to be his if he had any say about it.

Thunder rumbled in the distance, followed shortly by the white flash of lightning splitting the sky in half.

Aran growled low in his throat, circling the mountain lion on nearly silent feet. Sieh was wounded but more dangerous for it, favoring the right front leg. The sooner this was over, the better.

His footing slipped on the wet rock, and he staggered, regaining his balance. A moment slower

than he would have liked as the mountain lion pinned him to the ground, claws buried into both shoulders and one hind foot ready to tear through abdomen and internal organs, beyond what the naiad could heal.

Her powers were small and limited but she was still tied to the spring. Aran shoved with the last of his strength, pushing Sieh off his body. "D- Danu take you, wolf."

Neither of them were as tidy as they had been minutes before. Sieh had dark blood streaking his face from a deep cut over his eye. He'd lost the scrap of cloth holding his hair out of his eyes. Sieh's worn gray t-shirt was torn, looking like a knife had gone through the cotton of the front.

They were both breathing hard, unable to look away from the other until Aran lunged, pinning Sieh

against the ground with one forearm against the throat. That alone wouldn't have been enough to kill the other shapeshifter, but the water was.

Sieh had time for a momentary look of pleading before the knife went into his chest, crystal clear and glittering like the naiad's spring. Drawn from the same water and forced into an unlikely shape before being twisted in the shapeshifter's heart.

That would have ended the life of anyone mortal but with a shapeshifter of their power, it was always wiser to be safe than sorry. If he'd been fighting for his own life, it would have been more lethal and less certain of his survival, but he'd been intent on protecting his brother. At any cost.

There was water deep underground, not connected to the naiad's spring and he brought it up

to the surface, breaking the ground and sending little pebbles falling into the darkness of the rift as he knelt by Sieh's side, one hand on the shapeshifter's chest.

Sieh choked, spitting up spring water as his lungs filled with the liquid and he finally slumped against the mud churned up by their fight. The body he'd created giving up on the spirit he really was. It was only a few seconds longer before the shapeshifter's form returned to the wolf shape and faded from sight, returning to whatever spirit realm he drew his strength from. It would take him days if not a month or more for him to gather the strength to do anything but heal from the destruction of his heart and the drowning he had succumbed to.

Aran sat back on the balls of his feet, brushing sweat dampened hair out of his eyes. As reluctant as

he was to admit it, this had been hard fought – Sieh had had the advantage of being able to draw on the land for his power, he'd been forced to rely on desperation and the desire to protect his little brother. Wolves killed pups that didn't belong to them.

He stood, cautiously testing his balance before knocking on the cabin door. "Takara?"

Tristan peeked beneath the lace curtain and vanished a moment later, unlatching the door. His t-shirt sleeve looked like he'd wiped his nose on it and there were tear tracks running down his face. "H- he wasn't as scary as you were, Ari. Your…"

He trailed off, whimpering as he averted his gaze. "Your eyes are all white… w-what happened to the color? I liked it more than this."

Aran swore softly, taking a breath or two to push the instincts away and deeper into the little box they belonged to. This was his brother, not a rival that needed to be driven away. "Sorry. It – I… it happens sometimes. Your mother told you it was like this with me."

Tristan whimpered once more and backed into the darkened cabin, gaze locked on Aran as he wrapped his arms around his own body. "She did but I forgot. Who was the guy you killed?"

"No one." Aran paused, giving himself enough time for his eyes to adjust to the dimness of the cabin as much as it was for the color to darken in his eyes again. "He doesn't matter, kit."

Sieh was dealt with, but it was the stranger sitting as far as he could get on the bed away from the

light that disturbed him. "Forget Sieh, Tristan. Who's this?"

Guilt flashed across Tristan's face as he looked back, chewing on his lower lip. "Uhm… babysitter person, maybe? All he asked was that I keep the curtains closed for him and give him a treat."

He scuffed a small foot across the rough wooden floorboards, staring at the wood underneath his feet. "I wanted to help, he said it wasn't smart for me to run out between you and that guy while you were fighting."

"Probably smart of him." Aran gave the newcomer a wary look, wrinkling his nose in distaste as he placed what was wrong with this stranger. There was no scent clinging to him and though he looked like solid flesh and blood, there was no low murmur

of a heartbeat in the young man's chest. "I'd kill you like I did Sieh but that wouldn't serve much point, shadow. You're already dead. One of Hades, reckon?"

Who else was there? He had no interest or need of the dark-skinned Arabic or North African medical student who claimed to be Anubis. And that boy's master preferred his servants to be soldiers of one kind or another. Hades was more… tolerant of shades or ghost babysitters. "Go back to the crossroads, whoever you are."

Tugging on his hand forced him to look down at Tristan once more, hurt crossing the smaller boy's face. "Don't, Ari. He was only trying to help. Let him stay, pretty please? Dani's nice."

Dani. The shadow had a name it- he could remember? Aran snarled softly under his breath and relented. "Fine. But only until dark, and keep the curtains closed. I don't think he wants to face the danger daylight is to him."

"'kay." Tristan didn't look convinced by the promise, but he sat down to the ghost on the bed. "Will… you say more of the story you started?"

For his brother's sake, not for "Dani's". Aran sighed, turning a chair around so that his folded arms were resting on the back of it as he sat. "Sure. Might as well since it's a long time until dusk."

Something about the so-called babysitter's denim jacket, the hoodie and the military haircut bothered him though only the fates could have told him the reasons why that was so. It wasn't his place

to ask the dead university student directly. "Just don't interrupt me, either of you. Okay?"

Tristan nodded earnestly, stuffing half of a whole bar of chocolate in his mouth to silence himself. "Dani's" only expression was a mixture of resignation and careful reserve. Aran ignored him, focusing on his brother's face. The living concerned him more than the dead and the shadow had no place here, so far as he was concerned. "I couldn't go directly against Poseidon…"

Telling this part of the story mattered more than seeking answers for Sieh's challenge. They wouldn't come from the other shapeshifter, but someone who knew more of the wolf, likely. He could be patient and wait until they got back to Seattle though. He'd been waiting for over fifty years,

expecting this – a few more hours or a day or two wouldn't hurt much.

Chapter Ten

Early Helladic Period III – Approximately 2100 BC

He couldn't go directly against a god. That was a sure way to court death even for one like him, so he'd have to trick Poseidon or run and pray to whatever fate was looking out for him. They had never made their feelings on him clear, but it was far better an opinion than Poseidon's.

Danae and Theia were willing to accompany him to wherever he had in mind. Athira had refused to hear his attempt at persuading her that Poseidon wasn't the master they had been brought up to believe in. Her devotion was single minded and stubborn.

Whether that meant she would betray them or protect them wasn't his to know but it had been fifteen years of clinging to the coast of Thera and pretending to be the mortals they weren't. They could go no further inland than a day's walk without suffering from ill health, even if meant risking Poseidon's fury at their escape.

If he remembered them well enough to care. Fifteen years wasn't long enough to drop his guard and the memories of the drowned village haunted his memories. Not his dreams, he had no need for the mortal habit.

Every day was met with the fear that this would be the dawn when Poseidon would drown their adopted home like he had done with a forgotten human den years ago.

He braced himself on the opposite side of the little boat, cursing under his breath as he pulled the net into the boat. This would have been an easier task if he'd chanced using his gifts, but it would have raised a few questions from the mortal villagers. No one would have looked the other way if he'd dove into the water and stayed under for longer than they were capable of. If he was pretending to be human, that meant adopting human habits. Hunting or fishing for his family's meals. Driving their small flock of five sheep into the pasture and in the cooler seasons, butchering the creature for food.

Fifteen years on and he still struggled with keeping mortal food down. The taste, the texture of it in his mouth was revolting. Theia was no better at it than he was, forcing their daughter to do most of the

cooking for them. Of the three of them, she was the only one capable of tolerating mortal fare.

Danae's business was her own so he'd never asked her how or why she could when they couldn't.

He sighed, pulling on the oars as he turned the boat back to Thera's beach. There was fish to clean and a net to repair before dinner. Theia could handle that much but mending the net and leaving it to dry for the next day's catch was his responsibility.

She was there to greet him as he pulled the boat onto the beach, tying it off on a wooden stake pounded into the sandy ground. He embraced her for a second and then went back for his catch, stomach already turning at the prospect of eating what he'd pulled from the sea. "Danae?"

Theia's smile was wistful, resting one hand on the inside of his wrist before she dropped it back to her side. "Tending to the bees and speaking to them. There will be honey tonight, thanks to her."

"And our son?" Even fifteen years after the boy's birth, it was hard to picture himself as a father again. Much less to a young man like Iason. The pup was a shapeshifter, that much was certain, but he was closer kin to the mortal villagers than he was to his parents.

"Well enough." Theia's expression clouded, mirroring the disquiet he felt inside before she shook her head, half turning away. "He's never known anything but freedom. Let's not shatter that vision for him."

She let out a sigh, pulling the strap of her tunic up over her shoulder again. "Either way, no doubt. And we have a guest."

"A guest." He was wary, wishing he had thought to take more than fish knife with him. A sword or dagger would have been welcomed under his touch right now.

"A friend." Theia said. "No more than that. She means us no harm but I… thought to arrange something if Poseidon attempts to claim us again. Iason will have a sister to watch over him if we're taken."

They had precious few 'friends' in the village, keeping to themselves despite the whispers that lack of connection with mortals stirred in the village. "If you think it best."

Danae had left off her conversation with the bees nesting in the old snag and was now washing clothing in the pool of water she had brought up from the ground with the local naiad's blessing. It was a small thing and not strong enough to do more than the washing in but it was fresh water, not salt. Poseidon had no power over the springs and little streams of Thera.

It didn't make the ocean any less dangerous but that was a danger any sailor or fisherman dealt with on a regular basis.

He looked up, watching the bird circling overhead as the falcon went into a dive and came up short a dozen feet above the ground. It changed shape, light surrounding it before the young man

landed heavily in a crouch, one ankle twisting under his weight.

Iason stood a moment later, wincing as he took a step forward, crossing the distance between them. At fifteen he was a man grown but he bore little resemblance to his parents or sister. He forced a smile, taking in his son's appearance. The red hair was an odd contrast to the tanned skin and the boy hadn't done anything to make his eye color more human. They were still the falcon's golden color, not blue or hazel. "Iason."

"Yes?" Iason's expression slipped, darting a look towards Danae before fixing on his face again.

What could he say to that? He hesitated, looked down at his feet. Bare, unlike his son's, who

wore sandals. "Why don't you take your bow and go hunting? It could be a while before dinner is ready."

Iason snorted but did as he was asked, ducking inside the small house before coming back with his bow and quiver, arm guard strapped against his wrist. "Because Mother's meals are spoiled as often as not? I've never seen you or her eat, Father."

He shrugged, disregarding that. "Bring back a rabbit, kit. Please."

Iason snorted but there was no ill humor in the dismissal. "You just want me away from the beautiful hunter. And she is beautiful. Red haired…"

His voice trailed off, almost dreamy. "I'd mimic that hair color if it didn't make people believe she was my sister."

His son shook the thoughts off, sighing. "Ah well. I'll bring a rabbit back. Boar would be better but they need a hunting party to find and kill."

"Iason." He said it tightly, seeing his son's mood. If the boy didn't leave now, he never would.

"Yes, Father." Iason's good humor faded, replaced with resignation as he ventured around the back of the house and up the hill beyond it, vanishing a few moments later.

He watched for as long as he could before ducking under the stone lintel and seeing his wife and daughter sitting at the hearth. A pot of something bubbling over the low fire, meant for the evening meal. The third woman, the stranger was as red haired as Iason had described her as. No stranger to conflict

or defending herself, judging from the knife sheathed at her waist.

His gaze lingered on the weapon warily before he met her eyes. "I know that steel. Hephaestus forged that. How does a mortal woman come by it?"

She didn't flinch under his hard-edged words, mouth thinning instead. "Call it a gift from Agesander then. It was a desert god who saved my life once, now I serve him as often as I do the merciful one. It has been a duty I've had for the past eight hundred years."

Her eyes narrowed, barely hiding dislike. "Thais of Tiryns. We met, briefly a hundred years ago though we never had the… pleasure of an introduction then. I raised that child as my own until

she married. Until I saw her wedded, with child of her own and buried."

"You're mortal." His voice as just as flat as hers.

"I was, once." She folded her arms over her chest, wincing a little at the firelight. "Yes, my heart still beats, yes, blood still runs in my veins but don't call me a living woman. My brother took that from me when he… did what he did."

Theia stepped between them; hands slightly outstretched in a gesture meant to show peace as much to separate them before a fight could occur. "Please, save any childish disagreement for another night. You came here with some purpose, yes?"

Addressing Thais first before her warning glance settled on him.

He pinched the bridge of his nose between two fingers and relented, biting back on the ugly snarl that threatened to escape his throat. "You're a guest here, Thais. I won't hurt you."

She nodded curtly, laying the weapon between them. It wasn't out of reach of her hand, but the gesture was enough for him to relent and settle opposite her at the hearth. "If you have word, what is it?"

Thais looked away, seeking something in the hearth fire's embers. "Protection for your son, as much as I can. Your fate is yours alone, but he need not suffer for his parents' crime. My master relayed the message from his brother on that."

Her voice dropped, going tight. "You are found now if you ever knew how to hide to begin

with. Return and the Earthshaker may consider mercy. Refuse and he'll drown Thera, dragging it beneath the water."

"We don't have a choice then." He dropped his face into his hands, rubbing at the ache starting to form behind his eyes. "So long as the boy lives."

"He will." Thais put her hand on his arm, briefly touching the flushed, peeling skin there. "You need water. When-?"

"Father?"

Iason's question cut short Thais's and she glanced at the young shapeshifter, sighing as she shook her head. "There will be time to finish this later. If I might stay the day? You can bear sunlight without flinching. I... cannot. It hurts my eyes these days."

"Of course." Turning Thais away despite her warning was the last thing a good host did, even if the news she carried was troubling. They were found now and only a quiet discussion with his son would resolve matters. "Iason?"

They needed to have a word while hunting. Whatever the pup's intent had been, he hadn't strayed as far as hoped and had come back empty handed. "With me, please."

If Poseidon wanted them back, he would but Iason would be spared that fate if he went with the female hunter. There was a chance at hope for him, if not them and he didn't deserve to see his parents hurt or killed on the god's word. He deserved life, not a sword at his throat in waiting.

Chapter Eleven

September 19th, 1993, 8:00 PM. Seattle,

Washington

It was unlikely Sieh had been sent by anyone

but that didn't make the Alaskan shapeshifter's threat

any less troubling. And for that, there was no choice

but to go to the one man who stood a chance of giving

him answers. Or at least controlling the wolf.

Dead was relative when it came to their kind.

So long as their creator or anchor persisted, so would

they.

Aran shouldered his backpack, glancing

across the street to the seedy little apartment building

before crossing in the middle of the road. One car

veered sharply to avoid him, its owner flipping him

the bird along with a well-placed expletive. He

ignored both, glancing towards the front door before pushing the handle down.

Inside was dated, seventies or eighties in its design and not renovated since. Aran wrinkled his nose in distaste and hit the elevator button for the third floor. Coyote's apartment would be at the end of the hallway, smelling more of sage or sweetgrass than cigarette smoke. He could be home well before Tristan decided to demand the next part of the story. For now, he had business to attend to.

Their territories didn't intersect except when necessity brought them together. Coyote claimed Seattle and a good part of Washington state as his own. He was content with a stretch of the Pacific Ocean, so long as Coyote decided not to violate their unwritten agreement and take a swim there. It made

tolerating the other male easier, their territorial needs pushed aside for the sake of relative peace. They could stay out of each other's way as they wished or needed to.

If only that had been one of those days. He averted his gaze from the Native American shapeshifter, carefully looking away so the stone knife at his throat only drew the slightest bit of warmth as his blood trickled down his throat. "I'm no threat to you, Coyote."

Coyote's knife only pulled back an inch or two, the male shapeshifter's hand still balled in the collar of Aran's t-shirt. "The only way that were true was if you were as mortal as your little brother's, pup. I've seen you fight, your power matches mine."

"I didn't come here to fight you." Aran took advantage of the moment's hesitation and wrapped his hand around Coyote's wrist, feeling the small bones under the skin grate against each other as he twisted the hand away from his shirt. "Not this time."

"What then?" Coyote's eyes narrowed in dislike, but he lowered the stone knife back his side. "I believe you when you say you have no interest in fighting, but I know your power, you could drown Seattle if you ever lost control. It has… happened before, I've heard."

That stung and Aran snarled, baring his teeth as he took a step towards Coyote. The event the other man had mentioned had been at Poseidon's biding – he hadn't had the choice to disobey at the time. "I learned since then. I'm free of Poseidon's hold now."

He sat down on the worn, beige couch uninvited, eyes sweeping across the undecorated apartment walls. This was a place meant just for the roof over Coyote's head – it wasn't likely the other shapeshifter used it for anything but pretense. "And I can think of a century ago when your fight with Sieh burned the city. Only one died, sure but don't accuse me of threatening your home when you're just as likely to face another of our kind."

"Point." Coyote said dryly. He leaned against the living room doorframe; arms folded over his chest. "I should remember that you wee a slave to Poseidon once, you had no choice in your obedience to your former master."

A pensive look flickered across his face before he switched to Greek and sat down on the

coffee table, toying with the waist length plait, teasing the end of it around his fingers. "For privacy's sake, nothing more. It took me a year or two to master your tongue, pup. So tell me again, what do you want? Our paths rarely cross and if they did, the results may be disastrous for the humans here. We were both fortunate in choosing to hold back today."

Aran forced a shrug, grateful to be in a place where he wasn't obligated to understand human body language and gestures. Mariko and her husband had attempted to teach him the finer points, but he'd never been able to grasp the point or purpose of mimicking humans, except for something to imitate. The yellowing daisies on the coffee table next to Coyote's right hand were the only decoration in the living room. "Sieh could have killed Tristan the other day. It was only driving him off that persuaded him to stop."

"Ah." Coyote's eye color flickered, going from brown to a falcon's gold before the color returned to its natural shade. "I never sent him to test you. I think we know better than that. There are rules even we have to obey and breaking them…"

He pulled a daisy from the vase, looking down at it before placing it back into the water. "We're all governed by nature."

His mouth quirked slightly as he braced himself on one arm. "We're still no more than half civilized at the best of times, no? For all we pretend to be human, we're still feral. Spirits of whatever element brought us into life."

Dislike quickly replaced the brief moment of good humor as a crack of thunder sounded in the distance. "That said, pretend to be Mariko's adopted

son if you wish but you know our kind rarely have families as the mortals understand it. She is no more your mother than Poseidon was your father. Loyalty is wasted on them."

Those words stung more than the truth about their natures had. Aran snarled under his breath. Low, inhuman and nothing that could have come from a human's throat as he blurred, pinning Coyote against the nearby wall. Shards of the broken vase and flowers were scattered across the low table and graying, patchy carpet. He held what looked like a glass blade in his free hand, but it was water forced to hold an unlikely shape. "She may not be family by blood or birth, but she saved me that time. I owe her that debt even if you don't think it's worth it."

Coyote laughed though there was no humor in his eyes. "So be it. I thought you said you weren't interested in a fight. Next time we have one of our little… encounters, I'll be sure to ask you go come to Salt Lake City instead. Where I'll have the advantage. I won't touch the kit or hurt him; you have my word on that, so long as we continue to stay out of each other's way. I won't touch your brother or hurt him; you have my word on that. As long as we continue to stay out of each other's way."

He paused, voice souring. "And I'll be sure to remind Sieh of that agreement later once he's regained enough strength to remake his body – thanks to you. He's no pup of mine but I'm fond of the wolf despite any disagreements we may have had in the past."

It hadn't been said in so many words or even implied but Aran could guess at the meaning behind them. "You're making me leave."

He deflated, taking a step back as Coyote rubbed at his throat and dropped his hand back to his side. "Tristan's only a kit, he won't understand."

You look like a kit yourself, boy." Coyote crossed his arms over the faded, navy-blue t-shirt he wore. "Little more than seventeen, but I know you're older than that. Tristan will survive without you if his parents teach him to be self-reliant. I don't doubt they will."

"Just give me a little time to try explaining why I'm leaving first." Aran said. "He deserves that much."

"If you think it best." Coyote looked away, a shadowed look crossing his face at the broken vase on his coffee table. "But finish up quickly. Two of our kind in Washington state is tolerable – three. How many ways can a battle turn if we're all against each other?"

It was a question without an answer but fair all the same. Aran ducked his head, half turning away from the other shapeshifter and left Coyote to clean up the small mess their argument had caused. Tristan deserved an answer and an apology for what was to come.

Tristan clung to Aran's legs, wetness streaking his cheeks. "Don't go! Pretty please, Ari! You never finished your story!"

That was why he was back if only for a few days more. Aran disentangled his brother from around him and took a step back in the small hallway. "All right, just sit down at the table. I've got fresh milk and real cookies, not those damned Oreos you like so much."

Tristan's tears dried immediately though he sniffled, wiping his nose on his shirt sleeve. "'kay."

Cookies solved everything. Aran rolled his eyes and pulled the plastic container from his backpack. The milk was poured into a glass and set next to the double chocolate cookie on a chipped plate. "I don't want to leave but Coyote made his point rather clear. We're two very powerful shapeshifters trying to coexist in the same city. That isn't easy with how territorial we can get."

"But you aren't living in the same city."
Tristan took a bite from the cookie and chewed,
leaving crumbs behind on the tabletop instead of the
plate. "He's got the city; you got the strait and the
ocean! There's no crossover thingy."

"There isn't but do you really want to take the
chance?" Aran forced a smile at his own question.

"No." Tristan's expression fell. "But you'll
tell more of the story, right?"

"Yeah, I'll tell." Aran rummaged
halfheartedly through his backpack, finding a copy of
the photograph hanging in the upstairs hallway.
Mariko and her husband formally posed in it. His
adoptive mother in a kimono and her hair pinned back
in a bun, his father dressed in a plain white shirt,
sleeves rolled up halfway up his arms. He was

standing between them. His once dark hair pulled into a ponytail. Half Japanese, half white to avoid most of the questions about his parentage.

Tristan bounced impatiently in his seat, trying to reach for the photograph Aran held out of his reach. "Lemme."

Aran laughed, shaking his head. "If you want to but you'd barely recognize me in the photograph, kitten. Animal shapes aren't the only forms we're capable of. It can be appearance too as well, though some prefer the comfort of seeing themselves in the mirror each day."

Tristan accepted the framed image, tracing the younger dark-haired man in the image. "He looks a bit like me. Like Mom. You?"

It wasn't his son. Aran nodded reluctantly, unable to help thinking of Iason. The boy was lost or dead to him now, long enough that he'd never known a hint of Japanese culture or customs. "Yeah, once. From a time when people would have questioned a blond, fair skinned man ever being the son of a Japanese woman."

"Oh." Tristan clutched the photograph closer to his chest, hiding the long necked blue dinosaur on his front. "Thought it was you, maybe. 's the same expression in the eyes. Kinda tired."

Aran chuckled, gently pulling the photograph from his brother's grip. "No, you didn't. The boy in that picture is a stranger to you, someone I haven't been for nearly fifty years. C'mon. finish your snack

and I'll tuck you into bed. Maybe if you're lucky, I'll tell more of my story."

He planned on it either way, but the promise of the story was enough to put Tristan on his best behavior and finish the snack tidier than he had before finishing the milk. "kay."

Tristan was in bed, curled up with a patchy red furred panda in his arms beneath the coverlet. Aran sat down at the foot of the child size bed, seeing crayon drawings of his – their family taped to the walls. A fox with a balloon shaped tail, a stick figure that might have been their father. Something that only vaguely resembled a horse and a long tube-like thing that could have been a ferret or an otter, it was hard to say for sure. "Maybe you should stick with helping in

the garage. Drawing doesn't look like your strong point."

Then again, there was time – Tristan was only five. "Where was I?"

"Jason was safe, mos'ly." Tristan said. "You weren't?"

"Right." That was it. Aran sighed, enthusiasm for telling this part of the story fading. "Maybe we should wait until day? Don't want to give you nightmares, yeah?"

This part was as unpleasant to recall as it was to tell to a child but it was necessary for the story. Skipping over it wasn't going to change what had happened.

Chapter Twelve

Early Helladic Period III – Approximately
2100 BC

Fifteen years of hiding and all for naught. He was on his knees in front of Poseidon's disapproving frown. Theia knelt next to him and the only thing that was keeping their daughter from drowning or crushed beneath the weight of the god's watery home was the hand he had on her wrist.

Athira was standing a little ways apart from them at Poseidon's right hand. Her expression closed to all but those who knew her well.

He dared a look towards his wife and saw nothing but despair in her eyes. Someone had betrayed them, or accident and fate had finally seen fit to bring them back to Poseidon. All he could be grateful for, Iason was safe – at least for a time. Thais

had taken him to a place of safety. Somewhere that only she knew.

Poseidon sat on the golden throne, relaxed but ~~his eyes~~ were the gray of a storm-tossed ocean, barely hiding fury in them. "Did you really think you could hide from me?"

Lie and anger the god more than he already had or tell the truth and risk more of the same? He bowed his head, not daring to meet Poseidon's gaze. "I couldn't justify what you ordered me to do. I had no choice but to leave."

Theia's hand tightened on his before she swallowed, lifting her eyes for the first time. "Spare him, please. I questioned your orders first and persuaded my husband to see it through my eyes. I am the one to blame, not him."

Neither of the guards to either side of them could look now but he could see unhappiness in the set of their expressions, hands resting on their weapons. If it came to a fight, they would lose against their master. Strength came from knowing when to use it, and when to preserve their own lives for another day. Interfering on his and Theia's behalf wasn't cowardice, it was caution in front of a fickle god. "Theia…"

Her hand brushed across his, lingering for a moment before falling back to her side. "Don't, love. I know."

Poseidon leaned forward, chin resting on his hand before he looked away, pensive. "There must be consequences for betraying me, betraying your

companions but the two of you were my best soldiers until you abandoned my service."

He sighed, raking a hand through graying, shoulder length hair. "I have no wish to fight against either of you, but I cannot permit exile. You might find a master in one of my brothers instead. I am willing to give you a second chance at proving yourself, and your loyalty if you fight a warrior of my choosing."

It was no choice at all, loyalty, or a fight to come against one of his fellow soldiers but if it meant life, if only for a little while, he'd take that chance. If Theia was willing to do the same. Her expression was unreadable, head bowed before the guards stepped away from them, permitting them freedom if not an

unescorted departure from the hall. Away from each other.

The room was small, bare save for the blanket and pallet against the wall as his guard left him alone with his thoughts. An hour passed and then a second before footsteps sounded. Athira stood in the doorway, hesitating as she looked over her shoulder. "Father."

In human form she was a little past middling height, the top of her head level with his shoulder. In her natural horse form, it didn't matter where she stood. With the upper half of a muscular young woman and the remainder, a black mare – she was almost eye to eye with him, dressed in a shirt in place of a tunic.

Her gaze swept over him, and she bit down on her lower lip as she took in the plain tunic and the cloth wrapped around his forearms. "If you... return to Poseidon's side, he's willing to reconsider the fight. You need not prove yourself if you speak to him."

If only that was so simple. He dropped his head into his hands before glancing back at his daughter. "I lived among the mortals for fifteen years, long enough to see your brother become a man. They aren't as insignificant as Poseidon believes them to be. They..."

They loved, cared for their own and did the best they could to tend to the dead – they weren't mere mindless creatures easily washed away by a wave. "I cannot be Poseidon's anymore."

He knew too much of how their lives were like to go back to being Poseidon's obedient soldier.

"Then…" Athira's eyes narrowed as she trailed off. "You are lost, Father."

Her shoulders slumped at that as she put one hand on the doorframe. "I came hoping we could-could be a family again. Mother, you, my sister, and brother. I was wrong."

She closed her eyes, a little wetness trailing down her cheek. "You should know that your opponent tomorrow will be a woman. I won't say more than that, Amyntas."

It was rare that he heard his given name and this time it hurt more than he was willing to acknowledge. "Athira…"

She hesitated, indecision flickering across her face before resolve followed it. "Forgive me. I tried to help you see the light, but I failed you."

Her voice dropped a note or two as she looked away. "Father."

There was no true dawn or dusk in Poseidon's domain, just the play of light on water as the sun rose in the mortal world. One of the other soldiers handed him the weapon and he took it with a grudging nod. This was no game and whoever lost today, there was no chance at coming back from the death. He, or she would just cease to exist.

The scent was familiar, but he didn't know his opponent. She was as fair as he was, blonde hair plaited out of her eyes as she tested the edge of her

blade against the palm of her hand. Dark blood welled before she closed her fingers over the shallow cut.

He didn't give her time to reconsider or hesitate before he moved to attack, driving her back a step or two. It was his life or hers, and he had no intention of losing to a stranger.

She faltered before circling at a distance, looking for some break in his guard. He smiled briefly, showing her just a crack in his defense. If she took advantage of his weakness, he could turn it against her. Poseidon watched from his throne, pensive.

The female soldier's eyes widened in disbelief before she blocked his slash with her sword. She hesitated; he didn't as he pressed the attack. Her guard dropped, exposing her left side and he swept

his own sword at her side. It made contact, tearing through her tunic and the flesh and blood beneath the cloth. She stumbled, pressing her hand to her side and went to her knees with a soft snarl.

She let her weapon fall to the ground and shifted form, a pale wolf taking the place of the woman before she lunged at him – going for the throat. He moved too fast for her to make contact, bringing his forearm up to protect his throat as she brought him down.

He rolled, pinning her against the floor by the ruff as her back paws scrabbled, trying to right herself. It was his turn to change shape, abandoning the human mask for a wolf shape of his own. There was no finesse, no art to their fight now. Just two wolves trying to get the other to submit. Her teeth

sank into his side, and he snarled, tearing free of her hold, blood matting the dark gray fur.

He shifted back to human shape, seizing the forgotten sword and buried it halfway to the hilt in the female wolf's chest. She choked, sinking to her belly and light surrounded her, fading a moment later. Theia lay against the floor, one hand pressed to her chest, the sword she had pulled from the wound in her other hand.

Amyntas froze, staring at Theia as she tried to sit up and slipped in her own blood. Her scent had been too familiar but his own wife, he hadn't expected her to be the one he had been expected to fight. "Theia?"

Poseidon was unreadable, Athira had the barest hint of smile curving her lips as she slipped one arm around the god's waist.

Theia whimpered, forcing him to look away from their daughter as he dropped to his knees next to her. Blood stained his ruined tunic as he brushed a strand of Theia's dark hair out of her eyes. "Please…"

She lifted one hand to his face, tracing the line of his jaw and he clasped it in his own, trying to support her body in his free arm. Her fingertips were already dry, the skin raw and peeling as it spread across the back of her hand and over her arm. "Stay with me."

Theia choked, coughing a little as she fought to breathe. "No, Amyntas. You- you were always the stronger of the two of us. Sing for me?"

He swallowed, fighting the hard lump in his throat as he murmured the words to the lullaby Theia had once sung to their children. "Of course."

It was Theia's dying wish, he would do his best to give her what she wanted of him. "Forgive me."

She sagged in his hold, convulsing as the burning went deeper, past skin and into muscle and bone. There was no fire, but she was still burning in his arms, flesh falling away to reveal bone. Even that crumbled into dust as he held her close to his chest.

Danae was weeping, barely hiding her grief. Athira was cool, expressionless as she watched. He seized the abandoned sword, grip tightening around the hilt before he dragged Athira from her place next to Poseidon's side.

She fought him, snarling, nails dragging at the forearm he had around her throat. He didn't flinch at the scratches, balling his hand in her hair before he brought the sword up in his free hand and opened Athira's throat from behind.

Danae was on her knees, sifting through her mother's dust as wetness streaked her face.

He took no notice of her, letting the weapon fall as he went to his own knees on the tiled floor as he closed his eyes. If this meant his death, he'd accept it – his betrayal and flight from Poseidon's service – he was still a soldier. He'd accept any punishment placed on his head. It would have been a preferred fate to a lifetime without his wife.

The expected blow didn't fall, and he dared to lift his gaze to see Agesander standing by his

brother's side, a cool look directed towards the Earthshaker. Poseidon was scowling, not liking whatever his brother was murmuring in his ear.

Both gods vanished, whatever power Agesander had, overwhelming his brother's. Poseidon's fate no longer mattered to him – whether that was destruction or imprisonment in Tartarus.

Freedom from his master meant nothing when he had been forced to fight and lose his wife to earn it.

Chapter Thirteen

September 19th, 1993, 9:00 PM. Seattle, Washington

"That wasn't a very nice sorry." Tristan's voice was small, barely above a whimper,

interrupting the flow of Aran's words. "Posy's not very nice."

Aran sighed, warming his hands on the small cup of tea Mariko placed in front of him. "He was – is a god. They're always fickle. And I think I earned it in part, by betraying his trust and running away in the middle of the night. It wasn't cowardice or fear, just going AWOL on him. You understand that, right?"

Tristan blinked, uncertainty in his expression. "Maybe?"

He didn't but his brother was only five and he hadn't been raised or trained to fight. It was to be expected. Aran sighed, running a hand through his hair. Touching on the deaths of his family had been a mistake but one he needed to tell. I had a job to do

and I abandoned it when Poseidon needed me most. That's the part that counts."

"Oh." Tristan's expression fell at that as he clutched his teddy bear close to his chest. "'kay. What happened to her? Your girlfriend lady and your kids? An' I didn't even know your real name. Amy-something?"

"Amyntas. It hasn't been my name for a long time." Aran took a careful sip of the tea and set it aside with a slight grimace. "I won't be tied to that life any longer. Not with what he named me or in duty. They... died. Beyond what even our immortality could spare us from. Poseidon created Theia; he could just easily take it away from her. And did, Athira was only his... instrument. I

underestimated her desire to be a goddess or… her love for my master."

His memories of Theia's death and his daughters were blurred, fractured snapshots in time, not cause and effect in his mind. "I don't know why he spared me, if that was his choice at all, but the madness was enough of a punishment at the time. I…"

Aran trailed off, sighing as Mariko's hand tightened against his shoulder. Not in warning as much as an attempt at comforting him. "I don't remember much of the years after losing my family. It – I lost myself then and it took me years to recover. I was feral, let's leave it there."

Nightmares were the last thing he wanted to give his little brother so that part of the story would

go more or less unsaid. His natural shape may have been a black horse, but it wasn't the same creature he had been under Poseidon's command. More than one unlucky rider had found their death while attempting to ride him in the years after he'd finally found his way north to Ireland. No one had ever managed to put bit or bridle in the creature's mouth.

Tristan was still looking at him earnestly, though the fear scent still clung to his skin. "Wanna know."

That kit could be stubborn when he wanted to be. Aran looked into the Japanese style teacup, shoving a stray strand of hair out of his eyes. "Fine. It – I spent more than a few centuries as a kelpie. Your father's told enough stories about the creatures. Some... of those were about me before I met our

parents. I drowned my share of attempted riders and ate them. That was the madness, but it faded over the years. There's still a part of me that holds onto that instinct. Not so different from Sieh or Coyote, I guess. They both came the long hard road to something that looks like human decency. I had to find it again myself."

They weren't quite finished with the story, but they were more than halfway through it. Starting his story had been easy, almost a tale about a different man. Bringing it to a close, less so.

"You don't need to finish, Kaito." Mariko's words were in Japanese rather than English, using the name she'd given him a century ago. In return, he'd taught her all he knew of Irish. "I can tell the rest, as much as I know of it."

Aran took his adoptive mother's hand in his own and let it go a moment later. She wasn't without her own quiet sense of irony. Kaito meant ocean or sea. Given his past, it was fitting in an off-handed kind of way. "I'll finish. I just need some time to think."

Answering her in the same language as Tristan looked between them wide eyed and far too innocent for the story he'd been telling. "Thank you, Mariko."

She nodded, an abstract look crossing her face. "You should know, I met one of your kind in Chinatown when I was out. Small, red haired, with a Greek accent, yes? She said she was looking for you."

"She isn't my kind." Aran finished the last of the tea, leaving dregs behind in the cup. "If I know

who you're talking about, she was human once. Before she made a bargain with Osiris and Agesander- Hades."

It had been a long time since Hades's name had given him the fear it once had. That didn't mean they were on an equal level. Hades would always have more power than he could draw upon. "Where did you meet her?"

Mariko shrugged carefully, smoothing Tristan's mussed hair under her touch. "Below ground. She was hunting a vrykolakas. I joined her for an hour or two before dawn came. She said you would know how and where to find her, without my having to ask for an address."

"I do." Aran stood, bracing himself on the kitchen table as he suppressed the slight cough that

tore at his throat. "I'm going to need your father's sword."

Pain crossed Mariko's face at his request, but she nodded. "Of course. It's yours, my... son."

"Thank you." Aran inclined his head, grateful for her permission. He could have just taken the weapon, but he owed Mariko too much to be a thief of her father's sword. "I'll come back by dawn, if I can."

"No, not an if." Mariko said. "Please."

He nodded, turning away. "I will."

She waited for him on the rooftop of an abandoned apartment building, looking at the street below. "I thought you would come."

Aran snorted, scrambling onto the concrete ledge that was supposed to keep people from falling from the roof to the pavement six stories below where they stood. Heights had never been a worry for him. "You haven't changed, Thais."

"Tiryn. Thais died nearly five thousand years ago." She glanced back at him, tucking a strand of red hair behind one ear. "And I can't say the same for you. You're younger than when we last met. I wouldn't have even recognized you, were it not for the tone of your voice and the webbing between your fingers."

He braced himself, leaning back on one arm. "Need, not preference. It would be hard to explain having a little brother when I looked like I was in my

twenties. Twelve years difference is hard enough as it is. Why Tiryn? It isn't Greek."

That earned him a wry smile as she moved from playing with her hair to tangling it around her finger. "For Tiryns. It was my home once, but I didn't think a plural would make the best of names, so I dropped a letter from it."

She sighed, tiring of messing with her hair. "And because Thais would never have been capable of imagining such a world as this. She was a fisher's daughter, nothing more. All she wanted of life was to be a mother and pass away surrounded by children and grandchildren. She died and I took her place."

Her grip tightened on the hilt of a Greek blade before she shook her head. "It doesn't matter now. Your adoptive mother... seems kind. The kitsune."

"She lost family of her own fifty years ago."
Aran closed his hand around a pebble and let it fall,
heedless of who might be below them. "Mother,
father and brother in Hiroshima. She calls me her son
but I'm more certain that she sees me as the brother
she lost. Kaito."

Tiryn made a face, shivering beneath the thigh
length gray leather jacket she wore. "Was that his
name?"

"Mine." Aran looked away, not focused on
anything in particular around them. "It was always
Mariko and Sora when he lived."

"Give her my apologies then." Tiryn tugged
on her zipper, drawing it halfway up her jacket. "I
suppose that's her sword you carried with you?"

"Her father's. I'm just borrowing it." Aran unsheathed the blade and let the light reflect off the steel. "I keep telling her it belongs to Tristan, but I think she wants me to have it instead. He'll never use it. Just a guess on my part but if he ever learns how to use a weapon, he'll prefer a gun. Less skill involved."

"And you aren't Japanese." Tiryn shrugged, tilting her head to the side. "Aran could almost be that – to someone ignorant."

He rolled his eyes, sheathing the weapon again. "It's Irish, not Japanese but thank you, all the same. Did you come here asking for my help in dealing with a vampire or just to talk?"

She laughed, not offended by the question. "The hunt won't take long, I came more for the

company than your skills as a warrior. We're both so far from Athens…"

Tiryn trailed off, quieting. "I miss it. There's no history here, no culture except greed and financial gain. Russia had the grace to be beautiful at times. I'm sorry that you'll never have a chance to visit St. Petersburg. She's beautiful at dusk."

"Who's to say I haven't?" Aran drew back, smirking a little. "I prefer the Aegean, but I'm tied to water, not the sea specifically. The Neva's beautiful. The country is a little too Eastern Orthodox for my tastes, too Christan but I've had a century of looking at them as an American."

Tiryn laughed, shaking her head. "If I wasn't a lesbian by choice, not birth, I'd assume you were

flirting with me, Amyntas. I swore off men a long time ago after- after what my brother did."

"Aran." He corrected her reflexively, offering her his hand. "And I'm not sure that makes much of a difference, who you like to share a bed with. It's rare, but it happens. Men aren't the only sort to enjoy hurting others weaker than themselves."

Tiryn turned her blade over in her hands, averting her gaze. "You have experience with that?"

More than he cared to acknowledge but Tiryn deserved the truth he hadn't completely given to his little brother. "Unfortunately. Tristan asked, I told him as much as I could, but I edited to spare him the details. He's only five and doesn't need to know the truth until he's old enough to understand. I fought and

killed my wife, cut my daughter's throat for the part she played in manipulating the fight but-"

"But it was what came after." Tiryn said.

"Yeah." Aran pushed off his perch on the stone rail thing, leaning against it. "That. Let's go find your vampire and deal with it."

Tiryn chewed on her lower lip, gaze drifting to the pavement six stories below them before she put her hand on his forearm. "Forget the *vrykolalas*. This is a story you need to tell."

"Empath?" He lifted his gaze to meet hers, made wary by that.

"Empath." She shifted from one foot to the other, grimacing a little. "Osiris's thankless gift, not a skill I was born with. I only know what little you told

me years ago and what I can read from your emotions."

On one hand, she was a friend- one of the few he had. On the other, she was one of Osiris's hunters. Aran hesitated, uncertain before pushing the fear away. "Alright. I trust you."

"Was that in doubt?" Tiryn stuffed her hands into her jacket pockets. "You could drown me easily enough if you wanted to. I should be more frightened of you than you are of me. You're nearly a god."

Aran let his hands fall back to his sides, sighing. "Emphasis on nearly, but point taken. I just don't know where to start."

"Just after you fled Poseidon, perhaps?" Tiryn asked. "I knew you left, I was never clear on where, much to Iason's disappointment."

"Iason…" Aran drew back at that, all thought of the story forgotten at the mention of his son's name. "Is he?"

"No." Tiryn swept a few pebbles from the rooftop into flight before they vanished out of sight far below. "I'm sorry but he- he's gone. I've been hunting his murderer for over six hundred years now. That's why I thought to come to Seattle, I knew it was your last known home. Before or after 1912."

"I see. Thank you." That hurt more than he wanted to acknowledge in himself but at least it gave him a point to start from, for the part of the story he hadn't told Tristan yet. Their mother could do that on his behalf.

Chapter Fourteen

Ireland – Approximately 1500 BC

Hearing came to him first with the sound of unfamiliar birds squalling in the distance. Sight and touch were the next to return as he rolled onto his side, gasping for breath through a too dry throat. The air smelled different, heavy with rain as he glanced into a gray sky. Not Poseidon's hall then, or any place he knew as home.

He pulled in a breath and choked, one hand pressed flat against his chest as the pain flared, burning like fire from the inside. His head ached and he slumped against the rocky spit of beach, cursing it.

The emerald grass stretching for as far as the eye could see wasn't what he had experienced before as the rain went from a steady drizzle to a downpour, soaking him and plastering light brown hair to his scalp.

It was almost a relief against the pain and effort to draw a breath. He lifted his face to it, grateful when the pounding ache behind his eyes eased. "Thank you."

Whatever spirit was out there, he was grateful for its aid as he climbed to his feet. The tunic was a loss, a ragged edge finishing the knee length garment. Torn, somehow though the how remained a mystery he didn't plan on learning.

"Father?"

He started, hand going to a weapon that was no longer at his waist. The last clear memory he had was of Athira's hair in his hand and the dark blood staining his hands. Her blood. This didn't sound like her voice, gentler, softer and nearly pleading. "Danae?"

"I escaped as well, a…" Danae blushed, smoothing her hands over her skirt. "A lover I trusted more than my sister. He aided me, giving up his freedom to do so."

He hesitated and wrapped his arms around her waist as she rested her head against his chest. The wounds of Athira's betrayal and Theia's death would take years if they healed at all. It was a poor consolation, but they still had each other, that mattered. They wouldn't have to face such an unfamiliar land alone. "We're together, thank-"

"Thank the fates." Danae said softly. "Lachesis and her sisters did something for us. I had thought I'd lost you forever, Father."

He drew back, hesitating at the wobbly note in her voice. "What is it?"

Danae swallowed, her auburn hair just as wet as his own. "Mother's… death. Athira's- you lost yourself. It- they've been gone for five hundred years."

His hands dropped back to his sides, disbelieving. Five hundred years wasn't a long time for one of their kind but finding out that much time had passed without his being aware of it was frightening. "I- was it sleep?"

"No." Danae closed her eyes, pain flickering across her face. "Madness. You had no memory of me or Mother's death. I found you for a time before you left again. It was another century or more before I found you again- now."

"Tell me." He forced the words out of his mouth, hating them.

She sank down onto the soft grass, pulling her legs up to her chest. "Once you would have just killed in battle but since Mother's passing, you- you've become something else. I saw from a distance once. You were in your natural form, and you tempted a hapless rider onto your back before racing out into the water."

Her hand traced the line of between sky and water before she folded it around her legs. "I didn't follow but I'm almost certain you drowned and... ate what was left. The mortals have a word for that. Waterhorse."

"Waterhorse." He echoed her word, tasting salt in his mouth that had nothing to do with ocean water. "And there's no way to return to how I was before?"

"None." Danae looked away; shame clear on her face. "I tried to heal you of that, but I don't have the power I once did."

That was disappointing but not unsurprising either. His daughter had given up the nearly immortal life for a mortal one years ago. He clasped her hand in his, interlinking their fingers before he released it. "I have my mind now. And you, we can return to our home. To rest, heal."

Danae opened her mouth and closed it again, picking up a blue gray rock rounded by the waves and turned it over in her hands, studying the slight glitter of the stone. "You can. I... cannot. Lachesis gave me all that I sacrificed and more."

Her voice faltered. "Athira wanted to be a goddess and died for her desire. Lachesis gave me all

the power I had before I chose a mortal life, but I'll never travel beyond this island's shores again. I'm bound here. It is more my home now than the lives we had as Poseidon's soldiers. I tried to leave, to take bird form and fly beyond the horizon but something called me back here."

New made goddess or not, she was still his daughter. He wrapped an arm around her shoulders, tasting the sourness of unfamiliar trepidation in his mouth. "Then... I'll stay for a time. Perhaps we can watch over each other?"

He was hoping anyway. If they were bound here, however indirectly it was for him, they could keep the worst of their natures in check. Together. They had no one else to rely on anyway.

Chapter Fifteen

September 20th, 1993, 1:00 AM. Seattle,

Washington

"I suppose that explains the Irish accent." Tiryn left off toying with a woven leather bracelet around her rest, arms resting on the jacket she had laid across the concrete ledge. "If you spent as much time as you did in Ireland. Over a thousand years before Jesus. What made you decide to leave?"

That wasn't an easy question to answer and one he wasn't going to. Aran shrugged halfheartedly. "I got tired of all the rain. I wanted to see sunshine and white clouds for a while."

Tiryn arched an eyebrow at that, skepticism in her voice. "I'd call you out as a liar except that I know all of your kind lie out of reflex. It's part of your nature to tell a story and get away with it.

Thankfully, I'll always know the truth. Was it your daughter?"

Empaths. Aran let out an exasperated sigh, pulling the sunglasses from Tiryn's hair and letting them fall from his hand to the ground below. "Stay out of my head, Kokinos. Yes, it was Danae. She was... changing, by pieces. She's as much a part of Ireland as it's a part of her now. The two can't be separated without something being destroyed."

It hadn't been a pleasant discovery to find that Danae had become Danu and that she barely remembered him- the lives they'd had in Greece. A visit several centuries later had found her with more faith in the one Christian god than their own creator. "She was powerful enough to do something I thought

only Poseidon was capable of before she went to rest."

Tiryn's mouth quirked at that, almost becoming a short-lived smile. "I take it the Christian faith came when the missionaries did, but I know a little of Irish folklore. Less than I should, perhaps. The Tuatha de Danaan were hers?"

"Most, apart from the Wild Hunt." Aran rested his head in his hands, trying not to pick at the sunburned, peeling skin at his wrist. "No one knows where they came from but I'm going to guess Fenris and his folk had something to do with that, however small it was a role. Osiris wouldn't, would he?"

Tiryn sniffed, dismissal crossing her face. "He may be a southern god and a pagan to our beliefs, but he's civilized. He would never let his hunters run wild

like those savages. They're also fae and well outside his domain."

She turned away, slipping her jacket on. "We've spent too much time speaking as it was. Hunt with me or no? Night vision is no issue for either of us, but I could use your sense of smell and hearing in tracking this beast down."

Not all of Seattle's buried tunnels were meant for tourists. Those that were, were rarely home to the city's more nocturnal residents. Aran knelt, kicking his combat boots off as he balled the socks up inside the toe. The jeans followed a second later, folded neatly next to them on a nearby ledge. Tiryn gave him a pointed look, shrugging her backpack off and leaving it in their cache. "I know you, clothing was never an issue when you changed shape. So…"

"I'd rather not get them soaked through."
Aran shrugged, contemplating the oversized, gray cotton t-shirt in his hands before pulling it on over his head in place of the one he had worn earlier. "Denim takes forever to dry without a machine. And truth be told, I was always more comfortable in a tunic."

"Explains the shirt." Tiryn said dryly. "Well, at least it's long enough for some modesty. Can't say much for anything else."

Aran rolled his eyes, bracing himself on century old brickwork. "We're both Greek. I don't think modesty was something we were overly concerned with in those days. And if I remember correctly, you don't wear lingerie either. Except maybe for the bra, but that's mostly for when you do have to chase something."

Tiryn opened her mouth, closed it and bristled. "You really were one of Poseidon's make, wretch."

Aran laughed, pulling an elastic band from around his wrist and tied his hair back out of his eyes. "So long as you never call him my father, that's a compliment, not an insult."

He ducked the blow she aimed at his head, still laughing as he caught her wrist in his hand before letting go of it. "C'mon, we have your *vrykolalas* to find."

Tiryn sniffed, muttering a few words in Greek about male horses before she let him take the lead. Aran kept his hand on the katana's hilt, gaze sweeping from one side of the narrow tunnel to the other. Tiryn's night vision was good, his was better

and death wasn't something he needed to concern himself about. She was still fragile, still human despite the bargain she'd made with Osiris.

Aran dropped to a knee in the three inches of filthy water pooling along the tunnel floor, wrinkling his nose in disgust. "Humans."

The water smelled as foul as it looked, hints of refuse and waste drifting down to some unknown pit. If they could smell themselves sometimes, they'd take a little more care in where they disposed of their filth. And just a hint of coppery scent clinging to the still air, stronger in the right-hand branch of the tunnel. "This way."

Worse, he couldn't shift without betraying them. A wolf's or mountain lion's teeth and claws would have come in useful right now, save for the

soft glow that came with the change. "Damn the gods."

Tiryn's hand tightened briefly on his shoulder as she followed his gaze down the tunnel, no happier about the stink of wastewater than he was. "Let me."

"How?" Aran kept his voice low, barely above a murmur. "You're an empath and a hunter. Not a shadow witch."

"Perk of being tied to both Agesander and Osiris." Tiryn held a hand out, casting the already darkened tunnel into deeper shadow. "But I'm no shadow witch, you're right about that. Go on, change. It won't see you now."

The temperature dropped noticeably as frost nipped at her outstretched hand. Aran looked away and shifted form, taking a mountain lion shape. There

would be time to ask about her little shadow trick

later if they managed to deal with the vampire first.

He didn't give the raggedly dressed creature a

chance to turn and face them before he lunged at it,

bringing the vampire down into a puddle of filth.

Tiryn hung back, watching before circling to Aran's

left and dropping into a crouch to look at the hissing,

spitting thing as it struggled to free itself from

underneath his paws. This was her conversation with

the beast, not his but anything that involved his son

was worth listening to. Aran flattened his ears against

his skull, snarling softly until the vampire went still.

Tiryn gave him an approving look before

glancing at the vampire. "You killed the son of a

friend of mine years ago and ran, thinking you could

hide from me. Better that you have never tried in the

first place. It would have… made things easier on you."

The vampire tried to climb to hands and knees, failing when Aran growled again in warning. Tiryn pressed sword edge against its throat. "It's past time I sent you back to the shadows where you came."

Its laugh was a thin, raspy wheeze before it hissed, lunging at her. And missed, skidding on its chest and faceplanting into crumbling brick wall. Tiryn stepped out of the shadows, this time standing on Aran's right. "You might have been able to catch an unprepared hunter or a stupid one. I'm neither and I know my ways in and out of the crossroads better than most."

It hissed again, going into a crouch as flesh and muscle peeled away, revealing bone beneath rotting cloth. Aran took a step back, baring his teeth at the scent of grave rot and wastewater stink that clung to its body.

The rot was the least of its change as it bloated, growing to twice its size and losing definite shape as arms and legs fused with body. Aran shifted back to human shape, tasting bile as he tightened his hand on the katana's hilt. "You told me *vrykolalas*. You didn't say undead vampire slug creature out of Tartarus."

"Problem?" Tiryn backed up a step, keeping her gaze on the thing that had once been a man. "This wasn't one of Athira's toys, was it?"

"Unfortunately." Aran spoke through gritted teeth, regretting the memory Tiryn's question brought to mind. "I'd have taken Lycaon's kin over this… beast. At least they have a head to decapitate."

The vampire lifted itself from the ground, standing more like a serpent than the oversized cousin to the creature found in gardens as it let out a thin whistle. Aran snarled, slashing at the creature's exposed belly. "What I'd give for any talent involving fire. You can't- shit- drown a vampire!"

The brownish green blood that splattered against his shoulder and arm burned slightly, whatever acid that the liquid held was enough to hurt for a few moments, eating through cotton to the skin underneath.

Tiryn cursed under her breath, dropping to her knees as she fumbled for a rag, a glass bottle of some undefinable liquid and a lighter. "Duck!"

He went flat out, shielding himself as he rolled away from the source of the fire and the abrupt shower of the creature's decaying remains. Tiryn had thrown the bottle into the thing's open mouth as it moved to bite pointy barbs into his hip and side. It had bitten down by reflex and swallowed the burning bottle whole. Whatever passed for internal organs in the thing hadn't liked the idea of fire and reacted by exploding all over them.

He'd taken the worst of the acidic blood over his back and shoulders, wincing as he stood. "Molotov cocktail? I didn't know you had it on you."

Tiryn smirked, gingerly wiping her hands onto her jeans. "A girl never tells all her secrets, but this is why I was wearing a leather jacket. Their blood doesn't go through that as easily as cotton. It wasn't so much gasoline and a rag as it was naphtha and quicklime in bottle form. Athira's creatures tend to burn when exposed to this kind of fire. And this wasn't my first vampire fight."

"Good to know." Aran squeezed his eyes shut tight for a moment, ignoring the look of concern Tiryn gave him. "Let's find the cache again and get out of here, please."

The nausea was slight but present in the pit of his stomach as he pressed his arm against his side. "Iason can... finally rest, wherever he is."

Putting one foot in front of the other took all the focus he had, even with Tiryn's body supporting him. Aran went to his knees, panting in front of her as his vision swam. Her bottled fire trick hadn't hurt him but the burns from the vampire like creature's blood still itched across his back and shoulders.

She steadied him with one hand, concern crossing her face before her mouth tightened in unhappiness. "My home. Now."

He nodded, grateful that she had spoken in Greek. English was too messy a language and the weakness too much for him to find the words in it. "Thank you."

Their walk back to Tiryn's home was made one painful step at a time and up to the third story apartment building. She fumbled one handed for a

small, electrical taped key and forced it into the lock, turning it to open.

Aran steadied himself long enough to slump on an old tartan patterned couch, towel over his legs and a plastic basin in his lap. His back barely touching the sofa behind him. Tiryn knelt next to him in the space between coffee table and couch as she pressed the back of her hand against his forehead. "I knew shapeshifters ran warmer than humans but you're burning up."

She bit down on her lower lip, shaking her head as she rummaged through the small refrigerator in the kitchen. "Help me. What do you need?"

Aran coughed, sweat dampening his hair to his forehead before he retched into the container. What he needed was nothing Tiryn could help him

with. Only time or rest would do that for him. Tiryn cast him an anxious look over her shoulder before she kicked the refrigerator door closed and came back with a glass filled from the sink. A small bottle of liquid honey and salt in her other hand. "I don't know enough about how your body processes food to be confident this will work. All I know about you, personally, comes from our own folklore. And we both know how wrong that can be."

"Or right." Aran pressed a hand to the base of his throat, wincing as he accepted the offered glass and unscrewed the cap from the honey bottle, mixing a teaspoon or two of the liquid in with the water. "I don't eat. Never was a need for it."

He took a swallow of the water, breathing a sigh of relief as it eased the pain in his throat. At best

this was only a temporary solution, but it would help for a few hours. "Still hurts like shit but I feel like I can breathe again."

Tiryn sat down on the couch next to him, a cushion's length of space between them as she took his hand in hers. "How long has it been for you?"

Aran finished the water and emptied a little more undiluted honey into the glass before taking a cautious sip of the sticky treat. "Since I was anywhere near home? Or just swimming in general?"

"Both, either." Tiryn pulled the glass from his hands and set it down on the coffee table.

Longer than he would have liked, truth be told. Aran stood, wrapping the towel around his waist as he stood and walked over to the balcony window to stare out of it at the lightening sky beyond Seattle's

skyline. "Three months, maybe. I've been going off and on for a few days at a time, trying to balance my needs with my family's."

"May I?" Tiryn joined him at the window, pulling a spare set of sunglasses from behind an artificial potted plant as she gestured to the cloth bandaging wrapping his forearms with her other hand.

He placed his wrist in her hand, letting her remove the bandaging and discard it on the thin carpet by the balcony door. Tiryn's touch was gentle, but he still flinched as she brushed the sunburned skin blotching his arm.

She drew back, a little furrow forming between her eyebrows. "I'm not a medic or first aid responder but three months is a long time for you. You can't keep doing this to yourself, spending time

in Seattle and not letting yourself recover completely. It never works for humans; it won't work for you."

"Tristan…" Aran said.

Tiryn shook her head, bending down to retrieve the strip of cloth as she wrapped it around her hand and unwound it again. "Tristan nothing. You need a shower and my bed. The couch is comfortable enough. I'll sleep there for the day."

She gave him an arch look, biting lightly down on one fingernail. "You do sleep, yes? I was never clear on that for your kind."

Aran gave in, resigning himself to the 'doctor's' orders. "I don't but I'll do this if you promise to call Mariko while I'm in the shower."

"Done." Tiryn sat down on the couch, already dialing the number on the handset sitting next to an antique lamp.

That was as good as any. Aran closed the bathroom door behind him, pulling the ruined t-shirt off over his head, turning his back to get a better look at it in the vanity mirror. The burn damage was worse than what marked his arms. Tiryn kept burn cream in her medicine cabinet. He pulled the tube from its place on the glass ledge and dropped the towel on the tiled floor before turning the shower on.

The shower was cold, but he didn't feel the chill of it, just the relief of the water against his back. Tiryn's knock on the closed bathroom door broke him out of the reverie and he turned the water off with a pang of regret. He scooped the towel off the floor,

wrapping it around his waist. Tiryn wouldn't have anything to say about a state of undress, Mariko and the rest of his family might.

He drifted, trying to find the rest she had asked of him, head resting on one arm. Tiryn's coverlet was drawn up over his waist, stopping short of his back as she busied herself with the cream. "Stay with me?"

Tiryn forced a smile and shook her head. "You need sleep, as much as you can get. That's never going to happen if I share the bed with you."

She stood up from the side of the bed, capping the cream and left a glass of water on the nightstand, next to the bottle of honey. "I need sleep myself. I'll see you around lunchtime."

That was going to be a long four hours, but the battered paperback would occupy him for a little time if sleep didn't. "Thanks for helping."

If Tiryn heard his words, she didn't acknowledge them, reaching up for a spare comforter and pillow in her closet instead. She closed the door behind her with a soft click, leaving him alone in the bedroom and his thoughts.

Chapter Sixteen

September 20th, 1993, 7:00 AM. Seattle, Washington

Tristan bounced on the bed several hours later, nearly landing on Aran's back in the process. Aran bit back an Irish expletive and the following hiss of pain as he rolled onto his side. "Careful, kit."

"Sorry." The little shapeshifter had the grace to look shamed as he moved to a safe side of the double bed. "What happened? And how come your back looks… uhm… not sunburned. The other thingy."

Aran sat up, keeping the coverlet over his lap for privacy's sake. Tristan was too young to know that he'd taken Tiryn's offer of a nap but declined the men's sweatpants she'd laid out on a nearby chair. "You're looking at what Poseidon did to me. If I didn't obey him as he expected me, he wasn't unwilling to have another soldier handle the punishment. It was meant to keep them as much as me in line."

"Oh." Tristan quieted, small hand tracing one line of scarring that traveled across Aran's ribs.

"Mom says you're strong enough to heal all this without marks."

"Because I don't want to forget what he did." Aran folded the five-year-old's hand in his own before releasing it. "Where's Mom?"

Tristan bounced once on his knees and scrambled off the bed. "Talking to the pretty lady. Tirren?"

"Tiryn." Aran swung his legs off the bed, forgetting the coverlet he meant to use for modesty. Tristan's eyes went round, and he went the brightest shade of pink he could go before seizing a nearby pillowcase and putting flat side up over his head. Aran winced, cursing his carelessness, and reached for the sweatpants, pulling them on. "You can look now, I'm decent."

If barefoot and shirtless.

"Okay." Tristan peeked out from under the pillowcase and pulled it off his head. "How come you're starkers?"

Aran sat down on the edge of the bed ruefully. "Greek thing. Some day I'll meet you in London and I'll take you to the museum there. They've got quite a collection of old stuff there, some of them from my people."

He shrugged as the thought came to mind. "Never participated in them myself, it would have exposed myself too much but the human athletes used to compete without any clothes at all."

Aran went to the door, leaning against the frame as he ruffled Tristan's dark hair with his free

hand. "I don't think this is going to be likely but just wait until you see me throw one of Mom's plates."

"Really?" Tristan looked up at him, amazement in his eyes. "Can we?"

"Maybe later." Aran pressed his arm against his side, fighting the moment of nausea that overwhelmed him before fading. "I'm not feeling completely well right now. And I doubt she'll be happy to find us playing frisbee with her dishes."

"Awh." Tristan looked disappointed. "Okay. Can – can you tell more of your story?"

He was going to hurt the five-year-old more than he'd hoped to. "I've told you everything that's important, kit. I'm sorry. That's all there to it. There's something else I'm going to have to tell you and you probably aren't going to like it."

"'kay." Tristan wiped his nose on his shirt sleeve. "Is Tirren your girlfriend?"

"Tiryn." Aran corrected the younger boy tiredly. "Not exactly. She's an old friend of mine but she prefers women. I'm not really her type of partner. Why don't we go back to Mom? She's probably itching to get going again. You know how she is when she has to stay in one place for too long."

He rummaged through Tiryn's closet, finding a clean shirt in his size and pulled it on over his head. The cotton rubbed against the raw, peeling skin of his back and he bit down on his lower lip, drawing blood from the small wound. "Ow…"

His shoes were beneath a pile of Tiryn's dirty laundry, and he pushed it to the side, bending down to slip them onto his feet. "Good to go, kit?"

"Yep." Tristan darted through the doorway, making his way towards the apartment's front door. Aran was a step or two slower behind his brother, exchanging a tired look with their mother. At some point he was going to have a word with her about the prospect of leaving them for his true home.

It wasn't a prospect he wasn't looking forward to. "Hey, Tristan. Why don't you go play when we go home? Dad hasn't been out for a while – it's always been me or Mom lately."

And it would give him a few minutes freedom to talk with Mariko in privacy.

The kitchen hadn't changed much in a couple days, but it felt smaller than he remembered it being, lonelier. Tristan was chattering in the backyard, half signing half rushing his words to their father. Aran

watched them out of the corner of his eye and the screen door as Mariko set a fresh pot of tea down on the table alongside a pair of cups. "He's going to be okay."

Mariko sat down in the opposite chair, pouring some of the of the steaming liquid into her cup and sipped at it. "So you plan on leaving then?"

"I don't have much of a choice." Aran warmed his hands on his own tea, looking into the aromatic liquid. "I've been delaying things by going swimming every so often but that isn't working as well as I hoped it would. Tiryn helped a little earlier tonight with burn cream and insisting on a nap, but that vampire was a bit more than you thought it was."

"How so?" Mariko set her cup down, concern in her eyes.

He grimaced, taking a swallow of the tea contained inside his cup. It settled his stomach and he leaned back. "Halfway between slug and snake when it abandoned the human disguise. The best way to kill that thing turned out to be Greek fire in a bottle. I got its blood all over me when it exploded. That stuff burns on contact and all I was wearing was a cotton t-shirt."

"Pleasant." Mariko said dryly.

"Unfortunately." Aran looked towards the blue flower-patterned teapot. "It's dead now, no one will end up in the medical examiner's office missing a liver or kidneys. That was what you wanted, right?"

"It was, thank you." Mariko inclined her head, dark hair falling into her eyes before she tucked a strand behind one ear. "What will you tell Tristan?"

"I don't know." His expression fell as he set the empty cup down in front of him on the scarred kitchen table. "He's your son. Adopted or not, I'm just a guest of yours. It's been a century; I need a decade or two to think. To… heal. I've been a soldier for so long, I don't know any other life. Tristan has choices I never did. He's free. I'm still dealing with… that trauma and Poseidon's been imprisoned for years."

Mariko's hand covered his, turning it palm upwards to the light. "You need to tell him something. I agree you need to go back to where you belong but never telling him will hurt your brother. A letter or a word, something."

"I'll think about it." It wasn't even a promise, but it was the best he could offer the woman who had

helped him for years after his arrival in Seattle. "Just let me figure something out. Tiryn maybe, or Coyote. I know them best, aside from you. Tiryn's a friend and Coyote – I can't call him that, but I trust him more than I did Sieh. It was his life or mine and Tristan's if I hadn't killed him outside the cabin."

"I understand." Mariko rubbed small, comforting circles over the back of his hand as she looked away, seeking some inspiration from her reflection on the microwave. "Thank you for sav- protecting your brother then."

Her voice dropped a note or two as she released his hand. "Though I wish you didn't have to leave, Kaito."

Japanese again, not English. He switched to the same language out of habit, needing the

familiarity of the words. "It wouldn't have been my choice either if I'd been free to make it myself, but Poseidon was my maker. He made sure of the limits on my power and how I could use it. Enough to serve him as more than mortal, not enough to fight him on his own terms. Only the moirai could have changed that and they prefer to watch, last I'd heard of them."

He sighed, raking a hand through blond hair. "Besides, there's too much trouble with having me here to begin with. You were here when Seattle burned, you remember it. That was a fight just between Coyote and Sieh. I'm- we're too territorial. Sooner or later, there's going to be another fight for the land. Between sky and earth is well enough, put me and Coyote in battle and you might see a lot of the Pacific coast drowned. It's too much risk. I don't relate well to humans or like many of them but you're

still family of mine. I won't chance your lives by ripping open some underwater fault line, just to test a gang leader's control. I- I've done it once before."

He smirked bitterly, switching back to English. "And they gave the island the made-up name of Atlantis, thank you, oh great Greek philosopher. If it ever had a name, it wasn't that one."

"You're leaving?" Tristan stood in the kitchen door, a red baseball in his hands as he sniffled. "Why?"

"It's rude to eavesdrop." Aran scraped the chair back on the linoleum floor. "Tristan-"

"No!" Tristan tightened his hold on the ball and drew back, throwing it at Aran's chest. "You promised!"

Aran caught the ball reflexively, stopping its journey before it could strike. "There's only one way to hold me to a promise, kit and that's swearing on the Styx. I never promised anything and- this, I need to go home eventually."

"Don't care." Tristan pushed past him, going through the kitchen to the stairs leading to the second story. The bedroom door slammed a moment later.

Aran let out a sigh, pinching the bridge of his nose as Mariko cast him a resigned look. "Do you want to talk to him or is it on my head?"

"Yours, I think." She looked down at the table. "At least try. If he doesn't understand after that then I'll have a word with him, but you owe your brother more than this."

#

A cheap pine door shouldn't have been as intimidating as it was for him. He'd fought a vampire like creature, seen his share of conflict over the years in one form or another and yet he couldn't face a five-year old's closed door. Aran hesitated and turned the knob without knocking. "Tristan?"

"Go 'way." Tristan's voice was muffled, coming out from under the light blue coverlet he was hiding beneath.

"I'd love to, but I can't." Aran sat down on the edge of the child sized bed. "Mom made me swear I would try to talk at least. Explain myself."

Sometimes a lie about a promise was better than saying he'd come on his own. "Just hear me out, please."

Tristan emerged from underneath the coverlet though he stayed curled up into a tight ball, arms wrapped around his legs. "'kay, guess. But you promise right? Anything?"

"Anything." Aran put his hand on Tristan's shoulder. "As long as it doesn't risk your life to do it."

"Maybe." Tristan sniffled, wiping snot onto his t-shirt sleeve. "Do you have to go?"

"I think so." Aran swept his gaze around the small room, taking in a yellow laundry hamper of stuffed toys and a few books scattered across the graying carpet. "Wish I didn't have to, but it's past time. I've been with your- our parents for nearly a hundred years. Before them, the longest I spent

pretending to be human was fifteen years – and they weren't even born yet."

The words touched on the years he'd spent in hiding and the time just before Theia's death. "I could stay if I gave up the power I had but…"

"It wouldn't be you, would it?" Tristan wiped wetness away from his face. "I guess… don't change on me. I like you this way even if you're scary sometimes."

"Something like that." Aran pulled the little shapeshifter close, positioning him on his lap. "Am I forgiven?"

Tristan blinked, looking up at him as he snuggled closer. "Nope. Not yet. Swear on a stick that you'll take me for a ride. An' no takebacks. If you're

scared 'bout it. Bring your girlfriend lady. She's nice, even if she smells funny."

"Swear on a stick? Styx." Aran groaned, whacking the five-year-old with the nearby pillow. "Fine. I swear on the river but only if you let me ask Tiryn to watch over you. I'm not doing this with just you. Besides, you're too small to ride alone."

"Dealie." Tristan twisted around and hugged him. "When? You never said."

He was going to regret this, but he'd already made the promise and it prickled somewhere in the back of his thoughts, itching to be obeyed. Aran held his brother close, letting him snuggle deeper against his chest. "Tomorrow. It'll... give me a few hours to talk to Tiryn and ask about something I should have

earlier. And Mom will get her father's sword back. I think I left it at her place."

"'kay." Tristan wriggled off Aran's lap and bundled the coverlet around his shoulders. "One more thingy? No promises here. But…"

His voice wobbled, shyly. "How old are you? Mom never said to me. All I know is you looking really old."

"Seventeen isn't old." Aran rolled his eyes. "If we'd had this conversation a few years later, I'd be sneaking you into Coyote's favorite bar for an apple juice and a cookie. I'm not even legal by human standards yet. I could fake it a bit, match any twenty-one-year old's lost ID card if I wanted to but according to my nonexistent transcripts, I'm nearly out of high school."

Most of those words looked like they'd gone over his brother's head but that wasn't the point of them. Tristan was still watching him with an expectant look on his face. "How old?"

"You asked." Aran rested the back of his head against the white painted bedroom wall. "Based on what I'm able to do and what I remember of the people then, I want to guess at close to eight thousand, but it could be closer to Coyote's age. He was in America just after the last ice age."

He faked a shiver, ruffling Tristan's hair again. "It was out of my territory and way too cold for me. I was happy to stay in Greece, kit. Sun, sand and my wife. Feeling better now?"

Tristan hesitated and nodded. "Yep. A bit. But you'll come back, right?"

"I'll come back when you call, yeah." Aran stood, dog earing a kids' paperback as he skimmed the page. "Maybe I'll tell you a different story then. Laelaps and the Teumesian fox? It's got a bit of the fox and the hound story you like so much."

He smiled sheepishly, remembering the pair. "They were more like you, mortal but those two always seemed to find each other no matter how far apart they were. Laelaps was a flirt. C'mon. I still need to talk to Tiryn and get Mom's sword back. Just wait here?"

Tristan nodded, eagerness for tomorrow already showing in his eyes. "Okay. Maybe Dad needs help in the garage."

It wasn't a place he liked being in himself, but Tristan was cut from a different cloth. Aran stood to

the side, twisting at the doorknob. "Just as long as you remember that you're only supposed to pass him the tools. You're too little to be messing around with engines."

"'kay!" Tristan said.

That was one problem solved, one more that needed to be fixed. And that needed Tiryn's agreement beforehand. Aran reached for a jacket in the hallway, giving a passing look to Mariko. "This won't take more than a day but I'm returning the sword to you. Kind of... forgot it earlier."

Rare for him but the excuse behind the words was more important. "I'll be back."

Chapter Seventeen

September 20th, 1993, 12:00 P.M. Seattle, Washington

He knelt on Tiryn's floor, staring into the opened backpack in front of him. Something like this shouldn't have been so intimidating – he had been Poseidon's soldier after all, but something about it made him hesitate. "I can't do this."

"That's a first." Her words were blunt, the tone wasn't. "What in particular?"

"Leaving Tristan." He sat back cross legged with his back to her coffee table. "I know I have to go. I need it but..."

"He's family." Tiryn knelt next to him, sorting through the unnecessary items, and discarding most of them in a heap. "Homesick for Greece or not, that pup is still your brother."

"I'm not even sure I'll be in Athens." Aran quieted, turning a box of crackers over in his hands

before setting it into the unnecessary pile. "Or for how long. I haven't seen Danae for ninety years – she's not the most responsive of people these days but even knowing she's there. It's been a while."

"Ireland." Tiryn looked pensive. "Not my first choice but I don't have any right to tell you where to go. It's always been something in your head, not mine. You go where you're needed to be. If she's calling you home, listen to her."

Aran sighed, setting aside the spare change of clothes into the 'keep' pile. It wasn't necessary but having something clean to change into would be welcomed. "I'll worry about that later. Right now, what was that shadow trick you did when we were fighting the vampire? I saw your hands. Whatever it was, left you frostbitten for a few minutes."

Tiryn glanced at him, concern apparent through the brown tinted sunglasses she wore. "It meant nothing, we're both more concerned about each other than ourselves but I dragged a little of the crossroads into the daylight. It didn't like that, but it served its purpose in hiding that glow you do when you shift form."

If that was all it was, he had no right to press further as he pulled the zipper shut on a nearly empty backpack. "Fair. Little confession of mine. Tristan asked me to promise him a ride before I... left. I agreed, on the condition you come with him."

"Is that wise?" Tiryn's knuckles went white around the katana's hilt before she forced herself to relax and look away.

"Probably not completely but I swore it on the Styx. I've got no choice now." Aran made a face at that. "Kit pronounced it 'sticks'."

Tiryn laughed, shaking her head. "He'll learn, eventually. Someone will make him, or he'll see to it himself. Reading between the lines and the headache you're giving me, he wasn't happy hearing something you wanted to keep private until you were ready."

"Not really, which is where he managed to blackmail a horseback ride out of me." Aran stood, holding a hand out for the Japanese weapon. "I do need to return this to Mariko. It isn't mine. Tomorrow? Early in the morning? There's a little beach I know about three hours away from Seattle that'll give us enough privacy for the ride."

"Done." She got to her feet, gripping his forearm with her opposite hand before releasing it. "And it likely won't take me as long as that to get there. Time passes differently in the crossroads."

"Except that you'll have Tristan with you, and he doesn't have Osiris's or Hades's protection from them." Aran said.

Tiryn frowned and cursed under her breath. "I'd forgotten. Fine, I'll need to rent a car for that time. Damn it all to Tartarus. I need to make a call or two and I hate running your errands."

She half turned away, already dialing a number on her landline.

Aran shouldered the knapsack, pretending he couldn't overhear both sides of the conversation. What Tiryn did to borrow or rent a car for a few hours

was none of his business. His family and Tristan's safety was. Oath or not, there was little certainty in tomorrow. Only hope, and she was a bitch to deal with.

Epilogue

September 21st, 1993, 7:00 PM. Seattle, Washington

He hated the taste of metal in his mouth after changing but it was the only way to keep himself tame enough for his brother to ride. Without bridle and bit in his horse form – he couldn't trust himself to give what he'd promised Tristan.

The five-year-old was perched on his back, hands tangled in the black mane. "It's so high up…"

Aran flicked one small ear back at that, waiting until Tiryn had taken her place behind the

little shapeshifter, one arm wrapped around Tristan's waist. Her free hand held the reins slack against his neck. The strips of leather were only meant to steady herself, not control.

He took a step forward, aware of the weight he carried as he moved into a walk, Tiryn's cues guiding him more than the hated bridle. A pat against his neck and a slight squeeze against his sides and he sped up, moving from trot to canter and full out run. Almost freedom as the water splashed around them. Tiryn laughed somewhere behind him, giving him full rein. Tristan was whimpering, grip holding tight onto the black mane as he tried to tug at it.

Aran ignored the pulling and turned, going deeper into the water so that it just brushed his belly before slowing, spent at last. Tiryn slipped off first,

helping Tristan down onto the rocky beach before pulling the bridle off his head.

Aran shifted back to human shape, scooping a small handful of salt water, and using the taste to rinse the worse flavor of iron from his mouth before he spat it out. His shoulders and back ached from carrying the combined load he had. "That's going to hurt for a while. Neither of you are heavy but…"

Tiryn glanced at the sky, rubbing at his shoulders as she watched the last of the sun fade on the horizon. "You gave your brother what he asked for. He won't make that request again."

Aran stood, looking down at the bridle she still held her hand and pulled it from her grip. The leather straps were warm in his touch as he drew back and tossed the hated thing into the water. "I'm free."

Tiryn nodded, resting her head against his shoulder. "You are, yes. Go on, go find Danae."

Once that would have been so easy, but Aran hesitated, gaze drifting behind him to the small hollow where his brother was curled up, otter shaped and giving a squeaky little snore as he dreamed. "Tell him this when he wakes up. Call, or if he ever needs help and I'll come back. This time I'll willingly swear it on the Styx, he doesn't need to blackmail a promise out of me for it."

There wasn't a lot he wouldn't do to protect his brother. Even kill if need be. There had been a similar oath sworn to Theia and his own family and he'd failed to keep it. This one would be different, whatever the cost to him.

Shredding his t-shirt and jeans during the change wasn't something he needed to concern himself about when he could just shift form and reproduce whatever it was that he wanted to wear. That didn't make the act any less important for him. Not a journey to the underworld but still a katabasis of his own. Tiryn had been a stand in for the psychopomp this time.

She watched from a foot or two away, sunglasses perched on her head and expression unreadable as he pulled jeans and the wash abused gray t-shirt off, folding them into a pillow and blanket for the little otter's sleeping body. A letter torn from an old spiral bound notebook was tucked in beneath the tiny paws.

Aran waded out past knee high water, feeling the hunter's gaze on the back of his neck as he paused for a second. The desire to stay warred with the homesickness for Ireland. Homesickness won out and he let out a breath, pulling the last thing that tied him to the mortal lands from his hair. An elastic band was a small thing, easily forgotten by most people but it was still a reminder of the human mask he had worn for so long. Too long, in truth. Little habits, memories had crept in over the years, complicating things.

He broke eye contact with Tiryn, going deeper into the water and diving a moment later. The ocean was home and he'd been fighting the call to return for years. Aran closed his eyes, letting himself float, cradled by the water. Fair hair darkened to black as he let go of the human shape at last, the horse form taking place of the mortal.

No one could call themselves his master here, no one could command him in his element and after a century of being bound to obligation, he was home.

[Silver and Salt - Deleted Scenes]

10th April 1912

In appearance he was a third-class Irishman out of Belfast, the truth was somewhat more complex but there was few on board who were aware of that. He put his hand on the wall, letting his eyes drift shut for a moment. Either in prayer or a blessing but few would have recognized the Gaelic words he murmured to her.

She had no words, nothing she could speak aloud but the spirit within her body still responded to him. A small goddess made out of iron and steel,

given life by the humans who had dreamed her into being. "Mistress…"

It paid to be polite to her, however lacking in a verbal response she gave him. Aran smiled briefly and shouldered his backpack as he turned away. The lights and glitter of the first-class cabins held no interest for him. It was those deemed "poor" that he preferred. They were more real than those above.

#

Those in steerage weren't afforded the same luxury in cabins or entertainment but he didn't care about that as someone brought out a fiddle and a pair or two began the dance. All that mattered was the red-haired Irishwoman in a silvery gray dress across from where he stood with a cigarette in hand.

She smiled coyly, looking at him and away before she slipped into the crowd, easily skirting the spinning dancers. He laughed, following her wandering path until he caught up with her, one hand wrapping around her wrist. Few mortals would have noticed it but he was anything, but mortal and her skin just had the faintest scent of metal and oil clinging to it, just a taste of iron as his mouth brushed against the back her hand. All the things she had been created from. "Mistress,"

She smiled, caressing the side of his face as he released her hand. "Please, I am a child compared to the ages you have lived."

Aran chuckled, shaking his head at that. "We're both children of the sea, lass."

She blushed pink, hands smoothing over her dress. "You, a selkie and older than I? No, you were nature's creation. I was man's."

He shrugged, not caring for the distinction between them. "I never cared much for that difference."

The woman tilted her head to the side, contemplative. "Titania, if you please then."

"Aran," He pulled her into an embrace, not heeding the eyes of the crowd on them, or the catcalls offering them both good luck. "Come with me?"

#

It wasn't hard to change face and attire to make it up to the glittering lights of the upper decks and he found Titania leaning over the bow of the ship, watching the dark water below them. She was dark

231

haired now, a silver streak visible in the inky blue-black strands. She turned to look at him and hoisted herself so that she sat on the railing. "You asked if I would come with you, did you not?"

He laughed nodding and noted the silver and small diamond pendent at her throat. "A suitor?"

Titania touched it briefly, glancing away. "A gift from my captain, no more than that. You promised, did you not?"

He laughed, helping her stand on the narrow railing and supporting her there before he let the change take him with a soft glow of light surrounding his body. There was barely a ripple as the otter hit the water and curved, not caring about the crushing depths or the current surrounding him. No true shapeshifter herself but still capable of changing her

human form, Titania dove after him, newly golden hair drifting in the water of the North Atlantic.

He floated there, watching her through curious eyes and swam over, teasing paws through Titania's hair. She laughed, batting at him and he sailed a few yards back, tumbling until he regained control over his own body. She didn't know her own strength, but he didn't care about that. It was worth it just to swim with her.

#

11th April 1912

Titania seemed quieter than she had the other night, toying with the diamond pendant at her throat as he joined her by their usual meeting place. Aran frowned, sliding an arm around her waist. "What is it?"

She looked at him in concern, chewing on her lower lip in an oddly human gesture. "My... captain, he's asked for more speed and I worry I won't be able to give him that. I... sense things, danger but I do not know what it is?"

He'd sensed it as well though the how in their respective responses to danger were likely different. Titania likely only knew the captain was pushing her in the race to a mythical city called New York. He could tell something about the water and the small barely submerged pieces of ice surrounding them. "No, I fear it as well but the crew or the captain will not listen to an Irishman in steerage."

Titania sighed, breath puffing white in the cool night air. "I wish my sisters were here with me, but they are nowhere as aware as I am. Of the three of

us, I was the only one given a true life – they… just exist. Alive, aware but mute and blind. They are shells."

The disgust and fear in her voice was almost as chilling as the ice surrounding them. Aran slipped his hand over hers in a attempt to reassure her. She leaned into him, her scent holding a trace of coal and fire in it. "You're stronger than they are."

"Am I?" She wiped wetness away from her cheeks. "I wonder about that sometimes, whether I'll be able to protect my people or condemn them. I'm a flawed thing, A- Aran. I've seen the plans in my captain's cabin. Too few boats for all those I care for."

He closed his eyes, letting her cry onto his shoulder and comforting her as best he knew how.

Words were wasted here and unwanted. "You don't know what will happen, Titania."

She quieted, clinging to him before softly slipping away into the crowd of those going into the warmth of the dining room.

#

12ᵗʰ April 1912

Titania had been avoiding him, he couldn't say he blamed her, he couldn't say he liked it either but what else was one to do when that creeping sense of danger was stronger than it had been, and she lacked the words to tell him.

Aran looked down, losing his appetite for the simple fare in front of him and shoved it away only half eaten. "Titania?"

Her hair was dark again, that silver streak once more tucked behind one ear. Her dress was no longer the silvery gray thing she had worn before but more of a charcoal shade. Not quite a mourning black but not what he would have called a color of celebration either. Her familiar accent had shifted becoming more English than Irish now. "I believe we should keep from continuing our games, Aran. It would be for the best."

"For the best?" He echoed her, disbelieving and truth be told, a little hurt. "Titania…"

"No," Her shoulders dropped, betraying her own grief as much as she tried to deny it. "This is for the best, Aran."

He opened his mouth to speak but she was already gone. This time he didn't try to follow her. If she wanted company, she would ask for it, not before.

#

He saw her a few times but always at a distance and she was always quick to vanish into the crowd or turn away from him.

This time his swim was short lived and alone, chasing a dolphin or two though his heart wasn't in the games or their conversation they were engaged in. It wasn't long before he returned to the deck and his bunk in the cabin.

A few of the human Irishmen tried to catch him in conversation but he brushed them off as politely as he could without insulting them.

13th and 14th April 1912

He waited by their usual place for longer than he cared to acknowledge, or his limited patience normally permitted of him. Despite the dying hope in his chest and its flavor in his mouth, she failed to greet him in their secret little place between lifeboats.

Once more brokenhearted as he was left standing alone at midnight.

Aran turned away, prepared to go back to his place and stare blankly at the low ceiling overhead

"Aran?"

Titania's voice was soft, weary but she had abandoned her charcoal dress for a deep red. She looked older, lines touching the edge of her mouth and eyes. It only made her more beautiful, not less and it broke his heart to see her like this rather than

the playful young woman she had been at the start of their journey a few days ago. "I- am I forgiven?"

She tried for a smile, but it faded before it could show on her face. "There was nothing to forgive. You did nothing wrong, my… my love. I only came to give you my last gift."

He looked up and closed his hand reluctantly over the delicate silver chain and diamond he pressed into his palm. "This is yours; I can't accept it."

"It's a gift," She let out a breath, staring across the water at a fate only she could see. "Please, accept it, Aran. Keep it to remember me by."

What choice did he have at those words? He sighed, looping it over his own head and neck. "Very well, I accept."

Titania graced him with the lightest touch of her mouth against his before she turned away and walked into the darkness. He watched her go with a dry taste in his mouth, holding back the tears until he couldn't anymore. It wasn't a masculine thing to do, cry but he was male, not a man and he was a shapeshifter, not human.

#

The shriek that woke him from a relatively sound sleep had him drawing a knife from under his pillow before he saw Titania in his cabin. He was out of the bed and supporting her weight with his own almost before he could think, his knife abandoned and the four other men muttering expletives at the interruption.

He ignored their complaints, only seeing the tears streaking down her cheeks. "What is it?"

His voice was low but there was no point in concealing all but the broadest details from his fellow bunkmates now. "Titania?"

She clutched at him, breath hitching. "My- my captain. I trusted him and he…"

She hiccupped, swallowing past the hard lump in her throat. "He betrayed me. I couldn't have warned him, but I expected him to be a good man. We hit an iceberg, Aran. I fear for what comes next."

"They called you unsin- unflappable, Titania," He corrected himself hastily, gaze drifting around at the human men in the cabin. "Nothing frightened you."

Her laugh was small and yet still bitter.

"Everything has its fear, Aran. Please. That ice damaged me, and I'm frightened of what may happen next. I- I'm afraid of death. Of... my death."

"You won't die, not on my watch," He wrapped her arm around his shoulders and helped her to her feet. "Come with me. I'll take you away from here."

His words were more for the sake of the humans than Titania's comfort, as regrettable as that was. "Can you walk?"

She nodded tightly and put one foot in front of the other though it cost her to do so. He could see it in each labored breath and how she forced herself to keep going, more on his power than her own.

Aran let her sit down on a nearby bench in the second-class corridor, dropping into a crouch as he held her hands in his own. "Can you keep going?"

Titania swallowed and then retched into his lap. He ignored the wet, it was only salt water after all, not true vomit. It was several moments before she could speak again, her expression pained and miserable. "I'm – I'm drowning, Aran. I feel it inside."

He closed his eyes, fighting back tears of his own. Titania was the ship as much as she was the woman in front of him. The two were one and the same and there was nothing he could do to separate them. If she said she was drowning than the ship's compartments were filling quickly with icy water. "I'm sorry."

"No," Her hand was against his cheek, the skin on it paper thin and cool to the touch. "No apologies, Aran. Go, save yourself. I'm past saving even with the call my crew sent out to another ship. Just… remember me and that I tried to do what I could to save my people."

He nodded tiredly, getting to his feet, and letting her stay where she had chosen to remain. "I promise it on Brigid and Danu, I will."

Naming the goddesses was as good as a binding oath for him.

He slipped into the water, otter shaped and finally clinging to a small ice floe until a nearby boat drifted past. Its people were too in shock to notice the shapeshifter in their midst or how a peculiar otter shifted back to a human form.

The diamond pendant was warm in his hand and he looked down at it for a long moment before nearly tipping the boat in his dive from its safety. There was one more thing he could do before the end. One last thing he had to be witness to. Safety was little concern to him, he could always change, return to the oceanic spirit world he belonged to and resurface later. Death by cold, for him, was a minor thing.

The familiar red dress and silver-streaked hair caught his attention just as the bow portion fell past him to the ground yards below. The shadow of the stern followed a few minutes later, as far as his reckoning allowed it. He shifted back to human shape, desperate to wake Titania but the lack of bubbles at her mouth and response were telling enough.

He swallowed, not daring to breathe in any water of his own despite the chill even through his protection against it. Her shape wavered, faded around the edges, and was washed away as he watched. All that she had been, all that had been holding her to life, gone now. Without her ship anchoring her, she was lost. As near as one of their kind could get to a human death.

Aran looked away, finally swimming for the surface and scrambling on top of a piece of debris as the lights of another ship finally made them – itself clear in the darkness.

#

The Carpathia had none of Titania's soul or life in her construction. Aran sighed, wrapping his borrowed blanket around his shoulders. There was no

way to say he didn't need it, not without revealing who he really was but the rescuing ship had no feeling to her. Just cold steel and dead metal without a life or voice of her own. He pulled Titania's necklace from his pocket and turned it over in his hands before placing it back where it belonged. "I'm sorry…"

#

Halifax, Nova Scotia, April 14th, 2012

Canada wasn't home, he preferred the life and light of New York City, but he was doing this for a friend. Aran closed his eyes, murmuring a prayer as he put a flower down in front of the grave marker. History had painted Titania as a Tatiana, surname unknown and a second-class passenger but her story had been more than that once. She had been life and

soul of a ship lost before her time. A century gone and he still missed her. She had been friend and lover for as short a time as they'd had together now there was one last thing he could do for her memory.

He took a breath, steeling himself and dove off the edge of the Nova Scotia pier, seeking the watery spirit world to carry him faster than an ordinary otter could swim to the grave where Titania lay.

Her ship was in pieces, only the bow section still recognizable despite the sea life coating her railing and body. He circled, giving a sneeze like laugh at the sight seen through the murky water. Fate or luck had spared her name painted on the side of the bow. RMS Titanic was still more or less legible

despite the century past, as impossible as it should have been.

Her necklace was still clutched between his paws and he let it go, drifting downwards to tangle on the railing a few feet below. It was all the apology he could offer her for not being able to do more than he had. "I'm sorry…"

The words were unspoken but still there regardless.

58613334R00150

CPSIA information can be obtained
at www.ICGtesting.com
Printed in the USA
BVHW031658070521
606757BV00001B/33

About the Author

Photo Credit: Timothy Capp

Patricia J. Gallegos is a new author. *The View from My Window* is her first novel.

As a published illustrator, her pen and ink illustrations capture the wildlife and the landscape of the Four Corners in *Under the Indian Turquoise Sky*, Ye Galleon Press. This collection of Native American fables was shared, in the oral tradition, by respected Native-elder story tellers with young Native American students, who put these treasured fables into writing for the very first time. This treasury was compiled by Dr. Grace Nutley and Rosemary R. Davey.

As a Nationally Certified Sign Language Interpreter, Gallegos is a student of human nature and the language of what is unsaid but clearly stated. As a Doctor of Acupuncture and Oriental Medicine, she has the reputation of being the Shen whisperer, She-Who-Sees-Inside-the-Spirit. She teaches and practices Traditional Chinese Medicine in Portland, Oregon. Following her own native roots, she treads softly in the footsteps of her ancestral matriarch, who was an Apache warrior and practitioner of *curanderismo*.

About Atmosphere Press

Atmosphere Press is an independent, full-service publisher for excellent books in all genres and for all audiences. Learn more about what we do at atmospherepress.com.

We encourage you to check out some of Atmosphere's latest releases, which are available at Amazon.com and via order from your local bookstore:

The Black-Marketer's Daughter, a novel by Suman Mallick

This Side of Babylon, a novel by James Stoia

Within the Gray, a novel by Jenna Ashlyn

Where No Man Pursueth, a novel by Micheal E. Jimerson

Here's Waldo, a novel by Nick Olson

Tales of Little Egypt, a historical novel by James Gilbert

For a Better Life, a novel by Julia Reid Galosy

The Hidden Life, a novel by Robert Castle

Big Beasts, a novel by Patrick Scott

Alvarado, a novel by John W. Horton III

Nothing to Get Nostalgic About, a novel by Eddie Brophy

GROW: A Jack and Lake Creek Book, a novel by Chris S McGee

Home is Not This Body, a novel by Karahn Washington

Whose Mary Kate, a novel by Jane Leclere Doyle